How did this woman know him? How?

As he paused, crouching in the bushes while deciding what the hell to do next, she came. Morgan. Awakened by the alarm, she had gone directly to the study where he had been. As if she knew.

She stood in the open window, looking out into the darkness, her face completely confused, utterly vulnerable. She would remember their encounter only as a dream. The way she was staring out, squinting, searching the darkness, it seemed almost as if she were hoping to see him, rather than fearing she might.

The woman had no idea the kind of power she was playing with. No idea.

She had better hope she never had to learn.

She was turning, staring hard at the window glass, and lifting a hand to her neck.

Oh, God the reflection. She saw the wounds by night that would have vanished at the first touch of sunlight on her flesh. She saw the two punctures, the tiny ribbon of blood on her white flesh. She saw them and she knew.

MAGGIE SHAYNE

TWILIGHT HUNGER

MIRA

ISBN 1-55166-886-6

TWILIGHT HUNGER

Visit us at www.mirabooks.com

Printed in U.S.A.

Long ago, I was writing vampire stories
for Silhouette Shadows. When the line went away
(briefly, I'm sure, being a believer in reincarnation)
I thought for a time I wouldn't be able to continue
with the series I had begun. But there were people
at Silhouette who loved Wings in the Night
as much as I did, as much as its faithful readers did.

The leader of them all was my editor, Leslie Wainger.
She kept this series alive by having me do one story
as a Silhouette single-title release, another as a special
Silhouette Intimate Moments two-in-one. Because of that,
the popularity of the series never waned. She didn't give it
a chance to wane. And all the while she was working
behind the scenes to help me breathe new life into it,
until finally, MIRA Books was ready to take the dive
into the realm of the paranormal. Without Leslie Wainger,
I promise you, this series would have ended with
two books and a novella. Instead this is book number
seven, and I'm already plotting number eight
and thinking about number nine. Thank you, dear, dear
Leslie, for excellence in editing, for tremendous support
of your authors, for the little hearts and smiley faces and
comments you scribble in the margins of my manuscripts
(you'll never know how much those mean to me,
especially the "Damn you, I'm bawling" ones)
but most of all for "getting" me and the quirky work I do.

This book is dedicated to Leslie Wainger
from the bottom of my heart.

1

We children were supposed to be asleep....

But we woke, as if in response to some silent summons. We crept to the entrances of our tents and wagons, drawn like moths to the snapping flames of the central fire and the dark, leaping shadows the strange woman cast as she danced.

There was no music. I knew there was none, but it seemed to me that music filled my head all the same as I peered around the painted flap and watched her. She whirled, scarves trailing like colorful ghosts in her wake, her hair, black as the night, yet gleaming blue in the fire's glow. She arched and twisted and spun round again. And then she stopped still, and her eyes, like shining bits of coal, fixed right on mine. Scarlet lips curved in a terrifying smile, and she crooked a finger at me.

I tried to swallow, but the lump of cold dread in my throat wouldn't let me. Licking my lips, I glanced sideways at the tents and painted wagons of my kin, and saw the other children of our band, peering out at her, just as I was. Some of my cousins were older than I, some younger. Most looked very much like me. Their olive skin smooth, their eyes very round and wide, too thickly fringed for the eyes of a boy, but lovely beyond words on little girls. Their hair was uncut, like mine, but clean and raven black.

We were Gypsies all, and proud. The dancing woman…she was a Gypsy, too. I knew that at a glance. She was one of our own.

And crooking her finger at me still.

Dimitri, older than me by three years, gave me a superior look and whispered, "Go to her. I dare you!"

Only to prove myself braver than he, I stiffened my spine and stepped out of my mother's tent, my bare feet covering the cool ground by mere inches with each hesitant step. As I crept closer, the others, taking courage in mine, began to come out, too. Slowly we gathered round the beautiful stranger like sinners come to worship at the feet of a goddess. And as we did, her smile grew wider. She beckoned us closer, a finger to her lips, and then she sat down on a log near the fire.

"Who is she?" I whispered to Dimitri, for he had joined us now, too, ashamed of himself, I thought, not to have been leading us all from the start.

"Stupid, do you know nothing? She is our aunt." He shook his head disgustedly at me, then returned his enraptured gaze to the woman. "Her name is Sarafina," he said. "She comes sometimes…though I suppose you are too young to recall her last visit. She's not supposed to be here, though. When the grown-ups find out, there will be trouble."

"Why?" I too was entranced by the mysterious stranger as she lowered herself to the log, spreading the layers of her colorful skirts around her, opening her arms to welcome the young ones who crowded closer to sit on the ground all around her. I sat closest of all, right at her feet. Never had I seen a woman so beautiful. But there was something else about her, as well. Something…unearthly. Something frightening.

And there was the way her eyes kept meeting mine. There was a secret in that black gaze—a secret I could not quite see. Something shadowed, hidden.

"Why will there be trouble?" I whispered again.

"Because! She is outcast!"

My brows drew together. I was about to ask why, but then the woman—my Aunt Sarafina, whom I had never seen before in my life—began to speak. And her voice was like a song. Mesmerizing, deep, beguiling.

"Come, little ones. Oh, how I've missed you." Her gaze swept the faces of the children, the look in her eyes almost painful to see, so intense was the emotion there. "But most of you do not remember me at all, do you?" Her smile faltered. "And you, little Dante. You are…how old now?"

"Seven," I told her, my voice a mere whisper.

"Seven years," she replied with a heavy sigh. "I was here the day you were born, you know."

"No. I…didn't know."

"No matter. Oh, children, I've so much to tell you. But first…" She tugged open a drawstring sack that dangled from the sash round her waist, and from it she began to draw glorious things, which she handed around to one and all. Sweets and confections such as we had never tasted, wrapped in brightly colored paper. Shiny baubles on chains, and glittering stones of all kinds, carved into the shapes of animals and birds.

The one she gave to me was a stone of black onyx in the shape of a bat. I shivered when she placed the cold piece into my palm.

When the sack was empty and the children all quiet again, she began to speak. "I have seen so many things, little ones. Things you would not believe. I journeyed to the desert lands, and there I saw buildings as big as mountains—every stone larger than an entire Gypsy wagon! Perfect and smooth they are, and pointed at the top." She used her hands to make the shape of these wonders in the air before us. "No one knows who built them, nor when. They have been there forever, some say. Others say they were built as monuments to ancient kings…and that the bodies of those rulers still rest inside, along with treasures untold!" When our eyes widened, she nodded hard, making her raven curls dance and her earrings jangle. "I've been across the sea…to the land below, where creatures with necks as tall as…as that yew tree there, walk on stilt legs and nibble the young leaves from the tops of the trees. Yellow gold they are, and spotty! With sprouts atop their heads!"

I shook my head in disbelief. Surely she was spinning tales.

"Oh, Dante, it is true," she said. And her eyes held mine, her words for me alone, I was certain. "One day you will see these things, too. One day I will show them to you myself." Reaching down, she stroked a path through my hair and leaned close to me, whispering into my ear. "You are my very special boy, Dante. You and I share a bond more powerful even than the one you share with your own mother. Remember my words. I'll come back for you someday. When you need me, I will come."

I shivered and didn't know why.

Then I went stiff at the sound of the Grandmother's squawk. *"Outcast!"* she yelled, rushing from her tent and jabbing her fingers at Sarafina in the way that was said to ward off evil, the two middle fingers folded, forefinger and little one pointing straight out. She made a hissing sound when she did it, so I thought of a snake with a forked tongue snapping.

The children scattered. Sarafina rose slowly, the picture of grace, and I alone remained before her. Almost without thought, I got to my feet and turned to face the Grandmother. As if I wished to protect the lovely Sarafina. As if I could. My back was toward the woman now, and as her hands closed on my shoulders, I felt myself grow a full inch taller.

Then the Grandmother glared at me, and I thought I would shrink to the size of a sand flea.

"Can you not tolerate my presence even once every few years or so, Crone?" Sarafina asked. Her voice was no longer loving or soft or kind. It was deep and clear...and menacing.

"You've no business here!" the Grandmother said.

"But I have," she replied. "You are my family. And like it or not, I am yours."

"You are nothing. You are cursed. Be gone!"

Chaos erupted around us as mothers, awakened by the noise, dashed out of their tents and wagons, gathered their children and hurried them back inside. They acted as if a killer wolf had appeared at our campfire, rather than an outcast aunt of rare beauty, bearing exotic gifts and amazing tales.

My mother came, too. As she rushed toward me I tucked the stone bat up into my sleeve. She stopped before she reached me and met Sarafina's eyes. "Please," was all she said.

There was a moment of silence as something passed between the two women. Some message, unspoken, that left my mother's eyes sad and welling with tears.

Sarafina bent down and pressed her cool lips to my cheek. "I'll see you again, Dante. Never doubt it. But for now, go on. Go to your mamma." She gave me a gentle shove and let go my shoulders.

I walked to my mother, nearly hating her for making me leave the mysterious Sarafina before I'd had a chance to learn her secrets. She gripped my arm tightly and ran to our tent so fast that she nearly dragged me off my feet. Inside, she closed the flap and cupped my face in her hands, falling to her knees before me. "Did she touch you?" she cried. "Did she mark you?"

"Sarafina would not hurt me, Mamma. She is my aunt. She is kind, and beautiful."

But my mother seemed not to hear my words. She tipped my head to one side and the other, pushing my hair aside and searching my skin. I tired of it soon enough and tugged myself free.

"You are never to go near her again, do you hear me, Dante? If you see her, you must come to me at once. Promise me!"

"But why, Mamma?"

Her hand came across my face so suddenly I would have fallen had she not been gripping my arm with the other. "Do not question me! Promise me, Dante. Swear it on your soul!"

I lowered my head, my cheek stinging, and muttered my agreement. "I promise." I was ashamed of the tears that burned in my eyes. They came more from shock than pain. My mother's hand rarely lashed out in anger. I didn't understand why it had tonight.

She knelt now, her hands on my shoulders, her

worn face close to mine. "It's a promise you must keep, Dante. You endanger your soul if you break it. Mark me well." She drew a breath, sighed, and kissed the cheek she had so recently wounded. "Now, into bed with you." She was marginally calmer, her voice nearer its normal pitch.

I was far from calm. Something had stirred my blood tonight. I crawled into my bed, pulled the covers over me and let the tiny, cold stone bat drop from my sleeve into my hand. I held it, rubbed its smooth surface with my thumb, beneath the blanket where my mother could not see. Mamma watched over me for a long moment, then blew out the lamp, and curled up—not upon her own bed, but on the floor beside mine, a worn blanket her only cushion.

In the silence, I rolled toward the side of the tent and thrust a forefinger through the tiny hole I had made in the fabric, so I could watch the grown-ups round the fire long after they had sent the children to bed. I tugged the hole a little wider in the darkness. And through that tiny hole, I watched and I listened as the Grandmother, the crone of the band, the eldest and most venerated woman of the family, faced off against the most vibrantly beautiful female I had ever seen in my life.

"Why do you torment us by coming back to our midst?" the Grandmother asked, as the dancing flames painted her leathery face in orange and brown, shadows and light.

"*Why?* You, my own sister, ask me why?"

"Sister, bah!" The Grandmother spat on the ground. "You are no sister to me but a demon. Outcast! Cursed!"

I shook my head in wonder. What could Sarafina

mean? Sister? She could no more be the old one's sister than...than I could.

"Tell me why you come, demon! It is always the children you seek out when you return. It's for one of them, isn't it? Your wretched curse has been passed to one of them! Hasn't it? *Hasn't it?*"

Sarafina smiled very slowly, her face angelic and demonic all at once, and bathed in fireglow. "I come because you are all I have. I will always come back, old woman. *Always.* Long after you've gone to dust, I'll be coming back, bringing gifts to the little ones. Finding in their eyes and in their smiles the love and acceptance my own sister denies me. And there is nothing you can do to prevent it."

Before Sarafina turned away, she looked past the Grandmother and right into my eyes. As if she had known all along that I was there, watching her from the other side of that tiny hole in the tent. She could not have seen me. And yet, she must have. Her lips curved ever so slightly at the corners, and her mouth moved. Even though no sound emerged, I knew the word she whispered. *Remember.*

Then she turned, her skirts flying, and vanished into the night. I saw the trailing colors of her scarves like tails behind her for only an instant. Then the blackness of night closed in where she had been, and I saw her no more.

I lay down on my pillows, and I shivered in inexplicable dread.

It was me. My aunt had come for me. I knew it in my soul. What she wanted of me, I could not guess. How I knew it, this was a mystery. But I was certain to the core of me that she *did* have a reason for returning in the face of such hatred.

And the reason...was me.

* * *

Slowly, slowly, the smoke from the Gypsy camp-fire thinned. The light thrown by the flames dulled, and the heat—so real she had sworn she could feel it on her face—went cold.

Morgan De Silva blinked out of the fantasy. She was not looking at a Gypsy campfire through the huge dark eyes of a small boy. She was sitting on the floor of a dusty attic, staring down at the time-yellowed pages of a handwritten journal, bound in leather covers so old they felt buttery-soft against her hands. The vision painted by the words that spiderwebbed across the aging pages had been vivid. It had been...*real.* As real as if she'd been in that Gypsy camp in the distant past, instead of on the coast of Maine in the early spring of 1997.

Morgan turned the page slowly, eager to read on....

The ringing of the telephone, floating faintly from no small distance, stopped her. With a resigned sigh, she closed the large volume and returned it carefully to the aged trunk, atop a stack of others just like it. When she closed the trunk's lid, its hinges groaned and a miniature explosion of dust puffed out at her. Brushing her hands against each other, then her jeans, she blew out the candles that were the only source of light in the room and hurried down the narrow, steep attic stairs.

She hadn't expected to find a thing up there other than cobwebs and dust. Exploring more of the ram-shackle house had been an experiment in procrasti-nation, not an act of curiosity. If her own work had been going anywhere, she never would have bothered poking around this aging, sagging house at all.

And that would have been a crying shame.

She ran through the hallway, between walls of crumbling plaster, the lath beneath it visible in places, to the next set of stairs. These were wider, but not in much better repair than anything else around the place. The third step from the top was missing a board, and she skipped it automatically and trotted the rest of the way down as the phone kept on ringing.

If it were another lawyer or bill collector, she thought breathlessly, she would hunt them down and kill them.

The wide staircase emptied itself into a huge room that must have been glorious once, a century or so ago. Now it was filled with nothing but heartbroken echoes and a tangle of bare wires sticking out of the domed ceiling, where some magnificent chandelier must have once been. Beyond that room, through a pair of double doors, was her room. Her...*office*. For the moment, at least. But only until she earned back her fortune and returned to L.A. in triumph.

Pretty much the opposite of the way she had left.

Her heart was pounding from exertion by the time she got that far, and she was out of breath, slightly dizzy, and pressing one hand to her chest. Ridiculous for a twenty-year-old woman to tire so easily, but there it was. She had never been healthy, and she knew she wasn't ever going to be. But at least her condition hadn't begun to worsen yet. It was too soon. She had so many things to do.

Finally Morgan snatched up the telephone, which was as antiquated as the rest of the place. The handset weighed at least two pounds, she guessed, and the rotary dial seemed to mock her high-tech tastes.

If her "hello?" sounded irritated, it was because

she was dying to read more of those journals up in the attic, to find out more about their author. She might be on the verge of admitting that she was a talentless hack, but she still knew good writing when she read it, and what she had been reading upstairs was good writing. Painfully good.

"Morgan? What took you so long? I was getting worried."

Her irritation fled at David Sumner's familiar voice. Her honorary uncle—a title she'd stopped using long ago—was the only person who hadn't turned his back on her when she had gone from spoiled rich girl to penniless orphan in a matter of hours. He was the one person she didn't mind hearing from just now.

"Hey, David," she said. "I was just...exploring. This place is huge, you know."

"No, I don't know, never having laid eyes on it. You sound a little out of breath."

"Two flights of stairs will do that."

She noticed his hesitation. He tended to worry about her far more than he should.

"How is the place, anyway?" he asked at length.

"It's a wreck," she told him, her tone teasing, partly because she was trying to ease his mind and partly because she enjoyed teasing him. "Which serves you right for buying it sight unseen. Who does stuff like that?"

She could almost see his puckered face, the laugh lines around his eyes, his balding head. David had been her best friend for as long as she could remember. "A friend of the family," her parents had always called him. But it had seemed to Morgan that he'd barely tolerated *the family.*

Of course, he had known the truth about her parents

all along. She had only learned it recently, through tabloid headlines and courtroom vultures.

"I bought it for the location, and you know it," David told her. "And I trust my real estate guru on such matters. The building is coming down, anyway."

"Yes, it is," Morgan said. "As we speak."

He was quiet for a moment. "That bad, huh?"

She could have slapped herself. Sometimes she could be such a self-centered little... "It's not," she said quickly. "I was joking." She looked around her at the room she had chosen to inhabit. It had been somebody's library or study once upon a time.

She thought of the little boy she had been reading about and wondered if it had ever been his. In his older years, perhaps, when he had decided to write his memoirs.

From the corner of her eye, she saw him. A dark, broad-shouldered form bent over the desk, with a quill pen in his long, graceful hand. Her heart jumped, and she caught her breath and turned toward him. But there was nothing. No man, no form, no quill pen. Just her computer with its electric blue screen. Whatever she had seen was there and then gone. A vision. A thought form. A little overactivity of her imagination, perhaps.

A shiver worked its way up her spine, but she shook it away.

"Describe it to me," David was saying.

"What?" she asked, dragging her eyes away from the old desk.

"The house. Describe it to me."

She flicked her gaze toward the desk again. No one there. Sighing, she tried to comply with David's request. "It must have been incredible once. The scroll-work around the fireplace mantle is worn and faded, but lavish. I think it's hardwood. You're going to want to take that entire piece out before you tear it down. And there's hand-tooled casing that borders every one of the tall windows. This place has...I don't know. Something."

"It's far from what you're used to, though," David said.

"Yeah, well, it's not Beverly Hills, and we aren't having movie stars over for poolside parties...but I wouldn't be getting any work done that way, would I?"

"And are you? Getting any work done?"

Morgan looked at the glowing blue screen of her computer—which had only escaped the notice of the estate lawyers because it had been with her at UCLA when her parents had been killed and the true state of their finances revealed. They were broke, and so far in debt Morgan could barely wrap her mind around the actual numbers. She hadn't been able to make sense of it, at first. Her father was a successful director, her mother an actress who had reached her zenith a decade ago and had been doing smaller roles lately, but who had still seemed content with her life.

Or so Morgan had thought. She soon learned she had been living in a bubble. The level of cocaine in her parents' systems the night of the accident was so high the coroner wondered how they had even managed to drive.

They'd been addicts, their entire lifestyle a lie.

The house and everything in it had been sold to pay off a portion of their accumulated debt, and Morgan had to drop out of school. Her tuition had already been months overdue. And apparently her friends were as shallow as David had always tried to tell her they were, because once the truth came out, they had abandoned her like last year's wardrobe, while those she had always considered beneath her seemed secretly amused by her troubles. The last few days on campus, she had found tabloid pages tacked to bulletin boards in every hall, screaming about the secret, drug-infested life of the famous couple who seemed to have had it all. The nightmare behind the fairy tale, and the poor little rich girl left to pick up the pieces.

She had run from L.A. with her tail between her legs, with nowhere to go and nothing left besides the things she managed to take with her. She'd pulled into David's driveway with nothing but her Maserati—the registration in her name, thank God—and the stuff she had crammed into its minuscule trunk. He was her last hope, and she had half expected him to turn away from her in disgust, just like all the rest.

But he hadn't turned away. He'd helped her sell the car, buy a modest used one and pocket the difference. When she said she needed a hideaway where she could go to lick her wounds, he told her she could use this place in Maine, free of charge, for as long as she needed to.

Which wouldn't be long, she thought silently. She had always intended to become a wildly successful screenwriter. It was just going to have to happen a bit sooner than she'd planned. David was a producer. He would help her make the right connections, maybe even produce her screenplay himself. He'd promised to give her a shot. Help her all he could.

All she needed...was the material.

"Morgan?" David's voice jerked her away from

the path her thoughts had been wandering. "Did you hear me? I asked, how's the script coming?"

She blinked at the blank computer screen. The blinking cursor. "Fine. Great. It's coming great." So great that she had decided to go exploring this ancient wreck of a house rather than continue the battle with the blank screen. The only key on her keyboard getting a steady workout was the one marked "delete." She'd been producing garbage since she had arrived here. Garbage.

"You know, it's only natural you might have some trouble getting started," David said. "Don't push yourself. You've been through a lot. Your mind needs time to digest it all."

Morgan shrugged. "That's not it," she told him.

"No?"

"Of course not. It's been six months. I'm completely over it."

"Completely over losing your parents, your fortune, your home, your education and what you thought was your identity?" He made a clicking noise with his tongue. "I don't think so."

"Well, I am. And to tell you the truth, finding out I was adopted explained a lot of things. I mean, you know my parents were never all that...involved."

"That was the cocaine, hon. Not the adoption. Not you."

She cleared her throat when it started to tighten up, gave herself a mental kick. "As for the rest of it...I'm going to get it all back, David. Everything I lost. And then some."

She heard the smile in his voice. "I don't doubt it a bit."

"Neither do I," she said, glancing again at the

blank screen, feeling those doubts she'd denied nearly smothering her. Damn, why couldn't writing a blockbuster script be as easy as she had always thought it would be? She used to watch films with the feeling that she could do better in her sleep.

"So when can I expect the screenplay?" he asked.

Licking her lips, she wished to God she knew. "A masterpiece takes time...and it's...so unpredictable."

"I need a fall project. I'm saving a slot for you, Morgan. Three months. I need the material in three months. Can you do that? Write it over the summer and get it to me by September?"

Lifting her chin, swallowing hard, she said, "Yes. I'll have it finished by September. No problem."

Big problem.

"Great," David said. "You're gonna be fine, Morgan. You can get through this."

"Of course I can."

"Do you need anything?"

"No, no, I'm fine."

"Your funds still holding out?"

She licked her lips, forced the lie out. She'd cleaned out her accounts on David's advice, before the lawyers and creditors could get hold of her money, and she'd had the cash from the car. But while she had no rent here, there were other expenses. The phone, the electricity, and she had to eat. Truth to tell, the money in her checking account was dwindling.

"I'm fine," she said again.

"Good," David said softly. "Good. You let me know if there's anything you need."

"I will, David."

He was quiet for a moment. "How about your health?"

Drawing a breath, she sighed. "You know how I hate being thought of as sickly."

"Did I say you were sickly?"

"No."

"Well?"

She pursed her lips. "The brisk clean air up here is working wonders on me," she lied. What could she tell him? The truth? That it was cold and dreary and damp here, and that she resented having to think of a sixty-degree day in late April as a heat wave, when she would be basking in eighty-degree heat beside her parents' pool, working on her tan by now, if she'd been home?

But it did no good to wish for what she couldn't have.

"I ought to go, David," she whispered around the lump in her throat. "If I'm going to have this done by fall, I ought to get at it."

"Okay, hon. You just call if you need anything."

"I will, David. Thanks."

Morgan replaced the old receiver on its hook and gnawed on her lower lip. She turned the rickety wooden chair toward the computer screen, assured herself once again that no one was in it, and finally sat down. She poised her hands over the keyboard, told herself to write something, now, today, or else give up for good and go out and find a job. The problem was, she couldn't *do* anything.

Writing was the only thing she had ever wanted to do, and she'd been good once. Or…she thought she had. In school, her essays got raves. The theater group had even produced one of her plays. Everyone loved it. The campus critics, the local press...

But that was when she'd been Morgan De Silva, the brilliant daughter of a famous director and a beloved actress, the girl leading the charmed life and destined for success. Now she was Morgan De Silva, disgraced has-been, penniless, homeless, practically run out of town and staring into the face of a future more bleak than she could have imagined a year ago.

Now...now she just didn't know if her talent had ever been real, or if it had been her name winning her praise all this time. She didn't know anything anymore, not who she was, or what she was doing or why the words had just stopped coming. It was as if the well inside her had been a part of the illusion her life had been. As if it had dried up when that illusion had been shattered.

She lowered her hands, having put not one word on the screen. Outside, the wind howled; the lights dimmed, then came back. The old house groaned when the wind blew. Probably, if she was as old as it was, she would groan, too, she thought. And then she wondered just how old that was.

Those journals...there had been no dates inscribed, but it was obvious they'd been written long, long ago. At least a century...and maybe closer to two.

That thought brought her back to the one she'd had earlier, about the journal writer. Dante. Had he lived here, that man who'd been a Gypsy boy, entranced by his outcast aunt? Had he been in this very room, perhaps, pacing before a fire, his quill pen lying untouched on some polished antique desk? Had he courted his muse as impatiently as she did, grown frustrated when the words wouldn't come?

Drawn as if by an unseen hand, she rose and walked out of the office, through the ghostly front hall and up the wide staircase. She traversed the hallway, ignoring the doors that lined either side. She hadn't even ventured into most of the rooms up here. There were so many.

But her goal was none of them. Her goal was beyond, up the back stairway into the attic, where spiderwebs held court and dust ruled the day. She knelt as she had before and fished the book of matches from her jeans pocket, then lit the candles in the gaudy candelabra she'd found downstairs. As their soft yellow glow spread, she lovingly opened the hand-tooled chest, took out that first volume, stroked its cover and opened it slowly, careful not to break the brittle pages. Turning to the place where she had left off, she began to read. And once again she lost herself in the words.

2

It was fully thirteen years before I saw Sarafina again. Thirteen full years, during which I had learned many things. I had learned that no matter where we went, we would be driven out eventually. I had learned that no matter how honest we might be, we would be called thieves by strangers who knew nothing about us. So I learned to take what I wanted and wish them all damned. I might as well enjoy the fruits of the crimes attributed to me, I reasoned. If I were caught, I would pay for those crimes, whether I had committed them or not. Better I hang for my own offenses than for those of some pale-skinned whelp who pretended honesty and was believed without question, so long as there was a Gypsy nearby to take the blame.

But of all the things I had learned, one bit of knowledge eluded me, though I had sought it without end. I had never learned the mystery of Sarafina. Who she really was, how she was related to us, why she had been ousted from our band. Nor what was the nature of the curse she was said to carry.

Not until the night when my life nearly ended— *did* end, for all practical purposes. It *did* end—and a new one began. It was late autumn, and the year was 1848.

I was a young man then. Hotheaded and reckless.

My family was about to pack up and move on yet again. Not because we had grown tired of the place but because the locals accused us of stealing livestock, and we knew the law would be on us soon.

Before we left, I had decided I would extract a pound of flesh from our accusers. More than a pound, actually.

The moon was newly born that night; only a strand of silver gleamed in the sky as I crept into the farmer's barnyard. And even that light was blotted out more and more often as long, clawlike fingers of blue-black clouds reached across its slender arch. I didn't care what I stole that night, so long as I took something. It was retribution. It was repayment for the slander done to me and mine.

The first animal I came upon was a bearded billy goat. I remember it well…fawn and white, and shaggy. Horns curving back, away from its head. Hooves in sad need of trimming, like the too-long fingernails of an old man.

Slipping a rope around its neck, I led the goat away from the shed where it had been penned. Across the worn ground where, by day, the hens would peck and dig. Now they were roosting along the top rail of the fence and in the scraggly young saplings here and there. The goat came along easily, right up until I passed through the gate and started away from the barnyard. Then it stopped all of a sudden, planting its forefeet and bleating loud and long and plaintively. It was like a scream in the night.

I should have let the animal go. But pride in a young man is sometimes overblown, and in me it was combined with anger and fury and frustration.

So I kept tugging on the lead rope, dragging the

animal through the lush green grasses, which were damp with night dew. It dragged its feet, tugging and thrashing its shaggy head from side to side, bawling like a lost calf.

The farmer never called out, never ordered me to stop or release the goat or anything else. I never even knew he'd stepped out of his house. That was how silently death came for me that night. One moment I was cussing at an ornery goat, turning and tugging, the rope over my shoulder and the goat behind me. And the next I was facedown on the ground, my ears ringing from the explosion of the gunshot that had come as if from nowhere.

I could not believe it had happened so easily, so suddenly. Without fanfare or drama. The farmer had simply pulled the trigger of his black powder rifle, sending an earsplitting roar through the night and a lead ball through my back.

Shock and pain screamed in me in the seconds after I hit the ground. I felt, for a moment, the fire of the ball's path and the rush of the warm blood soaking my clothes. But then something far more frightening than pain came to me.

Numbness.

It began at my feet, as best I can recall. And I wasn't aware of it as it happened but afterward, when I heard the farmer's footfalls coming closer. I realized that I could not move, that I could not feel my feet. Within a second of that realization I felt the numbness spreading, creeping up my legs as steadily as a rising tide. My hips and pelvis, my belly. It rose further, and the pain that was like a fire in my back vanished. It simply vanished.

I felt nothing. I tried to move my arms, my legs, but I could not.

I gasped in shock when my body suddenly flipped, for I had not even felt the toe of the cruel farmer's boot as he used it to roll me onto my back. But I saw the hate in his eyes as he stared down at me, his weathered face like the bark of an aging cherry tree, white whiskers long and unkempt.

"Thievin' Gypsy scum," he said. He spat on me, and then turned and walked away, taking his goat with him.

He hadn't killed me.

The relief of that was soon overruled by the realization that he would have, had he not been certain I would die on my own within a few minutes. I could not feel the blood spreading beneath me, staining the grass. But I sensed it flowing from my body, felt myself weakening steadily from the loss of it. Felt myself…dying.

I heard his footsteps retreating. Heard the door of his ramshackle house banging closed. And then I heard nothing beyond the gentle wind of the night, whispering in the trees. Whispering my name.

"Oh, sweet Dante," a voice said from very nearby. Not the wind. Not this time. "You've brought this upon yourself far more quickly than I would have liked."

I moved my eyes, turned my head very slightly, but only that. For the most part, my eyes seemed to be the only part of me I was still able to command.

Sarafina stood beside me, silhouetted by the night, like some dark angel. Those black fingers of cloud stretched over the stars behind her. I tried to speak, but the words came so softly, I knew she could not hear them. Then she knelt and bent close to me, and with every ounce of strength in me, I managed to say, "Sarafina...I am dying."

Her soft hand brushed my dark hair away from my forehead. "No, Dante. You know full well I shall not let that happen."

"B-but..."

"Hush. It is almost time." She glanced down at my body, and I wondered what she saw. "You've nearly bled to death. It will only be another moment."

My eyes widened, and panic choked me. "Sarafina!" I rasped, fear giving my voice new strength, though it still emerged as little more than a harsh whisper. "Please!"

"Trust me, my darling. You will not die."

"But..."

"You will not die," she said again.

I lay there, fading, fading, darkness closing in around the edges of my vision. I realized dully that she looked no different to me than she had when I'd seen her last. No older. No different at all.

"There now. That's better."

My eyes opened, fell closed, opened again. My breaths came shallow and sparse, and I could feel my heartbeat. It pounded in my ears, ever slower... slower...slower....

"Listen to me, my special one," she said, and her voice seemed to come from very far away, as if she spoke to me from the depths of a cave. "You have a choice to make, and it must be made now. There will be no time to deliberate. Do you wish to die? Here and now? Or live, though it will mean living in exile, as I do? Hated by the family, outcast, and driven away."

I felt weak. As if I were becoming a shadow. I didn't understand her questions.

"Life or death, Dante? Speak your answer. If you delay, the choice will be gone. You will die. Tell me now. Which will it be? Life...or death?"

I strained to form the single word but never heard it emerge from my lips or felt them move at all. It was all I could do to think the word with the intention of speaking it aloud. *Life.*

"Good."

She moved. My vision was fading, so that I could not see where she went, what she did. Then she pressed something warm and wet to my lips and whispered, "Drink, Dante. This is the elixir that will make you live. Drink."

The warm, thick liquid touched my lips, and there was a quickening of my senses, followed at once by a shocking sensation of need. I closed my mouth around the font she offered and nursed at it like a suckling babe. Life seemed to awaken in me, along with a hunger such as I had never known. My arms moved, my hands clasping this bounty, holding it to my face, as I sucked at the luscious fluid that flowed into me.

"Enough!"

Sarafina gripped a handful of my hair and jerked my head away. And only then did I realize it had been her wrist at which I'd been so eagerly feeding. Her *blood* I had been drinking so hungrily. Even now, she pulled her forearm away, tugging a scarf from her hair and wrapping it tightly around the wound.

Horrified, I felt my stomach lurch, turning my head away from her and lifting my hand to swipe at my mouth.

"It's all right, Dante," she whispered. "It is the way the gift is shared."

I looked down at my hands, red with the blood I'd wiped from my mouth. But alive. Strong. I moved my fingers, made fists.

"What is this?" I asked her softly. "What...what does this mean?" And even as I said it, the numbness was receding down my body. The feeling rushed back into my torso, my legs and my feet, with heightened intensity.

My senses prickled with keen new awareness. My skin tingled at the touch of the very air. My eyes seemed to see more vividly, more precisely, than ever they had. And strength surged through my veins.

She tore my shirt away, making strips of its fabric as she spoke. "It is a gift, young Dante, though the old one calls it a curse. It is a gift I have given to you. You will never die now. Never grow older. And though your family will turn against you, you will never be alone, as I have been. For I will be with you. Always."

Looking over my shoulder at her, for she was now wadding the fabric and stuffing it into the wound in my back, which caused me immense pain, I shook my head. I did not understand. She tied several strips tightly around me, to hold the wads in place, then reached down, clasped my hand and helped me to my feet, and even as I rose, I saw the old man's silhouette looming just behind her.

I opened my mouth to shout a warning.

Before I said a word, Sarafina turned with such speed she seemed a mere blur. The farmer's rifle went sailing through the air, out of sight, firing harmlessly into the woods as it hit the ground. And Sarafina, the beautiful, gracious woman by whom I had been so entranced, gripped the farmer's shirtfront and jerked him forward. Before I could even react, she had fastened her mouth to his throat.

I heard the sounds.... I saw, very clearly in the darkness now, what she was doing. Drinking...his blood. Gorging herself at his throat. At first the farmer pounded her back and kicked at her...and then...then he simply surrendered. I heard his sigh, saw him close his eyes and even wrap his arms around her. He let his head fall backward, and I saw him grind his hips against Sarafina's as she continued to suck at his throat.

And then there was no life left in him at all.

She let go his shirt, and the corpse fell to the ground. Empty. A rag-poppet. Utterly drained.

With one of her scarfs, Sarafina dabbed delicately at her mouth as she turned to face me. I gaped at her, my mouth working soundlessly.

"Don't look so shocked, Dante. Are you telling me you're only just figuring it out? Hmm? We are Nosferatu. We are undead." She licked her lips, tilted her head and smiled very slightly at me. "Vampires," she whispered, and I swore the night wind picked up the word and repeated it a thousand times in a thousand voices.

Vampires.

A breeze from some unseen source made the candle flames leap and flicker. Morgan tore her eyes from the weathered pages and automatically looked behind her. But of course no one was there. Nothing was there. This wasn't real.

It wasn't real.

"Oh my God," Morgan whispered. "This isn't a diary. These aren't memoirs. It's…it's fiction. It's incredible, breathtaking *fiction!*"

Oh, maybe not to the man who had written it. The delightfully insane artist who had crafted this tale had, perhaps, even *believed* it. Imagine. A man who honestly thought he was a vampire. A man who had, in all likelihood, lived here. Right here. In this house.

Something scraped the window, and Morgan whirled, her hand flying to her chest as her heart leapt. But it was only a tree limb, bent and clawlike, scratching at the glass. Not some creature of the night who called himself Dante, come back to claim his diaries and his house. Of course not. Vampires were not real.

The sudden movement, the scare, left her slightly dizzy and made her chest pound. She waited for it to ease. The rush of breathlessness passed, as it always did. She drew a few deep, cleansing breaths and glanced at her watch. She had been sitting in the dark, musty attic for hours, lost in the imaginary world of a madman. When she should have been working on her own tales of intrigue.

God, how was she ever going to have a saleable script ready for David in three months? Especially now, when all she wanted to do was read more of this incredible tale.

Vaguely she wondered how long it had taken the imaginative Dante to pen *his* fantasies. Not long, she thought…if every journal in this stack were filled. And even then, she didn't know how he had managed it all in one short lifetime.

He was dead, though. He had to be dead, because she had finally come upon a date, so there was no doubt. And his words, his tales…they just lay there, untouched. So vivid, so wonderfully written, it was almost heartbreaking that they hadn't been shared with the world. God, if she had written something this good and it had never been seen, she would have been…

Oh.

Oh. The thought that just occurred to her! This could *be* her work. For all anyone else knew, it could all be *her work.* Who the hell would ever know the difference?

"No," she whispered aloud. "It wouldn't be right."

Wouldn't it? her mind argued. She had just decided it was criminal that this work hadn't been shared. She had just acknowledged that if she had been the author, she would have spent eternity regretting that the work lay here, undiscovered. The written word was meant to be read, after all. Not hidden away but…shared. Experienced.

She knelt again in front of the trunk, licked her dry lips. What harm would there be, she wondered? Dante was long dead, and no one else could possibly know of the existence of these diaries. Could they? Of course not! If they did, these journals wouldn't have been left here to molder in a dusty attic.

And there were so many of them!

"My God," she whispered. "This is a gold mine. I'm sitting on an absolute gold mine here." And as she sat there, staring down at the trunk full of stories, she knew that they were even more than that. They were the key to getting everything she wanted, to reclaiming everything she had lost. Wealth. Power. Fame. Her triumphant return to L.A. It was all right here. Almost like a gift...left just for her by some long-dead madman who'd called himself Dante and believed himself to be a vampire.

She took the first journal carefully, holding it to her breast like a lover as she straightened, and, turning, she carried it downstairs to her office.

This time, when she held her hands over the keyboard, Dante's journal was lying open on the table beside the computer. And this time, the words came.

3

Maxine Stuart was watching *JFK* for about the twelfth time on the little VCR/TV combo in her bedroom, a copy of *Catcher in the Rye* in her lap, a half-dead can of Coke on the bedside stand, when she heard the sirens. The sound stabbed her in the belly like an ice-cold blade and brought her slowly to her feet, though she couldn't have said why. She went to the window, pushed the curtains aside. She could see the flashing lights of the emergency vehicles passing on the highway in the distance. Heading south. Her gaze turned in that direction, and she narrowed her eyes on the faint red glow in the distant night sky.

A familiar Jeep bounded into her driveway, and about a second later she heard the front door of the small house open, heard her mother speaking to Max's friends as she let them in. Maxine shut the TV off, turned and opened her bedroom door as they came hurrying through the house.

Her two best friends came around a corner into the hall and stopped when they saw her standing there. Something was up. Jason didn't shake easily, and he looked shaken. Storm—her real name was Tempest, but she hated it—was downright pale. Maxine's mom was right on their heels.

"So what is it, what's burning?" Max asked.

"It's Spook Central," Jason said without even missing a beat. "It's bad."

"It's awful," Stormy added, and her round jewel-blue eyes were damp. "I don't think anyone got out alive."

Spook Central was Maxine's pet name for the large, nameless government compound just outside town. The main building was huge and sat well back from the road behind a large, electrified fence, surrounded by surveillance cameras and shrouded in secrecy. A research lab—that was the party line, anyway, and so the gullible locals believed. Medical research was done there—they were working on finding cures for cancer and AIDS, stuff like that. Good work. Almost holy. Too sacred to mess with or poke around in. Who would question such a saintly mission?

Maxine had her own theories, as she did about most things, and right now she hoped to God the one she had always considered the most likely—that the place was a military lab working on germ warfare and chemical weapons—was dead wrong.

Nightmare images from Stephen King's *The Stand* coiled and uncoiled in her mind until she shook them away and stepped into action. She turned, reaching back into her room to snatch a jacket from the back of a chair. Then she was striding down the hall. "Let's go."

"Go? Go where?" her mother asked, falling into step behind the three of them as they headed for the front door. When no one replied, Ellen got around them, stepping right into their path. "Max, don't you go over there. You'll just get in the way and maybe get hurt."

"Come on, Mom, I'm twenty years old. I'm not going to bother the firefighters. I just want to know what's going on."

"Then read about it in the morning paper, like everyone else."

"God, how can you be so innocent?"

Ellen Stuart sighed, looking worried, but also resigned. No one had ever really been able to change Maxine's mind once it was made up about something, and her mother ought to be getting used to that by now, having experienced it firsthand from the day she brought the three-month-old orphan home for the first time. "Be careful."

"Always." Maxine yanked a mini-backpack off the hook by the door. An iron-on patch with the words Trust No One and the *X-Files* logo decorated its front. She slung it over her shoulder, and the three friends trooped out of the house.

They all piled into Jason's creamed-coffee colored Jeep Cherokee. He liked to joke that he had picked the color to match his skin. And it did, pretty closely. Maxine took the back seat. Stormy, a pixie-sized psych major with short, spiky, bleached hair, got into the front with Jason, closing her door just as he backed out into the street and headed out of town.

Maxine sat on the edge of her seat, her head between the two in the front. "You can see the fire from here. Look at that."

They did. Stormy shivered, lowered her eyes. Jason stared as if mesmerized for a moment, then snapped out of it, flicking on the radio, turning the dial. "I knew you'd want to go," he said. "It came over my brother's scanner. If he wasn't a volunteer firefighter, I probably still wouldn't know."

"Still nothing about it on the radio, Jay?" Stormy asked. She was nervous; playing with her eyebrow ring was always a sign of that.

He kept flicking the dial, then gave up, shaking his head slowly. "I expected special reports, crap like that, but there hasn't been a word."

"They report what they're told to report," Maxine said. "Despite my mother's gullible belief in the system, the phrase 'free press' is an oxymoron in this country."

"I *like* your mom," Jason put in.

Max blinked at him as if he were speaking another language. "I like her, too. What the hell does that have to do with anything?"

"I just don't think you ought to be calling her gullible. She wouldn't like it."

Maxine closed her eyes, shook her head, then glanced at Stormy for backup.

"He's right," Stormy said. "Your mom is cool. You're so lucky."

"Of course she's cool! Hell, I would have gotten a dorm room or an apartment or gone to college out of town if she wasn't cool, instead of staying home and going to a local school. But this has nothing to do with my mother or how cool she may or may not be! I'm talking about the government here. Cover-ups. Covert operations."

Stormy shrugged, averting her eyes. Topics like this always made her uncomfortable. But Maxine wasn't uncomfortable discussing it. She was more uncomfortable having lived practically in the shadow of that huge, fenced in, well-guarded compound all her life, and never once knowing what went on inside.

She knew only one thing for sure. It wasn't cancer

research. She would have given her eyeteeth for a look beyond the tall, electrified fences of that place. Just one look. Now maybe no one would ever know the truth.

Jason drove on, pulling the Jeep over onto the right-hand shoulder before they got to the point where emergency vehicles lined both sides of the road. Highway flares lay across the pavement. Orange and white striped sawhorses with red reflectors were lined up behind them, forming a boundary that was supposed to tell them to keep out. They got out of the Jeep. Flames in the distance licked at the night sky, and Max could already taste the smoke in her mouth with every breath.

"This way." Maxine walked along the road's right shoulder, beyond the parked vehicles, and her friends followed. The burning compound was on the left, at the end of a long curving drive. She led the others forward until they were directly across the street from the entrance to the compound. Firefighters were across the street, partway along the drive, facing away from them. They were completely focused on their work, anyway. Maxine crouched near an ambulance, tugging the others down with her.

The fire trucks had apparently driven straight through the gate at the head of the drive. The guardhouse nearby was empty, the gate itself lying flat. The fence to the left and right of it was buckled and broken. The surveillance cameras that had been mounted on poles lay smashed to bits. Volunteer firefighters in yellow jackets marked with glowing silver reflective tape manned huge hoses attached to tanker trucks in the curving paved drive. Every time they beat the flames down a little, the trucks would roll closer, the men pushing farther into the fury.

"I don't know how they can stand it. God, I can feel the heat from here," Stormy said, pressing a palm to her face.

"I'm surprised their hoses aren't melting," Jason whispered. "If they move any closer…"

"If they move any closer, we'll be able to get in."

The other two looked at Maxine as if she had sprouted horns.

"What?" she asked.

"You gotta be out of your freaking mind, Max," Jason told her, while Storm just shook her head. "We can't go in there."

"No one's watching the entrance. They're all distracted, fighting the fire. We can get in without even trying."

"Okay, I'll rephrase that. We *can* go in there. But we shouldn't."

Now it was Maxine's turn to gape. "What are you, crazy? I've been *dying* to get behind those gates since I was old enough to see through that lame cancer research cover story they've been using."

"Which was when she was about six," Stormy muttered.

Max shot her a look but hurried on. "Don't you guys get it? This is our chance. No guards, nothing. We can finally see something besides the lie."

"And just what do you think there's gonna be left to see, Max?" Jason pointed at the place. "It's completely engulfed in flames."

"I won't know until I try."

He sighed, lowering his shaved head and running a hand over it. No one spoke again for a long time as they crouched and waited and watched. Twenty minutes went by before the firefighters pushed a few yards closer. Max shot to her feet, glanced both ways and ran across the street. Her two friends hesitated, then followed. They crossed the pavement and jogged through the opening, right over the mesh of the toppled gate, past the abandoned guardhouse and into the trees that lined the driveway. There were a lot of them. The better to block the place from the view of casual passersby, Max thought. Pines. Of course they were pines. Year-round-camouflage for whatever went on inside.

They ducked beneath one of the trees, and Max stared ahead. The fire was being steadily beaten down. Those firefighters were something else, she thought, wondering if Jay's older brother, Mike, was among them. They never gave up, even though they had to realize by now that it was a lost cause.

More sirens came, and Max looked back toward the road to see police cars, cops getting out, dispersing some of the curious onlookers who had now begun to gather on the road out front. "We just made it in time," she whispered.

"If they catch us in here, our asses will be toast," Jason said.

"If we get any closer to that inferno, they might be toast anyway," Stormy added.

The firemen ahead fought on, soaking the place down, beating back the flames and pressing ever closer. The trucks rolled forward a little more, and Max urged her unwilling comrades to do the same. "See that flagpole over there?" she asked, pointing. Jason and Storm looked at it, then at her.

"Once they get up that far, we can cut around the side of the building and make our way to the back."

"And then a flaming wall can come down on us, crushing us and roasting us at the same time," Storm said. Her gaze was fixed on the burning building, and the flames' reflection danced in her eyes.

Max swallowed any second thoughts she had about dragging her two best friends into this, beat them down the way the firefighters beat down the flames. It was for the greater good, she told herself. And besides, they wouldn't get hurt. She wouldn't let them get hurt. Maxine Stuart took care of her friends.

Movement drew her attention. "There they go!"

As the fire truck rolled ahead, Max ran forward, cutting off to the left and moving rapidly away from the pool of firelight that spread like an aura from ground-zero. The trees ended there, and she paused at the very last one. She tried not to feel a huge sense of relief when she realized Jason and Storm were still at her side. But she felt it anyway. God, they were loyal.

The distance from the front to the back of the rubble that had once been the main building was at least half a football field, without so much as a shrub for cover. But it was dark. Getting darker with every cloud of thick smoke that wafted from the fire.

"We can make it," Max said.

"They're gonna haul our asses to jail for this, Maxie," Jason said.

"Ready?"

Neither of them answered her. Max licked her lips and trusted them. "Go!" And she ran.

She was never certain they were following until she stopped when she reached what had been the far end of the building and they bumped into her in the darkness. Hands gripped shoulders as they steadied each other. Then they stood for a moment, catching their breath, squinting into the darkness. There were fifty feet between where they stood and the smoldering remains at the rear of the building. It no longer much resembled a building at all. It wasn't tall or square. It was a heap. Flames leaped up here and there, although most of the real fire had moved hungrily toward the front, having had its fill here, it seemed. There were glowing red shapes forming mounds underneath the charred forms of the skeletal underpinning. There were ashes, smoke. Were there people in there? she wondered. *Bodies?*

"This is close enough," Stormy whispered.

Max looked around. "You see that shrub over there? It's out of the smoke." She pointed. "You two wait for me there. I promise I won't be long."

"Don't, Max," Jason warned. He sounded pissed off. "Just...don't."

"Five minutes," she said. "Just five freaking minutes. This is once in a lifetime, Jay." She didn't wait for him to argue. She ran, instead.

They didn't follow this time.

It was hot. Damned hot, and the smoke was burning her eyes and her nose, and she kept trying not to cough too loudly and give herself away. She ran until she reached the rear of the building, and then she moved closer and closer to it, as close as she could stand to get. She figured her hair was probably getting a little singed, and she had to watch where she put her feet to keep from stepping on smoldering embers that would have melted right through the soles of her shoes.

She looked around, squinting through the veil of smoke and the shimmering heat waves. There were several things on the ground in one area. Large broken boxes—computers. Smashed to bits. Some burned and charred, others just smashed. Had someone thrown them out the windows in an effort to save them? Or maybe to destroy them? She kicked at one. What she wouldn't have given for a hard drive from one of those machines. God only knew what she might find. Bending, she reached out to pick through the pile of rubble, but the pieces were so hot they seared her fingers, and she jerked her hand away, sucking air through her teeth.

"Shit." She put her burned fingers to her lips, blew on them, drew them away and shook them in the air as she kept on walking. Her foot kicked something that rolled, and she looked down, frowning, looking closer. When she realized she was bending over a charred forearm and hand, she pulled back so suddenly she almost fell over. "Jesus!"

Her breathing quickened now, her lungs sucking in more smoke with every breath, but that couldn't be helped. She continued her search, spotting other evidence of human remains in the wreckage. More and more of it. Bodies. Parts of bodies. It was as if she had stepped into hell's dumping ground. Jesus, why hadn't anyone been able to get out alive? What the hell had happened here?

This was stupid. She had been a fool to come here. She started to turn, to go back, when movement caught her eye. Movement in the smoky distance. She went still, squinting, staring.

Gradually, the movement took shape. A man, his clothes burned, his skin so sooty she couldn't tell if he was black or white. He was hunched over, walking unevenly, bending and straightening over and over again. It looked as if he was picking things up, dragging himself away from the wreckage and picking things up as he went. She was about to offer to help him when she heard her name shouted from a distance.

The man heard Stormy's call, too, and he went stiff, jerking his head toward the voice. A tongue of flame leapt to life somewhere near him and illuminated his face for just an instant. His hair had been burned completely away from one side of his head, and the scalp and one side of his face was charred. Black, with pink showing through here and there. She tried to memorize his features, the rounded face, the shape of his chin. He tucked whatever he had been holding into his pockets and ran in a lumbering, uneven gait away from the voice and right toward Maxine.

She ducked down low, held her breath, willed herself not to move. She didn't know for sure that the man was dangerous, but if he were up to anything good, he wouldn't be running away. Maybe he was just a snoop, like she was. But probably not. He'd been inside that burning building. That much was obvious.

He limped past her, never even looking down at her as she sat there fighting not to shiver in fear. He moved so close she could smell his charred flesh, and it made her stomach clench reflexively.

Something fell from his jacket. Something—no, *two somethings*—dropped to the hot, rubble-strewn ground right at her feet. He never noticed, just kept going, dragging one leg, lunging with the other, until he vanished in the smoke.

Swallowing hard, Maxine reached for the items. One was a CD-ROM. The other, some kind of ID badge. She swore every nerve ending in her body tingled with electricity as she tucked the two still-warm items carefully into her pocket and, turning, ran back the way she had come. She refused to look again at the carnage. Refused to look behind her, even when she swore she felt the disfigured man's gaze burning into her back. She just hurried as fast as she could back to where she'd left her friends and fell to her knees near the shrub where they waited.

"God, thank God, you're back!" Storm said. She bent over Max, stroking her back. "Are you all right? What happened back there?"

"Did you find anything? What did you see?" Jason asked.

Maxine lifted her head, looked at them. "It's... there were...bodies."

"Oh, God," Storm said, closing her eyes.

Max gripped Jason's forearm, and he helped her to her feet. "Let's get the hell out of here, okay?" he suggested.

She nodded. They fell into step together, with Max in the center, her two friends flanking her almost protectively. They had made it almost all the way to the front gate when the sounds of rumbling motors flooded the night and vehicles came roaring along the street and into the drive. They ducked into the nearby pines, watching as camo-painted trucks and Jeeps with spotlights mounted on them bounded past. At least one vehicle had a machine gun mounted on a tripod in the back. Soldiers armed with weapons came spilling out of the trucks and fanned out onto the grounds.

Ten feet ahead of Max, a cop stood with his back to them, looking at the commotion with his head tilted to one side. *Her cop,* Maxine realized with a rush of relief.

Jason saw him at the same time, squeezed Max's arm, whispered, "Cop."

"It's okay. It's Lou Malone."

Jason sent her a frown.

"He teaches that women's self-defense course I take."

"You remember him, Jay," Storm put in. "He used to work our high school dances. He's the one Maxie always had a crush on."

"Oh, yeah. That one." He sent Max a look that asked if she still did, but she just rolled her eyes and looked away.

Someone spoke into a bullhorn, startling her so much that she jerked her gaze away from the back of Lou's head. "This is a government facility and therefore, a military operation. Local firefighters are to cease all activity at once. No one is to leave this site without clearance. Line up in an orderly fashion near the front gate and you'll be escorted off the premises. That is all."

"What the hell is going on, Max?" Storm whispered, clutching Maxine's arm. "They've got *guns.*"

"They're not going to use them." Jason tried to sound confident and sure of himself but missed that goal by about a mile. "I mean, they're soldiers. They *have* to carry guns. Right?"

They watched from their pine-scented blind as the soldiers tugged firemen away from their hoses. Some of the firefighters obeyed, moving to form a straggling line by the gate. Those who didn't move fast enough were searched where they were, then escorted to the front gate and through it. More soldiers searched the fire trucks, and the vehicles in the street, as well.

"Well, I'll be dipped," Officer Malone said to himself. "What the hell is all this about?"

Licking her lips, Maxine stepped out of her cover, walked up to Lou and cleared her throat. He turned fast, then gaped at her in surprise. She loved him. Had since tenth grade. And it didn't matter that his face was hard and lined, or that he was eighteen years older than she was, or that he saw her as little more than a pain-in-the-ass kid with a big imagination.

"Well, if it isn't Mad Maxie Stuart, my favorite redhead," he said, shaking his head slowly. "Why the hell am I not surprised to see you here?"

"Hey, Lou. I just wanted to see the fire."

"Uh-huh." He glanced at her friends. "Don't you two know better than to let her drag you into her schemes?"

They shrugged, said nothing.

"Lou, I don't like this," Max said. "This whole soldier bit. They're searching everyone."

"Yeah, I see that."

"Just an excuse to grope the females," Stormy said. "If they think they're gonna run their hands all over my body, they'd better think again."

Maxine watched Lou's eyes slide to hers as Stormy spoke and knew her friend had fallen on the right tactic. "I don't relish the idea of them copping a feel of my ass, either, Storm." Even as she said it, a soldier slammed a firefighter who resisted him up against the guardhouse. Lou saw it and winced.

"I'm scared, Lou. I just want to get out of here," Max said.

Lou Malone pursed his lips in thought; then, finally, he nodded. "It's not like you kids are any threat to national security. These guys are a little overzealous, I think. Look, there's a break in the fence, just past those pines. See that tallest one? It's near that. Go on, get outta here. I never saw you."

"Thanks, Lou."

He gave Maxine a worried nod, and, impulsively, she leaned up and planted a kiss on his cheek.

"Get your ass straight home, Mad Max. No more screwing around with grown-up stuff, okay?"

"I promise," she said. Then she ran off in the direction he'd shown her.

Max waited until Jason and Storm had gone home. She told them nothing about the man she had seen gathering evidence from the rubble. Nothing about the trophies she had recovered. She didn't want to tell them anything that could put them in danger or make them accessories if what she had done turned out to be a crime. Late that night, very late, she gently wiped the soot from the partially melted plastic of the name badge.

There was a photograph of a man, and the words, "Frank W. Stiles. Security Level: Alpha. DPI."

She knew what "Security Level: Alpha" meant. She had learned that the first time she tried to uncover the truth about UFOs and government cover-ups. Alpha was the word used to indicate the top-level security clearances in certain agencies under the auspices of the CIA. But in all her years of research she had never once come across any reference to any agency or operation called DPI.

Jesus, what the hell had she stumbled upon?

She was nearly shaking when she washed the soot from the CD-ROM and slid it into her computer, praying the heat hadn't ruined it.

It hadn't.

When she clicked RUN, the driver whirred and the screen went black. Red letters lit up the screen.

TOP SECRET DOCUMENTS

of

THE DIVISION OF PARANORMAL INVESTI-GATIONS

CASE FILES D145.9—H376.51

Continue?

The final word blinked its question at her, almost daring her to take it up on the challenge.

Stiffening her spine, she clicked on the word and brought up a table of contents. Names. They were simply names.

Damien, aka Namtar, Damien, aka Gilgamesh
Daniels, Matthew
Daniella
Dante
Devon, Josephina

Obviously alphabetical, the list began in the *D*s and ended in the *H*s. Some were first and last names, some only one name. There were maybe a hundred entries, as near as she could tell without counting. Clicking back to the top of the list, she began scrolling down it. Then she came to one that made her stop in her tracks.

Dracul, Vlad (See full bio for alias list.)

"What the hell?" Curious, she clicked on the name, and a graphic popped up. A drawing, not a photo, of a thoroughly modern-looking man, with long black hair and unusually full lips.

The most well known of the species, he was born in Carpathia and transformed, as nearly as we can tell, in his early twenties. Sired by an unknown enemy soldier, probably a Turk. Most recent sighting, May, 1992, Paris.

"Most *recent* sighting?" She blinked at the screen, her mind not quite digesting what she was seeing. "Ninety-two?"

Below the graphic, with its piercing eyes and pale skin, were more choices: Known Kills, Known Associates, Known Havens, Full Bio.

"What in the name of God *is* this shit?"

She hit the back button, clicked on another name in the list, and again was brought to a screen with an image of the person, this one an actual photograph labeled "taken before transformation" and a brief bio.

Josephina Devon. Born in Brooklyn, NY, in 1962. Transformed in the summer of her 30th year, June 1992. Sire: R-532 aka Rhiannon.

The vampire

"*Vampire?*"

was captured by DPI researchers in December of the same year. Held at DPI Headquarters in White Plains, NY, USA. Expired in captivity, 1995.

Again, the same choices were offered for further information, this time with one notable addition: "Tests Performed on the Subject & Results of Same."

This was not real.

This *could not* be real.

When she clicked on "full bio" she found a document more than a hundred pages long. With details that made her mind spin with the impossibility of it all. When she opened the file that referred to tests performed, she thought she was going to be ill. This person, this woman, had been a lab rat. Held and experimented upon in that very building. In her own town.

But no. It hadn't happened, because it wasn't real.

There were no such things as vampires. Much less a covert government agency devoted to researching them.

And yet, here was the proof that there were.

There *were*.

What the hell was she supposed to do now?

The next day, she still hadn't decided, when the doorbell rang and she answered it to find no one there. Just an unmarked manila envelope on the doorstep.

Her mother was already at work. Most days she left before Max was even out of bed. The odd delivery made Maxine curious, particularly after last night. She looked up and down the street. No strangers lurked anywhere. No suspicious vehicles with tinted windows slid past. The neighborhood was stirring to life. People opening their doors, picking up their morning papers.

Maxine picked up the envelope, looked at it, turned it over. Nothing. Not one word, not a label, not a stamp.

Frowning, she went back inside, closing and locking the door behind her. She took the envelope to the kitchen table, opening it as she walked, and she tipped it, dumping the contents out beside her bowl of corn flakes. Photos. What the hell? She frowned. Polaroids. Three of them. Then she blinked and snatched them up. That was Jason, sound asleep in his bed! She moved it to the back of the pile. The next shot was of Stormy, from the neck up, in her own shower. Maxine swore and looked at the third one. It was a shot of her mother, getting out of her car in the parking garage of the hospital where she worked as an R.N.

The telephone rang, and she damn near jumped out of her skin. Maxine clenched her teeth, dropped the photos on the table and went to pick up the phone.

"Do you like the photos, Maxine?"

The voice was a whisper so cold it sent a chill down her spine. "Who the hell is this?" Maxine reached for the answering machine on the table, jabbed the record button with her forefinger.

"Those shots were all taken in the past twelve hours, you know."

"Why?" Her hand was clenching the telephone so hard her knuckles were white. She wished it was this son of a bitch's neck. How dare he? God, he'd been in Jason's bedroom. In Storm's bathroom. And in that dark parking garage, alone with her mother.

"To show you how easy it is for me to learn everything about you, and how quickly and effortlessly I can get to the people you love. To shoot them. With a camera, this time, but—"

"You fuck with my family or my friends and you die. Do you understand me?"

"That's quite the threat, coming from a girl barely out of high school." He laughed, a deep, low sound that changed into a racking cough.

Max held the phone away from her ear, looking at it as realization dawned. It was him. The burned guy she'd seen at the fire. He must have seen her after all. He stopped coughing, and she put the phone back to her ear. "Why are you calling me? What do you want from me, anyway?"

"I want you to forget everything you saw last night. Pretend you were never there. Tell no one."

"Fine. I'll be glad to. If you'll tell me what happened there last night."

"I'm not making a bargain with you, Maxine. You'll do as I say. Forget you ever saw me."

"But—"

"Listen to me, you nosy little bitch!" She jerked in reaction to the anger in his voice. "If you so much as *mention* anything about seeing me at that fire to anyone, the next thing you find on your doorstep will be a body. Or a part of one. I'll just shuffle those photos and pick one at random. Are you following me now?"

"Yes!" She paused, took a breath, her outrage completely smothered by her fear. He would hurt her mother, her friends. "Yes, I...look, I don't know anything. I'm no threat to you. And I'm the only one that saw you. I didn't tell them. I didn't tell anyone. They don't know anything." She was shaking. She pressed a hand to the wall because her legs felt so unsteady.

"That's good. See that it stays that way. I'll be watching you, Maxine. And rest assured, I know how. I'm going to hear everything you say and see everything you do. Don't test me."

"I won't."

He hung up the phone.

Maxine wanted to sink to the floor. She looked around her, feeling exposed, vulnerable. She depressed the cutoff, then lifted it again. With a trembling forefinger, she punched the star key, then the six and the nine. Maybe she shouldn't. Maybe he wasn't kidding and would know she had tried.

"The last number that called this line was," the computer-generated voice said. Then it paused as its components worked. "We're sorry. That number is not available." It clicked off.

Swallowing hard, Maxine hung up the phone.

What the hell was she supposed to do now? Was he watching her? Could he see her even now? Were there bugs or hidden cameras in her own house? She searched her mind and mentally wondered what Oliver Stone would do.

She told herself to use her head. To think.

Okay. The guy had been in a fire last night. Wounded, burned. Suffering from smoke inhalation, too, by the sounds of his cough. He must have spotted her leaving, maybe even followed her home, and then followed Jason and Storm. He learned where they lived, went and got a camera, sneaked back and took the shots. Then he returned to Max's home and watched the place. He'd followed her mom to work in the wee hours of this morning and taken that shot of her. Then he'd come back here and dropped the envelope and made the phone call. Not from the pay phone, because that would have been traceable. A cell phone, maybe. She leaned over the answering machine, hit rewind and then play. As the tape played back, she heard traffic sounds in the background and some telltale static.

She stopped the machine, popped the microcassette out. He was on the road, on the move. He would have to be. He would be watching her, yes. If he were CIA, he would know how to plant bugs and cameras. But she didn't think he'd had the time to do those things yet. He probably figured he could scare her enough to keep her on the straight and narrow until he had all his ducks in a row.

Fine.

She went to her room, saved the contents of the CD-ROM to her hard drive, just in case, then tucked the CD and the name badge into her pocket along with the tape and headed out of the house. It wouldn't look unusual for her to walk to campus. She had classes today.

She wouldn't pursue this and put her mother or her friends at risk. She had no doubt the man would carry out his threats and then some. No doubt at all. God knew the government had committed far more serious atrocities and gotten away with them. Especially if the accounts on that CD were true.

But she wouldn't forget. And she would make sure

she had plenty of copies of this evidence tucked away in various places. Because someday she would be older and in a position to blow the whistle. Someday when she was established, with a Ph.D. behind her name, and a law license and some clout of her own. Then she would demand some answers.

But not yet. Right now she was just Mad Maxie Stuart, the twenty-year-old college student with the big imagination.

Imagination my ass, she thought. If she had ever needed proof that the government was up to no good in her hometown, she had it now. If that bastard on the phone thought his threats would put her off the scent, he was wrong. His threats were like the validation that had always eluded her. She wasn't a nut. She was right.

She had been right all along.

And she could be patient.

4

5 Years Later

Dante woke to the sounds of crackling flames and the smell of smoke. It was so like a fragment of his oldest nightmare that for a moment he believed it was just that, a dream memory come to haunt him, and he didn't stir. But then he felt the heat and the sting in his eyes. He sensed the angry flames and knew they were real.

He sat up fast, too fast, then had to blink in order to clear his swimming head. Night had not yet fallen, he realized dully. He was still weak with the languor of the day sleep. His limbs felt heavy as he turned himself sideways in the large bed and let his legs fall to the floor. They tingled in rebellion when he put weight on them, but he lumbered anyway, stark naked, across the lush carpet, toward the bedroom door. He didn't go far. He didn't have to. Flames snapped and snarled beyond the door, and its gleaming finish began to bubble and sweat.

Dante's nose burned with the smell, and his mind whirled with questions. This was not a coincidence. He turned toward the window, tugging back the heavy draperies, then ducking to the side as the sunlight seared his exposed skin. It hung low in the sky, that blinding yellow death, but it was there, dammit. If he went outside, he would roast.

If he stayed in here, he would do likewise.

The door groaned ominously, swelling inward before its pregnant belly burst, giving birth to hungry flames. Smoke wafted in like a great black ghost. His flesh sizzled. Growling deep in his throat, Dante tore the drapery from its rod, wrapped it around him like a shroud and dove through the glass.

The ground didn't give an inch but met him brutally, knocked the breath from his lungs, jarred his teeth and rattled his bones. He rolled, got to his feet and ran blindly as he felt the sun heating his skin through the fabric. There was motion to the left of him, then an impact as he slammed bodily into what felt like a car. Brakes squealed, and someone shouted a curse to the accompanying blast of a horn, but Dante just kept moving. He had to peer through the opening in the fabric to see where the hell he was going. Across the pavement, yes, this was right. He ran flat out, off the road, across the weed-strewn parking lot, his bare feet blistering with every searing step as he raced toward the shore. The sunlight beyond the drapery was beginning to penetrate now, and he could feel his flesh blister. Damn, damn, damn. Head down, bare feet pounding, drape clutched around him like a cloak, he ran.

There was a sound. A whirring sound, and then something skewered his arm. It felt as if a red-hot blade had driven straight through. He stopped dead at the stunning pain, groping beneath the drapery with his one functioning hand and feeling a shaft, like a dowel, embedded in his upper arm, warm, thick blood pulsing from the point of entry.

"I got him!" someone shouted. A man's voice.

A *dead* man, Dante thought viciously. He forced himself to keep moving. Then his feet touched water and he pressed onward, sloshing to knee depth, then mid-thigh. The cool salty wetness was like heaven on his flesh. God, he was baking. A few more yards and he pitched himself headlong into the Atlantic and swam deep. He let go the drapery, but it hung, tugging at the shaft in his arm until he tore it free. Pain screamed through him, but there was no time to acknowledge it. He swam, as deep as he could go, and still deeper, until he couldn't feel the sun heating his skin any longer.

Then he rolled, his body brushing the sand and shells and assorted litter on the bottom and stirring up a watery cloud as he looked above him, toward the surface. The sky beyond the water was still pale, but growing ever dimmer. The water cooled and soothed his heat-razed flesh, but his arm was alive with pain, and in a moment he realized the clouds in the water were taking on a pinkish hue. He glanced down at his arm. High on the outside, halfway between shoulder and elbow, the bolt he'd all but forgotten was still piercing him. Blood oozed steadily from around it, blossoming in the water.

The maniac had shot him with a crossbow.

Dante lifted his arm and saw the bolt sticking out the underside. Lovely.

Gripping the bolt with one hand, he pulled it free, swearing the damned thing was a mile long, grating his teeth at the intensity of the pain as it slid through his flesh. Jesus! Mortals would never know pain like vampires did. Never.

He dropped the bolt to the ocean floor, but the

blood still flowed. And it would continue to flow until he bled out, unless he found a way to stanch it. The wound would heal only with the day sleep. If he lived that long.

He reached down to the sea's bottom, scooped up a handful of the muddy sand and, mustering every ounce of tolerance he had, packed the stuff into the hole in his arm. The pain was excruciating. He howled with it, but in the depths, who could hear? He packed the sand in from both sides of the wound, then plucked a handful of coarse seaweed and wound it around his arm. Using his teeth and one hand, he knotted the rope-like stalks.

He was weak from the pain, his lungs starving for air, and though he would not die for the lack of it, it was nearly impossible to convince himself not to inhale.

When he looked up again, the sky was dark, and he whispered a silent thanks to whatever sorts of angels watched over the undead. He pushed his feet into the ocean bottom, just a little. Slowly, very slowly, he let himself float to the surface. When his head broke through, he sucked in a deep breath. It felt heavenly, filling his lungs, clearing his head. He pushed his dripping hair off his face and scanned the shoreline.

''He's got to come out sooner or later.''

Dante followed the sound of the voice to its owner, a man who stood on the shoreline, waving a flashlight around over the surface of the water. He was looking seventy-five yards too close to the shore. Thinking like a mortal, applying mortal limitations to a creature who laughed at them.

"If he does, he'll kill us both," said another man. "The sun's gone down."

"But—"

"We failed. You have to know when to admit defeat and walk away, Raymond. Otherwise you won't live long enough to try again. After dark, they're in control. You understand? The night is our enemy."

Gazing through the darkness, Dante spotted the second man on the shore. The left side of his face, between the cheek and the eye, was mottled and scarred, pulling the eye itself into a grotesque pout. Higher, there was a pink patch where no hair grew on his head.

"Put the light out," the scarred man ordered.

The other one, Raymond, obeyed. "How can he stay in the water that long? Huh? I didn't think they could breathe underwater like freaking fish or something."

"They can't. But it would take a very long time for one to pass out from lack of oxygen."

Dante pulled his arms through the water, moving silently, steadily closer, eager to rip out their throats and drain them dry. He'd lost a substantial amount of blood. He could replenish himself at their expense. The two were certainly courting his wrath.

But before he could reach them, they hurried away. He heard doors slam, a motor start up, and then saw the lights of a car as it left him. No longer bothering to move slowly or quietly, Dante swam until his knees dragged in the sand. Then he got to his feet and waded out of the cold ocean. As he stood on the shore, ankle deep in the water, stark naked and cold as stone, he looked back toward the flaming torch in the night that had been one of his favorite homes.

"I'm going to have to kill those two, whoever the hell they were."

"Dante?"

He knew that voice, and he waited there, dripping wet, his arm screaming in pain, until Sarafina stepped out of the shadows. She was beautiful, as always. Dressed in a full skirt of black lace, scalloped at the bottom. A white peasant blouse pushed down to bare her milky shoulders. Colorful silk scarfs at her waist and in her black, curling tresses, trailing her like comets' tails whenever she moved. She wore too much makeup. Always had. Thick black liner and dark shadow gave her a menacing appearance, and the long, curling bloodred nails added to that. But she was a Gypsy. She embraced the stereotypical image that went with the blood. It was her gimmick.

She moved closer, gripped his shoulders, making him wince, and kissed his face, his mouth. He felt her warmth and smelled a fresh kill on her breath.

"You're all right?" she asked when she finally released him.

"I've got a hole in my arm, but it will keep. The bastards burned my house."

"Did you see them?" she asked.

He nodded. "They're gone now, or they'd be dead."

"Did one of them have a scarred face?"

Looking at her sharply, Dante nodded. "You've encountered them?"

"Him, at least. He was following me one night in Rome. I'd have ripped out his throat if he hadn't realized I'd spotted him and run like a rabbit."

Dante sighed. "The man is a pest."

"The man needs killing."

Rolling his eyes, Dante managed a smile, in spite of his pain. "You think every mortal needs killing, Sarafina."

"Thirty of our kind have been murdered in their sleep, Dante. And other fires like this one have come close to claiming more. Someone knows our secrets."

A chill went through him—at her words, or because of the cold, he wasn't certain which. "Let's go someplace where I can get dry," he told her. "We'll talk there."

"Yes. You'll draw a crowd soon enough, standing out here naked."

Taking his arm, Sarafina led him to a black limousine that was parked around a bend in the road, put him into the back seat and slid in beside him. Dante almost smiled at the extravagance.

The driver said nothing of the sopping wet, naked man his employer had apparently plucked from the waves. He didn't even look directly into her eyes when she spoke to him. He was well trained, Dante thought. Very well. Maybe too well. Pushing a button so the glass partition opened just slightly, Sarafina said, "Take us to the apartment, pet. And turn up the heat back here."

The driver's only reply was a nod as the glass slid closed again. Then the car was in motion.

Sarafina picked up a large crocheted shawl and proceeded to rub Dante's shoulders, chest and hair with it. "I think it's that dreadful DPI," she said. "They have to be behind this."

Dante sent her a quelling glance, then jerked his head toward the man in the front.

"Oh, don't be ridiculous, love. He can't hear me

with the partition closed, and even if he could, he wouldn't repeat a word.''

Dante glanced again at the man in the front. He was very pale, very thin. His eyes seemed hollow. He couldn't see the man's throat, but the fact that he wore a turtleneck beneath his navy-blue jacket spoke volumes. Dante looked at Sarafina again. ''You're not supposed to use them as slaves, 'fina. It's bad form.''

She shrugged. ''At least I don't kill them outright. Unless they displease me. Stop changing the subject. What do we do about this organization?''

He shook his head slowly, debating whether to put the poor mortal out of his misery when the ride had ended. Then again, what good would it do? Sarafina would only find another whose mind she could bend to her will. The more often a vampire drank from a mortal without killing them, the more addicted the mortal became, until he was little more than a mindless subservient worm, like the driver, craving only the feel of his mistress's fangs sinking into his flesh.

''DPI was destroyed five years ago,'' he told her. ''The government stopped funding the project after that. It no longer exists.''

''Then who is hunting down vampires?''

He shrugged, looking away.

''More interestingly, who is giving them their information? How do they know where we rest, where we hunt, where we live? Even DPI, with all their research, didn't have this much information on our personal lives.'' She dropped the damp black shawl on the seat between them. ''That is the person we need to find, Dante. Whoever it is, we need to kill them...slowly, I think. I'd like to see them writhe for a while first.''

She pushed a button, and the glass between the front and back seats slid open once again. She leaned closer to it. "Your wrist, my pet. Your mistress is hungry."

Smiling wanly, the driver lifted his arm, poked his hand through the opening. The sleeve of his jacket was already rolled back, and several puncture wounds littered his forearm. Gripping his forearm with both of hers, Sarafina sank her teeth into him and sucked at him for a long while. Dante looked away but couldn't deny the hunger stirring inside him.

She lifted her head, licked her red lips clean. "Would you like some, Dante? My pet is quite delicious."

"You're cruel, Sarafina. Kill him and have done with it."

She lifted her brows as if wounded, then turned her attention back to her driver. She licked his forearm clean of the trickles of blood left behind and gently rolled his sleeve down again. "Here we are, love. Pull over right here."

He nodded, pulling the limo to a stop. Then he got out, came back and opened her door.

They were on a highway. Traffic rushed past in a blur of lights and motion. Sarafina didn't get up. Without so much as looking at him, she said, "I want you to do something for me, love."

"Anything," the driver whispered. He was a tall man, Dante noted. Dark hair sprinkled with gray, a thin, angular face and a beakish nose.

"I want you turn around, and walk out into the middle of the highway."

The driver stared at her, not directly at her eyes, but somewhere below them.

"Sarafina—" Dante began.

"Do it now," she said.

Dante closed his eyes and swore under his breath. The driver turned and stepped out into the oncoming traffic. His body was hurled about a hundred feet when it was struck. By then, though, Sarafina was behind the wheel and driving away.

She never even looked back.

"I just don't understand why you won't move back to L.A., Morgan. You have everything you wanted. You could return in triumph now, just the way you always said you would."

Morgan paced across the marble tiles of the great room, heels clicking with every step. She wore a loose-fitting teal blouse and matching pants in brushed silk that whispered over her skin when she moved. She loved the way it felt. "I like it here," she said. "Come on, David, even you have to admit I've done wonders with this place in five years' time."

"I'm beginning to wish I'd never sold it to you," he muttered, half under his breath. He eased his large frame into a claw-footed antique chair, looking around the great room as he did. She knew he had to admire what he saw. The plasterwork ceiling had been freshly redone, right down to the cherubic angels in the corners and filling the concave dome directly above them.

She took the seat across from him, handed him a glass of iced soda. Her own glass looked identical, but, despite the early-morning hour, there was vodka mixed with hers. She needed the strength. She loved David, but dammit, she wished he would just leave.

She didn't care about anything except getting back to her journals. To the fantasies and the man who had written them. God, to go a single waking hour, much less a day, without wallowing in his mind was nearly unbearable. She never left the house anymore. She never wanted to. And when she slept—oh, God, it was best when she slept. Because he was so much more real in dreams.

"I have to admit, I'm confused," David said, taking the soda, sipping it. "I thought it was all decided. You were going to hide out here, lick your wounds, write your blockbuster, make your fortune and come home to reclaim everything you'd lost."

"Ahh, yes. And restore honor to the De Silva family name." She smiled just a little.

"If I'd known you could write the way you can, and as quickly as you can, I have to admit, I'd never have let you come out here in the first place."

Morgan averted her eyes. "I couldn't write like that. Not out there. I found my...inspiration, for want of a better word, here. In this house. I couldn't work anywhere else. I can't, David. I won't."

"That's superstitious nonsense."

No, she thought. It wasn't. Dante was here. She felt him here. Her own beautiful madman. God, he— his diaries, at least—had given her back her life. And yet, they had stolen a part of it, too. The man who'd called himself Dante had captivated her mind, her soul, in some dark way she had yet to understand. He was real to her. He was more than a long-dead lunatic who had written down his insane delusions. He was *real.* He lived...inside her somehow. Inside this house.

But she couldn't explain any of that to David. Instead she stared up at the crystal chandelier she'd had installed in the great room and wondered how close she had come to the one that was there originally. When Dante had lived here.

It hadn't been easy to restore the house. And it hadn't been cheap. But thanks to the box office success of the first two films in her vampire series, she had been able to afford to do exactly what she wanted. And that included hiring period experts to help her plan her restoration, to make it as accurate as possible. Although much, *much* more luxurious.

Her third film had been out for exactly eight weeks, and it had already made Morgan wealthy beyond her wildest dreams. David, as well. And now they waited to see what other dreams might be realized.

Morgan glanced at her watch. "Isn't it time yet?"

"Close enough, I suppose. Come on." David got to his feet, held a hand out to her. She took it and let him pull her up. "God, Morgan, you've got to put on some weight. You're not an actress, you know."

She smiled at him, hiding the weakness in her legs, the slight rush of dizziness that often hit her when she got up too quickly. "You can't be too rich or too thin," she quipped. "Besides, if all goes well, I'll need to look good in some designer's idea of a dress in a few weeks."

Right. As if she would leave this place, even for that.

They walked across the tiles to the double doors that opened into her office. The fireplace had been converted to gas now, and the first thing Morgan did upon entering was turn it on. Lush oriental rugs covered the newly refinished hardwood floor. The desk was a reproduction, the computer state of the art. And the walls were filled with images of Dante. Charcoal sketches she'd done herself, rather than stills from the films. The actor who played him did a wonderful job, of course, but he wasn't Dante. She *knew* Dante.

There was a sketch of him as a small boy with huge dark eyes, peering up at a beautiful Gypsy woman who danced beside a campfire. There was another of him sitting at this very desk, brooding over his journals.

"This is almost creepy," David said, shivering a little as he crossed the large room, took a seat and picked up a remote control. "God, don't you ever get sick of him?"

Morgan paused near another drawing, her eyes locked with the staring, sightless eyes of the subject. "I know every line and contour of his face," she whispered. Then, as the silence drew out, she shook herself, forced a smile. "Of course that's impossible. It's all what my mind has created from the raw materials in the di—in the screenplays. But it seems real. I see him in my dreams as clearly as if he were real." She smiled. "I even know the sound of his voice."

"Writers," David muttered. He pushed a button, and the antique replica cabinet's doors slid open, revealing the big-screen television set behind them. He hit another button to flick it on, and one to set the channel. "I'd get sick of him," he said. "Real or not."

"I could drown in him and not get sick of him," she said. "Sometimes I think maybe that's what I'm doing. Drowning in him."

When David didn't answer, she glanced his way, saw him looking at her oddly. Morgan gave a little laugh to ease the worry from his eyes. "We creative types are supposed to be eccentric. Don't scowl like that, you'll wrinkle.''

He looked away with a sigh, but his gaze froze on the television screen, and he snatched up the remote, thumbing the volume up higher. ''Here it is!''

The famous couple at the podium took turns reading from a list, and Morgan thought the brief spot took longer than any two-hour feature she had ever sat through. She slugged back her drink and waited until they got to the part that interested her.

''In the category of best original screenplay, the nominees are…''

A hum seemed to fill her head, the room, her ears. She couldn't hear what they were saying any longer, but suddenly she saw her name on the screen along with four others. ''Morgan De Silva, for *Twilight Hunger*.''

David surged to his feet, hugging her hard against him, smiling and laughing and twisting from side to side as he held her. Morgan surrendered to the rush of darkness that swamped her brain and simply went limp in his arms.

She was lying on the chaise when she opened her eyes again. David sat close to her, patting her hand. ''There you are. It's all right. I guess this meant more to you than I realized.''

''It's not that…'' she began. Then she recalled what had just happened.

God, it was true. She was nominated for the top award in the film industry. For work that wasn't even her own. She had never expected it to go this far. And yet, she had, in a way, known it would. It had to. The stories were too good not to be recognized as such. There was something…transcendent about them. Something that touched the audience on a level that was almost visceral in its intensity.

"Are you all right?"

She nodded but didn't bother trying to sit up. This was very odd. She had expected to feel…jubilant at this moment. Wasn't this beyond her dreams? Wasn't this supposed to fix everything that had been missing from her life? Why did she still feel so empty inside?

"You're going to *have* to come back to L.A. with me now," David said. He pushed one hand through his thinning honey-blond hair, which was getting gray at the temples. "There are going to be parties. Receptions. Interviews. You should be seen."

The thought of leaving this place set her heart racing. She shook her head quickly, fighting back her panic. "I can't leave now."

"But—"

"The new one is at too delicate a point right now, David. I can't stop working on it without losing my momentum. And I can't work anywhere else. So I have to stay right here."

He closed his eyes slowly, as if attempting to digest her words.

"I should be finished with it by the time of the actual ceremony. I'll be able to come out for that. I promise."

His eyes popped open. "But you need a dress. And hair and…honey, people plan for months to get ready for this one, special night. God, if this had happened to the girl I knew five years ago, she'd have insisted I fly her to Paris to shop for a gown. And probably would have bought three of them before making a final decision."

Sitting up, very slowly, so as not to induce the

return of her familiar lightheadedness, she met his eyes. "I'm not that girl anymore."

"No," he said. "You're not. You've changed, Morgan. And not for the better. You've practically become a recluse."

She banked her anger. He was right, and if she spoke her mind, she would tell him to go home, so she could get right back to her reclusiveness. Crawl back into the velvet darkness of Dante's world. She hated not being enmeshed in it, missed him like a lover when she went a day without wading through his life, processing it through her own mind and soul, and onto her computer screen. Changing his memories, his deepest thoughts, into lines and stage directions, so that he could come to life on the screen. It was almost as if she were somehow trying to resurrect him from death by giving life to his memories.

Not enough. God, it was never enough.

"I've made you angry," David said.

"No. No, I'm just…overwhelmed." She smiled up at him. "So are you taking me out for breakfast to celebrate or not?"

Lifting his brows, he sighed. "Yes, of course I am. How soon can you be ready?"

She forced herself to look happy. To play the role of the excited honoree, eager to celebrate the achievement of a lifetime.

The truth was, she just wanted to get it over with and return to her house. *His* house. To be alone with the nonexistent man who haunted her, day and night. Heart and soul. Who possessed her mind.

Dante.

The man who had written volume upon volume in

the first person, and who had, she was convinced, believed every word he had written.

He had believed he was a vampire.

She almost wished it could be true.

5

Dante stood outside in the darkness, the wind in his face, tangling its cool damp fingers in his hair. Just a hint of rain looming. He felt its touch on his skin in that wind. He tasted it. The waves from the sea crashed to the shoreline just beyond the house. His house, or it had been once. Warm yellow light spilled from its windows, as if welcoming him home. But he knew better. Someone was inside. He could feel and taste them the same way he did the rain in the air. A woman.

When he had decided to come here, he hadn't even been certain he would find the place still standing. Last time he'd seen it, the house had been on the verge of ruin. But no more. Someone had gone to great pains to restore the house he had built over a century ago. The white flagstone walkway that curved up to the front door was just as he remembered it. The lampposts at the far end like sentries. Oh, they hadn't been electric, of course, as they were now. Nor had the lights inside the house. But the shutters were black, and the paint was white and fresh. And the chimney was the same size and shape, even though the bricks were all brand-new.

The door was different, he noted. It had been white, with four glass panes in a fantail pattern in the top. The new door was far more elaborate, wider, flanked

by tooled hardwood borders and a wide mantle arching over the top. Artificial flowers were affixed in that
arched mantle. It struck him for a moment, how false
that was. How ridiculous: The smell of plastic and
silk on the things made a mockery of the beauty they
tried to imitate.

Artificial flowers were a sacrilege.

An oval of stained glass stretched almost the whole
length of the door, and the handle was gleaming
brass. The place looked almost new again. Two cars
sat in the white gravel driveway, both of them foreign
and fast. Money lived here now. A woman with
wealth. And youth. He tasted that on the air, as well.

There was a man. Older. Robust. Strong. While the
female had a weakness about her. He didn't smell sex
in the air, so he assumed the relationship was platonic.

He was curious, he had to admit. Eager to see what
had been done to the inside of the place. And he
couldn't leave, anyway. Since his near miss with the
scarred man, he had found his every haven invaded,
his every familiar haunt under watch. The man knew
his secrets somehow. So Dante had come back here—
to a place he hadn't used in over a century—to find
safety and solace, until he could figure out what to
do.

Obviously, he'd stayed away too long. Someone
was living here.

Not that it mattered.

He walked around to the rear of the house, found
the willow tree still there, but so much larger than
before that he had to look twice. God, time passed in
a blur. Easily, he leapt onto a low-hanging limb and
began to climb. The smooth bark, flexible limbs, the
whisper of the dangling greenery, all these were fa-

miliar. He'd planted this tree here a hundred years ago.

As he neared the level of the master bedroom, he stopped, tipping his head to one side and opening his senses. He felt something. Not quite a scent on the air. Something else. Something…that stroked his nerve endings to life like a magnet moving over metal shards.

What *was* that?

He crept closer, climbing from the limb onto the railing that surrounded the balcony, his hand curling around its cool metal. Then he lowered himself down onto the balcony itself and walked closer to the closed glass doors. Sheer white curtains hung in those doors. Sheer enough that he could see through them, into the bedroom beyond.

The woman lay sleeping in a four-poster bed.

Her hair was the color of cinnamon, lush and long, and spread over the pillows. Her skin was creamy white, and as pale as if he had already tasted her. Naked arms rested atop the thin white sheet that he sensed was all that covered her. Her neck was long and slender. Dante licked his lips, and his desire stirred. He didn't make a habit of sampling innocent blood. He killed, yes. He could live on cold, stale blood stored in plastic bags, as some did. But he didn't really call that living. So he killed, but mostly only those who dearly needed killing. Other times, he paid for his desires to be sated. There were women who specialized in satisfying needs like his. They were discreet, and paid enough to keep them that way.

This woman…she wasn't one of them. And yet he was drawn to her, pulled. He wanted her.

He stood so close to the doors that his breath,

though cool, fogged the glass. He wiped it away, looking at her, and he wished silently that she would tug the sheet away, so he could see her more fully. Know for sure if she wore anything against her skin, underneath the covers.

Almost before the thought was complete, the woman lifted her hand to the top of the sheet and peeled it slowly away from her body. She was completely naked, as he had suspected. And for a moment all he could do was look at her and drink in her beauty. Small breasts, but soft, their tips rose-colored and plump. She was far too thin, ribs showing clearly beneath her skin. The hair between her thighs was the same burnished color as that on her head.

He let his gaze move up her body again. Let it linger on her breasts, and he thought about tasting them, and even as he thought it, her nipples stiffened. Frowning, Dante watched with some amazement. Could she be aware of his thoughts on some level? He could exercise mind control over a weak-willed mortal, he knew that, but he would at least have to be trying. The odd stray thought shouldn't...

He shifted his gaze to her face and wondered, should he happen to think about her creamy thighs parting for him, whether she would...

Her legs moved apart. Dante shivered with arousal and hunger, and not a little fear. It was as he was backing away that his mind cleared, giving him the answer he should have seen right away. Suddenly he understood what he'd been sensing earlier, that prickling awareness and attraction.

She was one of *them*. She was one of the Chosen.

He backed across the balcony, reached the railing and, turning, jumped it without hesitation. On the ground, he stood, looking around him and then out to the sea, as if it held the answers. If he'd had anywhere else in the world to go, he would have gone, and gladly.

But the sun would be up soon. And this place was the only haven he had left. He could create others, but that would take time. No, for now, he could only stay here.

But he was going to have to avoid the woman at all costs. Never had he experienced that sort of mind link with a mortal. Never. Nor had he with others of his own kind. What the hell did this mean?

He walked out toward the cliffs and, at the familiar spot, looked down at the stone ledge, some fifteen feet below. There was a small opening in the stone wall that backed that ledge. It was still shrouded by the vines he had planted ages ago. They sprouted around his feet where he stood and grew from the bits of soil along the cliff-face, draping downward to cover the cave's entrance like a curtain.

He hoped the passage that ran beneath the earth all the way back to the house hadn't collapsed by now. And he hoped the rooms hidden beneath the old house hadn't disintegrated to dust after so much time.

She was dreaming about Dante again.

He stood over her bed, staring down at her. Just stood there. He didn't say anything, and he didn't touch her.

She lay there, staring back at him, wishing he would do or say something. Anything. But he didn't.

She opened her mouth to speak and found she couldn't. So instead she looked at him. It was odd that she knew his face so well, she thought idly as she perused it in her dream. It was angular, and cruel. Longish and shadowed. His jawbone was sharp, his nose narrow. The eyes set deep, and so dark that he seemed to be looking out at her from somewhere deep within. From his soul, maybe.

He wanted to see her. Her eyes, once held by his, were locked there. And she knew what he wanted. All she wanted was to please him. She lifted a hand, peeled her covers away and lay there, completely naked and unashamed, as his dark, intense eyes burned over her. Every part of her.

Touch me, she thought. For the love of God, just touch me.

She blinked—and he was gone.

Just that suddenly.

Awake now, Morgan lay in her bed. Her covers were on the floor, and her body was alive. But she was alone.

God, these dreams were taking on a life of their own, weren't they? Maybe she needed to think about some sort of therapy. Not that she hadn't dreamed about him, over and over, night after night, since she had come to live here. But this time it had been different. It had been...*real.*

She sat up slowly, ran a hand through her hair and got to her feet. She pulled on a satin robe the color of cream, walked to the glass doors and opened them, stepping out onto the balcony, inhaling the night air deeply. It tasted good.

Then she paused and stared straight ahead.

A man stood on the cliffs, wind buffeting him as it was buffeting her. He was staring out toward the sea, and she couldn't really see his face. And yet there was something so incredibly familiar about him. The fall of his hair. His stance. Something.

A fist seemed to close around her stomach as clouds skittered away from the moon and, for just an instant, his face was touched by moonlight.

"Dante…" She whispered his name, breathed it.

And as if he had heard her, even though it was impossible from that distance, he turned sharply, looked right at her.

"It can't be…." Morgan closed her eyes, took three openmouthed breaths as her heart hammered in her chest. "It can't be."

She opened her eyes again.

The cliffs, the sea, the wind, and nothing else. No one was there. No one was there at all.

6

Maxine leaned back in the ergonomic chair and blinked her eyes several times. You didn't blink often enough when you stared at a computer screen all day. She'd read that somewhere. It wasn't good for your vision.

The front door opened, and Storm came in, a big white bag from the bakery in one hand and the morning mail in the other. "Time to take a break!" she called. "Carbs, calories and cream filling, just what the doctor ordered."

Max sighed, pushing the chair back. It rolled on its casters from the computer desk to the middle of the floor in what used to be the living room and was now an office. If you used the term loosely. It more closely resembled an explosion in a paper-and-file-folder factory. With computers. Lots of computers.

Storm dropped the bag on her own desk, sat down and peered inside. "Mmm, I got jelly and cream filled, and now I can't decide."

"How many are in there?" Maxine asked, lifting her brows.

"Half dozen." Storm didn't look up. The doughnuts had her mesmerized.

"Better go for one of each, then."

She looked up then, brows arched. "You think?"

"Oh, yeah. Far better than the risk of making the wrong choice."

"I like the way your mind works," Stormy said, smiling, as she reached into the bag to pluck out a doughnut.

Max got out of her chair and wandered into the kitchen, which was still a kitchen, where she poured two cups of fresh coffee. "Did you ever wonder just how screwed up I must be to be in the same town, in the same house, in the same rut, after all this time?"

"No."

Max smiled at the sound of the word, because it was doughnut muffled. She carried the two mugs back into the room in time to see Stormy taking another bite and closing her eyes in ecstasy.

Max set Storm's cup down in front of her and bent to help herself to a doughnut, knowing they would vanish if she didn't.

"You care to elaborate on that answer, or are you just gonna go with the one-syllable reply?"

Stormy swallowed, licked her lips, took a sip of her coffee. She still had a ring of powdered sugar around her mouth, but what the hell?

"Who wouldn't be in the same house? Shoot, girl, your mother gave it to you free and clear. You'd have been nuts not to take it. And I fail to see any rut. You're running not one, but two, businesses. Both turning a profit, I might add."

"Barely," Maxine muttered. She sighed, dunked her doughnut and took a big soggy bite. When she finished, she dropped the first of her two bombshells. "Web page design is getting boring, Stormy. To tell you the truth, I'm thinking about dropping it."

Stormy blinked. "Dropping it?"

"Closing it down."

Setting her coffee mug on her desk, Storm got to her feet. "Why would you do that? That's where you earn most of your income."

"Yeah, but it was never my life's work. I mean, it's okay. I'm good at it, but it's not my dream job. Never was."

"So what are you telling me? They're hiring over at Spies-R-Us?"

Max shot her a quick glance. "Don't even joke about that."

"Then what?" Storm threw her hands in the air, turning in a slow circle and searching the ceiling for an explanation. "I thought this side business of yours was enough to satisfy your inner snoop, Max. I mean, hasn't it been?"

"No, it hasn't. If anything, it's only whetted my appetite." Max had kind of stumbled into the realm of Internet crime investigations when one of her Web clients asked her advice in dealing with a cyber-stalker a year ago. Since then, she had helped track down a half-dozen others by tracing them through their super-anonymous, supposedly untraceable screennames. She had even helped to bust up several hoax rings revolving around so-called paranormal sciences. Scam artists who went online hawking everything from psychic readings to ghost-busting powders. Which was perfectly legal until you tied them to their partners, who harassed and sometimes frightened gullible people into believing they needed otherworldly help, then fed information to the scam artist, who used it to convince the client he was really in touch with "the other side."

All of this had given Max the opportunity to touch

base with her favorite cop now and then. Not that *that* had any bearing on her decision to move into this line of work.

"So what would you say if I told you I was thinking about embarking on another little enterprise?" she asked.

Storm turned to face her, searched her face warily. "A third business?"

"I'm dropping the Web designing services. So it would only be a second business. And, in fact, it would be more like taking the existing one to a new, higher level."

"What do you have in mind?"

Max wiped the doughnut sugar from her fingers onto her jeans and went to her desk. She opened a drawer, took out a sheet of paper, slid it across the surface. "Take a look at this and tell me what you think."

Storm came closer, leaned over it, reading aloud. "Maxine Stuart, Licensed Private..." Then she looked up. "Licensed private investigator? Since when?"

"It just came today. I sent in the application months ago."

"Maxie..."

"Look, I know. It sounds way over the top, but if you think about it, it's what we've been doing anyway. Just in cyberspace instead of real time."

"They can't shoot you in cyberspace." Storm rolled her eyes. "Who else knows about this?"

Max shrugged.

"Maxine Stuart, who else knows?"

Max lowered her eyes. "Well, Lou knows."

"Lou. Lou Malone. I figured as much. He probably encouraged this, didn't he?"

"Well, he, uh, helped me with the application process. He was one of my references."

"Uh-huh."

"Look, I'm good at this. And Lou's already got a few cases ready to toss my way."

"Hell. I don't know why you don't just jump that man's bones and get it over with, Max."

"I intend to. Just as soon as I can get him cornered." Stormy's eyes widened, and Max smiled in sheer nasty delight. "But one thing has nothing to do with the other. If I was doing this just to get closer to Lou, I'd have joined the force. It would have been easier."

"Yeah. Right. Isn't the old crock due to retire pretty soon?"

There was a throat clearing, and they both turned to see the old crock himself standing in the doorway. Max couldn't judge for sure how long he'd been standing there, how much he might have heard. She figured the man's bones would more easily succumb to any jumping she might attempt if she could sneak up on them. Take 'em by surprise, that sort of thing.

He was too thin, so his suit looked a little on the baggy side. "Am I interrupting anything?"

Stormy turned her back to him and made wide eyes at Max. Max ignored her. "Come on in, Lou. Did you smell the doughnuts or what?"

He didn't smile, didn't tease her in return the way he usually did. "It's, uh—kinda delicate."

Frowning, Maxine walked over to where he stood. He didn't wait. Instead he turned, stepped out onto the porch. When she joined him there and closed the door behind her, he said, "I'll buy you a cup of coffee. We can talk there. All right?"

"Sounds serious."

"Yeah. I need your help with something. It's sorta right up your alley, Max, or I'd never ask."

"Why not?"

"Why not what?"

"Why would you never ask?"

He drew a breath, sighed heavily. "'Cause you're brand-new at this kind of thing, and I sort of had it in mind to start you out with something a little more milk toast. Background checks on suspects, shit like that."

"Got that much faith in me, do you?"

"You're a kid."

"I'm twenty-five."

"Like I said..."

"Shut up, Lou." She yanked open his car door and sat beside him. He didn't take her to the coffee shop, as she had expected. Instead he pulled around the drive-through window of a fast food joint and got two large coffees, one black, one with two creams and three sugars. She smiled as he rattled off the order without asking her. He knew exactly how she liked her coffee.

His bones, she mused, were practically jumped already.

He drove to the nearest parking area, shut the car off and turned in his seat to face her.

"Gee, Lou, if you want to take me parking, maybe we should aim for something just a little more secluded."

His face colored. "Yeah, right."

"There's this old gravel bed south of town where

everyone used to go to make out back in high school. You know it?''

He avoided her eyes. ''Of course I know it.''

''Mmm. So you've been there?''

''Yeah. Shining lights on kids who ought to know better and sending 'em home to their mammas. Now, do you wanna talk business or do you wanna play, Maxie?''

She wanted to play. With him. Now. But she'd obviously pissed him off. He always got pissed off when she flirted with him, even a little bit. ''Fine. Business. Go ahead.'' She sat back in her seat and sipped her coffee.

''Okay. There's this woman. She's a friend of mine. A good friend.''

Fingernails raked across a chalkboard inside her head, and Maxine sat up straighter.

''Her name is Lydia Jordan. She runs Haven House.''

Max blinked now as her mind filled in the blanks. ''That's that girls' shelter downtown? For runaway teens in trouble?''

He nodded.

''But I thought that was run by a pair of former prostitutes.''

Again he nodded.

She lifted her eyebrows and stared at him. ''This friend of yours is a hooker?''

''*Was* a hooker.''

''And how the hell is it that *you* know her so well?'' she asked, and she really didn't care how bitchy it sounded.

He smiled at her. ''Hell, Maxie, if I wasn't old

enough to be your father, I'd almost think you were jealous.''

"You're nowhere *near* old enough to be my father.'' He was, technically, but she wasn't about to admit it.

He sighed, shaking his head. "I met Lydia the first time I picked her up for soliciting. I was a rookie, and she couldn't have been more than eighteen. I must have brought her in a dozen times over the years before she finally got herself straightened out. I didn't know Kimbra as well. But the two of them met on the streets, became best friends and helped each other start over.''

"That's the partner? The other half of the dynamic duo?''

He nodded. "They got legitimate jobs, took classes, and once they had themselves taken care of, they reached back down to help other girls like them. I think they'd both spent some time at Haven House before they took it over. Anyway, none of that matters right now.''

"Of course it matters. Just how close are you to this Lydia person, Lou?''

He sent her a look she rarely saw on him. An angry one that told her very clearly that she was crossing some unseen, unspoken boundary line and that she'd damn well better back off.

She sighed and looked away.

"Kimbra Sykes is dead. Murdered. And Lydia has somehow got it into her head that some kind of supernatural forces were involved.''

Maxine was unimpressed. "Did a lot of drugs while she was turning tricks, did she?''

"No. But she's always been incredibly superstitious."

She wanted to ask him why the hell he thought she should care how superstitious this ex-whore might be. She hated the woman. Instantly, automatically hated her. "So what makes you think I can do anything to help her?"

He put a hand on her shoulder. "Max, have I done something to make you mad at me?"

"No." She didn't even look at him as she spoke.

"Well then, how come you're sitting there puckered up like a prune?" He only sighed when she refused to answer. Then he shook his head. "I just thought that—hell, you know all about this kind of stuff. Remember that woman who thought her house was haunted, and how she hired that Internet ghostbuster to come clear it out for her?"

"And it turned out he was the one haunting it? Yeah, I remember."

"You knew. You knew right off the bat it was a hoax. And you were able to convince that woman, mostly because you knew so much about the subject. You went in there telling her that a *real ghost* would never behave the way hers was—remember? Had her eating out of your hand!"

She shrugged, warming just a little at his praise. "I'm pretty good when I know my subject."

"And you know this subject. You and your skeptical mind, always having to dig into anything you come upon that doesn't seem quite right. Learn all you can about it and then proceed to debunk it."

She shrugged. "It's not that I don't believe in the paranormal. I just know that ninety-nine percent of the ghosts, goblins, psychics and channelers out there are con artists. I believe what I can see with my own eyes, not what people tell me. And even when I see it with my own eyes, I don't believe much of what the government or any other authority figure tells me. If that makes me a skeptic, then I'm a skeptic.''

''You're a skeptic.''

She shrugged. ''I still don't see what you want me to do for your...friend.''

''I want you to convince her that her best friend was not murdered by a vampire.''

Maxine's head came up very slowly. She met his eyes, looking for the hint of humor that would tell her he was joking. But it wasn't there.

''Vampire?''

''Yeah. Is that the craziest freaking thing you've ever heard or what?''

She nodded vaguely, but in her mind, she was back at that burned-out building, five years ago, with the soldiers, the lights. Hell. She had always known it would come back to haunt her. She knew things she shouldn't know. Things no one should know.

''When can I meet this Lydia person?''

''Then you'll do it?'' he asked.

She met his eyes, swallowed hard. ''For you? Sure, Lou. You know I can't say no to you. I just wish you'd get around to asking me for something a little more fun.''

He laughed uneasily, patted her on the head and looked away. Then he started the car up again and drove her back home.

7

Dante woke in the sour-tasting darkness of his tomb and looked around, seeing everything.

It wasn't really a tomb. Not exactly, though all it would need to make it mirror one was a rotting corpse or two. The square concrete room was large, window-less, airless. Down here, one inhaled stagnant dank-ness and mold rather than oxygen. The subterranean room held only a handful of items: a kerosene lantern on a rickety old table and a coffin. And while he found sleeping in the thing to be a laughable cliché, it had its advantages. First and foremost, it would dis-courage anyone who might somehow find his way in here. Anyone other than a vampire hunter, that was. Secondly, coffins were built to last. This one was as well preserved as it had been when he'd been here last. The padding inside was still soft and intact, if a little less-than-fresh smelling. It sat on a bier that was a rectangle of concrete, rising up from the floor. Built for just that purpose, the bier was the third advantage. Hollow inside, it led to a secondary tunnel. He had never yet needed to use the trap door in the bottom of the coffin, but it was good to know it was there, should he need it.

This place was secure. Safe. But it had never been meant for habitation. It was a last resort, nothing

more. That he had been forced to retreat to this place
should only spur him to take action that much sooner.

He needed to learn who these new vampire hunters
were, where they were getting their information. He
needed to stop them.

Smoothing the wrinkles from his clothes, he
glanced just once at the cement spiral steps that led
up to a solid ceiling. There was a hinged doorway in
the floor there, completely invisible from above. But
when he'd opened it, curious to see what the woman
had done to his house, he'd found a wooden barrier.
Someone had apparently laid a new hardwood floor
over the old one in his study. Oh, he could have
smashed through it easily enough, but announcing his
presence was the last thing he had in mind.

Bad enough she had glimpsed him that first night,
just before dawn.

Looked right at him and whispered his name. He'd
heard her clearly, despite the distance. His senses
were honed by centuries of immortality and, he
thought, blood drinking. Living blood was raw power
to his kind.

She had said his name. And he'd heard her, physically heard her, but also heard her mentally. He had
felt that whisper echoing within his mind. And he'd
felt the intense yearning that had been wrapped
around it. He had even felt an answering tug at his
own heart, and yet that made no sense. He didn't even
know the woman. But she, apparently, knew him.

He wondered about that. It ate at him. Had she seen
his name on some stray scrap of paper that had been
left lying around the house? It wasn't on the deed—
he'd used a false name then.

And if she had simply seen his name somewhere,

that did not explain how she could connect that name to the stranger she had glimpsed standing on the shore in the dead of night. She had recognized him. How that could be, he didn't know.

She was one of the Chosen, those few special mortals with the rare Belladonna Antigen in their blood. The same antigen all vampires shared. They were the only mortals who could be successfully transformed. And they drew his kind like magnets. Many vampires found honor in watching over the Chosen. Protecting them. To Dante's way of thinking, that was foolhardy in the extreme. Being drawn to mortals, caring for them in the least, would only make a vampire vulnerable, weak. It was said that it was nearly impossible for a vampire to harm one of them, unless he were insane or mad with passion. The bloodlust, perhaps.

He knew he had to find out all of that and more about the woman in his house. Despite the fact that he felt, already, that legendary attraction between her kind and his. He could fight that. It was information he needed from her.

She probably didn't even know about the antigen in her blood that made her different from other mortals. He didn't know much about it himself, except that all vampires shared it. And that there was a psychic attraction between mortals with the antigen and the vampires who could smell it on them like a perfume.

He smelled it now!

Footsteps padded across the floor over his head, and Dante looked up sharply, listening. It was *her*. He *felt* her. Her feet were either bare or clad only in something soft, socks or stockings or thin cloth slippers. She stopped walking, stood in place. Right in front of the fireplace, if the fireplace were even still there.

Unable to resist, Dante moved directly beneath the spot where she stood and lifted his arms over his head. He pressed his palms to the ceiling, closed his eyes and opened his mind.

Morgan leaned over to turn the knob on the gas fireplace. It flared to life, and she stood there for a moment, admiring the flames. And then, suddenly, the bottom dropped out of her stomach. The blood seemed to drain from her head, and a rush of shivering cold shot up her spine.

She braced her hands on the mantle, leaned forward and dragged in one ragged breath after another. "What the hell was that?" she whispered.

Then she went very still and lifted her head slowly. Blinking, she turned and glanced behind her. "Who's there?"

No one answered. The house remained still, silent, empty. David had left for L.A. hours ago. And yet she had the most powerful feeling she was not alone.

Drawing a deep, steadying breath, she told herself she was imagining things. Just as she had been imagining that man on the cliffs last night. That man who looked like her mental image of Dante, the madman who'd lived in this house a century ago. Maybe she was spending a little too much time immersed in his journals. Of course she was. But why shouldn't she, when she no longer wanted to do anything else?

She forced herself to walk across the floor to her desk, though her feet seemed oddly reluctant to move at first. The uneasy feeling fled as she sat down in her chair, booted up her computer, opened the file. She worked better at night than she did during the day. No wonder, given the subject matter.

The scene she wrote was one she felt in every cell of her body. She had lived it as she had read the account in his journals. And she lived it again now, as she transferred the tale onto her computer, only this time she told it from the point of view of the woman. Dante's victim.

The woman had seen the dark stranger watching her at night—but she would never approach him. There was a dangerous air about him, and yet he exuded something—something sinful. That drew her, spoke to her, tempted her to impure thoughts she could barely contain.

And then one night he came to her while she lay sleeping in her bed. His mouth on hers was what woke her. Although she wasn't really awake. A voice in her mind told her that this was just a dream. A dream in which she was helpless to resist him. And so she responded willingly, even eagerly, to his touch, his commands. It was all right, because it wasn't real. And in the morning she would remember it as a guilty dream and nothing more.

In her mind, as she wrote the scene, Morgan became that woman. Dante's love slave unaware. She felt every touch she described. Tasted his mouth on hers, felt his tongue invading her, its texture and cool wetness when he laved a path over her jaw and neck and, lower, to her breasts. She sucked in a gasp, shocked when he closed his mouth on her breast, without removing the nightgown.

The impulse to push him away, the shame, the guilt...

But it's only a dream. You can't move, love. It's but a dream.

Pleasure melted through her when he suckled her, then pinched her nipple between his teeth while she winced in ecstasy.

Morgan's heart beat faster as her fingers flew over the keys.

She lay in the bed, still, paralyzed by her dream state, as Dante's hands deftly removed the nightgown, then skimmed over her flesh, teasing and touching places she would never have dared let any man touch. He invaded her private places. He invaded *her*. And she liked it. All of it. And wanted more.

His eyes. God, his eyes, how they burned when they stared into hers. Willing her, commanding her to be still. To surrender. It's only a dream, she thought. I can't wake, and I can't move. So it's all right. It's all right to let him do as he will, because I have no choice.

He slid his fingers into the moist wetness between her legs and then moved them in and out. His thumb found the most sensitive place on her body, and pressed and massaged it as his fingers drove into her again and again. She found she could move after all as she parted her legs to him. He leaned closer, reaming her mercilessly as her entire body jerked against his hands. His mouth parted, and he kissed her throat, sucked the skin between his teeth, bit down. His teeth sank into her throat, and the orgasm screamed through her.

Morgan cried out loud, her entire body trembling, her hand flying to her neck at the sensation of a mouth feeding there. Her heart pounded, and she was wet and close to orgasm herself, though she had not been

touched. She sucked in a sharp breath and stood up
unsteadily, backing away from her computer. God, it
was so real. She'd felt the sensation of incisors punc-
turing her skin. His mouth on her, his hands on her,
his fingers…

And then that brief, sharp, delicious stabbing bite.

Shaking all over, aroused beyond belief, she drew
her hand slowly away from her throat and looked at
her palm. She fully expected to see traces of blood
there. But there was nothing.

"God, what is this? What is happening to me?"

Turning around on legs that wobbled, she glanced
at the clock and realized that time had flown past.
The page number in the corner of the screen told her
she'd composed a dozen pages of sheer dark erotica,
and she wondered how the hell it was going to translate onto the big screen.

No. It wouldn't.

She looked back at the pages and pages of description, and finally highlighted it all and hit the delete
key. In its place she inserted the stage directions from
which the actors and the director could build what
they would. "They have intense sex without inter-
course. He drinks from her. She remembers it as a
dream the next day." When she finished, she saved
the file, shut the computer down and stood there
blinking at it, wondering what the hell had possessed
her just now.

She had gone on a journey. A flight of pure imagination. In her mind, she had felt every touch. And
while she had fantasized about Dante before, about
making love to him, or, rather, to the character he
played in his insane ramblings, it had never been so
vivid. So real.

She was wet. Her skin was hot to the touch, her breasts firm and sensitized. And the blood pulsed rapidly in her neck where she had imagined his mouth.

She walked upstairs rather unsteadily, ran a cool bath and told herself she needed to get laid before long. She must be more sexually frustrated than she realized.

Dante had moved when she had moved, pressing his hands to the floor beneath the place where she sat, sensing her on the other side of that wooden barrier and opening his mind to hers.

What he'd found there held him fast. She was imagining herself. And because she could see herself clearly in her mind, he could see her there, as well. In her mind she wasn't as thin or as pale as he knew she was in reality. She was healthy, shapelier. Her hair was the same, burnished red and long and thick. Her eyes—he'd never had the chance to look into her eyes before. They were emeralds, sparkling beneath a layer of sheen.

She lay on a bed, surrounded by sheer white curtains, and he, Dante, stood over her, staring down at her. He saw his own face quite clearly in her mind, and though it shifted and hid behind the mists of her imagination, when she focused hard, those mists parted. His features were precise. It had been a long, long time since Dante had looked at himself in a mirror. But this was very much as if he were doing just that. He'd forgotten how shadowed his face appeared. How deep set his eyes were. How wide his mouth was.

It stunned him to see himself there in her mind, in her vision. And for just a moment he pulled back a bit, unable to breathe while so completely immersed in her. He blinked, seeing only the dull room again. Very faintly, he heard tapping. Rapid, uneven tapping, broken now and then.

And then he felt the woman shiver, and he turned his attention back to her again, to the vision unfolding in her mind while that odd tapping rushed on in increasing tempo. He saw himself undressing the woman, heard himself telling the woman in the bed that this was all just a dream, that she had no control over what was about to happen and therefore no responsibility for it. That because it wasn't real, she could allow herself to feel things she would never feel, without guilt or shame or fear of any sort. He asked her to surrender her will to him, and she sighed her consent. And then he knelt beside the bed and slowly undressed the woman while she lay there, helpless to resist him, and not wanting to, anyway.

He watched this scene unfolding, mesmerized, trapped, unable to pull his mind free as the phantom Dante touched and caressed every part of the woman, first with his hands, then with his lips. He felt every sensation that passed through her in her fantasy, could smell and feel and taste her. And when he saw himself take her throat, saw his teeth sink into her delicate flesh, he bit down unconsciously, and for one glorious moment he tasted her blood on his tongue and felt her release ripple through his body as she screamed his name aloud.

Then the fantasy shattered. The woman above shot to her feet; he heard them hit the floor. The room was black again, and he stood there, beneath her, shaking, bodily, from his head to his feet.

Leaning back against a cool concrete wall, he

fought to catch his breath. What the hell was the woman doing? How did she know his face, his voice, much less understand the powers he possessed? How could she know what he was?

Did she *want* this thing she dreamed of in such vivid detail it had been as if she were describing the scene aloud, like some Gypsy storyteller of old? Was that what this was about? Desire? Lust?

He was hard and aroused and hungry. Damn hungry. He knew far too little about these Chosen mortals and their link with the undead. But already he sensed it was far more powerful than he had ever understood.

He needed to know more.

He needed to feed. And not on her. God, if the fantasy had been that mind-numbing, what would the reality be like?

He would kill her. If he touched her, he would lose all control and take everything she had. Her body. Her blood. Her life.

Shaking off the lingering images of the woman's fantasy, but unable to so easily rid himself of the arousal it had stirred in him, he strode to the arching steel door at the far end of the room, slid the bolt free and stepped into the cave-like tunnel that led to the outside. Then he headed into town.

To feed.

Morgan soaked in the cool water of her opulent bathroom, and tried to erase the images from her mind. Oh, she had dreamed of Dante before, but it was always very clear that it was just that. A dream. And she saw through his eyes and thought with his mind every day when she wrote down his stories, embellishing to her heart's content. But when she did, she always knew it was only make-believe. All writers lived in the heads of their characters. But they knew what reality was. And what it wasn't.

This time she had felt him. This time she had felt his hands on her skin, his breath on her neck, his teeth piercing her flesh, his mouth sucking at her throat.

It had been real.

And it had been incredible.

Sighing, she sank lower into the water, closed her eyes, tried to think about something else, *anything* else.

The awards ceremony. The dress she still hadn't chosen. The time she would need to spend in L.A. Minimal time. Something was happening here. Something she needed to explore fully until she understood it.

She wasn't going anywhere until she did.

What the hell, she might as well begin now. She closed her eyes, visualizing again the scene she had just written. Bending her knees until they rose up out of the water, she slid her hand down her thigh, touched herself and imagined it was his hand touching her. She shivered and whispered his name. "Dante..."

He could travel very quickly when the need arose, and it had indeed arisen tonight. In an hour's time he was in Bangor, walking the streets, his eyes sharp and watchful.

He found her easily enough. She didn't need to work, not with what he paid her to be available to him. And he didn't have time to seduce an innocent, or to hunt down a victim deserving of death. Not tonight. Tonight he needed his gratification given swiftly and unquestioningly.

She opened the door when he rang the bell, smiled at him. "It's been a while."

He nodded, stepped inside and closed the door behind him.

"You want something to—"

"No. Come here."

Blinking, she seemed a bit afraid, though she shouldn't be. This was something they'd done often enough before. He supposed, however, that his mood had something to do with the flash of fear in her eyes. He tried to soften his expression, even attempted a smile. "Come here."

Swallowing, she stepped closer. Her hands pressed to his chest, slid up his shirt, curled around his neck. She let her head fall backward.

Dante didn't hesitate. He bent and bit into her. She gasped, went stiff, then relaxed very slowly and melted against him. Her blood rushed over his tongue, coating his throat, filling him, warming him. Life coursed through his veins; he felt it tingling there, making him alive with it. Sexual desire stirred in him, and he arched against her as he drank, his hands sliding lower to cup her hips to him. God, how he needed, craved, hungered! Her blood pulsed into his mouth with every beat of her heart—but then it began to slow.

Alarm shot through him, and he lifted his head away, licking his lips—God, she was delicious—and looking down at her.

The blond woman's head slumped to one side. Her eyes were closed, and her skin was very pale. There were two tiny holes in her neck, a thin ribbon of blood twisting from each of them.

Jesus, had he killed her?

"Belinda? Come on, wake up." He shook her gently, patted her face.

Her eyelids fluttered but didn't open. Sighing, he scooped her into his arms, carried her to her sofa and laid her down. He propped her feet on pillows, then tucked a blanket around her.

By then she was stirring, her eyes slowly opening. Her smile was weak. "Damn, you do me good," she whispered.

"Are you all right?"

Inhaling slowly, she seemed to take stock. "Dizzy. Lightheaded as hell. That's never happened before." Her words were slightly slurred, as if she were drunk. He'd taken too much.

"I'm sorry," he said. "My fault. I…it won't happen again."

She smiled weakly. "I like it. I just wish you'd take me the other way while you're at it. I'd like to fuck you raw, baby. Why won't you let me?"

He shook his head slowly. "Not part of the deal." He drew a breath, sighed. "You're going to be fine," he said. "Just sleep, all right?"

"Whatever you say, baby. You're the boss." She closed her eyes, and he sensed her falling asleep almost at once.

Getting to his feet, Dante tugged ten one hundred dollar bills from his pocket and laid them on the coffee table. A bonus for Belinda, who used to sell her body for a living but now sold her blood and made ten times the money. She was his personal whore. He made a point never to get too close, to spend much time, to touch her any more than was necessary. And he only fed from her a few times a year. He had others, around the country, in Europe. Belinda willingly moved between three East Coast cities so she could be where he needed her, when he needed her. He kept her in lush apartments, paid her a generous monthly salary. She never complained.

He didn't know what she or the others like her thought of him. Whether they realized what he was or believed he was simply a rich man with a vampire fetish. He did know they would never breathe a word. He paid them far too well, and he had made it clear well in advance that the money would vanish, as they themselves would, if they spoke of him or his peculiar appetites to anyone.

He'd found them on the streets. In the gutters, for the most part. When you pulled someone up from such misery, they were usually grateful enough to be loyal. You couldn't trust anyone who had been born rich. That had always been his opinion, at least.

That woman, back there at his house in Maine. She had been born rich. He smelled it on her.

He didn't trust her.

And having sated his blood lust, he thought he would be safe to return there now. To have a closer look at this woman who knew so much about him.

To begin the task of learning her every secret.

8

He came to her again that night. And again she knew it was only a dream.

She'd gone to bed after her bath. And she had left the balcony doors open, almost as a challenge. Almost as if some ridiculous part of her mind clung to the fanciful notion that he might, somehow, be real.

Fictional characters did not come to life and visit their authors, she told herself. Why, then, did she brush her hair until the repeated movement of her arms had made her breathless? Why did she wear the small, sheer black peignoir to bed?

She was a fool. She was obsessed. In love with a man who didn't exist. In fact, she was probably in love with a man who never had, except in the mind of a deluded writer. The dark loner, Dante, immortal, utterly sexual creature of the night, had never been real. He was a figment of the journal writer's imagination.

And yet she was completely and utterly obsessed all the same.

She lay awake for a long time, silently begging him to come to her dreams, if only as a way to ensure that her own mind would comply and bring him there while she slept. Finally she drifted off.

And then she felt a cool breeze wafting from the

open balcony doors, and she knew he was there. In her dream, she opened her eyes, and she saw him, standing at the foot of the bed, staring at her, his gaze onyx fire. And again it wasn't like the dreams she had had before. If she didn't know it was impossible, she would have believed this to be real.

"Dante," she whispered.

He lifted his brows as if surprised. "Most women would react quite differently to waking and finding a stranger staring at them as they slept."

"You're not a stranger," she whispered. "I know you."

"So I have gathered." His voice was exactly as she had known it would be. Deep and very soft. Erotically soft. But clear and rich, too. "What I would like to know is...how?"

Her dream self sat up in the bed. She let the sheet fall away from her. Let him see her. She wanted him to see her. "How?"

He responded as she had wished he would. Of course he did. This was her dream. His gaze slid down her body, lingering on her breasts, clearly visible beyond their sheer black filter. "How do you know me?"

She closed her eyes, felt her body respond to his gaze as if it were a touch. "I'm not sure myself. It's as if I'm completely possessed by you." Opening her eyes, she fixed them to his. "Or perhaps it's just that I want to be."

"Do you?"

She nodded very slowly. "It's odd, you know. I've never felt for any man what I feel for you. And you—

you're just a fantasy. Just a dream." Looking away from him, she said, "I suppose that's just as well. Better, maybe. No one gets hurt."

He tipped his head to one side. "A dream, am I?"

She nodded.

He smiled just a little. "Is that what you want me to be? A dream? Like the one you had earlier in the evening?"

Her eyes widened, and she felt a rush of desire and fear coursing through her in a heady combination. She didn't answer, but he moved closer to her, until he stood beside her bed. Reaching out with one hand, he took the sheet and tugged it slowly down her body, slowly exposing her hips and legs and feet.

"Tell me all I wish to know, and I might just comply with your...request." He sat now on the side of her bed. She was half reclining, back against the headboard, and he reached out, dragged the back of his hand over her breast, his knuckles just grazing her nipple. "Beginning with your name."

"Morgan. Morgan De Silva."

"That's very good." He turned his hand, gave her nipple a tiny pinch, her reward, and she gasped in pleasure.

"I wonder, Morgan, would you be so submissive if you thought I were real?" he asked, lazily stroking the nub now, squeezing, tugging now and again.

"If you were real, you would make me as you are."

Those words seemed to startle him. He paused in his ministrations to her breast, his eyes shooting to hers. "Why would I do that?"

"Because we were meant to be together, Dante. You're a part of me, and I am a part of you." She lowered her eyes. "Fantasy, yes. But if you were real, then these feelings would be real. And you could no more resist them than I."

For just a moment she thought there was a flash of fear in his eyes.

She covered his hand on her breast with her own. "But you're not real. Even though this fantasy of mine has suddenly become more real than it has ever been before." She looked down at his hand on her breast. "I can feel you."

His fingers resumed their steady, delicate manipulations.

"I want to feel everything with you, Dante. Everything I have imagined."

He drew his hand away. "Impossible."

"Of course it's possible. Anything's possible in a dream."

"I must leave." He got to his feet, but before he'd gone a step toward the door, she was on her feet, too, clutching his shoulder, turning him.

He turned, reluctantly, as if he would rather not have, and when she had his attention, she slid the straps of the peignoir from her shoulders, pushed it down and let it fall to the floor. She stood there, naked, and his eyes moved over her body, boldly inspecting every inch of her. Taking his hand, she tugged him back to the bed, then lay down on her back.

"Take me, Dante." She pushed her hair away from her neck. "Taste me. I want to feel it again, the way

I felt it earlier. Possessed by you, blood, soul and body."

She saw him tremble, but she still had hold of his hand, and she pulled him gently closer. Again he sat on the edge of her bed, and this time, she sat up and pressed her mouth to his, her arms twisting around his neck.

He kissed her, fed from her mouth, suckled her tongue, nipping it with his sharp teeth and drawing tiny droplets of blood. As he did, he pressed her down again, until his body pressed hers to the bed, and he devoured her mouth. One knee was wedged between her legs, parting them, and she felt his erection now, beyond the barrier of his jeans, pressing to her naked, open center.

Reaching down, she grabbed his zipper.

He covered that hand with his own and gently pulled it away as he broke the kiss.

"I'll hurt you," he whispered.

"You can't hurt me. It's my dream."

Sitting up, panting for breath, he whispered, "Close your eyes, Morgan. And I'll give you what you want."

Lying still, she did as he asked. She closed her eyes.

He leaned close to her again, and his lips now were very near to her ear. "Surrender to me," he whispered, slowly, repeatedly. "Open to me. Let me inside you. Inside your mind."

"Yes," she whispered. Her legs parted, but he didn't touch her. And yet he did. Somehow, he did. Without touching her, he caressed her. Like phantom fingers on her skin, he stroked and rubbed and slid around her body, touching her nowhere and everywhere at once. She could see it in her mind, feel it as if it were real, but she knew he hadn't moved. Not a muscle. He was sitting as he had been, staring at her.

"That's it," he whispered. "Give yourself over. Feel me, Morgan. I'm inside you, around you. Do you feel me?"

"Yes!"

"Around you, inside you, possessing you, owning you. Your body is mine to command at this moment, isn't it, Morgan?"

She nodded, as she twisted and writhed on the bed, craving more, craving so much more.

His lips very close to her ears, he whispered, "Come, Morgan."

The orgasm broke through her like an explosion. She screamed his name, her arms lashing around his neck and pulling him close. And then she felt it, his mouth parting and snapping closed on her throat, his teeth piercing her skin, and then the delicious sucking.

"Yes, yes, yes," she whispered as the climax went on and on, driven further by his drinking from her.

And then she faded. She faded and vanished, lost herself utterly in him.

Dante licked the blood from his lips and lifted his head away. He shouldn't have tasted her. Dammit, he hadn't meant to. Her arms fell away from his neck. He eased her onto her pillows. Straightening away, he pulled the covers over her, then turned and closed his eyes.

Already he was hungering for more. He had only meant to pleasure her with the power of his mind. But God, it had as potent an effect on him as it did on her. And when she'd pulled him to her, cradling his face to her neck as she shivered and bucked with her climax, he had lost himself in the scent of her. The blood, rushing just beneath the skin, her hands pressing him closer, her neck arching toward him.

And so he'd taken her. Just like that, he'd plunged his teeth into her luscious flesh and drunk.

Only a little. God, only a little. But the power of it was beyond understanding. It rocked him, the force of her life inside him. It made him shudder. It made him want more.

Rising from the bed, Dante took two staggering steps toward the window before he caught himself in a grip of iron will. No. He couldn't leave, not now. She was asleep, and while he had seen very little inside her mind while he'd been there, probing, he had seen pages of what looked like his own handwriting and a room—a familiar room. His study.

He didn't know what it meant, but he had come here to find out.

Glancing back at the bed, where she slept deeply, he made his decision. He refused to let the heated affections of some strange mortal female sway him from his task. And yet he had trouble drawing his gaze away from the two tiny holes in her neck and the trickle of red from each of them. He nearly leaned down to lick the stray droplets away, but he resisted. God knew he could as easily rip out her throat.

He moved silently, soundlessly, past the foot of her

bed, toward the door. Then he opened it and slipped into the darkened hall, pulling the bedroom door closed behind him.

And then—then he went still, as the mists of time parted and he seemed to be looking a century into the past. The hall's hardwood floor gleamed with finish so new he could smell it. And the wide stairs, wider at the base than at the top, spilled downward into the great room that was exactly as he remembered it. The vaulted dome ceiling housing the crystal chandelier. The pristine woodwork with its intricately carved trim. God, he had missed this place.

As he walked slowly down the stairs, his palm gliding over the highly polished bannister, he saw the differences. The paintings on the walls were not the ones he'd put up himself. The chandelier was electric, not gas powered, as it had been when he had lived here. The furniture was different. Oh, she had the period right. How she knew he'd decorated the entire place in rugged-looking reproductions from the time of the Norse invasions, he couldn't begin to guess. But she had done likewise. The chairs were like the thrones of a barbarian king. Solid square legs and arms, with the heads of bears or lions at the ends. Boxy tables to match, and in the corners stood pedestals of granite bearing sculptures of legendary warriors. Eric the Red, with his two-horned helm. A muscled valkyrie astride a winged horse.

His choices hadn't been exactly the same. But that she'd chosen this culture, the Vikings, as her theme was beyond coincidence. The woman knew him. Study of the period had been a hobby of his. A chill whispered up his spine. He glanced toward the dark-wood double doors that led to his study. Or had once. It had been his haven. His shelter against the world.

He was almost afraid to go in there, almost couldn't make himself do it. But then he did. He moved to the doors, gripped the brass handles, turned them and pulled the doors open.

His study opened out before him as if he were looking again into the past. The fireplace on the far wall had been restored to its original design. The huge antique desk in the corner was not exactly like his, but the size was right. The chair before it was modern, of course, with casters, and the computer on top of the desk seemed completely out of place.

It occurred to him suddenly that that must have been the spot where she had been earlier tonight, when he'd been inside her mind. When he had felt her fantasizing about him. Felt everything she imagined as if it were real.

Before he could dwell on that for much longer, he caught sight of something else, something that drew his head around fast and then captured his full attention.

Drawings on the walls. Some in frames, some just tacked up haphazardly. God, there were a dozen of them. And they were all…him.

He stared as if stricken, moved closer against his will, and scrutinized every line, every shade and shadow that made up the contours of his face. And as he did, he ran his hand over his own chin and cheek and jawbone. So unnatural to be able to look at himself this way, when he had been unable to see his own reflection for so long. Centuries. Was his face that angular? Were his eyes that deep, that shadowed? God, he looked haunted.

How did this woman know him? How?

The room suddenly seemed too small and felt like a vacuum. He sucked in a breath, then another, but couldn't seem to find enough air. The shock, he supposed, of seeing himself depicted so clearly. He opened every desk drawer but found no evidence, and he scanned the bookshelves, as well, to no avail. The computer mocked him. He knew very little about the machines. Searching its contents would be challenging. And still, he supposed, he was going to have to attempt it.

But first, air. He was still having trouble digesting all of this. Particularly when he glimpsed the drawing of him as a child, near the campfire of his family, while Sarafina danced. His breath caught in his throat then.

Dante dragged himself to the nearest window, flipped the catch at the top and opened it easily. Then he took a deep drink of cool, bracing night air.

A shrill, piercing tone split the silence of the night and shattered his renewed composure. Hell, it was some kind of an alarm. He clasped his palms to his sensitive ears and lunged through the open window, running from the house into the welcoming arms of the night.

As he paused, crouching in the bushes while deciding what the hell to do next, she came. Morgan. Awakened by the alarm, she had gone directly to the study where he had been. As if she knew. God, how connected they were.

She stood in the open window, looking out into the darkness, her face completely confused, utterly vulnerable. She would remember their encounter only as a dream. And yet she knew someone had been inside her house. The way she was staring out, squinting, searching the darkness, it seemed almost as if she were hoping to see him, rather than fearing she might.

The woman had no idea the kind of power she was playing with. No idea.

She had better hope she never had to learn.

He started to leave, but then he saw her move, and something about the way her eyes changed caught his attention. She was turning, staring hard at the windowglass, and lifting a hand to her neck.

Oh, God, the reflection. She saw the wounds by night that would have vanished at the first touch of sunlight on her flesh. She saw the two punctures, the tiny ribbon of blood on her white flesh. She saw them—and she knew.

9

"**P**ersonally," Lou said, "I think Lydia's just been watching too many movies. This paranormal bullshit is all the rage on the big screen lately."

"Yeah?" Max glanced across the front seat at him. He was driving his beat-up Buick, and there was a console in between them holding his foam coffee cup, his sausage-and-egg croissant, a small notebook, several candy bar wrappers, and numerous other bits of paraphernalia. The man spent way too much time in his car.

"Sure," he said. "What, you don't know? I figured you probably saw every new monster movie the minute it came out."

She sent him a smirk. "I don't like poorly done horror," she said. "It just isn't what it used to be anymore. All slash and no class. You know what I mean?"

"Sure I do."

"Besides," she said, "I don't like to go to the movies alone. And there's not exactly a steady stream of potential dates beating a path to my door."

He shook his head from side to side. "I can't imagine why not."

"No? Well that's nice of you, Lou. But you're just saying that. I'm not really very pretty."

He made a grunting sound and blurted, "The hell you aren't."

Max averted her face, pretending to look out the passenger side window so he wouldn't see her shit-eating grin. "Well, maybe I'm passably cute," she ventured. "But cute isn't the same thing as sexy. Men don't tend to see me as sexy."

"Blind men, maybe."

Her smile grew even wider. She forced it into hiding, made her eyebrows arch in delicate surprise, and turned to look at him. "You mean *you* think I'm sexy, Lou?"

"I...?" He closed his mouth, drew his brows together, saw right through her. "You know, you shouldn't tease an old guy like that. It's not nice."

"I'm not—"

"Look, here we are," he said, wheeling the car toward the parking lot as if it were the safe zone in a life-or-death game of tag. "Now remember, hon. This lady is an old, dear friend of mine. I care about her feelings. She's just lost her best friend in the world, and I gotta tell you, that's the least of the losses she's been through in her life. So you be on your best behavior. I'm talking manners, Maxie. Show some respect."

"Sheesh, you act like I'm going to go in there and spit on her or something."

"I just want you to ease her mind. That's all. Disabuse her of this farfetched notion she has about bloodsucking night stalkers. And be convincing. Okay?"

She lowered her head, lifted her gaze and fluttered her lashes. "Anything you say, Lou."

Lou rolled his eyes heavenward as he pulled the

car into the first empty space in the lot outside June's. The place had a bar in one half and a dining room in the other. It was pretty dead at midmorning on a weekday, which was, Max figured, why Lou had chosen it.

She got out her side, not bothering to lock the door, which Lou remedied for her with a look of exasperation. The way Max figured it, if someone was so desperate for wheels that they would make off with Lou's rustmobile, more power to them. He would do better collecting the insurance.

They walked up the steps to the diner's entrance. Lou opened the door for her, and she made damn sure to brush his body with hers when she went through it. He pretended not to notice.

A woman looked up from a table when they came in, her eyes skimming Max quickly, lighting on Lou, and warming as she got to her feet and smiled. It was a weak, watery smile. And Max probably would have felt a rush of sympathy for anyone else who smiled like that. Except that this woman was a buxom bleached blonde who would look good in a feedbag, and she was sending that wet smile to *her cop*.

Max quelled her urge to scowl at the woman as Lou led her to the table.

"Lydia," Lou said. "How you doing, hon?" He reached out for a gentle hug as he spoke to her, and Max felt her blood throb in her temples.

"I'm all right. Thanks for coming, Lou." She eased her grip on him and glanced at Maxine.

"Lydia, this is Maxine Stuart, the girl I was telling you about. Maxie, Lydia Jordan."

Lydia's smile didn't falter, didn't turn into one that seemed forced or strained, as Max had expected it to.

She probably thought Max was too young to be any competition for Lou's affections. Well, she damn well better think again.

"I can't tell you how grateful I am that you agreed to meet with me, Maxine," Lydia said, reaching out to clasp Max's hand in both of hers. "Lou says you know more about this kind of thing than anyone he knows. And I so need the opinion of someone like you, whose judgement I can trust beyond question."

Max blinked, a little surprised. So Lou had sung her praises, had he? Cool. That was good to know. She shot Lou a look, but he avoided it and waved at the chairs. "Let's sit and get on with this."

Max sat on one side of the small square table, Lou on the other, with Lydia in between them. Lovely. A waitress appeared to fill the coffee cups waiting on the table, left menus and quietly vanished.

"Gee, she was talkative," Max commented.

"I told them we wanted as much privacy as possible." Swallowing as if she had a lump in her throat, Lydia looked Max in the eye. "I understand Lou has already told you the basics. My partner...my...my best friend in the world, Kimbra Sykes...was killed on her way home one night two weeks ago."

"I've seen Lou's notes on what happened," Max said, keeping her voice down in case anyone might be listening in. She wouldn't want to get Lou into trouble for the world. "They found her the next morning in an alley."

Lydia nodded, her blond hair moving with every motion. She wore too much makeup, Max thought unkindly. Old broads tended to do that. Pile it on in an effort to cover up the ravages of time.

"Lou's going to be mad as hell at me for this,

Maxine, but…'' Lydia pulled an envelope from the
black leather attache case at her side, slid it across
the table. ''I got copies of the crime scene photos and
the autopsy report before the F.B.I. took over the
case.''

''Oh, for crying out loud, Lydia, how the hell—''

Lou broke off as Max started to open the envelope
and Lydia held up a hand to stop her. ''I'll go freshen
up, give you time to look that over.''

Max paused with her hand inside the envelope.
''Sorry, I wasn't thinking.''

''That's okay. Go ahead, that's what I brought it
for.'' She got to her feet, headed for the rest room in
the back and vanished from Max's line of vision.

''You didn't know she had this stuff?'' Max asked,
sliding the documents and photos from the envelope.

''No, and I have no idea how the hell she got her
hands on it, either. The freaking Feds came in, took
all the evidence and destroyed any copies we'd
made.''

Max looked up at him. ''They did?''

''Yeah. It just happened. There's something going
on, Maxie, but I'll be damned if I know what. My
best guess would be maybe a serial killer using this
same M.O. But if you breathe a word of that, I'll deny
it.''

''Thank goodness Big Brother keeps the public so
well informed,'' she muttered. She laid the stack on
the table, flipped over the top page and stared down
at the crime scene photographs. A woman, very tall
and lean, maybe in her early forties, lay on the ground
in an alley. She wore khakis and a forest-green
sweater with a V-neck. Her light brown hair was
twisted into a neat knot.

"Not a hair out of place," Max muttered. "Look at her clothes, Lou. They aren't dirty or torn. Her makeup isn't even smeared."

"I know."

She flipped through the photos and got to the autopsy shots, which were routine until she got to the closeups of the woman's neck. Two tiny punctures marred the lily white skin there. Again she flipped pages rapidly, until she got to the autopsy report. "The woman died from blood loss," she told Lou. "It says an impossibly small amount of blood remained in her body, but that she didn't have a single injury anywhere. Not a cut, not a bruise, no internal bleeding, nothing—except for those two puncture wounds at her throat." She skimmed the page, then went back to the first stack of photos, flipping quickly through them. "And not a drop of blood at the crime scene, either."

She lifted her gaze, met Lou's eyes. Then, beyond him, she saw Lydia approaching slowly and took her cue, shoving the stack of papers and photos back into the envelope. No one should have to see their best friend looking like that.

"Well?" Lydia asked, stopping, standing near the table. "What's your opinion?"

"Can I keep these?" Max asked, holding up the envelope. "I'd like to study them a little more."

"Of course. I made copies. But…what do you think, Maxine? Am I completely insane to think it could have been…I mean…"

"You're not insane at all. Either someone was trying very hard to make this murder look like the work of a vampire…or else it actually *was*."

"Maxie..." Lou looked as if he wanted to throttle her.

"Sorry, Lou, but for crying out loud, do you have any better theories?"

"A hundred! Alien abduction would be a better theory than that. Jeez, Max, I brought you here to make things better, and you've only made them worse."

"Don't yell at her," Lydia said. Her voice was soft but firm. "I wanted her to give me her honest opinion, and she did that, in spite of the fact that she must have known it would piss you off, Lou. Let her be." She turned her attention to Max. "What do you think I should do now?"

Maxine felt herself grow a little taller. The woman was asking her advice as if she were someone important, someone whose opinion mattered. And the fact was, Max realized, she *was*. No one could help Lydia more than Max could. But damn, this was one can of worms she'd been secretly hoping she wouldn't have to open again—at least, not yet. She remembered the burned, sooty face of that man and the sound of his voice, threatening her loved ones on the phone.

She shook herself and realized Lydia was still waiting for an answer. "The first thing, the most important thing, is that you are to tell no one about this. No one. Pretend you don't know. Pretend you're swallowing whatever cock-and-bull tale they spin for you about Kimbra's death. Thank them and don't argue. Don't question. I swear to God, that's vital."

Lydia looked surprised but was nodding emphatically. Lou, meanwhile, had narrowed his eyes on Max and was staring at her as if she'd lost her mind.

"Other than that, just go about your daily business as normally as you can. Stay off the streets, behind locked doors at night. Some company wouldn't be a bad idea. I mean, just in case."

"Yeah, right," Lou said. "I suppose you're gonna suggest she hang garlic and crucifixes around her bed, too, huh, Maxie?"

She shot him a glance. "I don't think they really work."

He rolled his eyes, shook his head. "Lydia, go home and forget about this meeting. I should have known better than to bring Mad Maxie Stuart in as the voice of reason. Let the authorities handle this, and I promise you, you'll get your answers in time. You just need to be patient."

He turned then. "And as for you—"

"Lou, please," Lydia said.

Max slumped in her chair. "It's okay, Lydia," she said. "Go ahead, go back to your routine. Trust me, I'm on this." Then she sighed. "Maybe you should go now. I think Lou wants to yell at me alone for a little while."

Lydia looked at her, finally nodded. "Looks like you can handle him."

"I can."

"Thank you, Maxine. Thank you. I'll be in touch."

Max yanked a business card out of her pocket and handed it to Lydia almost as an afterthought. "It's, uh—one of my old ones. Haven't had new ones made up yet."

Lydia nodded, tucking the card into her pocket. Then she gave Lou a hug and left the diner.

Max got to her feet. "Come on, Lou."

"Come on where?" he asked.

"My place. There are some things you need to see. And if you still want to yell at me after you've seen them, then you can feel free. I'll welcome it. But if not—then you gotta help me figure this out."

"There is nothing you can show me that will make what you just did to that woman all right, Maxie. I'm never gonna forgive you for this."

"Yeah, you will."

He reached for the envelope, but she snatched it off the table before he could grab it. "That's classified material," he said.

"I know," she said. "I've got reams more of it at my place. So this will fit right in."

He stared at her, waiting for the punch line, and when it didn't come, he lifted his brows and widened his eyes.

"Come on," she said. "I'll explain when we get there."

Lou noticed the change in Maxie right off the bat. Man, she'd taken him by surprise, encouraging Lydia's delusions instead of debunking them. Max was wild, yes. Impetuous, that, too. Irreverent, and a little bit self-involved. But damn, he'd never thought she would turn on him when he was counting on her.

He was more than a little disappointed. Then again, she was a kid. What could you expect?

But now he was getting worried. When they left the diner, she acted as if she thought someone might be watching them. She looked up and down the road, looked underneath his car before she got in, checked the back seat, and then kept checking the rearview mirrors as he drove.

"What the hell is the matter?" he asked her.

She glanced at him, shook her head. "Stop at the bank. I need to get something."

He frowned at her, but pulled into the bank's drive-way. "Drive-through window?" he asked.

"Safe deposit box."

Okay, *that* sent a little chill up his spine. What the hell was Mad Maxie up to? He parked the car as she dug through her purse and finally came up with a key. Then he followed her inside, and damned if her behavior didn't set his antennae on high alert. He'd seen her cynical, skeptical and ridiculous, but he'd never seen her paranoid. And there was part of him—a small part—that thought maybe she had reason. He found himself watching her back as if she were his partner and they had just entered a roomful of cut-throats.

She noticed it; he knew she did. Saw the way her eyes warmed in appreciation. She had hellacious eyes, Maxie did. Big and green and shiny. Went with the fiery red hair. She was a Technicolor female. In spirit as well as looks. She sent him a wink and a secretive smile as a teller led her into a back room. Lou grated his teeth and moved in closer, put his back to the door she'd gone through, kept his eyes on the place and tried to ignore his slightly increased pulse rate.

Maxie, he realized, had no idea what it did to him when she flirted the way she did. Constantly. She thought he was too old to react to her, thought he was no threat, no danger. A gelding. Hell, it wasn't exactly flattering, but to be honest, Lou *liked* that she felt safe with him. He was damned ashamed of himself for the reactions, in both body and mind, that he couldn't always prevent. He would rather be shot than admit that to her, though. He didn't want her knowing he was just another dirty old man.

Eighteen years between them. Technically, he was old enough to be her father. Okay, a young father, but still…

She came back out and he didn't see anything in her hands that she hadn't had when she'd gone in. Then he noticed that her handbag was plumper now than before. Jesus, she was being careful.

He led her out to the car, put her in, got behind the wheel and put the vehicle into motion again. "You ready to tell me what this is all about yet, Max?"

She glanced up at him, licked her lips. "You're the only person in the world I trust enough to talk to about this, Lou. No one can know. No one. I haven't told my mom or Stormy or anyone."

"Understood," he said.

"I wanted to tell you a long time ago, but I was afraid it would get you into trouble. And I knew it could put you in danger."

He snapped his head around toward her.

"Let's go to your place, okay? Mine's too busy. Storm's in and out all day, and besides, they know where I live."

"Who knows where you live? Jesus, Maxie, you're starting to scare me."

"You have a computer at home, right? With a CD-ROM drive?"

He nodded, and his mind wandered briefly to the condition of his apartment, but that was trivial. Something had really frightened Max. And she wasn't a stupid girl. He didn't think she would blow something completely harmless this far out of proportion.

"Is that what was in the safe deposit box, Max? A CD-ROM?"

"And an ID badge."

He lifted his brows. "What kind of an ID badge?"

"Kinda like yours. Only instead of City Police, it says DPI."

"Never heard of it."

"I'm pretty sure it was a secret unit within the CIA, and it used to be headquartered right here in White Plains. Before it burned to the ground, anyway."

He sat there for a full minute, processing what she had just told him. Then he got it. "You mean the cancer research center that burned five or so years back?"

She nodded. "Yeah. Only it wasn't cancer they were researching."

He swung the car into his space and gripped the wheel with both hands, facing her. "You were there, snooping around, that night. I remember when you asked me to—" He broke off as it came clear. "You took this stuff from the fire that night, didn't you, Maxie? That's why you needed me to help you get around those soldiers who showed up."

"Now you're getting it. And it gets even better, Lou. Someone besides you saw me snooping around there that night."

"Who?"

"The guy who belonged to the ID badge, I think."

"Holy freaking..."

"Don't freak on me yet, cause this is just the believable part of the story. Come on. If I tell you the rest, you'll have me hauled away to a mental ward before I get very far. You gotta see this stuff for yourself."

She opened her car door, got out, hitched her purse up onto her shoulder.

Lou got out, too, but his head was spinning. He couldn't believe Max had stolen secrets from some kind of government agency. My God, people went to prison for less.

He took her arm, led her up the outside stairs to his second-floor apartment. "I don't know what the hell you've gotten yourself into this time, Max," he said softly. "I just hope to Christ I can get you out of it."

10

Morgan worked endlessly, long into the nights, typing away on her computer, or pacing and talking to herself, as Dante watched her every move.

He never saw her eat. She drank constantly, though. Vodka, mixed with whatever soft drink she had on hand. Whatever she was writing had her obsessed. And he sensed it had to do with him. He did not want to believe it had to do with his secrets being revealed to his enemies.

His nocturnal visit had worsened things, he thought. It might not have, had she not seen the evidence of his kiss of possession with her own eyes. It had been gone the next day. She might even have believed she had imagined it all.

But obviously she was afraid she had not.

He couldn't get into the damned study to find out what she was working on—not without setting off alarms, which would alert both her and the police. Even if he could gain access, finding what he wanted would be difficult. He'd been watching her, night after night, writing feverishly. She saved everything on CDs and stored them in a large safe that hadn't been there before. It was hidden behind a mock bookcase. Its door opened away from the window through which he observed her every move, so he hadn't been able to see what else might be inside.

Tonight he watched her typing frantically, just as he watched her every night. He had tried again, putting his hand to the floor beneath her to help him connect with her mind, see what she was seeing there, but without success. She had erected barriers of some kind. At least when she was awake. She wouldn't be able to sustain them while she slept. But damn, he was afraid to go to her in her sleep again. Afraid he would lose control.

He almost had, the last time....

She worked long into the night, and when she stopped, she leaned back in the chair as if utterly drained.

God, she was beautiful. Skin like alabaster, long straight hair in a shade of copper that shone as if it were a light source all its own. She was so thin. It had been three days since he'd been in the same room with her, touched her—and he was determined not to do so again. He would just watch her from outside, and sooner or later she would forget to turn a lock or set an alarm, or perhaps she would leave the house. His chance would come.

But not tonight. She rose at last, glancing at her watch. He knew by the proximity of dawn, which vampires always sensed, that it must be near 2:00 a.m. She was unsteady on her feet. He was beginning to think she was ill. In fact, whatever weakness he had sensed in her that first night seemed to be worsening by alarming degrees, as did the unnatural pallor of her skin. It worried him. God, it made his mind reel.

Even feeling poorly, though, Morgan remembered to take the CD from the drive, slide it into its protective sheath and put it in the blasted safe. It was frustrating as hell that he couldn't see the numbers she punched in. Almost as frustrating as being unable to see the computer screen as she wrote for hour upon hour upon hour.

Neither of those things was as frustrating as being so close to her and yet unable to touch her again. Or as sensing she was ill but not knowing why.

He dreamed of her when he rested by day. It was unnatural for a vampire's day sleep to be plagued with dreams. Unheard of, in his experience. He had never dreamed—not once from the day Sarafina had brought him over into the realm of night. Not once— until he had first sipped from the font of Morgan De Silva.

She shut the computer off and went upstairs, and he had to admit to feeling a surge of relief as he rose from his position outside the study's window and went around to the rear of the house, clambering up the tree to watch her as he did every night.

Sarafina would probably laugh at him if she could see him behaving this way. She would probably attribute his childish antics to lust—and she wouldn't be completely wrong. But there was something more than desire at work here. There was this bond—he denied it, but he felt it all the same. He had to know how this woman knew him.

She entered the bedroom and walked straight through it into the adjoining bathroom. When he had lived here, the bedroom had been a two room suite. What had been his bath, she had converted to a walk-in closet. What had been an entire sitting room, she had converted into a bath fit for royalty. Most days she settled for a fast, brisk shower in the morning. The room had a three-sided, frosted-glass enclosed, corner stall for that. But this time, she didn't go to the shower. She went to the huge tub, cranked the faucets on, then paused, sitting on the edge as if exhausted by that simple motion.

She didn't close the door. She never closed the door. Why the hell should she, up here on the second floor? Why should she expect to be seen up here?

He wanted to stay. To watch her bathe. But if he did, he would likely smash through the windows and go to her in spite of his determination not to. Gathering his resolve, he leapt down to the ground. He went to the ocean to bathe himself and spent an hour walking along the beach, reasoning with his own mind, grappling with his own desire. By the time he returned to her balcony, he fully expected her to be in bed, sound asleep.

She was sound asleep. But not in her bed.

She was in the bath. Her pale body was limp, her head hanging to one side, hair dragging in the water. He thought she was dead when he threw open the balcony doors and raced inside, through the bedroom and into the bathroom. "Morgan?"

She didn't respond at all.

He went to the tub, scooped her up into his arms, dripping wet, and carried her to the bed, snatching up a towel on the way. She was alive. He knew that at once, sensing the life in her, hearing it buzzing through her cells, that singing energy no one could name. It stopped singing at death. It sang louder and more clearly in the undead.

She lifted her head weakly from his shoulder. "Dante?"

"I'm a dream. I'm only a dream," he told her.

She relaxed in his arms. He carried her to the bed, toweled her off a little, and laid her down, quickly pulling the covers over her so he wouldn't have to look at her skin. "Why are you so ill, Morgan?"

She smiled very softly. "I'm dying. Didn't you know?"

He went very still, his hands still clutching the blanket near her shoulders. His eyes shot to hers. "Dying..."

"I have this rare blood type," she told him. "The doctors say everyone who has it dies young, but no one can seem to figure out why."

"The Belladonna Antigen," he whispered.

"Yes, that's the one." She let her head sink into her pillows, sighing. "I didn't expect it to get this much worse so soon."

"I'm sorry," he whispered. "I didn't know it was...I didn't know it was fatal."

"Of course you did. You live inside me. You know everything about me."

"Not this."

She smiled very slowly. "I'm so tired." Her eyes fell closed, her head tipping sideways and a lock of hair falling over her eyes. "I hope it isn't tonight," she whispered. "I hope I have...just a few more weeks. I need to finish...and then the awards...."

She drifted off, muttering words that might have made sense to her but made none to him. He tried to look into her mind once she fell asleep. It was no longer closed to him, but she was so tired, there was nothing to see. She slept like the dead. And that was no cliché in her case.

Dante tried to sense the life force in her, to guess how long she had. It was weak. Hell, he didn't want to increase the bond between them still further, and yet he was compelled, for some odd reason, to help this woman.

He knew better, his mind told him. It would strengthen the bond between them. It would make this longing even more difficult to resist.

And yet, she was weak. She was fading. He sensed it.

It came down to the simple fact that he did not want to let her go. He pushed back his sleeve, brought his wrist to his mouth and bit down. His incisors sank into flesh, popped through cartilage, pierced the vein, but not too deeply. Just a nick. He slid the thumb of his free hand over the wounds, held it there as he moved his wrist to Morgan's lips. In his mind, he created the image of what he wanted her to do and sent it to her with the force of his will. Then he pressed his wrist to her mouth.

She drank. Her lips parted and closed over the punctures, warm and wet, and she suckled him like a baby at its mother's breast. Desire shot through him like an electrical charge. She licked, swallowed, sucked harder. His breath came faster, and he grew hard with arousal. Finally, teeth grated in sweet anguish, he held her forehead with one hand and pulled his wrist away. He yanked a scarf from the nightstand, knocking a book to the floor in the process. As he twisted the scarf around his wrist, he glanced down at the title. *Psychic Self-Defense*. Dion Fortune, no less. No wonder he could no longer so easily read Morgan's thoughts. He tied the scarf in a knot, tourniquet-tight. It would do until dawn. Dawn was not far off, in fact.

He glanced down at the woman on the bed. Her

skin was pinker now, and she felt warmer to the touch. She would feel stronger tomorrow.

But again, she couldn't know why. She had to remember him only as a dream. And dammit, he had to make some kind of progress in figuring out why and how she knew as much about him as she did.

Maybe she was psychic. Maybe that was the explanation that so eluded him. Perhaps she'd picked up some kind of trace emanations he had left in the atmosphere of this place.

Again he looked at her. There were traces of his blood on her lips. Dante leaned forward, pressed his to them, kissed the droplets away.

Her eyes fluttered open. "How can I love a man who doesn't exist?" she whispered. "I do, you know. I love you, Dante."

He felt his eyes widen in alarm. "The last woman who said those words to me nearly cost me my life."

"I know," she whispered, rolling onto her side, eyes falling closed again. "Laura Sullivan, the lass from Dunkinny."

Dante went utterly rigid. "How do you know that name?" But she didn't answer. "Morgan?" But no. He could wake her, but that would be too risky. He would have to wake her completely in order to get any straight answers out of her. And then he would never convince her that this had all been just a dream. Instead, he laid his hands on her head, focused on her mind, probed and sought.

What he found was her, beautiful, healthy, staring into a man's eyes—his eyes—and whispering, "I'll never betray you the way Laura Sullivan did, Dante."

Then he saw a screen behind them both, alight with moving pictures that retold the tale. He saw the woman he had loved, the only mortal he had ever trusted with the truth of what he was. He saw her, and she looked the way she had looked then. She led a mob of the villagers, all of them bearing torches, and she shouted at them, "He's a beast, I tell you. He tried to drink my blood and admitted to me what he is—and his friend Donovan, too! We have to destroy them!"

Then the others shouted "Burn, burn, burn, burn" as they hurled their flaming clubs at the castle he shared with Donovan O'Roarke, his young protegé.

The screen went black. In her mind, once again, there were only the two of them. "I already know what you are, Dante. I love you all the same." She leaned up in the dream, her lips pressing to his.

Dante backed out of her mind in a rush, shook himself.

It was true. She knew all of his secrets. All of them.

11

She slept heavily, late into the afternoon. But when Morgan finally did wake, she woke all at once. Her eyes opened wide, and she sat up with a gasp, as if something had shocked her out of a deep sleep.

Nothing had. She sat there blinking, pressing her hand to her forehead in anticipation of the rush of dizziness that always came when she sat up too suddenly, or stood up too suddenly, or ran up the stairs, or a thousand other things.

It didn't come, though. And as she sat there, she slowly became aware of the way she *felt*. She felt...better. Almost good. Frowning, she flung her covers back and got to her feet, testing her balance, waiting for the weakness. It occurred to her that she didn't remember getting into bed last night. In fact, the last thing she remembered was the bath, and...and then the dream.

Closing her eyes slowly, she let her breath rush from her lips. Dante. He had come to her again in her dreams. Squeezing her eyes a little tighter against the rush of sweet pain the memory brought, she tried to recall the details to her mind. But nothing came clearly. Just the memory of his voice, speaking in its deep velvety hush, soothing her. His hand, cool on her face. His nearness. His *realness*.

Oh, and his taste!

God, had she really dreamt *that?*

She was losing it, she knew that. Completely enmeshed in the life of a man who didn't exist. Living his stories by day, dreaming of him by night. My God, she was an acclaimed screenwriter. And yet she didn't care. She cared about nothing except him, a man who did not—who *could* not—exist!

Something compelled her to check the French doors that led out onto her balcony before she did anything else. They were locked. From the inside. Of course they were. What had she expected? Sighing, she turned and walked into the bathroom.

She stopped in the doorway, staring in at a tub still full of water. "That's so odd." More than odd, a voice in her mind warned. It was completely unlike her to leave water in the tub. She was meticulous about this house, had been ever since she had first come to know its one-time owner. To her, this place was Dante's headstone. His memorial. His marker. She honored it.

Another sign of her looming nervous breakdown, she supposed. And what on earth had possessed her to sleep all day long? Hell, she shouldn't complain. As good as she felt, she would be able to make up for lost time long into the night.

Heading back into her bedroom, she decided to get out of the house for a little while. Outside, in the brisk spring air, maybe go for a walk down the beach and into the Norman Rockwell town a mile away. It would do her good. Besides, she couldn't remember the last time she had felt capable of walking on the beach.

She showered quickly, threw on a pair of jeans and a cozy sweater, dressed her feet in a pair of white ankle socks and lightweight tennis shoes. She only towel dried her hair, then left it loose. And she grabbed a handbag she rarely used, and a jacket, just in case.

Then she trotted down the wide staircase with a sense of anticipation she couldn't explain and didn't want to. At the bottom, she caught herself, slowed her pace, mentally reminding herself that she would be breathless and panting if she didn't. She wasn't, though. Her heart wasn't even pounding hard.

Maybe she was getting better. Maybe the sea air or those herbal supplements she'd been taking were finally kicking in. Maybe...

She walked briskly through the house, out the back door and down across the sloping green lawn toward the cliffs. For a moment she simply stood there, staring out at the horizon. The sun was setting on the other side of the world. If she were on the West Coast, she could watch it go down over the ocean. A huge blazing ball of fire, quenching itself slowly in the cool embrace of the sea. She hadn't watched the sun set over the Pacific in years. But she could watch it rise over the Atlantic. And tonight she could watch the darkness gradually stealing over the water, changing its color, as the sun set far, far behind her.

She thought about the words that could capture such a sight and describe it. The way the water kept changing, racing, it seemed to stay a shade darker than the sky. The sky went from robin's egg to lilac, navy to midnight blue. The sea from turquoise to purple to ebony.

The wind picked up as the sun sank lower. Salty and ever cooler, it pushed Morgan teasingly, daring her to push back. She stood there for a long time as the first few stars winked to life in the darkening sky. Sighing in appreciation, she inhaled the night air. It tasted good. She wasn't ready to go in just yet. Turning, she headed down the path along the edge of the cliffs to where it rolled downward to the shore at a gentler angle. When she reached the level of the shore, she followed the stony, sandy shoreline southward toward town.

Easton was small. Picturesque, but not enough so that it had become a tourist trap—not yet, at least. The sidewalks tended to roll up early. Morgan veered away from the beach onto the town's main road, just north of the downtown area. She took the sidewalk and walked along, looking in the shop windows, most of which were already closed.

A crowd drew her attention, and she glanced ahead, saw the line forming outside the movie theater, its small, lighted marquee above their heads. The theater was small, two screens, a couple of hundred seats. No surround-sound or giant screen. It was closed until showtime, and the doors opened a half hour before each show and not a minute sooner.

Glancing up at the scrolling marquee, Morgan couldn't help but smile. Her latest film was showing, and underneath the title the colored lights spelled out a message that scrolled past repeatedly. ''Easton's own Morgan De Silva has earned a Best Screenplay nomination! See the film tonight!''

She blinked happily. Gee, it seemed she was something of a celebrity around town. Odd that no one had been out to the house to bother her. Of course, she kept a very low profile, rarely ventured out, had an unlisted phone number and a whole lot of electronic security. Maybe people just respected each other's privacy out here?

There had to be more to it than that. Part of her knew what, but most of her refused to acknowledge what that part of her knew. It was silly to believe that people avoided going anywhere near her house because it still emanated the predatory energy of the man who had once inhabited it.

She still carried her jacket. Now she put it on, tugging up its lightweight hood and tucking her long hair inside it. She dug into her purse for the case that held her designer sunglasses and slipped them on, as well. Then she moved ahead and took her spot at the end of the line.

She felt a shiver go up her spine, as if a cold breath had just whispered across her nape, and she turned fast. But no one stood behind her. There was someone standing on the sidewalk, though, several yards away, in the direction from which she had come. A man. He stood in the shadows, all the way at the end of the block, on the corner. And the moment she looked his way, he slipped around the corner and out of sight.

His stance…his silhouette, nothing but a dark shape in the night. And yet she thought… No. She was letting her imagination run away with her again.

"Miss?"

She turned, realized it was her turn to step up to the ticket window. "Sorry. One please, for *Twilight Hunger.*" She slid a ten across the counter, waited for the change, which was a crisp clean five with her ticket on top. She'd been out so few times since coming here that the low ticket prices still surprised her. She tucked the five in her jeans pocket and held on to the ticket as she moved inside.

She got a seat in the back and sat quietly while the previews began to roll.

Morgan had thought she was the last one in, but the doors opened a few minutes into the previews, and someone else entered. Again that chill danced over her spine, and Morgan turned to look his way.

He was already making his way to the opposite side of the theater, but, like her, he took a seat in the back row. He wore a long coat with its collar turned up around his face, and he, too, had dark glasses.

It was foolish to think of Dante when she saw the stranger. It was just some other lonely soul who preferred to keep his identity to himself. Dante didn't exist. The Dante of those journals, the one who haunted her mind, had *never* existed. Only a slightly deranged man with a wild imagination and an excellent way with words. The Dante whose life was about to unfold on the screen at the far end of the room was a fictional character. A figment of his creator's imagination, enhanced, perhaps, by Morgan's own. But he wasn't real. And she had to get that through her head. He was not real.

Just because she'd been having vivid, visceral dreams about him...

And just because she had hallucinated those marks on her neck that night...

They were there! her mind insisted. *I checked in the bedroom mirror, and they were there.*

But gone without a trace in the morning, she reminded herself. And as vivid as her dreams had been lately, how could she be so sure that seeing those marks hadn't been just another part of one of them?

"Dante isn't real," she whispered to herself. "And

he most certainly isn't sitting in this dark theater, watching me watch this film.''

Why, then, did she feel herself sinking more deeply into her seat as his story began to play out for the audience—and as the words across the screen told them all that she, Morgan De Silva, had created it?

12

Lou got a call before Max could show him what she had on the CD, and then he managed to avoid her for a couple of days—hell, she wasn't even sure why, unless he was doing some research on his own.

Finally she caught him by waiting for him at his apartment after his shift. And then she sat him down and made him look at his computer while she manned the mouse and showed him the vampire files of the organization known as DPI.

When they finished, Lou looked as if Max had popped him between the eyes with a two-by-four. He sat there blinking at the computer screen long after she had closed the file and removed the CD from the drive.

"Do you think if you stare at Bill Gates' brainchild long enough you'll find your way back to that logical world where everything makes sense?"

He glanced at her vaguely.

"Believe me, it doesn't work. I spent a couple of hours staring at the Windows logo myself after I saw what was on that CD. It didn't help a bit."

"It's nuts. It's a prank."

"The man I saw outside the fire that night was no prank, Lou. He was real. And he dropped the CD and the ID badge. That place, that so-called research center—it was for research, all right. On vampires."

He shook his head.

"I never told you what happened the next morning. The morning after the fire."

"Something happened the next morning?"

"I had an envelope delivered to my front door."

His brows rose now as he studied her. "What was in it?"

"Photos. My friends, Jason Beck, asleep in his bed, and Stormy in her own shower. And there was one of my mother, in the parking garage at work. It had been taken that morning."

"Any note?"

She shook her head. "No, he called instead."

"He *called* you?"

Maxine nodded. Lou was getting riled now. She had known he would. He was the most laid-back guy on the planet until someone he cared about was threatened or harmed. Then he got damned dangerous. And he did care about her, even if he was too dense to realize it.

"The same guy you saw that night?"

"I think so, yeah. I mean, it had to be him."

"What did he say to you, Maxie? Did he know you took those things?"

She shook her head slowly. "Nope. But he knew I'd seen him there. He made it clear that he could get to my friends and my mother at will, told me to forget I'd ever been there, that if I so much as mentioned seeing him or being in that place the night of the fire, he would find out and make me regret it."

"He said he'd hurt your mother."

She nodded. "And I believed him. I still do. And I kept the tape of that call, Lou. You can hear it for yourself." She was nothing if not prepared. She took the tape out of the envelope, popped it into Lou's machine and let it play.

Lou muttered a string of cuss words under his breath. When the tape finished, he said, "I need a beer."

"I could use one myself." She left him sitting where he was—on the edge of his camelback couch, elbows braced on his knees—walked into the kitchen and opened his fridge. As she had expected, it was well stocked. All the beer, coldcuts and cheese a man could eat. A few bottles of ketchup, mustard, salsa, hot sauce and horseradish. *Horseradish?* She took out two long necks, twisted off the caps and carried them back into the living room of the three-room apartment. She handed him a bottle, then flopped onto the couch beside him and took a long drink from her own.

Lou was looking at her oddly as she swallowed.

"What?"

He shrugged. "Never saw you drink before."

"I've been legal for years, Lou."

"Sure. I just never think of you that way."

"I hadn't noticed," she said, loading on as much sarcasm as the words could carry.

He was quiet for a long moment, sipping his beer, studying her sipping hers. Made her feel damned self-conscious. Finally he set the bottle on the coffee table, no doubt adding a fresh new water ring to the collection that had accumulated there. "You must have been scared half to death, Max."

She shrugged, took another gulp. "It shook me up some, yeah."

"You should have told me about this."

"And what could you have done, Lou? File a report? This guy worked for some offshoot of the CIA, Lou. The C-fucking-IA.''

He sighed. "Even if that's true—"

"It's true. And if I'd told you about it, he would have known. If you had filed a report, he would have known, and maybe you'd have been getting threats, too—or worse."

He sat back a little. "You were protecting me." He said it deadpan.

"Not just you. Myself, my mother, Stormy and Jason."

"And me."

She shrugged, looked away, because it was true. "Maybe I just don't trust cops."

"I *know* you don't trust cops. But you trust *me*."

She smiled just a little. "Yeah, and you trust me, too, don't you?"

He pursed his lips. "You're sharp. You don't lie, and you're damn tough to lie to. What's not to trust?"

"You trust me," she insisted. "So trust me on this. There's not a passably sane person in the entire civilized world who believes vampires exist. But if they don't, then why does the government have volumes of research on them? Why does it know them by name and have life histories on so many of them? This is real, Lou. They exist."

He shook his head. "I can't wrap my brain around that one, Maxie."

"You will. Hell, it's taken me the better part of five years. Unfortunately, you don't have that kind of time."

He glanced at her, and she knew he was wishing she wouldn't finish the thought, but she had to.

"Lydia Jordan's friend was killed by one of them, Lou. There's no getting around that."

He shook his head slowly. "She was more than a friend. And you can't tell Lydia about any of this, regardless."

"Why not? What's the point in keeping this secret?"

"I don't know what the point is, but there has to be one, or the government wouldn't have gone to so much trouble to do it!"

She widened her eyes and bobbed her head at him.

"Hell, Max...just let me think, okay?"

"Fine." She polished off her beer, leaned back on the couch and absently reached for the newspaper strewn on the coffee table, picking it up, leafing through the sections. She picked out the magazine section, which she always read first. She flipped it open, paused and shook her head. "Speak of the devil."

"What?"

Sending Lou a lopsided smile, she held up the page so he could see the article's title. "Vampire Thriller Garners Coveted Nomination."

He rolled his eyes, shook his head. "Figures."

She licked her lips as she began to skim the article about the film and the reclusive screenwriter, until she got to the short synopsis of the story, and there she paused. "Uh...Lou?"

"I'm still thinkin'."

"Yeah, well, think about this. Wasn't one of the names on that CD-ROM 'Dante'?"

He glanced at her sharply. "I think so. Why?"

She licked her lips. "Maybe we'd better take another look at the file on that one. And, uh—then we ought to think about going out. Maybe even catching a movie.''

In the theater, the story, a prequel to the earlier two films, unfolded on the silver screen. A young man, a Gypsy, lay on the ground. The makeshift bandage was torn and bloody. But there was no longer any pain, and his strength was returning. More than returning, it surged in him, singing in his veins like a thousand violins. He tore the bandage off, balled it up and threw it to the ground beside the rest of what had been his shirt. He stared at his Aunt Sarafina. Her black eyes gleamed in the night, though there was no light for them to reflect. And he saw more now than he had seen before, as if he were seeing her through new eyes now. How he'd ever missed something so obvious before, he couldn't imagine.

Sarafina was not human. Her skin was too smooth. No pores, no flaws. Her lips were too dark, and her eyes had that glow, that luster, as did her hair. There was something else. Involuntarily, instinctively, he tipped his head back and, without sniffing, he smelled the scent on her. Something pungent and exotic, like a mingling of sex and blood. Her scent.

''Your scent, too,'' she said softly, her voice a rich combination of tones in harmony, not one flat pitch as he had always believed voices to be. It was as if he had never truly heard before.

Then his wonder faded as he realized she had been reading his thoughts. His eyes widening, he turned from her, started off through the woods.

''And where do you think you're going, Dante?''

''Home. Back to the village. Where I belong.''

''You can't go back there now.'' She didn't follow

him. She stood where she was, and since she wasn't shouting, he didn't understand why he could hear her so clearly, just as clearly no matter how far he walked from her. "You're outcast now, just like me."

"You lie!" he shouted, and he ran faster and faster.

As he approached the village, the young man was surprised that he heard no music. It was their last night in this camp. In the morning they would move again. All the items they could pack had been packed. Tonight there should be a huge fire, with music and dancing, and stories of past adventures told with excited anticipation of what new ones might lie just ahead.

Instead, there was silence. He heard the fire crackling, smelled it long before he should have. But of voices, there were almost none. Mere whispers now and again, and the gentle brush of fabric as his people moved around the camp.

He emerged from the trees and paused to stare at his family. The Grandmother knelt near a large boulder, grinding herbs with her mortar and pestle. His cousins didn't run or play but instead sat around watching her, their eyes damp, shoulders slumped. The men were grouped together at the far end of camp in a huddle of angry faces, muttering quietly in a way that made Dante wonder who had angered them. They looked as if they were plotting violence. The women were clustered around the tent belonging to Dante and his mother. And beyond them all, he could hear his mother's soft, broken crying coming from within the tent.

He was drawn forward, into the light of the flames. "Mother?" he called. "Everyone, what has happened?"

Heads snapped up fast, eyes widening and turning in his direction. He heard his mother say his name on a ragged breath, and then she was pushing her way through the women as she emerged from the tent.

The Grandmother stepped into her path, putting herself directly between them. "Stay away!" she commanded Dante, and she held her hands up, forefinger and pinky extended, hissing as she poked the sign at him repeatedly. "Stay back, I say!"

Dante blinked at her in shock. "Grandmother…what's wrong with you? It's me, it's Dante. What…?"

His mother pushed the older woman aside then and came closer. "Is it really you, my son? Dimitri said you were killed. Shot dead when you tried to steal a goat."

"If you lied to us about such a thing…" The deep-voiced threat came from Dimitri's father.

"I didn't lie! I saw it, I tell you. He was shot, both barrels of the old man's shotgun."

"You weren't even there!" Dante said, instinctively denying the truth. Knowing somehow that if he admitted what had really happened, his family would believe him to be some kind of demon. A vampire, just as Sarafina claimed he was. But it wasn't true. It *wasn't!*

"I followed you, Dante." Dimitri's eyes were narrow on him now, untrusting, perhaps even afraid. "I knew you were out for adventure. I planned to join in when the old man came out. I saw him fire. I saw you fall."

"And then you ran, didn't you?" Dante asked, grasping the idea like a drowning man clutching a limb. "Admit it. You heard the gun, and you ran and left me there to die."

"I ran." Dimitri lowered his black head in shame.

"You see?" Dante forced a nervous smile as he glanced at his mother and the Grandmother, and then at the men who were gathering around. The women had gathered their children and were standing as far from him as possible. So many huge brown eyes on him. "He didn't stay long enough to see that the man's shots never hit me. Only frightened me, so I fell down. I was not even hit, much less killed."

Several of them glanced toward Dimitri for confirmation. His head came up slowly, and he stared at Dante. "I saw the blood. You are as a brother to me, Dante, and I love you, but I saw the blood."

Dante shivered, knowing how frightened Dimitri must have been to witness such a thing. He looked for support from the other men but found only suspicion in their eyes. And several of them were not even there, he realized.

"Turn around, Dante," the Grandmother told him. "Let me see your back."

"You'll find nothing there."

"Turn!"

One did not disobey the Grandmother. Dante turned, praying he had managed to wipe all the blood away, wishing he could see his own back. Everyone looked. He craned his neck to look over his shoulder at them, saw his mother inspecting him closely. "There is no wound," she said. "And I see no blood, only there's so much dirt it is hard to be sure."

"Why can you not take my word?" Dante asked. "Dimitri was mistaken. Mother, you wept for me when you thought I was dead. Can you not rejoice for me now that you see me alive?''

She stared at him, hope lighting her eyes. Trembling, she lifted a hand toward his face, and he closed his eyes as he awaited her warm touch.

The forest beside him came alive as men emerged from it, the men he'd noticed missing from the crowd before. When they saw him, they gaped as if seeing a ghost, and Dante shot a look at his mother.

"We sent them out to bring your body home to us, Dante," she explained.

"Tell us," the Grandmother commanded. "What did you find at the farmer's shack?"

The oldest of the group, Alexi, lifted his hand from his side. A ball of material was in it, and as he unfurled the mass, Dante realized what it was. He could do nothing to stop Alexi from holding it up for all to see. Dante's shirt, a hole rent in its back, strips torn away, the entire thing soaked in drying blood.

"The farmer was dead," Alexi said softly. "Two holes, right here." He used his fingers to poke himself in the throat, and young Dante remembered seeing his aunt, Sarafina, drain the old man by biting him there.

"Nosferatu!" the Grandmother shrieked, tugging Dante's mother behind her and jabbing her fingers at him again. "Leave us, demon! Go your way and leave us!"

As one, the entire village pulled away from Dante, moving nearer the fire. He shook his head, lifting a hand toward them in appeal. "Please! I am not a demon! I am just as I was before. I am Dante." He found his mother's eyes in the crowd. "I am your son!"

''My son is dead.'' The words were low, deep, reverberating with pain.

''No!''

''It was Sarafina, wasn't it, boy?'' the Grandmother asked him. ''She came to you as you lay dying. She passed her curse on to you. Didn't she?''

''No!''

The Grandmother spat on the ground. ''We shall see, young devil. For the sun rises soon. Our Dante's soul will find peace when your body burns!''

Dante's mother spun toward the east, and she stared off into the paling sky. Then she raced to him, put her hands on his chest and pushed at him. ''Go, Dante! Go now. I cannot bear to lose you twice.''

''Mother? I don't—''

''Go! Cover yourself!''

''You do him no favors, child,'' the Grandmother muttered.

Then Dante felt something he had never felt before. A heat, searing from somewhere deep within him as the first rays of the sun pierced the sky, shooting like arrows from the horizon, stabbing him deeply and burning there. ''Ah!'' He clutched himself, gritted his teeth. Thin spirals of smoke began to rise from his flesh.

''Run! Into the woods. Find shelter!'' his mother screamed.

The burning was unbearable. Dante turned, and ran. The trees offered relief, but only for seconds as he lunged headlong, deeper into the forest, seeking shelter from the sun, his heart breaking, his mind racing, but all of it secondary to the searing pain of his burning flesh. He dove into the first cover he saw, a pile of deadfall, and burrowed deeper, pulling leaves and brush over and around him as he dug to the very bottom of the mound.

And then he sat very still, waiting for the pain to ease, waiting. He had to think. He had to understand why this was happening to him.

But his head was suddenly heavy. Far too heavy, and his eyes, though tear-filled, were closing. He fought to stay awake. God, how could he sleep when his entire world had just been turned on its head? But there was no resisting this sleep. In fact, it didn't seem at all like falling asleep. It seemed, he thought, panic gripping his heart, like dying....

Morgan got up and ran from the theater. Dante, who had been watching the events of his own life play out on the screen in a state of utter disbelief and increasing anger, saw her go, and he rose slowly and followed her. *She* had done this. Somehow that woman knew his secrets. And she had told the entire world.

She was going to have to pay. Tonight.

Lou had read the entire DPI case file on the alleged vampire who went by the name of Dante before they managed to find a theater still showing the flick that Mad Maxie was so hot on seeing. It had been released a couple of months ago, but now, with a Best Screenplay nomination, a few places were showing it again. Maxie managed to locate one while he read, and then she came and read over his shoulder, since it was two hours before the next showing.

So they both were fairly up on the bullshit in the file as they sat in the theater. Which meant that he knew, and he knew that she knew, that what was playing out on the screen was pretty much an adaptation of several key parts of the file. Not as dry, of course. Goddamn riveting, actually.

But the high points were the same. Gypsy kid, shot for stealing a goat, transformed into a vampire by an exotic aunt who never aged. Right. The fiction on the screen was cold hard fact, according to this crackpot government agency. The only difference was, the film was slanted in sympathy with the creature. He came off as wounded and lonely, cursed and hunted. The files made him sound more like a vicious animal that needed putting down.

Lou knew damned well he would *never* convince Max that both versions were bullshit. Not now.

"Now do you see what I'm talking about, Lou?"

He walked beside her, back up the carpeted slope out of the theater. Someone bumped into her, jostled her, and he automatically grabbed her upper arm. "All I see is that your top secret information seems to be not so secret after all."

"If that were the case, it would be public knowledge. Some investigative reporter would be all over this stuff."

"What, you didn't see the latest *Enquirer?* I'm sure they covered it. Right next to the baby they found inside an uncut pumpkin, still on the vine, and the rash of alien abductions in Upper Butthole, Nebraska."

She sneered at him. "If it were public knowledge, it would make the *Times.*"

"Um-hm."

"Lou, this is real. We've got the same set of facts from two separate sources now. This woman, this screenwriter, she knows more about this than either of us. We've got to talk to her.''

He led her to his car, put her in it and got behind the wheel. ''I don't want to talk to you about this anymore. Tomorrow morning, I'm gonna call in a few favors.''

''No.''

''I have a buddy who works for the CIA. Low-level guy, but still…he'll know who to ask about this…this DPI garbage.''

''Lou, no.''

''I'm a cop, Max. I'm not swallowing a bit of this. It isn't in me to swallow it. Not without proof.''

She caught his face between her flattened palms and turned him to face her. She was close to him. So close he could feel her breath on his mouth. It smelled like hot buttered popcorn and was every bit as tempting.

''Don't tell anyone. Lou, please. It's too dangerous.''

He looked at her. She had those huge green eyes, and right now they were scared. He didn't see Mad Maxie Stuart scared very often. When he did, it meant something. Damn, he just wished she wouldn't get so close. Sighing, he lifted a hand and tousled her short red hair, moving her face away from his in the process. ''Okay, all right. Fine. I won't say anything.''

''And we'll try to trace the screenwriter. Morgan De Silva. And just talk to her.''

He sighed, pulling the car up in front of Maxie's house-slash-office. ''I'll think about it.''

''I'll do it with you or without you, Lou.''

''Now, listen, Maxie, you be patient. Give me a few days to sort through all this.'' He waggled a finger at her, father-like. "And not a word to Lydia in the meantime. Understand?"

"Not a word to Lydia about what, Lou?" a voice asked.

He swung his head around and saw Lydia herself standing on the other side of the car. She had apparently been waiting for Max to get home.

"Come on inside, Lydia," Max called, getting out of Lou's car and heading toward her house. "I'll explain everything. See you later, Lou."

"But…"

"Bye, Lou," Lydia said, sending him a smile.

Lou gave his head a quick shake, wondering how the hell he had managed to lose control of the situation so quickly. "Listen, Lydia, whatever she tells you is pure conjecture. You gotta know that up front."

Lydia rolled her eyes at him and joined Max, walking up the steps to the front porch and across it toward the door.

"Don't either one of you *do* anything without calling me first. Understand?"

Maxie looked at him over her shoulder, sent him a wink. "Of course we won't. Wouldn't be any fun without you."

Then she opened the door, and the two of them went into the house.

Lou went back to his car. But he didn't go home. He went back to the station instead, because that was where he kept all his business-related phone contacts. He looked up the number of his CIA buddy and gave the man a call. As vaguely as he could manage, he asked his friend to find out what he could about an alleged secret CIA unit known as DPI.

Then he drove back to Maxie's house and parked outside to watch the place for the rest of the night.

13

A soft hand fell on Morgan's shoulder as she sat there on the beach, sobbing.

"Why do you cry?"

It was a woman's voice, deep and rich, slightly accented. Morgan lifted her head and swiped her hands across her cheeks. She could barely see the woman who'd walked up beside her. She was a tall, slender blur. Dark hair, cranberry-colored coat. "Oh, God, you must think I'm an idiot."

"No. I, too, had a very strong reaction to the film. Not as strong as yours, however." She sat down in the sand beside Morgan.

"You...you were at the theater?"

"Mmm. I saw you run off, weeping, and I was concerned."

Finally Morgan cleared her eyes enough to look at the woman who was sitting beside her on the sand. Her wine-colored trench coat reached to her ankles and was buttoned all the way down. Long black boots on her feet, hugging her calves. Her hands were gloved in matching black leather, and her face was partially hidden by exquisite masses of black curls. She wore a lot of makeup. Way more than Morgan would usually find tasteful. And yet she had the presence to pull it off.

She stared out over the waves, not looking Morgan directly in the eyes.

"What made you run from the theater that way?"

Lowering her head, Morgan shook it slowly. The woman didn't seem to know who she was, and she preferred to keep it that way. Her sunglasses and head scarf remained in place, and she was grateful for them. "The story seems very real to me," she said softly. "I've seen it play out a dozen times." More than that, in her mind. "And every time I have the same reaction when his family rejects him that way. Sending him out into a world of darkness all on his own. I guess it just hits me on some level."

"Mmm. Me, too. I was treated much the same way by my family." She turned now and seemed able to lock on to Morgan's eyes right through the sunglasses. "You also, I would guess?"

"Yes." She spoke without meaning to. As if the words were drawn out of her. The woman had stunning eyes. Dark, maybe black, and somehow luminous. The sun had long since set, and the waves lapped gently at the shore beneath a star-dotted night sky.

"Tell me," the woman said, her voice soft and low. Compelling.

"I…was never close to my parents. It was only after they died that I learned I was adopted."

"Ahhh," she said on a breath. "Poor thing. And you wonder, then, about your real family. Your blood." As she spoke, she reached out a hand, gently moving Morgan's long hair off her shoulder, letting it fall down her back. Her eyes slid over Morgan's chin, touching her throat, and the skin there heated as if the touch were a physical one.

"Yes," Morgan said. "I do wonder about them. What they were like."

"Perhaps this history of yours is why you feel such empathy with Dante—the vampire in the film."

"Or maybe it's just that I live in his house."

The woman started, her eyes widening slightly and jerking up to Morgan's again. The spell of her quiet voice was broken. It was sharper now. "Whatever do you mean by that, child?"

What was she thinking? God, a slip like that could annihilate her budding career. She could never, *never* admit that the character in her films had been someone else's creation—much less that she lived in the home that had once been his. If she did, the rest would come out, too. That she had plagiarized his mad ramblings to create her award-nominated work. She tried a false smile, shaking her head in self-deprecation. "The house in one of the films reminded me a lot of my own, that's all."

"Oh."

She had the distinct feeling the woman didn't believe her. Getting to her feet, she brushed the sand from her clothes, turning her back to the woman as she did so. "I should go, it's getting late and…" She turned back again.

But there was no woman there.

Morgan blinked rapidly, searching the beach in one direction, then the other, scanning the water and the distance back toward town. Nothing. No one.

My God, had she imagined the dark woman? She pressed a hand to her forehead, closed her eyes. "Maybe I need to get away from here for a while. Just for a while." But even as she said it, she knew it wasn't possible. She couldn't leave. It was no longer a matter of simply not wanting to. The moment the words left her lips, she felt sick inside, a sense of panic stirring at the mere thought of leaving here. Leaving...*him.*

"What the hell did you think you were doing with that girl, Sarafina?" Dante demanded, and his tone was harsh. Too harsh, perhaps, as it caused Sarafina's perfectly arched brows to lift in question.

"Then you know her. Mmm. What is she to you?"

"Nothing." He snapped his answer without looking at her, lest she see too much. "What are you even doing here? I couldn't believe it when I sensed your presence in that theater."

Sarafina shrugged innocently, though he knew too well there wasn't an innocent bone in her body. She gave her head a shake, taunting the wind with her riotous hair. "I came to see you. I couldn't help but feel you in the theater as I passed through town, so I went inside. Imagine my surprise when I saw our history being played out on the screen."

He closed his eyes, unable to reply to that. He'd been shocked to his core to see his own life in that film. And it felt far too much like a betrayal. Especially now that he knew the truth. It was Morgan. She had written the screenplay.

Once again a woman who claimed to love him had betrayed his secrets to his enemies. To everyone. To the world.

"Apparently it had an equally upsetting effect on the girl, whoever she is. The way she ran out of there." Sarafina locked her black eyes on his. "I'll ask you again. What is she to you, Dante?"

"She's an innocent mortal, nothing more." He

didn't tell her that he had been nearby, listening to every word of her conversation with Morgan. He had fully expected to have to intervene.

"Oh, she's far more than an ordinary mortal, my love. Far, far more." She took his hand, and they walked side by side along the beach, a mile from where Sarafina had been talking to the girl. "But we'll get to that," she said. "Why did you interrupt me when I was having such an illuminating discussion with the whelp?"

"To stop you from ripping out her jugular, dear gentle aunt. She's a local and would be missed."

Truth to tell, he'd been following Morgan with half a mind to do just that himself—to destroy her. But when he'd seen his bloodthirsty Sarafina with her, he'd felt a stab of fear and an undeniable instinct to protect. He had shouted to Sarafina with his mind, and she had responded by rushing to his side in a blur of motion too fast for any human eye to follow.

"It goes to show just how poorly I've taught you, doesn't it?" she asked. "And how isolated you have made yourself all these years. I couldn't have harmed her if I'd wanted to. She's one of the Chosen."

He nodded. "That much I had put together on my own. But I admit I know very little of just what that means, aside from the fact that she shares the same antigen we all do, and that she can become as we are."

Sighing, Sarafina nodded. "I knew she was in the theater before I'd been there a heartbeat," she said. She stopped walking when she came to a large boulder, took a seat upon it like a queen taking her throne. Dante stood nearby, watching her as she stared out at the sea. It was the blue-black hue of wet slate. "We can feel their presence. This much you know. We cannot harm them.''

''Cannot?'' He pondered that for a moment. ''I thought it was more that we tended not to want to. What would happen, do you suppose, if we tried?''

She glanced up at him quickly. ''You have some reason for wanting to do the girl harm?''

''I barely know her.'' He looked away as he said it.

Sarafina shrugged delicately. ''If we tried—well, I'm not sure what would happen. The truth of the matter is, we're more often compelled to protect them when we encounter them in passing.''

That explained his urge to come between his aunt and the weeping Morgan.

''They have abbreviated life spans, you know.''

His head snapped up. Morgan had said as much, but he hadn't wanted to believe it. ''No. I didn't know that,'' he lied, unwilling and unable to let his aunt know how much he and Morgan had communicated in her dream.

Sarafina only nodded. ''Mmm. Rarely live beyond thirty mortal years. She looks as though she's deteriorating already.'' She shrugged.

''What can be done?'' he asked, searching Sarafina's face.

''Nothing. Bring her over or let her die. It's a simple choice, really.'' She shrugged. ''They say that for each vampire, there is one of the Chosen with whom the psychic bond is stronger. I've always found it to be so much hogwash. Romanticism and nothing more.''

''Oh, do you? You're saying your bond with me wasn't like that?''

"My bond with you was *nothing* like that, Dante. You were my family. My nephew. The only one of my clan with any kind of link to me. I loved you because of that." She stared out at the sea, and the wind lifted her curls from her shoulders. "No, this other bond, this one that is spoken of in whispers among the undead, is said to be intensely more. It manifests itself as an extreme psychic link between the minds. Some claim a vampire can communicate mentally with their special mortal, and he or she with them. It also creates an extreme sexual hunger between the two that becomes even more heightened should they share blood."

She swung her gaze to Dante, and he quickly averted his eyes. "Is she living in your house, Dante?"

He schooled his expression, guarded his thoughts. "Yes."

"Then where are you staying?"

He did not want her seeing the inside of Morgan's house, he thought. She would realize Morgan was the one writing the stories for the screen—a secret it would be difficult to keep for very long anyway, if Sarafina were to stay in town. But the longer, the better. He thought that if anyone could get past the instinctive distaste for harming one of the Chosen, it would be Sarafina. And she would, if she knew the truth. She would kill the girl and let the consequences be damned.

"A cave. Nothing that would suit you, love."

She crooked a brow. "There is a house for rent only a mile or so from here. Shall we procure it for our use?"

He nodded vaguely, thinking how very badly he

wanted to see Morgan tonight, wondering how the hell he was going to rid himself of Sarafina in the meantime.

"Then that will be our mission tonight," she said. "Tomorrow night, we'll see that film again. All of it, this time. And we must find out who is telling our tales to the filmmakers, and how he got the information. Apparently a native of this place, if the theater marquee is correct. Though likely he's moved to some glamorous city by now."

"He?" Dante asked, frowning.

"Morgan...something or other. I'll get the full name tomorrow." She smiled at him. "But tonight, that house. It's quite isolated. We can stay there tonight, and no one will be the wiser."

Dante nodded slowly, thinking as he did. "Go ahead of me," he whispered. "See about the house. I'll join you by dawn. I have...to feed."

She crooked her brow at him. "The house will be ready. It's a mile north, on that road that runs along the coast. A once proud Victorian that has been painted a ghastly yellow, with pink-and-green trim."

He nodded, recalling the exact place she meant.

"Frankly, I'm surprised you didn't rent it for yourself already."

Why would he? He'd been living beneath the feet of the woman his body craved. And now he knew for certain why he craved her so, but that did nothing to ease the hunger.

"I require very little in the way of comfort, 'fina."

Leaning close, she clasped his collar in both hands and kissed him on the mouth. "Come before dawn, love, or I'll come looking."

"I will."

She left him. He waited until his senses could no longer detect her anywhere nearby, and then he went to find Morgan. He couldn't play with her anymore. He needed answers. Now.

It was 4:00 a.m. when Lou's cell phone bleated, jerking him out of what had damn near been a little nap. He'd been sitting in his car all night, watching Maxie's place. He thought maybe Lydia was sleeping over, because she hadn't left yet. And hell, he didn't blame her, if Max was telling her vampire stories in there.

He picked up his phone. "Yeah?"

"Malone, where the hell are you?"

He frowned at the familiar voice of his longtime partner, back when they'd had the manpower to put two cops in every car. "Denny?"

"They've been looking everywhere for you, Lou. Listen, you'd better get over here, pronto."

"Jesus, I'm not due in for another..." He glanced at his watch.

"Not the station. Your place, Lou. There's been a break-in, and...it's not pretty."

He frowned, and a tiny sliver of ice jabbed him in the chest. He knew just by Denny's tone that he would get no more than that over the phone, so he didn't bother asking. "I'll be right over."

"If, uh, you've been with anyone tonight, you might just want to bring them along, too."

Lou blinked, drawing the phone away and staring at it, then bringing it slowly back to his head. "Are you suggesting I might be in need of an alibi, Den?"

"Might not be a bad idea."

Lou swore softly. "What the hell is going on over there?"

Too late. Sgt. Dennis Kehoe had already disconnected.

Someone tapped on Lou's car window, and he damn near jumped out of his skin. It was only Maxie, though, grinning at him and holding a coffee cup in her hand. He set the phone down, rolled down the window.

"If you want to spend the whole night watching me, Lou, you could just say so. It's not like I'd object. But it would be more fun if you'd do it from closer range."

He stared up at her as she shoved the cup into his hands. "So you know I've been here ever since I dropped you off?"

She shook her head. "You left for twenty minutes or so right after. Remember?"

"Shit." He did remember. That drive to the station, the phone call to his friend at the CIA. Hell.

"What's the matter, Lou?"

He glanced at her, noticed she was still dressed. If you could call it that. She never wore much. Thin-strapped T-shirts that were tight fitting with smart-ass remarks across the front, or loose silky blouses that were even sexier. If it got cold, she tossed a jacket over them. "Where's Lydia?"

He saw her face tighten up just a little. "She's sound asleep. Why?"

"Get in, would you? I need to go to my place for a sec."

"Okay, okay, Lou. Fine." She came around the car, got in. "You don't look so good. You okay?"

"I'll let you know when we get to my place."

As it turned out, it wasn't okay. It wasn't at all okay. He knew that when he pulled up and couldn't even get into the parking lot because of all the police vehicles. Yellow tape criss-crossed every entrance, and an ambulance was just pulling away.

"What the hell…?"

Lou put a hand on Maxie's shoulder to calm her down, stopped the car and then got out. "You'd better wait here. I'll come get you if I need you."

"Uh-huh." She opened her door and got out, walking so close to him that her thigh and hip seemed to have melded to his, and she wrapped an arm around his and held on tight.

"Malone." Captain Howard Dutton, Lou's boss, lifted the crime scene tape for Lou to duck underneath. "I need to know where you've been tonight. All night."

"He's been with me." Maxie spat out the words before Lou could so much as open his mouth. "Who was in the ambulance?"

The captain blinked, and Lou knew he wasn't used to being questioned by a mite of a thing like Maxine Stuart. He shifted his gaze to Lou's again. "You've been with this woman all night?"

"No," Lou said. "I dropped her off at her place around ten. Left to go to the station to find something I'd left in my desk. Then I went back. All told, I was gone about twenty minutes."

"Anyone see where you were during that time? Can you verify that you didn't come back here, to the apartment?"

Lou felt his stomach clench. "No."

"Yes, he can, Captain." Maxie cut in yet again. Both men looked at her sharply. Max shrugged, focusing on Lou. "Look, I admit it. I thought you were sneaking off to meet some other woman—"

"Other woman?" What the hell was she talking about?

"—so I followed you. I saw you go into the station, and I waited until you came back out. Then I followed you back to my place."

"And Officer Malone didn't see you, ma'am?"

"I, uh…I parked in back and went in the back door. He never even knew I'd been gone." She crossed her arms over her chest. "Now, will you please tell us what's going on here? Who was that in the ambulance?"

The captain sighed, again addressing Lou and shutting Max out, which Lou knew pissed her off. "We responded to a report of a prowler in your building, Lou. When we got here, your apartment door was open, the place was trashed, and there was a woman on the floor. She'd been shot in the head at close range. We found a twenty-two on the floor nearby, no prints." He turned. "Denny, where's the weapon?"

"Right here, sir." Dennis held up an evidence bag as he hurried closer.

Lou looked at it and damn near puked but tried to keep his poker face. "It's mine. The spare I keep in the closet."

"I thought it probably was," Captain Dutton said. He turned, leading them forward up the stairs toward the apartment. "We're gonna need you to look around, see if anything's missing."

Lou nodded. He walked right behind the captain, Max still close beside him. "What about the woman?" Lou asked. "Is she dead?"

"They're going through the motions," Dutton replied without looking back. "They don't expect her to last the night, though. We figure she'd been lying there for five or six hours. We never did find any prowler, but one neighbor heard what could have been a gunshot around ten p.m. She thought it was a car backfiring and wrote it off. The ID in the victim's bag read Jones. Tempest Jones. You know her?"

Max stopped walking. Lou turned to look at her even while processing the name, which seemed vaguely familiar. Then he forgot about it when he saw Max's face, which had gone utterly white. Her jaw gaped, worked soundlessly, and her grip on his forearm tightened like a vise. Wide green eyes stared into his, moistening, and she whispered, "Stormy."

Shit. Maxine's best friend. Max damn near went backwards down the stairs when her knees gave. Her hand on his arm went lax, and she sort of sagged, but he grabbed her quickly, pulled her in close, figuring it was okay at a time like this. The captain turned. "Then you *did* know the victim?"

. "She's a friend," Lou said. Max's arms had snapped around his waist, and her face was pressed into his shirt. He felt wetness there, but she cried silently. "Listen, Captain, can you just secure the place, post a man on it? I need to take Max to the hospital."

The captain made a face but nodded. "Yeah, sure, fine, but one thing, Lou. How well did you know this girl? This Tempest Jones?"

He shook his head. "Well enough to share doughnuts and coffee with her. Not well enough so I recognized her legal name right off. That good enough for you?"

The captain sighed, inclined his head. "Go on."

"Thanks." Lou moved Max's body around his own, like shifting the position of a belt. He got her around to the side and managed to shuffle the two of them back down the stairs and past the tape to the car. Someone opened the passenger door for him, and he glanced up at Denny, gave him a nod of thanks.

Denny looked worried and maybe a little surprised. Sure he looked surprised. It must seem to him, to everyone here, as if he and Mad Maxie were some kind of couple. As if *that* could happen.

He eased her onto the passenger seat, and she still clung to him. "Hon, you gotta let go now, okay? Just for a minute, so I can drive us to the hospital. Hmm?"

Sniffling, she nodded against his chest, but it still took long seconds for her to loosen her grip on his neck. He put her seat belt around her, snapped it in place and closed her door. As soon as he was behind the wheel, she latched on to him again. Head on his shoulder, clutching his arm. Made it tough to drive. Not that he minded.

"What the hell happened?" she asked him as he drove. "Why would Stormy go to your place?"

He licked his lips. "I don't know. I just don't freaking know, Max." Then he lowered his head. He didn't like thinking what he was thinking. But all of this had happened after he'd made that phone call to his old friend at the CIA. And Stormy Jones was one of the people Max had said had been threatened by that goon five years ago.

It couldn't be connected, though. Goddamn, it couldn't be.

14

Dante did not intend to creep up to her window tonight, as he had done in the past. He planned to stride
right up the walk to the front door, ring the bell and
introduce himself when she opened it. Yes, it would
shock her. But though physically fragile, he sensed
she had emotional strength she hadn't yet tapped. She
would deal with the shock. And then she would answer to him for what she had done.

He climbed the sloping ground from the shore onto
the grassy hilltop, then nearer, crossing the back lawn
and circling the house. But when he got close his skin
prickled, not with the attraction he always felt as he
drew close to her, but with warning.

Alert now, he looked around, seeing the strange
vehicle in her driveway. He didn't smell exhaust in
the air. It must have been sitting there for at least a
short time. Whoever was in the house with Morgan
had been waiting for her when she had finally returned to the house.

Closing his eyes, Dante attuned his senses. As always, Morgan's essence was clear and easy to locate.
The other one was far more difficult to perceive. It
took effort, almost as if the man—yes, it was a man—
had constructed a wall around his mind. There was
something about the stranger Dante didn't like. He
felt…dangerous.

Dante went up to the house, walked slowly around it, drawing one palm over the wood as he stepped around and between the plants and shrubs. They had not gone into the study. He didn't know why, but he felt like congratulating her on that.

And then he did. Without even quite meaning to, he sent the message. *Good thinking, Morgan. He doesn't need to go in there.*

It stunned him to the marrow when he heard her mind's reply. *That room is my special place. Mine…and Dante's. No one goes in there.*

She spoke to him and thought she was speaking to herself. Carrying on that internal dialogue that people tended to have with themselves. Never knowing that one side of the conversation was coming from someone else.

I don't like this man, she was thinking.

He's dangerous, Dante warned, quickly focusing on what was important. *Be careful of him.*

He knew she was nodding to herself, to him, even though he couldn't see her. And then he reached the outer wall of the sitting room and felt the hum of her energy right through the wall. He stopped there, turning to face the side of the house, pressing both palms flat and probing his way deeper into her mind. And still deeper. When he felt resistance, he whispered in her brain, *Open to me, Morgan. It's only me. Let me come inside. You know I won't hurt you.*

And she did. With a shuddering sigh, she relaxed and let him in, all the way in. He found himself seeing through her eyes. Hearing with her ears. He didn't take control. Wasn't even certain he could if he tried, but it didn't matter. That wasn't the purpose of his being this close to her.

Protecting her was. Which was odd, considering he had come here furious enough to kill her himself. At least, he had convinced himself he was furious enough to do her harm. Now he wondered.

The man, the stranger, was standing with his back to Morgan, studying the layout of the house in false admiration, nodding in false approval. "Very nice, what you've done with the old place."

"I like it," she replied. "But you said you were here to interview me about my work, Mr. Stiles."

"Please, call me Frank. I realize I should get moving on this. I'd never have bothered you at four a.m. if I hadn't seen you coming in. I don't doubt you're tired. It was awfully good of you to let me come in at all."

"Well, you did say you had driven six hours to get here in time to meet your deadline. But as I said, it's going to have to be brief. Will you have a seat?"

She didn't offer him refreshment. He didn't ask. Instead, he turned as he took his seat in a massive hardwood chair with lions' feet and a velvet cushion. Dante saw his face through Morgan's eyes and felt his heart skip. Or was that Morgan's heart?

The left side of the man's face was mottled with pink flesh that looked like a melted rubber doll. The eyelid drooped, the cheek sagged, the lips twisted, and the ear was a misshapen lump. He wore a hairpiece on that side. Dante hadn't spotted it at first, but now he could see that the hair was a slightly different shade and a bit less coarse on one side of his head than on the other. It was a good job. Good enough to fool a mortal.

The scarred man smiled at her. To her credit, Morgan smiled back. But she, too, was sensing something off about the man, and it wasn't due just to his appearance. She kept thinking it might be, chiding herself for being nervous because of a scar. The man couldn't help that. But she kept sensing something wrong beyond the surface.

"You must be very excited about your award nomination," he said. "I think it's well deserved."

"Thank you. Yes, I am quite overwhelmed that the film has been so well received."

"It's a good film." He pulled out a notepad from a pocket, and then a pen. It looked exactly like the notepad you would expect a reporter to carry. Which was another red flag, as far as Dante was concerned. "But then again, so were the first two. Why do you think this one was so much more well-received?"

Dante's heart seemed to stop beating. *The first two?*

"The first two films were much lower budget," Morgan said. "But even so, they gained a cult following that was beyond all our expectations. That, of course, led to our being able to release the third in a much bigger way."

The man nodded. "Is there a fourth in the works?"

"Of course."

The man nodded and scribbled and smiled, while Dante's heart twisted itself into knots. "I think these films have a realism about them that other vampire films—indeed, nearly all horror films—tend to lack. The Dante character...he's completely believable. Very real."

Morgan swallowed uncomfortably. *He* is *real—to me,* her mind whispered. Aloud she said, "Well, that's the key to good fiction, you know. Making it believable."

"Indeed," the reporter said. "But this is beyond

believable. It's…well, it's almost as if it's a true story. And when I stumbled on the fact that your home was once owned by a man named Dante, well, I have to admit, I got curious.''

Every nerve in Morgan's body went taut. ''What are you talking about, Mr. Stiles?''

''Oh, come on. It's a matter of public record.''

She shook her head slowly. ''No,'' she said. ''It's not.'' Then she seemed to catch herself. ''I don't know where you got that information, but it's incorrect. This place was abandoned by its former owner, a Mr. Daniel Taylor. The state claimed it when he died without an heir, and my uncle David bought it from them.''

''Daniel Taylor was one of many aliases the vampire Dante has used over the years.''

She made a face. Dante couldn't see it, but he could feel her twisting her lips and bending her brows, as if she thought the man were speaking of something too stupid to even contemplate. ''My goodness, you have a big imagination.''

''It's fact, Morgan. Just as the things in those films of yours are fact.''

She got slowly to her feet. ''You're insane if you think vampires are factual, Mr. Stiles. And I don't like entertaining insane strangers in my house in the dead of night. I think it's time for you to leave.''

''And I think it's time for you to tell the truth. Vampires are real, Ms. De Silva. You know it, and I know it. Dante is real, and he's going to be mad as hell when he finds out you've been making major motion pictures out of his deep dark secrets.''

She strode across the room, even as a cold shiver

worked through her body. Across the foyer, toward the front door. She reached for the handle.

The man was close behind her all the way, and he put his hand over hers on the door knob. "I'm not a reporter," he told her. "I work for the government. I've spent my life studying creatures like Dante, Ms. De Silva, and I know enough about them to know that you are in serious danger. If he finds you—"

"Get out." She jerked the door open despite his hand on hers. "Now, Stiles!"

"How did you learn all that information about him? Tell me."

She glared at him. "If you don't leave, I'm going to call the police."

"I'm not going to let you do that."

Her hand moved, quick as a heartbeat, to the little numbered panel on the wall, fingers dancing over the security system's buttons before he could reach to stop her. "There. The police will be here in five minutes."

"I'm trying to help you. He's a monster, Ms. De Silva. He'll find you, and trust me, he'll kill you unless you let me help."

She leaned toward him. "There are no such things as vampires," she whispered. Then she smiled as a siren sounded in the distance. "Hmm, quicker than I expected."

The man sighed his frustration, turned and ran out of the house, his gait uneven. She saw his car as he drove away and made a note of the license plate quickly before she closed the door, turned the locks. Then slowly, very slowly, she went still and silent as her mind replayed the words the man had said. That Dante was real. That he would be furious with her for sharing his secrets with the world. That he would kill her.

But he couldn't kill her, she thought in an unfocused and vague way. He loved her. No, no, she corrected herself. She loved him. If he were real, he would love her, too, because there was no denying the power of that bond. But he wasn't real. He didn't exist. So he didn't love her. And he certainly couldn't hurt her.

Closing his senses, Dante retreated from her mind, slowly feeling his own flesh again. He opened his eyes, blinking his vision into focus. He moved his hands, clenching and releasing his fists a few times. The sirens were getting closer. Stiles was long gone. But now the police were on their way. So was the dawn, in a few more hours. And yet he didn't go to Sarafina, or the house she had no doubt made ready and waiting. He didn't go very far at all.

"He said he was a reporter," Morgan told the police officer who'd shown up. The way his siren had wailed, she'd half expected a small cop army to come crashing in on her. Instead, there was just the one fellow, a rather innocuous looking grandpa type. If he'd had a hair on his head or face, he could have played a convincing Santa. As it was, though, he had only the ready smile, the twinkling eyes and the belly. His uniform was midnight blue, almost black. He didn't wear a hat, and his head was as shiny and pink as his cheeks. He'd introduced himself as Sandy Gray, which sounded more like a color than a name, she thought.

"So you let him in," Sandy said. "Did he show you any ID?"

She shook her head. She and Officer Sandy were standing in the foyer, face-to-face, he a hair shorter, she feeling less than reassured, and more tired by the minute. "Do you mind coming in where we can sit down?" she asked.

"Of course not." He followed as she led him through to the same sitting room where the man had been.

"I went for a long walk today. It made me realize how out of shape I am. It really wiped me out." She sat in her favorite chair. The cop remained standing, and she figured she could understand that. At last he was taller that way. She didn't even mind.

"You said the man gave you his name," he prompted, drawing her back to the subject.

"Yes. Stiles. Frank Stiles. It didn't seem like a made-up name at the time."

He jotted it down.

"He had a notepad, like yours there. A pen, instead of a pencil. Said he'd been waiting for the chance to interview me about the award nomination, and that he'd driven six straight hours just to interview me in time for a morning deadline."

The man nodded. He knew about the nomination. Since seeing the theater marquees, Morgan realized that everyone in town knew about it by now.

"Then what happened?"

She drew a breath. "I brought him in here. He sat over there." She pointed. "Asked me a couple of questions. I started getting the feeling he wasn't really a reporter at all."

"Really? What did he say to make you suspicious?"

She blinked. "I don't know. Nothing, really, it was

just a feeling.'' She shrugged and moved quickly past the topic. ''I asked him to leave, and he refused. He seemed vaguely menacing, and so I hit the security panel's alarm button. As soon as he realized what I had done, he ran off.''

He nodded. ''So he didn't harm you in any way?''

''No.''

''And he didn't take anything?''

''No.''

He folded his notebook. ''I don't really see that a crime has been committed here.''

She tipped her head to one side and stared at him.

''Well, not leaving right away when told to isn't exactly criminal behavior.''

She sighed. ''I suppose not. But this is not your everyday situation, Officer. I mean, I'm not trying to be a bitch here, but I am something of a celebrity. I think he wants something, and I think he'll be back.''

He studied her face. ''Obsessed fan? That sort of thing?''

''Sure. It's possible, isn't it?''

That, more than anything else she had said, seemed to work. The officer turned it over in his mind and nodded.

''Why don't you give me a description, ma'am? We'll have everyone keep an eye out for this character.''

She nodded and proceeded to describe Frank Stiles in exquisite detail, from the scarred face to the clothes he was wearing. But she never once mentioned that he claimed to work for the government, or vampires or the accusations of plagiarism the man had made.

Even so, the cop looked more and more skeptical

as she concluded her description. "I, um…I got the license plate number as he drove away."

"Did you?"

She nodded, pulled the slip of paper on which she had jotted the plate number from her pocket and handed it to him. He looked it over, then looked at her. "Maine plates?"

"No. New York."

"Hmm." He tucked the scrap into his own pocket. "You gonna be okay here alone for the rest of the night, ma'am?"

Oddly, the thought popped into her head that she wasn't alone. But that made so little sense that she wasn't even sure where it had come from. "I'll be fine. I'll set the security system, and this time I won't let any strangers inside."

"That's a good plan," the cop said. "We'll have a patrol car drive past a few times tonight, okay? If anything looks off, he'll stop."

"Off?" She gave her head a shake. "You mean, like body parts strewn on the lawn, the doors and windows smashed in, that sort of thing?"

He pursed his lips. "It's not gonna come to that, ma'am. You sure you're all right? I could drive you into town, put you in a room somewhere if—"

"No. No, I'm fine. That was my twisted sense of humor there." He still didn't crack a smile. "Thank you, Officer Gray." She walked him to the door and locked it behind him, resetting her security systems.

Then she went upstairs, took a quick shower, put on a cool nightgown and curled up in bed with another of Dante's journals.

But she couldn't lose herself tonight, not even in the spellbinding words of her phantom lover. The

words of that other man, the scarred man, kept coming back to her again and again. *Vampires are real....*
Dante is real, and he's going to be mad as hell when he finds out....

She sighed, pushing the covers back, forgetting for a moment the precious book that lay there in her lap. It hit the floor with a thud, and dust rose from it. It had landed on its back, open wide, and when she lovingly bent to pick it up again, some of the words from the time-yellowed pages caught her eye.

Trap door...
Beneath the house...
Coffin...

Shivering, she picked the book up. It was the eighth volume, and this was a section she hadn't read before. As she scanned the yellowed pages, a cold chill worked through her body. At last, something that could be verified. Proven. If she had the nerve.

Closing the book, sliding it carefully beneath the pillows, she turned and walked back downstairs, pausing at the double doors of her sanctuary, the room that had been Dante's study. His favorite place, and hers, as well. Swallowing hard, she stepped inside and moved toward the fireplace. She peeled away the oriental rug, rolling it back, baring the hardwood floor underneath.

It was unmarred. Unbroken. No hinges, no outline of a trapdoor where one had been described in the book. But the floor might have been covered over many times since those pages had been written. She recalled the sensation that had rinsed through her, the feeling that Dante was close to her, touching her, inside her mind—how many times in the past few weeks? Often when she was right here in this room.

Reaching for the iron poker, she walked across the floor again, from one wall to the other, tapping the floor with the poker as she did. Tap, tap, tap, tap, tap, *thud.*

She stopped, frozen in place, wondering if she had heard a difference or only imagined one. Again she tapped, and again the sound changed near the place where the trap door was supposed to have been. As if it were hollow underneath.

Licking her lips, Morgan knelt down. She jammed the tip of the fire poker between the floorboards, then tipped it back to pry them up. The boards resisted the effort, of course. She jabbed the thing harder, deeper, pried again, leaning into the effort with all her weight. And again and again. Until finally a single floorboard came free, breaking jaggedly in the middle.

Breathless, sweating, Morgan stood there, leaning on the poker, staring down. Underneath the floorboard was an older, rotting board, and a single tap of the poker stabbed a hole straight through it into the dark void underneath the house. Still unable to catch her breath, Morgan raced to her desk for a flashlight and returned to the hole she had made. Flicking it on, she shone its beam down through the opening. An old curving staircase was directly below her. Leading from the very floor on which she knelt down into the bowels of the earth.

Straightening away, her heart pounding with so much force she thought it would explode at any moment, she stared at the floor. ''My God, could it be true? Could he be…real? Dante?'' she whispered.

Then she snatched up the poker again and pried up another floorboard; and then another. She bashed in the rotted trap door—and yes, that was what the boards underneath had been. It was clear now—she could see the rusted hinges—and finally she made an opening big enough to fit through.

Swallowing hard, nodding firmly, she clutched the poker in one hand, gripped her flashlight in the other, and lowered herself through the hole and down to the stairway.

Morgan was not in her bedroom when Dante peered in from the balcony. He had changed his mind about striding up to the front door and confronting her. After the scare she'd had tonight with the scarred man, it would be too much.

She wasn't working with him. Wasn't feeding him information—at least not consciously. He was furious with her, yes, eager to confront her and rage at her for what she had done. Equally eager, though, to visit her in her dreams as he had done before. To make love to her with his mind, even though it was sheer hell on his body. It was release, of a sort. He was hungry for her, craving her, even as he wanted to throttle her until she was silenced forever.

But she wasn't in the bed awaiting his phantom touch or his vampiric rage. And she wasn't in her bathroom showering or bathing so that he could watch the water beading on her alabaster skin or possibly drown her in it. In fact, his senses told him she was far from this area of the house—and agitated in the extreme.

He thought of her earlier encounter with the scarred man, and worry gnawed at his gut. Idiot that he was, he felt every cell in his body aching to go to her, protect her, save her. He didn't sense the man's presence. But he knew that Stiles, as he called himself, was trouble. It was he who had been hunting Dante and his kind for months now. It had to be the film that had led him to Morgan. Stiles would use her to get to him if he had to.

Something was wrong, terribly wrong, with Morgan. Dante felt a twisting pain in his gut that wasn't his own, a hitch in his breathing, a chill of fear—no, terror.

No time now for caution. He responded to irresistible instinct, lunging through her room, into the hallway, following the magnetic pull of her being on his. He raced down the stairs. The study doors were open this time, and when he surged through them, ready to defend her from whatever was the matter, he was brought up short by the sight of broken boards lying on the floor beside the bunched-up rug and the gaping black opening beyond.

"Oh, sweet Jesus, no..."

Dante didn't know what the hell to do. He stood there frozen in time for an instant. And then he heard her scream.

15

Morgan walked warily down the curving wooden staircase hidden beneath her floorboards, placing her feet slowly, cautiously, shifting her weight gradually. The stairs groaned in protest as if they could give way at any moment. But they didn't, and she managed to make her way to the bottom. She found herself in a dank, dark room. A basement—one that didn't exist, according to every record on the place. God knew she had gone over blueprints and plans and age-old titles during the remodeling as she tried her damnedest to restore the house to its original appearance. She had learned the colors of the decor in several of the rooms. There had been a sketch of the chandelier, and an aging photo of the gardens in back.

But nowhere had there been mention of a cellar. In fact, the lack of one was mentioned more than once in those documents. Almost apologetically, as if it were an inexcusable oversight on the part of the builder. The builder—Daniel Taylor.

Daniel Taylor is one of many aliases the vampire Dante has used....

Oh, hell.

Taking a breath of stale air that had never seen sunlight, Morgan flicked her flashlight on, moved its beam around. Wooden beams crossed the low ceiling above her head. The walls were built of flat stones, piled on top of each other. She didn't know how the hell they stayed upright. An arching opening stood at the far end of the smallish room, and she went toward it, shining her light. No spiderwebs. She found it odd that there were no spiderwebs sticking to her face as she tiptoed, barely breathing, over the dirt floor.

She moved closer and finally stepped through the archway into the smaller, even darker room, this one made of concrete. The beam of her light arced around it to the left, falling on a small table, a kerosene lantern, a book of matches. She could smell the fuel. The lantern's globe was clean.

Blinking, she made her way to the lantern, and then, anchoring her flashlight under one arm to keep its beam where she wanted it, she found the lever that lifted the lantern's globe, struck a match and touched it to the wick. As she lowered the globe into place again and adjusted the flame, soft yellow light filled the room. It was such an incredible relief to have a more helpful source of light that she sighed as she turned to see what the place looked like now that she could see.

On the far side of the room, on a platform that kept it raised off the floor, was a box made of time-dulled wood so dark it seemed black, with tarnished silver handles on the sides.

She stood there staring at it, her mind refusing to process the information her eyes were sending for the drawn-out space between two heartbeats.

And then her mind whispered the truth to her. A coffin. And a scream ran in terror from her lungs, bouncing off the walls and diving back into her own ears to hide.

She bit her lip to silence herself and fought to catch

her breath as her heart galloped. The coffin's lid was closed. It looked old. How long had this thing been here? God, what was inside? Her mind wanted to know. It told her body to move closer, touch the wood, open the lid and see....

Him. Dante.

The rest of her wanted to run. Every cell, every muscle, tingled and twitched with the urge to turn and flee from this place. But her body refused to do either. Her legs were trembling so hard she could barely stand on them. Stress tended to do her in as quickly as physical overexertion, and today she had experienced both in levels beyond what she'd been capable of withstanding for over a year now.

It's not real. This is another of those vivid dreams. That's all.

But no. In her dreams she was always strong, vital, bursting with energy. And she never felt fear. In the dreams he loved her.

God, could that scarred man have been right? Could those journals be real? Could her Dante be lying right here in this casket? Perfectly preserved. Immortal? *Undead?*

"Maybe not," she muttered. "Maybe he just had himself secretly buried here. Maybe that's all this is. The hundred-year-old rotted corpse of a wealthy, eccentric lunatic is probably all that's in that box. Just bones by now. That's all." And when she saw it, when she saw the proof that Dante had been an ordinary man with a vivid imagination and a gift for writing, maybe that would be enough to break the spell he had cast on her. Maybe she could free herself of the sticky web her own obsession had spun to entrap her.

Catching her breath, she forced her feet to move closer. One step, then another. She wasn't even sure she could bring herself to open the lid when she got to it. Then again, it might be sealed. It *should* be sealed, shouldn't it? They didn't just toss bodies into boxes and leave them unlocked.

Then again, they didn't usually hide them underneath houses, either.

She was at the coffin now. She told her hands to rise, and they did, though she was almost surprised to see them obey. She lowered her hands gently to the coffin. It was cold to the touch, and a layer of grime lay between the smooth wood and her palms. Drawing a breath, she told herself to open the lid.

"Don't." The single word came in a deep, rich, hauntingly familiar voice from behind her.

Morgan froze at the command and closed her eyes. He had entered silently. She hadn't heard a sound, not a footstep. Nothing.

"Let it be, Morgan. There's nothing in there that you need to see."

Eyes still closed, she whispered, "Dante?"

"I…" The voice hesitated, and Morgan opened her eyes and knew that his next words would be lies. She knew it as surely as if she were the one about to speak them, making them up as she went along. She felt him groping, searching his mind for a convincing lie. "Yes, I am Dante, but not the one you think I am. He was my great-great-grandfather."

"And he is buried here." She said his next line for him.

"It was his last wish."

She nodded. "And why are you here?"

"To see you." He paused, breathed, and she felt

him searching and spinning. "That film of yours is
so like the old man's delusions that when I learned
you were living in the house he had built, I knew you
had learned of his fantasies somehow and used them
to create the script."

She didn't turn to face him. She couldn't. Not yet.
"You're saying they're not real?"

He forced a laugh, just a breath, really. It was the
most false thing she had ever heard. "Of course
they're not real."

"And you came inside my house without knocking?"

"I...was about to knock when I heard you
scream."

"From outside."

"Of course."

"And yet you set off no alarms when you came
in?"

He didn't speak. Morgan swallowed hard, and in
one swift act of will, pushed upward on the lid. The
coffin lay empty, white satin lining beginning to yellow with age. The lid stayed up when she let it go
and turned slowly to look on the face of her fantasy
lover for the first time.

He stood there dressed in black trousers and a black
silk shirt buttoned all the way to the collar, no jacket,
no tie. He was dark. Everything about him...dark.
Empty. Hollow. His face just as sculpted as she had
imagined it, the hollows of his cheeks, the endlessly
deep wells of his ebony eyes.

He took her breath away. Because she loved him.
Because she was bound to him in ways she didn't
even understand. Because he was so exactly as she

had known he would be. Familiar. Beloved. He was hers.

"You're real," she whispered.

He stared back at her in silence. She felt him then, stealing into her mind. Felt him planting the certainty that this was just another of her dreams, willing her to believe it. She opened her eyes wide, shook her head hard. "Stop it. You're not a dream. I won't believe you are."

"How can you be so sure?"

"It's no use, Dante. Even if you could do whatever it is you do to my mind, the broken floorboards, this room…they'll all still be here when I wake. Even you couldn't make it all go away in the time left before sunrise."

He studied her, his eyes probing and narrow. "You're either very brave or very foolish, Morgan. Don't you know how angry you've made me? I should kill you for what you've done."

"Then do it."

She saw the shock ripple through him. She didn't let it stop her. Her hands went to the high collar of her nightgown, and she ripped it open, popping buttons all the way to her waist. She tipped her head back, closed her eyes. "Do it, Dante."

Her pulse beat in reaction to the touch of his eyes on her throat. She felt him shiver, felt her own heat rise. She wanted something she couldn't name, as little sense as it made. She knew she was dying anyway, and soon, judging by her symptoms of late. If she had to die, why not in the way he had described so erotically in his journals? The way she had experienced so vividly, if only slightly? Why couldn't she die in utter ecstasy as her essence flowed into him?

And suddenly he was there, his arms tight around her, pulling her body hard against his as he bent over her. His mouth closed on her throat, and she whispered, "Yes...." He bit down without breaking through and suckled her skin. She arched her hips against him, felt the arousal pressing back. Morgan had never felt such fire burn in her body as she did then. Her hands tangled in his hair as she twisted and writhed in his powerful arms, pressing her body closer, arching her throat to his hungry mouth. She felt his lips, warm and wet on her skin. His tongue, stroking and tasting. The delicious pinch of his teeth biting down, just a little.

And then suddenly he wrenched himself away from her so violently that she stumbled and fell to the packed earth floor. Breathless, she remained there, knees bent awkwardly, arms braced on the floor behind her as she stared at him. At his eyes, gleaming now with an odd luminescence that didn't seem to come from the glow of the kerosene lamp. At his face, drawn tight in some kind of unnamed anguish.

"You have no idea what the hell you're playing with, Morgan," he said, his voice coarse and unsteady.

"I know," she said. Her words came less forcefully than she would have liked. Her chest moved rapidly as she fought for breath in between. "I know you...better than anyone ever has, Dante.... Or ever will."

He went very still, his eyes narrowing on her. "How?"

She closed her eyes, let her head fall backward. Then her arms bent, and she was lying flat on the floor. God, she was so weak suddenly. It was all too much.

He swore softly and bent to gather her up into his arms. He carried her out of the place, up the rickety stairs, and managed to get up through the jagged hole in the floor. "Are you hurt?" He asked the question almost reluctantly as he took her through the house, obviously knowing his way around.

"No."

"But you are ill," he said unnecessarily.

She nodded, resting her head against his chest. "You're changing the subject."

"Am I?"

They were in the hall now, where he turned and carried her unerringly to her bedroom. To the bed. Then he lowered her onto it, but when he would have straightened away, she locked her arms around his neck and held on. "You want to know how I know about you?"

Leaning over her, one knee on the bed, his face only inches from hers, he nodded. "I have to know."

"Then make love to me, Dante, and I'll tell you."

His eyes flared hotter as he stared into hers. "I cannot do that, Morgan. You're too weak."

"Not for that. Never for that." She lifted her head from the pillows, using him as leverage, and pressed her lips to his. "Please."

Groaning softly, he returned the kiss, folding his arms beneath her and lifting her upper body to his chest. His tongue traced her lips and, when she parted them, slipped inside to taste her. His breaths came harder, faster, and he slid his mouth from hers to trace her jawline down to her neck and kiss her there, where he had before.

He let her go, let her fall. "I can't...."

"You have before. You have. I know it was real. It wasn't a dream. Dammit, Dante, you've been with me, night after night."

"It wasn't real. It was in your mind, in my mind. It wasn't real."

"Then make it real!"

His muscles were so tense he was shaking, and his jaw was rigid. Then he glanced toward the window, and she followed his gaze and realized the dawn was at hand. "Tell no one what you've seen tonight. I swear to you, Morgan, if you breathe a word, you'll die. Do you understand? I'll have no choice in the matter."

"Do you really think I would betray you? My God, Dante, I would never—"

"You already have."

She blinked and realized he was referring to the film. "It's not the way you think it is."

"You've told my secrets to the world, Morgan. Some of my dearest friends have died because of what you revealed about me and my kind in your films. I'm being hunted because of you, my every step hounded by that man you met earlier tonight."

She felt her eyes widen. "I didn't know. I never would have told your stories, Dante, if I had known they were real. You have to believe that!"

He got to his feet, went to the window. "I have to leave."

She surged from the bed, weak, nearly exhausted, and clutched at the back of his shirt. "Then come back. Dante, promise you'll come to me tonight. I'll tell you everything, I swear."

He glanced back at her. "Or maybe you'll have the scarred man here waiting when I arrive?"

"I would let him kill me first...."

She dropped to her knees, suddenly too weak to stand. Her head falling forward, she drew a shallow breath. "I would die, Dante, before I would betray you." It was a string of words floating on a breath, a mere exhalation, not even a whisper.

"Words I've heard before, Morgan." Dante knelt, clutched her shoulders, lifted her chin to search her face. Then he folded her to his chest, held her there with one hand, and took something from his pocket with the other. She saw it shine as it flicked open. A small pointed blade, like a leather punch. He drew it to his own throat and jabbed it in, grunting in pain as he did.

Morgan gasped, her eyes fixed on his corded neck as he drew the blade away and a scarlet strand of blood unwound from the puncture wound, trailing over his skin. She licked her lips. The scent of it touched her nostrils, and a feral lust twisted in her gut. His hand was in her hair, at the back of her head, pulling her closer, but she didn't need it. She knew what she needed.

She buried her face in the crook of his neck, closed her mouth over the wound and sucked the blood from his body. She drew on the opening, her tongue darting to catch any drops that escaped her hungry lips. She lapped at him there until he pulled her away, pressing one hand to the wound in his throat. For one insane moment she fought him, pressing closer, clawing at his hand, trying to steal more of this drug she craved. She could have ripped his throat open with her own teeth in that moment, like a wolf. She could have killed him.

He held her off easily enough. But when she looked into his face, she saw the same bared teeth, the same breathless hunger, the same feral gleam lit his eyes. My God, he wanted to devour her in exactly the same way. Like an animal. Like a predator.

He flung her toward the bed, lunged out onto the balcony and vanished over the side. Morgan lay where she had landed, half on the bed, half off, panting. Her body was alive, tingling, her heart beating loudly and strongly. She didn't feel weak anymore. She felt alive, more alive than she had in years.

This, she realized, must be a glimmer of what it felt like to be…to be what Dante was. To be a vampire.

She wanted it. Suddenly she wanted it with everything in her. She wanted to be a vampire. And she wondered if she would be, now? If drinking his blood would make her what he was.

Dante made his way to the house Sarafina had told him about with all due haste. He found her there, pacing, waiting for him, but he only muttered a terse greeting before moving past her into the basement. She had tossed some blankets into a pair of crates to make do.

She was on his heels instantly, of course. "Where have you been? What's kept you, Dante? Jesus, is that *your* blood I smell?"

"A minor accident."

"There's no such thing!" She gripped his shoulder to stop him, but he kept moving anyway, climbing into the box she'd prepared for him, pulling the lid

over himself. She caught the lid in her hands to prevent him covering himself fully and ranted on. "You
know how easily we can bleed out, Dante. What the
hell happened to make you so careless?"

"I had a run-in with our scar-faced vampire
hunter," he told her. Because if she ever knew the
truth, she would explode. And nothing, not even her
bond to their kind, would protect Morgan from Sarafina's wrath. She was incredibly possessive. Not only
of the slaves she kept, but of him. He was her only
family. That meant a great deal to Sarafina.

"The scarred man? He's in town?"

"Yes. So be careful." Dante gave the cover another tug. "The sooner I sleep, the sooner the reju-
venation process can heal my wound, 'fina."

Sighing, obviously still filled with questions, Sarafina secured the lid over him. He found the latches
that had been affixed to hook from the inside, and he
hooked them. Then he listened while Sarafina made
her bedtime preparations and climbed into her own
box.

He lay very still, closed his eyes. Waiting. Sleep
was a long time in coming, though. Even when it did
finally sweep over him, he couldn't stop the images
from playing through his mind. Images of him—and
Morgan. Naked, entwined. His body buried to the hilt
in hers. His teeth sinking into her flesh. Her blood
flowing into his body. God, he wanted her. He wanted
to possess every part of her. Her soul. Her flesh. Her
blood.

And he knew it would be worse now. She had
drunk from him not once, but twice. He had tasted
her, and he knew damned well that he would do it
again if he wasn't careful. If he made love to her, he

would drink from her. Drain her, maybe. He wouldn't be able to stop himself. And in her weakened state, he would kill her. He would *kill her*.

God, he didn't want to kill Morgan De Silva. He wanted…he wanted to love her.

Too bad he was incapable of loving anyone at all.

16

Maxine and Lou were sitting in the hospital waiting room, where they'd been sitting for the past four hours. It was daylight now. Stormy's parents had been notified and finally taken into a private room to await word. None had come. None whatsoever. It was the cruelest form of torture Lou could think of. The CIA ought to use it. Just refuse to tell some parent how their wounded child was doing until they gave up every secret in their possession. Hell, it would work every time.

"I've got to get hold of Jay. Jason Beck," Max said. "He would want to know."

Lou didn't like seeing his normally spunky Max this way. She was pale and shaken. Like someone had hit her smack between the eyes with a fucking two-by-four, and no wonder. He remembered the kid she referred to. He had been the third part of their inseparable trio all through high school and college. "Do you know where to find him?"

She shook her head slowly, stayed quiet for a long time. Then finally she spoke again. "It's probably just as well," she said. And it took Lou a moment to realize she was still talking about Jason Beck. He wondered vaguely how she'd managed to lose touch with someone she'd been so close to. But time passed. Shit happened.

"Why do you say that?"

"Come on, Lou. You know what this is about as well as I do. They found out that I'd told you what I knew about DPI."

He averted his eyes.

"It's the only thing that makes sense. They kill Stormy and frame you. It's a message to me. A lesson for me. It serves to make sure I won't ever tell anyone else. They destroy two people I lo—care about. Just like that Stiles guy told me he would. The question is, how does he know I told you?"

Lou licked his lips, lifted his gaze to hers slowly. "I made a call last night."

She went very still. Didn't say anything, just stared at him, begging him with her eyes not to tell her what she had to know he was going to tell her.

"To the friend of mine who works for the CIA. I asked him to find out what he could about DPI. Told him I suspected they'd been running some kind of covert op out of White Plains until the HQ burned five years ago. I didn't mention you or the man you saw."

"You didn't have to." She swallowed hard. "I asked you not to talk to anyone, Lou. How could you do this to me?"

"Hey, Max, come on. I had no reason to think it would result in anything like…like this."

"No reason? You had one reason. You had my word. I told you they threatened my friends and my mother, and you went right ahead and—" She stopped there. "Oh, God. Oh, God, my mother."

She was on her feet and heading for a pay phone before Lou could stop her. He leaned back in his vinyl seat, pushed a hand through his hair. She was right;

she was dead right. If it had been another cop asking him to keep quiet about something like this, he would have taken them at their word and done it. But he'd underestimated Max. Mad Maxie the conspiracy theorist, always seeing trouble where there wasn't any.

Well, hell. Maybe for once she wasn't so far off base.

There was a dull ping, the elevator doors off to the left slid open, and Lydia came hurrying from them, eyes wide. "What happened? Lou, are you okay? Where's Max? God, is it Max?"

"No, no, she's fine. I'm fine." He was on his feet and met Lydia halfway, hugged her good and hard.

"I woke up this morning and no one was at Max's. So I called your place and got some cop who told me I could find you both at the hospital. Jesus, Lou, I was scared half out of my mind."

She looked it, he thought, stepping back a little. Her hair was a mess, no makeup. She looked her age for a change, which was kind of refreshing. But totally unlike her.

Then she lost interest in him completely when she saw Max coming back from the pay phone. Lydia walked up to the kid and hugged her as if they'd been friends for a long, long time instead of only a few days. "Honey, you look like hell."

"I feel it."

"How's your mother, Max?" Lou asked.

"Fine. Maybe she's safe down there. Maybe they don't know where she is. Or maybe they don't have the manpower to be down there and up here at the same time. Or maybe there's only the one man, the one I saw. Maybe it's just him, working alone." She pushed a hand through her hair. "God, I don't even know what we're dealing with here. I don't know who to be more afraid of. The vampires or the vampire hunters.''

Lydia let her go and stepped back, staring at her.

Lou looked up and down the hall to be sure that remark hadn't been overheard. "Keep it down, will you? Someone will show up waving a one-way ticket to the mental ward with your name on it if you keep this up.''

She glared at him.

"Will someone please tell me what's happened?''

"It's my friend Stormy. My partner in the business. She was found at Lou's place with a bullet in her head. They left her for dead, but she wasn't quite. They trashed Lou's place, and they used his gun. Tried to set it up to look like he'd done it.''

"My God." Her gaze shot to Lou's, but then she turned it inward. "Wait a minute. Stormy? There was a message on your machine from someone named Stormy this morning when I got up. I saw the light, thought it might have been something from you, letting me know where you were, so I played it.''

"I never looked at the machine when we got in last night." Max gripped Lydia's hands. "What did she say?''

Glancing around her, Lydia lowered her voice. "She said she had an odd call from Lou asking her to come to his place. That she wanted to let you know, in case he was in trouble. She said he sounded funny." She gave her head a shake. "I think that was all, but it's still on the tape in your machine.''

"That machine records the time the call came in. Do you remember what it was?''

"Around nine p.m.,'' Lydia said.

She nodded. "It wasn't Lou. Lou was with me, seeing a movie, and then sitting outside watching my place. Someone called her. Lured her over there and met her at the door with a twenty-two."

"Thank God it was a twenty-two," Lou put in. "Anything bigger would have killed her."

"But why? Why would anyone want to do that?" Lydia was baffled.

"It has to do with—" Max broke off as a doctor finally emerged from the room where Stormy was being treated. At the same moment a nurse came from the private waiting room with Storm's parents behind her. Everyone crowded together in the center of the waiting area.

"She's alive," the doctor said. "But she's in a coma."

Storm's father, a blond man whose normally healthy tan seemed to have turned to gray, lifted his head, met the doctor's eyes. "Is she brain dead, Doctor? Just tell us the truth."

"No. She has brain wave activity. It's minimal, but it's there."

"How long will she be in the coma?" Max asked, stepping forward, clasping Mrs. Jones's hand. "I mean, a day? A week?"

"We have no way of knowing when or…or even if she'll come out of the coma," the doctor said. "But as long as she has brain wave activity, there's hope." They all waited for him to say more. Lou knew what they wanted to hear. Exactly how much hope? Exactly what were her chances, and when would they know anything more for certain? He could see by the doctor's weary face that he didn't have any answers to give them.

Sighing, the doctor led them all to chairs, urged them to sit, sat opposite them. "Look, there have been cases where a coma has lasted months, even years. Sometimes they wake up, sometimes they don't. The longer she stays comatose, the lower her chances of recovering will be. But there have been cases where people woke up after extended comas to make nearly full recoveries. There's just no way to know."

"And what about when she does wake up?" Mrs. Jones asked. "Will there be brain damage?"

"We can't even begin to tell until she does wake up, ma'am. Again, though, the sooner she regains consciousness, the better."

"She'll wake up," Max said. She said it to the doctor, and then she said it again to Storm's parents. "She will wake up, and she'll be fine. They say comatose people can hear you talking to them. Is that true, Doctor?"

He nodded. "In some cases. I've seen reactions in the EEG readouts when loved ones speak to comatose patients."

"Then that's what we should do," Max said, in typical Maxine-Take-Charge-Stuart fashion. "I think someone should be in there with her all the time, talking to her. And if no one can be there, we can have tapes of our voices playing, or music. I know all her favorite music. Nothing slow, though. I mean, we want something hardcore and powerful, like Godsmack, banging in there. We won't let her slip away. We just won't let her."

"Some of those might be very good ideas," the doctor said. "Keep in mind you'll have to give her a chance to rest in between."

"If she wants to rest, she can damn well wake up." Maxine's eyes were brimming with tears.

Mrs. Jones cupped a hand to Max's face. "You're a good girl, Maxine. A good friend." Then the woman looked past her at Lou and lowered her eyes.

"You need to know, Mrs. Jones, that Lou was at my place last night. I wasn't lying when I told you that. You know how much I love Stormy. I wouldn't lie to you about this. Someone set him up."

Mrs. Jones nodded.

"We've known Officer Malone a long time," her husband said. "It would take a lot more than what we've been told so far to make us believe him capable of anything like this."

"I appreciate that," Lou told the man. "And I swear to you, I'm gonna do everything I can to find the SOB who did this to your daughter and put him away for a long, long time."

"Yeah. And so am I." Maxie sent Lou a look when she said that. And he knew what it meant. They were going to do this her way from now on. With his help or without it, Maxie was going to track down that screenwriter and pump her for information about— God, he could hardly think it without smirking—vampires.

And when he glanced at Lydia, Lou knew she was going to be attached to Max at the hip until they got the answers she wanted. This was not even close to what he had hoped to accomplish by bringing the two women together. Not by a long shot. In fact, his entire goal had been derailed by all this nonsense. He had fully expected Max to reassure Lydia that there were no such things as vampires and end that part of the entire arrangement. After that, they were supposed to get to know each other as friends and maybe later make a few discoveries on their own. The same discoveries he'd made himself, entirely by accident.

It was all blown to hell now. Christ.

"She may need another blood transfusion, Mrs. Jones," the doctor said, and as soon as she started to get to her feet, he held up a hand. "No, ma'am. You can't donate any more today. We have supplies, don't worry."

"I'd prefer to know the source," the woman said. "I know, I know, the blood supply is safer than ever, but still…"

"I'm A-positive," Maxie said.

"Me, too," Lydia put in.

The doc shook his head. "Not what we need for her, though you're welcome to donate anyway. Anyone for A-neg?"

Lou raised his hand like a schoolkid.

"You're elected." The doctor sent Lou off with a nurse, and he thought it pretty ironic that he was entertaining the notion that vampires might be real even as he let some pretty young thing drain a pint from his veins.

"Can we see her?" Stormy's mother asked.

The doctor nodded. "Absolutely." He led the two parents away, and Max noticed with a wrenching ache in her belly the way Mr. Jones held his wife close to his side, all but holding her up, like he was loaning some of his strength to her.

She sighed and turned to Lydia. "We need to talk."

"You poor thing." Lydia hugged her again. "I

know what you're going through. When Kimbra died, I just…"

"She was more to you than a best friend, though, wasn't she?"

Lydia looked at her for a moment, smiled gently, sadly. "Am I that obvious?"

"I saw the photo you have in your wallet when you opened it the other day. The two of you, arm in arm. The way you were looking at her."

"I loved her," Lydia said softly. "She was my whole life. And even though it's not the same, I can see you love Stormy. I can see the hurt in your eyes. God, it's like looking into a mirror a few weeks ago."

Max swiped at her eyes. "We don't have time for a pity party here. We need to get our stories straight about last night. And then we need to get rid of that tape in the answering machine."

Lydia frowned at her. "Get our stories straight?"

"Lou sat in his car outside my place all night long," Max told her.

Lydia nodded in agreement. "Right. I remember when you spotted him out there. I thought it was real sweet of him."

"Exactly. So that's two of us who can swear that Lou never left our sight."

"Except that he did," Lydia said softly. "Remember? After he dropped you, he took off for a while? He was back in no time, but—"

"Yeah, and the damn fool told them so." Max licked her lips. "I had to think fast, so I said that when Lou left, I followed him. Made up some line about suspecting he was seeing some other woman and being jealous. I confirmed what he told them, that he'd gone to the station and then come straight back to my place.''

Lydia nodded slowly. ''I didn't know you and Lou were—''

''We aren't.''

''So you lied to the police.''

''I know he didn't do this. You know it, too.''

Lydia turned away, drew a deep breath, finally blew it out with a sigh. ''Of course I know it.'' She turned to face Max again. ''I was there, after all, when you left to go follow him. I tried to tell you Lou was a one-woman man, but you just had to make sure.''

Max bit her lip. ''You could have been sleeping upstairs. You could have no knowledge one way or the other.''

''Two witnesses are better than one. Especially if they think that one is the suspect's lover, Maxine.''

Max nodded. ''Thank you.''

''No need. I like Lou. We've been friends a long time.''

''He doesn't know I made it up. He would never let me do it.''

''Understood,'' Lydia said. ''You mentioned the answering machine?''

''Yeah, we need to erase the message.'' Then she shook her head. ''But there might be a clue in it. I should find a way to keep a copy.''

''We could just put in a new tape,'' Lydia suggested.

''It's not on tape. It stores the messages electronically.''

''Buy a new machine,'' Lydia said. ''Take the old one and stash it somewhere safe.''

Max nodded slowly. ''It's a good plan. Later I can

transfer the message to tape and destroy the machine, just for good measure. But for now, that's the fastest solution. And we have to get it done before they decide to search my place.''

''I'll take care of it. Stay here, see your friend.''

Max nodded. ''Use cash. And buy it someplace busy, like Wal-Mart, where they won't remember you. And don't make your appearance too memorable.''

Biting her lip, Lydia frowned hard at her. ''Just what are we dealing with here, hon?''

''The government. A part of the CIA, I think. A secret part that may not even exist anymore, but the man who shot Stormy was a part of it.''

Lydia nodded slowly. ''You called them...vampire hunters.''

''That's exactly what they were. Maybe still are.'' She sighed. ''Look, I'll tell you everything I know. But you can't mention it to a soul. That's what got Stormy shot.''

''Okay. Understood. But not now. This isn't the time or the place. I'll go take care of that machine of yours, and we'll talk later.''

''May as well meet up at the police station,'' Max said. ''They're going to want sworn statements from all of us.''

''Noon?'' Lydia said.

''Noon's good.''

''See you then.''

After Lydia left, Max waited around until Lou finally returned from donating blood with a bandage on his arm. He looked at her as if checking her over, like he was searching for signs as to how she was holding up, and while her independent-woman side thought it was hopelessly old-fashioned of him, the rest of her loved it that he worried.

"I'm okay," she told him before he bothered to ask.

"No, you're not, but I don't see how you could be." He looked around. "Where's Lydia?"

"Had some things to do. She's gonna meet us at the station at noon, so we can give them our statements."

"And then what?"

She shrugged. "I'm gonna go home, make some tapes of my voice for Stormy's mom to play for her, gather up a few CDs and my programmable player, and get it all set up in her room. Then I'm gonna pack."

"Pack?"

"I hate to leave Stormy, Lou. But according to what I've been able to find out online, that screenwriter lives in Maine. And we really do need to talk to her. She's the only lead we have right now, besides Stiles, and we can't find him."

"If he knows about the films, we're as likely to find him in Maine as anywhere else."

She blinked twice, then stared at him. "We? Does that mean you're going with me?"

"Yep."

"Will they let you, before this case is solved?"

"Nope. I'll just have to be sneaky. Good thing I've got an expert to help me on that." He gave her a smile, lopsided and sad, but real.

She thought about hugging the big lug, but Storm's parents came walking up to her then, her crying softly, him holding her. "Go on in, Maxine," Mr. Jones said. "We cleared it with the doctor, and we both think hearing your voice will do her a world of good.'' He pointed her down the hall. ''Two-oh-seven.''

''Okay. You two ought to get something to eat, and maybe rest a bit. I know you want to be here, but you're gonna need time off, too. If you go getting sick, you won't be much help to Stormy, after all.''

''We'll be fine. Go on, go see her now.''

She glanced at Lou. ''Go ahead, Maxie. Take your time. I'll be here waiting.''

Sending him a grateful nod, she went down the hall, searched for the door marked 207, and found it. There was a moment, though, when she almost couldn't go in. She stood with her hand on the door, not pushing it open, and she wondered if some deluded part of her mind thought this wouldn't be real until she saw it with her own eyes. Or if she was just afraid Stormy would die while she was in there.

Didn't matter. Stormy mattered. That was all. She swallowed her fear, pushed the door open, peered inside.

It did not look like Stormy lying in that bed, and for the barest instant Max thought she had the wrong room. But then logic made her look more closely. Yes, she was more still and pale than she had ever been, and her eyebrow ring had been removed. Her short, bleached hair had vanished. It might be swathed by the skullcap of bandages she wore, or it might have been shaved. Max didn't know.

But the elfin face and fine-boned features were Stormy's. There were leads going from her head to a monitor, from her chest to another, from her nostrils to an oxygen pump, from her wrist to an IV bag, and from somewhere under the sheets to a bag at the foot of the bed, which she did not want to think about.

The nurse smiled at Max. "Well, Tempest, you have a visitor. Isn't that nice?"

"Call her Stormy," Max said firmly. "Make sure you tell the other nurses, too. She wouldn't answer to Tempest even if she was fully awake."

The nurse nodded, turning with her hands on her hips. "And here I was thinking what a gorgeous name you had. I love Tempest!" Then she shrugged. "I suppose Stormy is nice, too, though." She was leaning in, adjusting the covers and talking to Stormy as if she were wide awake and hearing every word.

Max liked the nurse. She liked her attitude. She liked the caring in her eyes. "I'm Maxine," she told the nurse, as she came closer.

"And do you have a preferred nickname, too?"

"Mad Max, but don't spread it around."

The nurse laughed, patting Stormy's shoulder. "Did you hear that? Mad Max. Girl, I like your friends. Well, have a seat Mad Max, and I'll give you two some private time."

Max sat down, and the nurse left. The constant beeps of the monitors were drugging. Steady and almost hypnotic. "Man, we're gonna have to get them to turn off the sound on these contraptions, Stormy. You think?" She leaned closer, clasped Storm's hand. "It's Max, honey. I'm here, and I know what happened, okay? I know it wasn't Lou. I don't want you to worry about that."

No response. She lay there completely silent and still.

"I know you're in there, Storm. I know you can hear me." She spoke louder, more firmly. "Everything is fine. Your parents are fine, I'm fine. And the man who did this is going down. Understand?''

Still nothing. Just the monotonous beeps.

''You have to focus, hon. Focus every ounce of your energy on waking up. You hear me? That's all I want you thinking about. And you might as well know you aren't going to get a moment's peace until you do. I'm getting your favorite CDs, and someone's gonna be in here talking your damn multiply pierced ears off until you wake up. No one's gonna leave you alone. You got that?''

The beeping patterns changed. Picked up speed a little.

Max glanced around her at the machines, as if she would know a damn thing by looking at them. But something had agitated Stormy. What had she just said? No one's gonna leave you alone. She licked her lips. ''Being alone worries you, does it?''

Again the pace picked up.

''No one will leave you alone. I'm gonna have someone guarding your door, and someone else in here with you, twenty-four-seven. I promise you, you're safe here. Okay?''

She couldn't tell if she had eased Stormy's mind or not. But the beeps slowly resumed their former pattern.

''Keep trying to wake up, hon.''

The nurse came back in, told Max it was time to go. Max nodded. ''I gotta leave for a bit, babe, but I promise you're not gonna be left alone. I promise.'' She turned to the nurse. ''Can you stay with her until her mom gets back?''

''Of course I'm staying. It's almost time for my program!'' She reached for the remote, flicked on the room's television, and pulled up a chair. "I hope you like *Passions,* girl, 'cause I never miss it," she told Stormy.

"She loves it," Max said. "I'll see you later, Storm. Don't be scared, hon. I've got your back, okay?"

The nurse nodded in approval, and Max left the room. Back in the waiting room, she went to Lou, leaned against his chest and hoped he wouldn't complain. He didn't. He hugged her instead. "We need to get guards on her room, Lou. If he finds out she's alive, he might come back."

"He would have no reason to."

"What if she saw him?"

"Hon, you saw him. You already know what he looks like, as well as his name. Being ID'd is not on his list of worries for some reason."

"Still…"

Sighing, he nodded. "I'll get right on it."

She closed her eyes. "We have time to get some breakfast?"

"Yeah. I phoned in, told them we'd be coming in at noon to talk to IAD and give our statements. We have a couple of hours yet." He took her arm, and they walked to the elevators together.

17

Morgan slept through most of the day again. It was afternoon when she woke, stretching her arms above her head and arching her back, feeling good. She opened her eyes, and everything that had happened the night before returned to her. She felt a delicious sensitivity at her throat, and, flinging back the covers, ran to her dressing table to examine it in the mirror.

A purple bruise and the marks of his teeth. No punctures. No. He hadn't tasted her blood, but he'd fed her his own. She could still taste him on her tongue.

What did it mean? she wondered yet again. How did one become a vampire, if it were possible at all? Was she already changing? Was this vitality singing in her veins a part of it, or only a temporary side effect from drinking him? This sleeping through the day, waking only late in the afternoon, was this a sign that she was becoming as he was?

She only knew she'd been getting steadily weaker until he had first come to her. Now she felt stronger, as she had the last time. She thought, the way she had been feeling, she might well have been dead by now without his intervention. His…his blood. He was keeping her alive.

But for how long? She had to know. And she knew where to find the answers. Or hoped she did. Dante's journals. There were still one or two she hadn't read completely through. That was what she would do for the rest of the afternoon, she decided. Read. Research. She had several hours before dark, and that was precisely how she would fill them. She stripped off the torn, buttonless nightgown, pulled on her white satin robe, tied it and moved down the stairs to the study, where she kept the journals locked away in a safe.

But when she stood in the open study doors, she saw the mess on the floor and realized she had other work left to do. Broken boards lay beside the hole. If it were true that the scarred man was hunting Dante, and if he were to come back here and somehow see this…

Damn.

Her afternoon passed more quickly than she would have liked. She had to shower, dress. Then, taking one broken piece of wood with her, she drove into town to the nearest lumber yard and purchased matching pieces of the correct length to patch the damage she had done. She bought a hammer and nails, a small crowbar and a handsaw.

When she returned home with her purchases and faced the task before her, she felt a hint of doubt that she would be able to pull it off. Ordinarily this kind of physical labor would be far too much for her to tackle alone. She'd toyed with the idea of hiring someone to do the job but realized she had no idea who she could trust. How would she explain the need to keep it quiet, and even if she did, wouldn't that just make the worker more likely to tell? Her being who she was, he would probably sell the tidbit to a scandal sheet for a few thousand dollars.

Besides, she didn't *feel* as if the job was too much

for her. Not today. Shrugging, she knelt on the floor, took up the crowbar. She would never know until she tried, she decided.

It took her an hour to pull out the old nails that held the broken scraps of lumber to the main beams underneath and remove the bits of wood. Then more time as she measured the hole and marked her new boards at the right length.

Now the test, she thought, as she took up the saw. If she could manage this, it would be a miracle.

Swallowing her doubts, she laid the sawblade across the line she'd drawn and drew it backward. Then she began to pump the saw back and forth, as smoothly as she could. The short end fell away, clattering to the floor, and she looked at it in something like shock. She drew a hand over her brow, felt sweat beading there. Her heart was pounding, her body warm with exertion. God, when was the last time she had felt this way?

She continued to work, sawing the boards, fitting them in place, nailing them as she went along. When there was only one board to go, she paused to kick all the scraps, the old lumber, the broken pieces, the sawdust, the bent, used nails, into the hole. Then she nailed the final board into place.

It didn't look perfect when she finished. The boards were a different color, lighter, newer looking, unfinished, and the joints were less than tight. But it was the best she could do at the moment. Her newfound energy seemed to be starting to wane.

She got a broom to sweep up the remaining bits of sawdust and dirt. Then she pulled the oriental rug back down to cover the new boards.

Brushing her hands and straightening, she was finished.

Only an hour now, until sundown. She looked down at herself, realized she was damp with sweat, and had sawdust clinging to her skin and her hair. If he came back—God, she hoped he would—she didn't want him seeing her like this.

"I need to get ready," she whispered. "For Dante." Yet more of the day wrested from her hands. She would barely have time to read at all. Still, it was important.

A half hour later, she returned to the study, freshly showered, her hair clean and lavender scented and blown dry, flowing loose down her back. She wore the white satin robe that tied at the waist and hung all the way to her bare feet, and she carried a pot of herbal tea and a cup with her. It was a special blend, supposedly good for boosting one's energy. Hers was running low, though still higher than it had been before Dante had come to her.

She turned on the gas fireplace, then went to the safe in the wall, took out one of the precious journals, one of those she still hadn't read all the way through, and curled up in the big armchair nearest the fire. Filling her teacup, she flipped through the pages until she found the place where she had last left off. And before very long, she was immersed once again in the tales of the vampire, hearing them as clearly in her mind as if they were spoken in Dante's deep, rich voice.

Sarafina tried to warn me. "Never mix with mortals. Never." She said it early in my education and repeated it often. "Our kind must live alone."

"What about the Chosen?"

I knew the term. That surprised her to some extent, I think, because I hadn't heard it from her. We sat by a fire that night, in a grove of trees, the way we had done in our mortal lives. I think that at the beginning, that was what Sarafina envisioned. A band of two—two Gypsy vampires, living the way we had before. She was trying, I think, to recapture some of what she had lost when she had lost her family, her tribe. But of course it was impossible. I accepted that long before she did.

"The Chosen are humans with a connection to us. Something about the blood," she told me. "We know which ones they are because we sense them. We feel drawn to them, and sometimes they to us. But we do not make ourselves known to them, Dante. That must be understood at all costs. We do not."

"They can become vampires. Like us," I said.

"They can. And do you know what happens when they do?"

I shook my head.

"They go mad."

She said it so simply, as if it were an established fact. "All of them?" I asked, even though I knew better. I hadn't gone mad, nor had Sarafina.

She didn't answer that. "Some become so morose they refuse to feed until their bodies become dormant, brittle shells that lie as if dead for untold centuries, their souls trapped inside. Some become giddy with their newfound vampiric power and go on gluttonous killing sprees, leaving so many bodies in their wake that the mortals realize what is happening and hunt us like animals in their vengeance. They die, too. We kill them ourselves. We have no choice, unless the mortals beat us to it.''

I sat there listening, rapt with attention.

''Some simply open a vein and let themselves bleed to death. Others walk deliberately into a fire like this one and burn to ash.''

I studied her for a long time. The way the fire danced on her face and in her eyes. ''I was one of the Chosen,'' I said. ''You sensed it in me and transformed me.''

''I had no choice. You were dying.''

''You had a choice. You could have let me die.''

She averted her eyes, shrugged as if my words were of little consequence.

''I think you planned to transform me all along, Sarafina. I think that's why you came back to the family, singled me out.''

She looked at me again, pierced me with her eyes. ''Perhaps I wished for that, Dante, but I would not have done it without careful consideration. This life is not an easy one. I know it must seem so to you at this point, but it's not.''

''You think this life seems easy to me? I lost everyone I loved, 'fina. My own mother, my family, my very way of life. Everything I knew was torn from me that night. It's been far from easy. Yet I have not gone mad, or ended my own life.''

''It will become harder.''

I mulled that over for a moment. How certain she sounded. Was she so unhappy, then? I began to realize how very lonely she must have been all those years before I had crossed over to join her in darkness. ''Most mortals cannot bear the shock of the change. The loss of all they were. Even those who do adjust and accept do not all last. A hundred years, perhaps two, and then the reality of eternal life begins to reveal itself to them as it really is. As much curse as blessing. As much pain as pleasure. And they, too, often choose not to continue.''

''And what of those who do?''

She was silent for a long moment. ''Those who do continue, I suppose, find a way to make peace with what they are. They stop fighting it. They stop hoping for a cure to make them mortal again. They stop looking for rhyme or reason to explain their existence or justify it. And they simply accept.''

''Have you reached that point?'' I asked her.

Meeting my eyes, she shook her head. ''No. But I've seen that acceptance in the eyes of some of the old ones. I've heard them speak of it. And I am determined to survive, on my own terms and in my own way, until I find it for myself.''

And she would, I thought. But for now, she was restless. Seeking something, maybe this peace she spoke of, maybe something else. I couldn't know.

''Then what do you do, 'fina?'' I asked. ''For... companionship?''

''We have each other for that.''

''That's not the kind I meant.'' I had to look away, still not comfortable with the lustier aspects of what I was, still not understanding it, as this was very early in my preternatural life. I couldn't face her as I spoke. ''When I feed from the humans...especially the women, though sometimes with the men, as well...I feel...''

''Desire,'' she said, finishing the sentence for me. ''I see now what it is you need to know. How to sate it.''

Eyes fixed on the fire, I nodded.

"Do not be embarrassed, Dante. We are sensual creatures. It is our nature. Every physical sensation is heightened to degrees far too intense for mere mortals to bear. We feel everything a thousand times more keenly than we did before. Pain, yes. To the point where it can paralyze us. But pleasure, too. God, the way we experience physical release is beyond comprehension."

My throat went dry, and I felt a stirring of desire at her description.

"The blood lust and sexual lust are very closely bound in our kind," she went on. "You cannot experience one without the other. Should you attempt to have sex with a mortal, you'll end up biting deeply into her flesh before you've finished, drinking her into you. The two go hand in hand. The ecstasy of the drinking enhances the orgasm, and the orgasm enhances the ecstasy of the blood. The combination of the two is such potent, mind-numbing pleasure that you give yourself over completely to sensation. You hurt them. You kill them."

I studied her through narrowed eyes. "I don't think I believe it."

"No?"

"No. Certainly I sense that some of what you're saying is true, but not that physical pleasure could drive me beyond the ability to control myself. Certainly not that."

"Perhaps," she said slowly, drawing out the word. "It's less likely you'd kill one of the Chosen, though still a risk. It's best to stick with other vampires, or make for yourself a few slaves."

"Slaves." I said the word with contempt. She always kept several at her disposal. Mortals, not of the Chosen caste, whom she had made virtual zombies, utterly devoted to her. She drained them, but not to the point of death. Then replenished their bodies with a modicum of her own cursed blood. She did this over and over, keeping them captive for days at a time, until the bond was forged. One night she would rise to find them utterly hers. Ready to obey her every command, their very existence based on their desire to please her. I did not know how she managed to mate with these mindless drones without killing them. I think she usually did end up killing them in the end, but how she kept them alive in the meantime, I do not know.

I hated them. I hated the sight of them. And I had no desire to know the details of what she did with them.

But for me, I knew my own soul. And I knew that I could never become so drunk on pleasure that I would kill an innocent. "I don't believe you," I told her. "I think you only want to keep me from being close to anyone other than you."

She lifted her brows. "Do you now?"

"Yes. Perhaps you don't have the inner strength to control your lusts, to have sex without murdering your partner. But I do."

"Well. That's very good to know."

I was not to know it then, but my dear benefactor had a plan in mind to teach me, once and for all, the truth. It was weeks later. We were staying in a fine home, guests of some wealthy old man who was utterly smitten with Sarafina. I disliked mixing with the mortals this way. Living among them, making excuses for the hours I kept. This did not bother Sarafina. She didn't mind living with them. She kept herself hidden away behind a patina of lies. No part of her, body or soul, ever touched them. Not on any level beyond that of predator and prey. She was playing make believe as their friend, their guest. She felt nothing for them. Nothing. And I was fairly certain she had been hunting peasants in the nearby village. Three people had gone missing since our arrival.

I did not like to think that my aunt was murdering the innocent. However, it was her choice. Not mine. We did not sit in judgement of the acts of another vampire unless they directly endangered us as a whole. So long as she was careful to dispose of the bodies and didn't kill too many in one town and draw suspicion on herself, I had no business telling her it was wrong, much less trying to stop her. She would have to deal with her own guilt, or karma, or sin, or whatever were the results of her actions. It was not my place. This was one rule among our kind, and the first my aunt had taught me.

It was as I contemplated these things in my rooms one night that a gentle tap sounded on my door. I didn't bother opening my mind to gather impressions, a mistake I made often, I fear, in my early days. I simply assumed it was 'fina and called, "Enter."

The door opened, and the serving maid I remembered from the late dinners where 'fina and I pretended to eat with our host and various guests, night after tiresome night, stepped inside. She wore very little. A nightgown of fabric so sheer that every inch of her warm mortal flesh was visible, and she carried a candle. Her hair, masses of it, honey blond and wildly curling, was loose and tumbling. Her lips wet and parted. Her body full and lush.

Forcing my gaze to her face, her eyes, I said, "What is it you want of me?"

"You've got it wrong, m'lord. I've come to ask that very question of you." Her accent was of the lower classes, though not quite Cockney. She'd trained herself to lose the harshest edges of her natural speech, I guessed. Imitating instead the more pleasing tones of her employers.

"I'm afraid I don't know what you mean."

She stepped farther inside, setting her candlestick on the bureau, closing the large door behind her and then eyeing me calmly. "I see the way you look at me, m'lord. At my breasts when I lean close to pour yer tea. And at my arse when I bend to pour anyone else's. I got tired of waitin' for you to ask, thought I might be bold and make the offer."

It was true enough. The wench wore necklines scooped so low I had wondered more than once how she kept those delightfully plump tits contained. They swelled above the fabric of her dresses, and she made sure to wave them under my nose as often as possible. I'd been tempted. I'd been intrigued.

"Surely yer not shy, now, are you, m'lord?"

"No. I'm not shy."

"You'll find I'm not, either." And she proved it, while walking across the room toward me, tugging at a tie at her neckline and shucking even the thin garment she'd been wearing. It floated to the floor, and she stood proudly naked, not a foot from where I still sat in a chair near the fireplace.

I could smell every scent of her. She was clean, freshly bathed, just for me, I thought. Her hair smelled of henna, her skin of aloe. And I smelled her arousal, too, and knew she was damp with the juices of it. And I'd yet to even touch her.

I licked my lips in anticipation. God knew it had been years since I'd known a woman in the way she wanted me to know her. I'd devoured many, yes, drinking from them in small, restrained draughts that left me craving more and left them quivering with desire. I went to them by night, commanded them to remember me as a dream.

Sarafina had told me I could do no more without killing them. I didn't believe her. Surely I could… touch….

The wench dropped to her knees, stroked her hand over my groin and felt my aroused state. She smiled up at me, then tore my breeches open and bent to lick at my root. I shuddered in pleasure, desire blazing through me at the first touch of her tongue, but then she took me into her mouth, warm and wet, took me deep. Her arms twisted around behind me to hold me to her, and she bounced up and down on my cock, sucking with all her might. Even as the semen rose in my rod, so the blood lust rose in my veins. I felt it, like a dark hunger, growing stronger with the pleasure she gave, until I could hear the blood rushing beneath her skin. I could smell it. I had to have it.

Gripping a handful of her hair, I pulled her head from me, pulling her onto her feet and forward, so she straddled me. I grabbed her hips and slammed her down, stabbing deeply into her, so deeply she cried out—in pain or pleasure or some mingling of the two, I do not know. I didn't care. Again she began bouncing up and down on me. I'd had her throat in mind, her sweet jugular, but the swollen mounds of those succulent tits bouncing in my face changed my mind.

I reached out and caught one like a prize, sucked hard on the nipple and then bit down. She shrieked in delight, and I pierced the very tip with an incisor and sucked hard at the thin trickle of blood that came.

It touched my tongue, and I was lost. Sensation, need, that powerful hunger that overwhelms all logic, burned through my brain as I sucked harder, bit deeper to increase the blood flow, ignoring her shrieks as I held her to me and took what I wanted, even then knowing it wasn't enough.

I got up, my cock still embedded in her, her legs anchored around me, her bleeding nipple tight in my teeth, and I walked to the bed, tumbled us both down onto it crossways, landing hard atop her. I let her breast go at last as I rammed myself into her so powerfully the heavy bed thumped and jerked, inching across the floor with my thrusts. She was crying out now, too loudly not to be heard in her passion. I silenced the wench with a hand to her mouth and sank my teeth into the other breast, biting deeper this time, plunging both fangs in to the hilt and drinking, sucking. I fucked her hard and sank my teeth into her delicious flesh over and over again, her shoulder, her arms and, finally, her throat. My razor-sharp teeth sank through her flesh as if it were butter, broke through the cartilage with a popping sound, and then the jugular gave up its bounty. I drove my shaft to the hilt as her heart pumped the blood into me in willing sacrifice. I devoured her and I climaxed, and it was magnified a thousand times from the climaxes I'd known as a mortal. A million times. My body nearly shook itself apart. I was momentarily blind. Deaf. My entire being was focused at the two places where we were joined—my cock inside her and my teeth in her throat. Between the two arced bolts of lightning. And that was all I was. Sheer mind-bending pleasure so intense it was agony. I cried out with it, releasing her throat, drawing my head back to roar in savage delight.

When the sensations finally waned, I still lay there on top of her, relishing the feel of her life thrumming in my veins and the satisfaction of sexual release. I was high, soaring on the aftermath of such intense gratification. I was warm, her blood pumping through me, empowering me.

Gradually I became aware of a slow, rhythmic clapping from somewhere in the room. Blinking out of the buzzing energy in my head, I lifted my eyes, focused them, and saw Sarafina standing on the far side of the room, applauding. "Well done, Dante. Very well done."

I looked down at the woman beneath me. Her eyes were wide open and glazing already. And her throat—God, I hadn't simply punctured it, I'd torn a wide, gaping wound. I'd ripped her flesh, severed the vein, torn through the muscle, baring her windpipe. I scrambled off her, backing away, but I saw it all. There were smaller wounds on her breasts, her arms, her shoulders, even her jaw. They'd bled, but only a little. I hadn't let much of that nectar escape my hungry mouth. Her center was torn, bloody from the force with which I'd pummeled her.

I brought a hand to my mouth in shock, but it came away with traces of scarlet adorning it. It was on my face, I knew. I'd buried my face in that wound, slavering to get more of her into me. And I must be wearing a lot of the evidence still.

It was on my hands, my chest.

Turning in shock to Sarafina, I whispered, "Why didn't you stop me? Why?"

"Stop you?" She shook her head. "I sent her to you, Dante. Some lessons are only learned by doing. Now you know what will happen if you spend your passion on a mortal. Save it. Slaves or other vampires are the only safe options if you're determined not to kill. Then again, perhaps you've changed your mind about that, now that you've seen how good it is."

"I don't kill."

"You do now. Like a wolf or a shark or any other predator, you've had a taste of it, Dante. You'll do it again. We're predators. It's what we do. But that argument is for later. Now we must leave this place before tonight's work is discovered. Wrap the slut in blankets and go wash yourself up. I'll gather our things."

"But—"

"But nothing. She already composed a note, informing the household that she has run away with a stable boy. I actually had her believing you would want to take her away with us once you'd sampled her luscious body." She tipped her head back, laughing delicately. "I vow, Dante, you did her nicely. I had no idea you were such a stallion."

"Shut up, 'fina." I saw where her eyes were and righted my breeches. "You're my aunt, for God's sake."

"God has nothing to do with it, boy. And I'm not only your aunt—your great-great aunt—I'm also your mother and your sire and your sister. The blood ties of the past mean nothing. We are a new kind of family now. And I could take what you gave to her and more without sustaining any damage at all."

I stared at her coldly. "The blood ties of the past still mean something to me, Sarafina. And I promise you, we will never be together in that way."

I saw the hurt and the anger in her eyes. Perhaps she had been undead for so long that the propriety of mortals meant nothing to her, perhaps she had even forgotten it. But I hadn't. I hurt her with those words. But I meant them. And while I hated what she had done to me that night, I knew that I had learned an important lesson.

Never to have physical relations with a mortal.

Morgan closed the book, blinking in shock. There had been exceptions. Something about slaves, which she didn't find the least appealing. Something about "the Chosen," which she understood even less. And other vampires.

Nothing about how one made other vampires. Nothing about anything helpful—except that she now knew why Dante refused to sleep with her.

And she thought it might be for the best. She certainly didn't want him to kill her.

She glanced down at her attire, licking her lips in trepidation. Quickly she jumped to her feet, returned the journal to the safe, closed and locked the door, and then closed the false bookcase over it. Then she ran out of the study, hurrying up the stairs to her bedroom, slamming the door behind her. She had to change. She didn't want to tempt him to do...to do *that* to her.

But the moment she closed her bedroom door, she heard him. Not aloud, but, in some strange, fascinating way, inside her mind.

Morgan.

She ignored the voice in her head and tugged open a bureau drawer.

Morgan!

The French doors flew open, blasted by a gust of wind. She spun around, gasping in shock. But he wasn't standing there on the balcony, as she had half expected. Trembling, she went to the doors to pull them closed, and that was when she saw him. He stood on the back lawn, halfway between the house and the sea. And she felt him looking right at her.

Come out here to me. Now.

Could she really be hearing him without a sound? She thought about calling down that she would be just a minute, but the final word came again.

Now.

It compelled her. She couldn't convince herself not to obey. Turning, Morgan walked out of her bedroom, down the stairs and through the house to the back door. She stepped out onto the flagstone patio and down three more steps, until her bare feet were sinking into the damp, cold grass. It sent a chill through her, and still she walked on. She walked until she stood facing him, an arm's length between his body and hers.

His gaze slid down her body. She felt it like a touch, shivered with cold and with awareness.

"Now we have time. All night, in fact. And you're going to tell me, Morgan, how you know about me."

She met his eyes and found herself incapable of coherent thought. There was nothing in her mind beyond submission. Obedience. It took an act of sheer will to break the hold of those eyes on hers, compelling her to tell him everything he wanted to know, but she did it. She looked away, past him at the sea.

Her mind whispered that if she told him about the journals, he would take them away. And, God, she couldn't lose her only link to him.

Or *were* they her only link to him?

"How did you do that?" she whispered.

His eyes closed for a moment as he sought patience. "Summon you here?" he asked, and when she nodded, he sighed. "I'm a vampire. An old one."

It wasn't an answer. "So you've learned mind control over the years?"

"To some extent, yes."

"Then you could summon anyone to come to you, make them come even if they didn't want to?" She was looking at the ground now, anywhere but into his eyes.

A finger hooked beneath her chin, tipped her head slowly up. "You wanted to."

A shiver worked through her body.

"It's more difficult to convince someone to do something they don't want to do. But I have the feeling, Morgan, that I could convince you to do just about anything I asked."

"I..." Her breathing quickened, and he noticed. She knew he noticed—she saw it in his eyes—and she almost thought he could hear her heartbeat speeding up, too. "I heard your voice in my mind. As clearly as if you were standing beside me, speaking to me."

He nodded.

"Does that happen with everyone, too?"

He broke eye contact this time but didn't look away as she had done. No, he just shifted his gaze to her lips. "I came here to ask questions, not answer them."

"I have questions, too," she said. "And I need answers as badly as you do."

He squared his shoulders. "Your conditions have changed, then?"

"I don't..."

"Last night you offered to tell me everything I wished to know if I would take you. Tonight you're ready to trade information instead of sex."

When he said the words "if I would take you," a shiver worked through her and heat pooled in her center. It brought vivid images to mind. *Take you.* It implied her submission, willing or otherwise. His mastery, his possession of her in any way he desired. She wanted it, and more. She craved it. She could see it so clearly in her mind. His hands holding her wrists, his mouth moving over her body, kissing and tasting and nipping, sampling her flesh and her blood while she whimpered in pain and pleasure.

"Stop it!"

His voice, harsh and sharp, brought her to attention. He had turned away, his hands pressed to his temples and his eyes closed.

"I can see your thoughts as clearly as you can, Morgan. And I warn you, my restraint is running low."

"I'm sorry."

He stood there for a moment longer, gathering himself, she thought. Finally he drew a breath, straightened his back and turned to face her again. "I beg of you, tell me what I need to know. The more time I spend near you, the more you place yourself at risk."

She quelled the fear in her belly. "At risk of what, Dante? Being killed? It's a small risk, I promise you that. I'm dying anyway. I'm not sure I'd have made it through the day if you hadn't..." She remembered vividly drinking from his neck and quickly slammed the door on the memory. "I need to know some things first."

"So you can use them in your next screenplay?"

She lowered her head. "When I wrote the script, I didn't know you were real. I thought I was mining the delusions of a crazy old man who was probably long dead."

Sighing, he turned and began walking toward the cliffs. She fell into step beside him, but his strides were long and powerful, and she had to take two steps for every one of his. "You have to believe me, Dante. I would never betray you. Not now."

"And why not?" he asked.

"Because I am in love with you."

They had reached the cliffs, and he stopped walking when she said the words, just stood there, facing the sea. "You don't know me. You don't know what I am. What I truly am. Your writer's mind has spun some sort of fantasy from the romanticized myths and legends you've heard and read. But you don't know the truth, and you need to get it fixed firmly in your mortal mind, Morgan. Vampires are predators. Killers. And mortals are their prey."

"Is that the way it was with Laura Sullivan? Was she your prey?"

He shot her a heated glance. "I was young. In love. I thought I could overcome my natural tendencies with her. She turned on me before I ever had the chance to find out." He lowered his head. "It was the second part of a vital lesson, Morgan. Mortals and vampires are mortal enemies. Do you believe for one moment that a mongoose could love a cobra? And even if it did, they would be doomed. One of them destined to destroy the other.''

She swallowed her fear. "What does it mean to be one of the Chosen?" she asked.

He turned his head to stare down at her. "Where did you hear that term?"

"The same place I learned all the other things I know about you. I know that certain humans are called the Chosen. I know that it's something to do with their blood, and that vampires sense them and feel protective of them."

He looked away. "Then you know as much as I do."

"Not quite."

"This is a waste of time. I'm leaving." He turned his back to her.

"Am I one of them, Dante? And does it mean I don't have to die?"

He went utterly still.

She moved closer to him, slid her hands up his back and curled them over his shoulders. "When you fed me from your body, Dante, I felt…alive. Every sense heightened, every nerve ending awake and feeling everything. But it didn't last. I want to feel that again. All the time. I want to be what you are."

"So now we come to the heart of the matter at last. You seek entry into the world of the undead. That is what these declarations of love and desire are truly about." He turned to face her. "You don't have a strong enough mind to bear it, Morgan. You'd be dead inside a year."

"That's a year more than I have now."

He shook his head. "I won't do it to you. I refuse to visit this madness on another."

"Then it is possible. I am one of the Chosen!"

He pushed a hand through his hair in frustration. "Yes. Dammit, yes. You carry the Belladonna Antigen in your blood. You're one of the Chosen. It's why you're wasting away so soon. Your caste do."

She nodded, processing the information and reviewing the tale she had read in her mind. He would be far less likely, his evil aunt had told him, to harm one of the Chosen. "How is it done?"

His eyes gleamed softly in the night. He was angry at her for forcing this and yet aroused at the prospect. His gaze danced over her throat. "I sink my teeth deep into your lily-white throat, Morgan, and I suck the very lifeblood from you. I gorge myself on you until you hover on the very brink of death. If I take a little too much, you die. You lie there, hovering between life and death, until I decide to feed you from me. If you have enough strength remaining in you to drink, then you do. You drink from my veins. You swallow my curse."

The wind blew in harder from the sea. "And that's all?"

"You sleep. You wake. You feed. And it's complete."

She nodded firmly. "All right then." She pushed her hair behind her head, held it bunched there in one hand and tipped her chin up toward him. "Do it."

He looked down at her, a feral gleam in his eyes. Tracing the back of his forefinger over her throat, he growled very softly, like an animal in the night.

"Yes, you want to. You know you do," she whispered.

His breath came harsh and raspy. But she felt him fighting her, fighting his hunger and his desire. And then she remembered what she'd read. How closely the hunger for blood and sexual desire were linked.

He turned his head away from her.

She tugged free the sash of her robe and let the wind part it for her, driving it from her shoulders, down her arms, and then tearing it away. She stood naked, arms outspread, the cold wind razing her.

Dante's gaze came back to her. Riveted to her breasts as they pebbled in the cold wind. She moved closer, slid her arms around his neck and, standing on tiptoe, pressed her mouth to his.

With a shuddering sigh, he kissed her. His mouth tasted hers, their tongues twined and mated, and he held her body nestled against his almost tenderly. His lips left hers to trail over her jaw, onto her neck, where they suckled and kissed, and then he lifted his head as if with great effort. "Please, don't make me hurt you. I couldn't bear it, don't you understand? And I will hurt you. I will."

"It will be different with me. I'm one of the Chosen. I love you, and I know. I won't let you hurt me, Dante."

"You couldn't stop me."

"I have nothing to lose, don't you see that?" She tipped her head back again, her hands pressing to the back of his until he shivered and let her push him lower. His lips brushed her flesh. He groaned softly. "Please, please, Dante, please…"

Growling, he opened his mouth and sank his teeth into her. She felt a stabbing pain and then only warm waves of increasing ecstasy as he nursed at her throat. He suckled her, drank from her, and her body vanished. All that remained was that place where his mouth possessed her throat and his teeth pressed into her flesh.

There was a sound. A hiss of air and a thud. Dante grunted in pain, and let her go, staggering backward. Morgan slumped to the ground, dazed, weak.

"I've got you now, you bloodthirsty bastard!" a voice shouted.

Morgan looked up and saw a rod embedded in Dante's shoulder, blood oozing from around the wound; then her gaze shot the other way, and she spotted the scarred man running toward them, a crossbow in his hand.

"Morgan…"

"I'm fine. Run, Dante. Go. Now!"

He did. Vanishing in a single burst of movement over the edge of the cliff. When he jumped, Morgan screamed from sheer instinct. And then the hunter was kneeling beside her, looking over the edge in search of his quarry. She looked, too, but Dante was nowhere to be found.

She pushed herself up onto her knees, swung a weak blow at the man. "Damn you! What the hell is wrong with you?"

The man looked at her. His gazed moved down her naked body in the darkness. Damn him, he looked as much as he wanted. Getting to her feet, weak and dizzy but determined not to show it, she looked around, and found her robe hanging from the gnarled branches of a geriatric apple tree. She walked unsteadily toward it, snatched it free and tugged it on.

"I just saved your life, you know!" the man shouted, hurrying after her.

"You shot my boyfriend and probably killed him," she snapped. "I'm calling the police."

"You're not calling anybody." He gripped her shoulder and spun her around. She clutched the robe tight around her, especially the wide part around the neck. "Not until you let me have a look at your throat, anyway."

"You had a look at everything back there," she replied. "Should have looked your fill while you had the chance, because you won't get another."

"He was drinking from you. You were letting him. Fucking bloodwhore!"

"You're insane." She started toward the house again, but her knees buckled and she had to stop, lean against a tree and breathe deeply.

"He's taken too much," the man said. "He'd have killed you if I hadn't come along."

"It's the shock of seeing my boyfriend shot with a crossbow and knocked off a cliff, you lunatic!" She was vaguely aware of a car pulling into the drive out front. She heard it clearly, saw the headlights. Heard a door slam.

He grabbed her arm again. "Tell me the truth, dammit."

"Let go of me! Help! Someone help!"

"Hey! What's going on out there?" a man's voice called. There were running feet, and then she saw forms in the darkness, coming around the side of the house. Three of them. It was too dark to make out faces at a distance. The newcomer in the lead said, "I'm a cop, mister, and you'd better let that lady go before I decide to put a bullet in your ass."

The scarred man released her arm, turned and ran into the night.

The new man muttered a cuss word and took off

in pursuit, while the other two, both women, rushed to either side of Morgan, asking if she were all right.

She kept her head down, clutched her robe tight, not wanting to reveal the telltale punctures on her neck to anyone. "I don't know who you all are, but I'm glad you came along when you did," she muttered.

"Just point us to the nearest door, hon," said one of them. "We'll get you inside."

She nodded, pointing to the back door, and she got her knees steady again. They helped her inside, through the back door into the kitchen, and she kept her head down, face averted, as she hurried through ahead of them. "Just wait here, will you? I just need a minute...."

She felt their eyes on her—curious, no doubt—as she hurried through the house, but they did respect her request. No one followed her. She paused at the study to lock the doors, and then she dragged herself upstairs to her room.

God, she was so weak. That bastard. His interruption might very well be the end of her. She shed the robe, dragged open a closet and located a silk pajama set. She pulled on the bottoms, slung the top on the bed and went to a dresser drawer, digging until she found a black turtleneck. She pulled it quickly over her head, then put on the pajama top and added slippers for good measure. When she stood in front of her full-length mirror, she saw a pale, frail woman. Curling her fingers around the neck of the shirt, she tugged it down, leaning closer to her reflection. The two punctures were there. Tiny, purple.

Swallowing hard, she eased the collar back into place against her skin, reached for a hairbrush and wondered who these new people were. She was going to have to go back downstairs and face them in a matter of minutes. How, when she could barely stand upright?

She would manage.

God, where was Dante? He'd vanished over the cliff but had never hit the water. She was certain she would have heard the splash if he had. What, then? God, was he all right?

Tears welling in her eyes, she tiptoed onto the balcony and looked out at the night sky. "God, Dante, are you all right? Tell me you're still alive. Tell me something, somehow. If you died because of me..."

Morgan.

His voice came clearly in her mind. And with it was a bolt of pain that was nearly blinding. She pressed her hands to her head, dropping to her knees.

I'll come to you again.

It was a promise, given with another blast of unbearable pain.

"Dante, where are you?" she said aloud. "Let me help you. Let me do something."

But there was no reply. Nothing. And she knew he wouldn't say more. Because when he sent his thoughts to her, he sent his agony, too. God, that they could be this connected—ah, but he had drunk deeply from her tonight. That might have something to do with it.

"I love you Dante," she whispered. "I swear I didn't know that man was coming. I swear it. And I'll kill him myself to protect you. I will." She had to prove it, though. She knew that. God, what he must be thinking! That she had planned this, set him up for that animal to shoot down.

Tears rolling down her cheeks, she backed inside but left the doors open so he could return to her if he were able. And then she turned, squared her shoulders and went to face the strangers downstairs.

18

Maxine paced Morgan De Silva's large kitchen, taking in every detail, from the tiny square marble tiles that lined the walls to the larger marble slab in the exact same pink and gray swirls that formed the surface of the island in the center. The oblong island had four flat burners and a sink on one end. The other end was bare, with stools arranged around it. Lydia occupied one of them, but Max couldn't sit. Not with Lou out there in the night, chasing after God knew who—or what.

"Did you see what I saw?" she asked. Really just to fill the silence. There was no doubt in her mind that Lydia had spotted it.

"What?" the older woman asked.

"On that white robe she was wearing? The collar?"

Lydia looked at her blankly, then shook her head.

"Blood, Lydia. Just a little, a drop or two. But it was there. And so was the way she clutched that collar around her neck."

"I assumed she was cold, or shaken. Maybe both."

Max shook her head firmly. "She was hiding something. Did you see how fast she hurried out of here?"

"She was upset, Maxine."

"Ten to one she comes back here wearing something that covers her neck.'' She paced toward the back door again, parted the curtain to peer out. ''God, I wish he'd get back here.'' Max sighed in frustration, gripped the knob. ''To hell with this. I'm going after him.'' As she jerked the door open, Lou came puffing tiredly up the steps.

Max managed to keep herself from flinging her arms around him, but she did give him a good look. No damage that showed. ''You catch him?''

''He's long gone. I didn't even get within sight of him.''

''Damn.''

Lou sank onto a stool, only to rise again when the woman they had inadvertently rescued reappeared in the kitchen. Max's gaze went straight to her neck, and when she saw the black turtleneck, she sent a smug look at Lydia. But Lydia wasn't looking back at her. She and Lou were both staring at the woman as if seeing a ghost.

Frowning, Max looked back at her. Then she blinked and stared. ''My God...''

''Who *are* you? What is this?'' the woman asked, gaping at Max.

Max knew the feeling, because the same questions were spinning in her mind.

''You two are almost identical!'' Lou said it as if he thought no one else had noticed.

No, they weren't, Max thought. Morgan De Silva was pale as a ghost, so thin she was bony, and her hair was long, endlessly long, and perfectly smooth, shiny. Maxine was no stick figure. Her hair was shorter and tended to curl if she let it grow at all. And she had color. At least enough to distinguish her from a corpse. But aside from those differences…this woman could have been her twin.

Max sank onto a stool, and that word, "twin," played and replayed in her mind. God, was it possible?

"You're Morgan De Silva," Lou said. It wasn't a question.

"Yes. But I don't understand what this is all about. Why…what…?"

"Ms. De Silva, please, this is as much a shock to us as it is to you," Lou said slowly. He was still standing. Morgan De Silva was, too, though it didn't look as if she would be much longer. Hell, Max had to wonder how those skinny legs carried anything at all, much less an entire human being. Even one as scrawny as her.

Right on cue, she wobbled. Lou took her arms in that way of his. Non-threatening, easy. "Come on, sit down," he said. She did.

He glanced at Max. She wasn't sure if he was nudging her to speak or checking to see if she was okay. Maybe a little of both. She looked back at him, not knowing what the hell to say.

Nodding almost imperceptibly, Lou took the lead. "I'm Lou Malone," he told Morgan De Silva. "I'm a cop from White Plains, New York. This is Maxine Stuart, and over there is Lydia Jordan. They're friends of mine."

Looking at Max unblinkingly, Morgan said, "Are you a cop, too?"

"P.I.," Max said.

Licking her lips, Morgan turned her gaze inward. "You were adopted?"

"Yeah. You?"

Morgan nodded. "Your birthday?"

"May 4th, nineteen—"

"Seventy-seven." Morgan lifted her head slowly.

Lydia was getting up, Max noticed with the part of her brain that was still capable of noticing anything beyond the woman sitting in front of her.

"Lydia?" Lou asked.

"This is private, Lou. They ought to be alone."

Nodding, Lou pressed a hand to Max's shoulder. "We'll take a walk by the water. Yell if you need us."

She nodded, not really even processing what he was saying. When the door closed, she was alone with a strangely pale, frail woman who could have been her twin. Who—maybe—*was* her twin. "This is really tough to wrap my mind around. I mean, I always knew I was adopted. But no one bothered to tell me I had a twin sister running around somewhere."

Morgan stared at her. "You mean this little surprise visit isn't the culmination of some kind of search?"

Hell, she sounded a little hostile. "No, it's not the culmination of anything. Until I saw your face, I had no idea."

"You hadn't seen my face before?"

"I've never even been to Maine before."

"I meant in the press. On TV."

The light dawned. "That's right. You must be kind of famous now, with the nomination and all."

"Kind of," she said. She seemed to be striving for some sort of authoritative posture, head up, spine straight, eyes focused. But Max could see the struggle, and it ruined the entire effect. "So if you didn't know about me, what are you doing here?"

"Jesus, does it matter?" Max got to her feet and

moved just a little closer. Lifting a hand, she touched Morgan's face with her fingertips. "We're sisters. I can't even believe this, it's…"

Morgan lowered her eyes. "We shared a womb for nine months. It's not that big a deal."

Max let her hand fall to her side again. "Is that all this means to you?"

"Our mother obviously didn't think it was all that important. Why the hell would she have given us up—much less split us up—if it meant anything to her? It's a biological coincidence."

"You're one cold bitch, aren't you?"

Morgan's eyes snapped to Maxine's. "Why don't you just tell me what you want from me so we can get to the point here."

"What I *want* from you?"

The pale woman lifted her brows and waited.

Max rolled her eyes. "Oh, I get it. You've got money. Success. You think that's why I'm here, that I'm after a cut."

"I was just nominated for a major award. I've had a lot of press. Are you telling me that has nothing to do with your sudden interest in me?"

"I told you, I didn't know you existed until I saw your face." Max said the words as firmly as she knew how without shouting them. "The reason I came here has nothing whatsoever to do with your money or your damned award nomination. God, who the hell raised you, anyway?"

"A pair of glittering Hollywood cocaine addicts, not that it's any of your business." She closed her eyes, and her head fell forward. She didn't try to fight it this time. Just let her long red locks hang in her eyes. "Once more, why are you here?"

"I'm here because my best friend is lying in a hospital bed with a bullet in her brain, in a coma from which she probably won't recover. And I want the son of a bitch who put her there."

Morgan blinked. It seemed to Max she had perhaps finally penetrated the shell around the woman's soul. "I'm sorry. But I still don't see what that has to do with me."

"It has to do with vampires, Morgan."

She flinched. Max saw it clearly. She tried to cover it, but it was too late. "That's ridiculous. Vampires don't exist."

"Oh, I'm not talking about the fictional ones. I'm talking about the real ones. You know. Like in your film."

"I've had a very difficult day," Morgan said softly. "I hate to be rude, but I'm going to have to ask you to leave."

The woman honestly didn't look well. "I'll leave right after I tell you a very short story. All right?"

Meeting Max's eyes only briefly, Morgan nodded. "So long as it's very short."

"So short it has no ending. Not yet, anyway. There was a compound in my hometown. Supposedly a government-run research center. It had been there for as long as I could remember, but five years ago it burned to the ground. I sneaked past the firefighters, hoping to finally get a clue what had really been going on there all those years."

Morgan interrupted with a short burst of air. "What made you think anything was going on there, besides research?"

"Armed guards. Surveillance cameras. Vehicles with government plates in and out all the time. Electrified fence. Dogs. You name it. I found two things when I got inside: an ID badge and a CD filled with information on vampires. Years worth of information. One of the vampires was called Dante, and the information about him recorded on the CD is very similar to the background of the Dante in your films.''

Morgan stared attentively at her now. She no longer looked as if she were suffering the tale just to be rid of the teller. She was rapt. ''And the ID badge?''

''It belonged to Frank W. Stiles, an agent of the Division of Paranormal Investigations, which I suspect is a secret division within the CIA.''

''Frank W. Stiles.'' Morgan whispered the name.

''The reason I found those things is because they were dropped by a badly burned man as he dragged himself out of the rubble. The next thing I knew, the place was surrounded by military. I managed to slip away, but what I didn't know was that the man had seen me. And the next day he let me know that if I breathed a word about having seen him, or about anything else I might have seen that night, he would kill my best friends and my mother. My adoptive mother.''

''Is this the same best friend you said was shot?''

''Yeah.''

''And you think it's connected? You said yourself this incident was five years ago.''

''There's more. Just recently there was a murder in our town. A woman who was very close to Lydia Jordan. It looked like the work of a vampire, and I realized I couldn't keep the information I had to myself any longer. Not if people were dying. So I told Lou what I knew, showed him the CD. The next thing

I know, my friend is found in Lou's apartment. She'd been shot in the head with Lou's gun. I know Lou didn't do it, but it was pretty clear someone was setting him up. I know it was Frank Stiles. I *know* it.''

"When did this happen?"

Max wondered why it mattered. "Last night between nine and ten p.m. Why?"

"And how long did it take you to drive here? You did drive, didn't you?"

"Yeah, we drove. About six hours, give or take."

Morgan nodded slowly, no longer in a big hurry to get rid of her newfound sister, it seemed. "So who is it you're after? The vampire who killed Lydia's friend or the scarred man who shot yours?"

Max blinked. "I didn't say he was scarred."

Morgan lowered her head, shaking it quickly. "You said he was badly burned. Same thing."

"No, it's not. Not really."

"I just assumed—"

"You've seen him. Hell, of course you have. He probably made the same connection I did when he saw the film."

"You're putting words in my mouth. I never said—"

"All I want is the truth," Max said.

"I don't *know* the truth!" Morgan's knees seemed to give, and she clutched the countertop to hold herself upright.

"You look really ill, Morgan. Have you been sick?"

"It's a...condition. A certain blood antigen. Belladonna. Although, if we're twins, I would have expected you to have it, too."

"Plain old A-positive."

"Is that even possible?"

"I don't know," Max said. "I suppose we'd have to ask a doctor or...something." She lowered her head, then raised it again. "Who was that, attacking you out there tonight? Was it Dante?"

Morgan shook her head slowly, pacing away from Max, her gait unsteady, feet almost dragging. "It was the scarred man—Stiles. Like you, he thinks Dante is real and that I can lead the way to him. But you're both wrong. There is no Dante. And even if there were—"

Her legs dissolved, and as she slumped toward the floor, Max grabbed her and held on, eased her down rather than letting her fall.

"You knew, didn't you, Lou?"

He looked at Lydia's face as they walked along the cliffs outside. Her hair had been pure honey gold once, but now a few strands of gray had appeared in its waves. Her face was sharper now, harsher, having lost the plump-cheeked look of youth. And yet she was still beautiful.

The grass fell away just beyond where they walked, vanishing into the face of a steep rocky cliff that plunged to the shore below. He liked the ocean up here. It smelled good. Salty and fresh, and the sea breeze wasn't as cold as he would have expected it to be. It seemed to roll in with the waves.

"I suspected," he admitted at length. "About Maxie, anyway. That's why I introduced you two. I honestly didn't expect her to take off with this vampire theory the way she has. It was just an excuse to put the two of you together and give you a chance to see what was obvious to me."

"And Morgan?" she asked.

"I had no clue whatsoever, Lydia. I swear."

She licked her lips. "You should have told me. About Max, I mean."

"I thought it was something you two ought to put together on your own." He put an arm around her shoulders. "I'm sorry if I did it wrong, hon. You know I want the best for you."

"I know you do."

"You gonna tell them?"

She sighed. "I don't know. I need to think."

They both turned as Max's voice shouted for Lou from the house. Lydia gripped Lou's arm. "Could he have come back?"

"Come on," Lou said, taking her arm as they ran across the wide expanse of back lawn toward the house. "We haven't been out of sight of the house," he muttered. "He could have come in another door, I suppose, but—"

They reached the house, rushing inside to find Morgan unconscious on the floor and Max kneeling beside her, cradling her head and looking scared to death.

"Jesus, what happened?"

"She just collapsed!"

Lydia ran forward, knelt beside Max and touched Morgan's face. "She's so cold."

"I think she's sick," Max said. "Lou, can you get her into her bed? I'm gonna see if I can find a phone number for a doctor or something."

Nodding, Lou bent to scoop the woman up. She didn't weigh more than a minute. Then he carried her up the stairs and started hunting for the right bedroom.

Max sat by the strange woman's bed and stared at her. It was 2:00 a.m. Lou was long asleep in one of the guest rooms, Lydia in another. This place had a half-dozen spare bedrooms, all made up, that apparently got very little use. Thin films of dust in the spare bedrooms told Max that her odd little twin didn't have much company.

She had been unable to sleep a wink herself. So she'd come in here, and now she sat and watched the woman sleeping like the dead. The bed was a huge four-poster, with white lace coverlets over mounds of blankets and thick pillows all around her. Four people could sleep in that bed with room to spare.

This place was gorgeous. Huge and gorgeous. The adjoining bathroom was bigger than Max's bedroom. Hell, so was the walk-in closet. And the *clothes!*

She rubbed her arms against a chill. When she had come in here, the French doors with the creamy sheer curtains had been open, the chill autumn night breeze wafting in. Max had closed them. But it was still too damned cold in here.

But of course all those thoughts were just trying to distract her from the real reason she was here. Oh, she told herself a thousand lies. That she just wanted to try to get used to looking at a face so like her own. That she wanted to be nearby in case Morgan awoke, to explain why they were all still here, invading her home. That she was worried the obviously ill woman would take a turn for the worse before morning.

But none of those were the real reason.

She wanted to see underneath that turtleneck collar.

Licking her lips nervously, Max leaned forward. Morgan lay on her back, just as still as stone, her face startlingly white in the darkness, her hair spread on the pillows around her. Sleeping Beauty. Max reached closer with her hand, and it hovered just above Morgan's neck. Then she moved it closer, very slowly. Her fingertips touched the black fabric.

Careful, she told herself. *Don't touch her skin, or she'll wake. Careful...*

She pinched the edge of the stretchy fabric between her thumb and forefinger, and pulled very gently out and downward. She leaned closer over Morgan, trying to see behind the collar.

They were there. Just as she had thought they would be. Two tiny marks, deep maroon in color.

"Dante, nooo," Morgan moaned in her sleep.

Max jumped so suddenly she let the collar snap back against the other woman's neck as she jerked backward.

"Stay away!" Morgan rasped. Her head began to turn to one side and the other on the pillows. "No, Dante, don't come here." There were tears squeezing out from beneath her closed eyelids now.

Max couldn't help but feel a twist of pain in her gut. This was her sister. And she had been attacked by a vampire. Max didn't know why the hell Morgan insisted on denying it, but the evidence was there, from the marks on her neck to the words of her nightmares, begging the monster not to come back.

"No, no!"

Max leaned in again, clasping Morgan's shoulders this time. "Easy. It's all right. You're safe."

The woman stopped struggling. She went still, her breath rushing in and out a bit more slowly than before.

"It's all right," Max whispered.

Morgan blinked her eyes open. It seemed to take

her a moment to remember who Max was. That brief instant of shock was followed by one of dawning realization. "You're still here?" she asked softly.

"You passed out downstairs. Lou carried you up here."

She nodded, her eyes falling closed. "I'm fine. You can leave now."

"That's not what your friend David said."

Her eyes flew wide again. "D-David? You've spoken to—but how?"

"I was trying to find a phone number for your doctor or a family member or someone, and not having much luck, when the phone rang. It was a man named David Sumner, who seemed very worried about you. I explained what had happened—"

"There was no reason to do that," Morgan whispered.

"He'll be here in the morning. He asked me to stay until he could arrive. So I did."

"I don't need watching over."

"I know about Dante," Max said flatly.

Morgan's gaze shot to hers. "So do I. He's a fictional character in some films I wrote."

"I meant the real Dante. The one who left those marks on your neck."

Morgan's hand flew to the spot on her neck, but when she felt the collar there, she frowned. "There are no—"

"Save it, sister. I peeked."

Sighing with everything in her, Morgan said, "You don't understand."

"Why don't you explain it to me?"

Morgan sat up then, slowly. Max automatically leaned in to plump the pillows behind her, and when their eyes met that time, she felt a connection, the first one. "You don't have to deal with this alone anymore," she told Morgan. "You've got family here now. That means something to me, even if it doesn't to you. You're my sister. I'm not going to let anyone hurt you."

Leaning back on the pillows Max had arranged for her, Morgan lowered her eyes. "It means something to me, too." She said it as if with great reluctance. "I just...I was shocked. I didn't mean to be...cold."

"You'd had a rough evening."

"But it wasn't Dante. He wouldn't hurt me."

"No?" She tried not to show her jubilation that Morgan had finally admitted—or all but admitted—that Dante was real.

"No. It's the scarred man. He's the enemy. He's the one who attacked me. He had..." She had to pause there, battle down a sob. "He had a crossbow."

"That must have been terrifying."

"It was. God, I was so afraid. And I still don't know if he's..." She stopped there, bit her lip.

"You don't know if he's what? Coming back? You don't need to worry about that, Morgan. You've got a cop, a P.I., and a counselor for runaway teens in the house. Between us, we can handle just about anything that comes up. He's not going to get near you again."

Morgan looked at Max for a long moment, almost as if she intended to argue, but then she simply nodded. "You really aren't after anything from me, are you?"

"No. I'm really not." Max closed a hand around one of Morgan's thin, cool ones.

Morgan returned the squeeze.

"Rest now. You'll feel better in the morning."

Nodding, Morgan closed her eyes and sank into sleep.

19

It was late morning, and Max had fallen asleep in her chair when the creaking of the bedroom door made her jerk herself awake. She twisted toward the door, half expecting to have a fight on her hands. But it was neither a dark vampire nor the scarred Frank Stiles who walked quietly into the bedroom. It was Lou, and he was with a big, sandy-haired man who stared at Max as if he couldn't quite believe his eyes.

"Maxie, this is David Sumner," Lou said. He couldn't quite manage a whisper, but his voice came out softly all the same.

Nodding, Max got to her feet, and only then did she realize she was still holding Morgan's hand. She gently let it go, placing it on the bed and giving her newfound sister one last lingering look before she turned back to the men. "Let's talk downstairs, can we? She's sleeping so soundly, I hate to wake her."

Lou nodded and started to leave, but Sumner didn't. He moved closer, leaned over Morgan and looked at her, his eyes troubled. He touched her very gently, just laid his hand lightly on her face. She sighed deeply, but other than that didn't respond at all.

Lowering his head, the man nodded, turned and walked out of the bedroom. Max followed, closing the bedroom door behind her, and it was a good thing, because Sumner began asking questions almost immediately.

"What happened to her? Why does she look so pale? My God, her skin is as chilled as if she's been on ice overnight. And—"

"One question at a time, Mr. Sumner," Max cut in, holding a stop-sign palm toward him and pressing her other hand to her head. "I haven't even had my morning infusion of caffeine yet, and I didn't exactly get a lot of sleep last night."

Sumner offered an apologetic nod. "God. I can't get over the resemblance. Officer Malone—"

"Lou, it's Lou."

"—told me about you as soon as I got here, but I just—I can't get over it."

Max understood the reaction only too well. "I've been looking at Morgan all night, and I still can't get over it, either," she said. "I didn't know I had a sister at all, much less a twin."

"Neither did I," Sumner admitted.

They reached the kitchen, where Max smelled coffee brewing and made a beeline for it. She didn't see Lydia anywhere and wondered where she'd gone. The two men sat at the table, and she poured herself a coffee and joined them. "I'm sorry, I guess I'm still unclear on your relationship with Morgan, uh, David, is it?"

"Yes, David. I'm…well, an honorary uncle. I've known Morgan ever since she was a year old. If they'd been religious types, I suppose I would have been named Morgan's godfather, but that was never formalized. When they died…well, I was all she had."

"You also produced her vampire films," Lou observed, picking up a cooling, half-empty cup of coffee and sipping its contents.

"Yeah, well. I'll tell you, I didn't expect them to be as good as they were. When I saw that first script, I swear to God, I told her she should shop it around. Get a bidding war going among the real heavy hitters, you know? But she wouldn't do it. She wanted me to make her first film. So I cut her in for half the profits and did the best I could with it. She deserved more. But as it turned out, the films grabbed a following right out of the gate, and the momentum built to the success of this third one."

Lou nodded slowly. "So how was she, the last time you saw her?"

"Not like this." David glanced at the watch he wore. "I can't reach her doctor before ten. I'll call him then."

"Then she *has* been ill?" Lou asked.

David drew a deep breath. "Listen, Morgan's star is just starting to rise. I don't want this getting out."

"We're not looking for a story to sell to the scandal sheets, David," Max told him. "If we were, then the missing twin angle would be plenty. There's something not right here, and I—we only want to help her."

Lowering his head, David said, "I'm afraid there's not a lot that can be done for her. She, um...she has a rare condition. An antigen in her bloodstream that has medical science baffled. No one seems to know why, but individuals who have this antigen in common begin to weaken and fade in their mid to late twenties and rarely live beyond their early thirties."

"What...what are you saying?" Max whispered, meeting his eyes. "That she's..."

"I'm sorry. I know this must come as a shock." David sighed, lowered his head and pinched the bridge of his nose. "She's known about this since she was a teenager," he went on without looking up. "Hell, it's what made her so driven, and why she was so determined to get a screenplay produced right away, at such a young age. She knew she didn't have a lot of time."

Max sat there staring at him. Her eyes were burning. Her mind spinning. "That's…that's wrong, that's not—that can't be true."

"Max," Lou began.

"That's not it, Lou!" She shot a look at David Sumner. "You're telling me she's *dying?*"

"We didn't expect it to get this much worse this soon, but—"

"Oh, God," Lou muttered.

Max just sat there, getting angrier and angrier. Finally she pounded a fist on the table. "This doesn't make any sense whatsoever. Look, I don't know what else might be wrong with her, but the reason she's in the state she is right now is because she was attacked by a vampire last night."

David Sumner was silent, just looking at her, then Lou, then her again. "That's not very funny."

"I saw the marks on her throat. I looked while I was sitting up with her and she was asleep, and when she woke up I called her on it, and she admitted it to me." She was speaking too rapidly now, and she could see that she was scaring the shit out of Sumner. "Dante is real. She admitted it! Although she insists he's no threat to her."

Sumner got slowly to his feet, looking nervous.

"Maybe now that I'm here you two should move along. I'm really grateful for your help but—"

"Now he thinks we're crackpots, Maxie. Sheesh, you ever hear of being subtle?"

She shot Lou a look. "You brought the CD, didn't you?"

"I brought it."

"Well, show him. Just fucking show him."

Nodding, Lou got up as if his limbs ached. They probably did, from that chase the night before. He glanced at David Sumner. "Give me a half hour of your time, Sumner. If you still think we're a pair of lunatics when I finish, we'll leave. No fuss, no muss. Okay?"

Sumner licked his lips, looking from one of them to the other. "I...suppose so."

"Good. Is there a computer around this place?"

"In the study, but Morgan keeps it locked. She hates anyone going in there." The words made Maxine's antennae quiver. "I have a laptop in the car," the big man added.

"Then let's go get it." Lou glanced back at Max. "You better go take a nap, huh? You didn't sleep all night. The bed in your room was still made up this morning."

She nodded, her eyes heavy. "Maybe I'll do that," she said. "Where's Lydia, anyway?"

"Went out first thing. Into town for supplies, she said. She'll be back."

Max frowned and thought about going for a walk around the grounds—maybe the fresh air would wake her up. But her eyelids and muscles disagreed with that plan, so she sucked down her coffee as if it were lifeblood and refilled her cup again. She had no intention of taking a nap.

Morgan was weak, groggy, when she woke. And there was an empty, hollow feeling emanating, echoing, from somewhere deep in her center. A yearning...for Dante. It was beyond simple desire. It was beyond human love. It was an ache, a desperate, endless need. The soul-deep hunger of a woman on the brink of death by starvation.

Clenching her teeth against the emptiness, she got up, took note of the daylight still flooding in through the thin curtains on the French doors and silently cursed it. Even if Dante had survived—*God, please!*—he wouldn't be able to come to her. Not now. Not in daylight.

She dragged herself tiredly into the bathroom, wanting a fast shower, knowing she lacked the energy to take one. There was no hopping in, scrubbing down, rinsing off and hopping out. No, but she did manage to crank on the taps and peel off her clothes. She stood under the spray with her hands braced on the shower wall and her head hanging down. She couldn't get through the day like this. Jesus, she needed...

She knew what she needed. She needed Dante. She needed him inside her, his fire burning life through her veins. He had taken too much from her. Not to hurt her, God, she knew that. He was going to do what she asked. Make her what he was. Drain her and then refill her with his own life. Stiles's interruption had cost her dearly.

Something, some sense that was very much like

hearing a sharp noise but not quite, made her lift her head and listen. Was someone else in the house?

God, those strangers from last night? Were they still here?

She had to admit to a softness toward the woman who claimed to be her sister. But anyone who meant Dante harm was her enemy. She would protect him, no matter what. No matter who she had to fight.

Reaching for a towel, she stepped out of the shower, feeling cleaner but no stronger, and only a little more awake. She paused to look into the full-length mirror at her body, dropping the towel to the floor and wondering how Dante could want her as she was. Skinny. Weak. Pale. Lifting her chin, she looked at the place on her throat where he had pierced her. Her body tingled all over at the memory of the sensations that had rushed through her then. The ultimate possession. She had been completely his—and relishing it.

Then she narrowed her eyes, her fingers dancing over the skin of her neck. There were no marks. No punctures, as she knew there had been the night before. Moving closer, she looked again, frowning. Very faint marks, barely pink against the white of her skin, betrayed the place where his incisors had been embedded in her flesh. The holes and the bruising around them were gone. The marks that remained…even they seemed to be fading before her eyes.

"It was real," she whispered. "I know it was."

She pulled on a robe, a different one, scarlet satin, hoping to draw energy from the color. She brushed her hair, although the act was exhausting, and finally she crept down the stairs to face the intruders. She had to convince them that she was all right and get rid of them. Otherwise Dante would never be able to come to her again.

At the bottom of the wide curving staircase, Morgan paused, staring across the foyer to the open doors of her haven. Her study. The place she let no one invade. She thought of the floorboards beneath the rug, the hidden space below, where, for all she knew, Dante might have taken refuge last night. Her heart stuttered, and anger pushed it into a faster pace than before. She surged across the foyer, into the study.

Maxine stood there, looking beautiful and alive and healthy. She was staring at the drawings of Dante that lined the walls, not touching anything, not searching, just staring.

"These doors are kept locked for a reason," Morgan said, her voice low, her anger in check.

Max jerked in surprise, her eyes wide as they met Morgan's. "You're right, I'm sorry, I just...couldn't help myself." She came forward, a hand going to Morgan's arm. "You shouldn't be up. You're still so weak."

"I'm fine." She pulled her arm away, willed herself to stay angry, not to soften again toward the woman. "This is my private study," she said. "I don't let anyone in here."

"So I was told. That's why I had to come in." She shrugged. "Look, I know I invaded your privacy. I thought maybe I'd find something in here that might help me save your life."

Morgan couldn't hold Max's eyes then, because the sincerity she saw in them touched her, though she didn't want it to. "Nothing can do that. There's nothing."

"You have to have more time," Max said. "You have to, Morgan. I just found you."

Morgan turned her back and denied the bolt of pain those words sent through her. "I spent a lot of time wanting that to be true. It only leads to disappointment, Maxine. I don't want to want it again. I've accepted the facts." And she had, she thought. But not the facts as her sister knew them. Morgan knew that living a normal life was no longer an option. She had thought accepting death was her only choice, but now she had another option. A new life of endless night. It might be possible. If she could only last long enough to make it happen.

Max was silent for a long moment. When she spoke again, her voice was thick. "These drawings—they're stunning."

Morgan turned, managed to face her again now that Max was attempting a lighter subject. "Thank you. They're just what my imagination tells me my character looks like."

Max blinked. "Come on, Morgan, we're past that. You admitted last night that he was real. Don't you remember? When I saw the marks?"

Pasting an innocent expression on her face, Morgan lifted her chin, let her hair fall back and parted the collar of her robe. "What marks?"

Max frowned, moving closer and inspecting her neck. "But...but they were there. You covered them up." She reached out and dragged a forefinger across the place where the marks had been, but when she looked, Morgan knew, she saw no traces of makeup. "I don't understand."

"You don't need to."

"Morgan, if this vampire is...is feeding on you,

then whatever time you have left will be even less, don't you see that? David said the last time he saw you, you were—"

"David?" Morgan flinched. "David?"

"Don't you remember? I told you last night he was coming."

Morgan frowned, trying to sort out the confused muddle of her mind.

"He's here," Max said. "In that small parlor off the living room with Lou."

Morgan started out of the study, then turned to take Maxine's hand and tug her along. "How did you get into the study?" she asked.

Sheepishly, Max tugged a key from her jeans pocket. "It was on your nightstand. A lucky guess."

Taking the key, Morgan turned to close and lock the study doors. Clutching the key in her palm, she moved slowly across the parquet to the small parlor, wondering what was going on between Lou, the policeman, and her beloved David. When she walked in, the two men were huddled over David's familiar laptop, and they both looked up.

"David," she said, forcing a warm smile.

"Oh, baby." He surged to his feet and wrapped her in a warm bear hug. "Honey, how are you? You looked so bad when I arrived that I—"

"David, I need to talk to you. Alone." She turned to Maxine. "Please."

"Sure. We're not the Gestapo, Morgan. We only want what's best for you."

Lou got to his feet and left the room, joining Max in the living room. Morgan closed the door on them and turned to David, a man she knew would do anything for her. Anything. She met his eyes and said, "I want them out."

Max was stunned when a quiet, slightly guilty-looking David Sumner asked them to leave. Morgan had gone straight back to her bedroom, barely sparing her a glance on the way, and then David stood there in the large living room and told them they were going to have to leave.

Lou nodded just slightly. "I understand."

"I don't!" Max scowled at the man. "And you shouldn't, either, David. Not if you care about her. My God, I'm her sister. The sister she didn't even know she had. Her twin, for God's sake!"

"I know. I'm sorry, Maxine, it's just—it's what she wants."

"Do you really think that was her talking to you in there? It wasn't," Max insisted. "It was him. That vampire. He's got her under some kind of—"

"Max, come on." Lou cut her off gently. "I'm on your side, and even to me that sounds over the top."

"You think so?"

David touched her shoulder, so she switched from glaring at Lou to glaring at him. "I have to admit," David said, "the evidence you two have is...well, it's compelling. I'm not saying I believe it, but I can see where you might. But Morgan is extremely agitated and totally unlike herself."

"Gee, I wonder why," Max muttered.

"I just think, given her condition, it would be better if we humored her in this. At least until we can get to the bottom of what's going on here."

Max stopped frowning and slowly lifted her brows. "It sounds like you don't really want us to leave."

"Frankly, I don't." He pushed a hand through his hair and paced away from them before turning back. "I know phonies when I see them, and you people are the real deal. I know that. It's just that she's so damn sick, and so out of it right now. I don't know if I can handle whatever is happening to her on my own."

"And yet you're throwing us out."

"Out of the house, yes. But I'd like you to stay in town for a couple of days. Can you do that?" He held up a hand when Max would have replied. "I'll pay whatever you want for your time. And I'll put you up in town. There are some accommodations that are really quite pleasant."

Max felt a hint of relief. "I'll take you up on the room. But not on the—"

"She'll take you up on all of it," Lou cut in.

"She's my sister," Max said.

"She's rich. You're getting by, I'm retiring, and Lydia's scraping." Then he frowned. "Where the hell is Lydia, anyway?"

"She hasn't come back yet. We'll have to find her before we leave," Max said, a hint of worry gnawing at her belly. Then she turned her attention back to David. "You're going to have to watch her closely. Especially at night. We could come over, you know. Stake the place out, keep our distance."

Drawing a breath, David cast a nervous glance toward the stairs. "It seems wrong, spying on her. And yet...I'm worried." Sighing, he said, "I don't want to betray her. I'll watch her closely. Maybe even get her doctor to prescribe something when she sees him this afternoon. A sedative, something to help her sleep through the night."

Max wanted to argue. Lou stopped her. "We'll go. Just be sure you call us if you need to. And we can't stay up here indefinitely, either."

Max drew a breath, shaking her head. "I don't like this."

"I don't either, to be honest," David said. "Why don't you go on upstairs and say goodbye, Max?"

"If she wanted to say goodbye to me, she'd have said it down here." She looked from one man to the other, then sighed in exasperation. "I'll try."

David began telling Lou about the hotel where he sometimes stayed while in town, at times when he didn't want to interrupt Morgan at work, as Max headed for the curving staircase and started up it. It occurred to her that Morgan had everything. She was stunningly beautiful. Odd that the same face could look so different on two people. On Max, it was average. Passably pretty, no more. Morgan had reached the pinnacle of success in her career. Max still wasn't sure what her career was, although she thought the P.I. thing was her calling. Of course, she'd thought the same about Web design and Internet investigations. Both had gone stale for her. Morgan was wildly wealthy and had a dream house she could obviously afford to decorate exactly as she liked. Max was living in her mother's house and paying not a dime for the privilege. Morgan had a Mercedes sitting in the driveway, though it looked as if it rarely escaped from beneath its custom car cover. Max drove a VW Bug. An *original* VW Bug. Forest green. Got almost forty miles to the gallon. When it ran.

And yet Morgan was ill. And because of that, the rest of her wealth seemed like nothing at all.

Max tapped on the bedroom door only once. "Morgan, it's me. I'm coming in.'' She gave her a beat or two, then opened the door. Morgan was sitting in a chair near the French doors, staring out them.

Max walked across the room and stood beside her. "It's a beautiful view from here." And it was, a wide strip of verdant green grass, then a deep, midnight velvet band of sea, all dotted with whitecaps right now, and finally a robin's-egg blue sky with puffs of cloud floating past.

Morgan didn't speak.

Max said, "I'm leaving, Morgan. David said you wanted us out, so we're going. I only came up here to say goodbye."

Nothing. She didn't even look up at her.

"I guess you really don't give a shit, though, do you?" Max sighed, turned on her heel, headed for the door. "I don't know why I bothered trying."

"I'm sorry, Maxine."

She stopped halfway to the door. "Are you?" When Morgan said no more, Max turned slowly. "Why are you throwing us out, Morgan?"

Morgan met Max's eyes only fleetingly, touching, then dancing away before darting back again. She couldn't hold her gaze steadily. "Who raised you?" she asked at length.

Blinking, Max said, "John and Ellen Stuart. The most wonderful middle-class suburban couple in the world."

Morgan nodded very slowly. "And what was it like, growing up with them?"

"It was wonderful. I mean, it was a family. They loved me. The only bad time I can remember is when my dad died. That was the year I started college. It was his heart."

"And they were...involved? In your life?"

"Mom was on every committee at school, chaperoned field trips and sometimes school dances. Dad never missed a ball game or a school play." She almost smiled. "Yeah, they were involved. I always knew I was adopted. It was a non-issue. We loved each other."

"I loved my parents, too," Morgan said very slowly, choosing her words carefully and as if it were an effort. "But I'm still not sure why they adopted me. They didn't have time for me. It was almost as if I were an accessory they purchased to go with their image. I had nannies and tutors and instructors and a driver. And I had David. But my parents were uninvolved. Took trips without me. Tried to make up for it by showering me in money, expensive gifts, cars, clothes. I had my own credit card before I was fourteen."

"I'm sorry you had it so rough," Max said.

"Are you being sarcastic?"

"Surprisingly, no. I meant it. I feel sorry for you."

"I don't want your sympathy. I'm just trying to explain to you why it is that the word 'family' doesn't have the same connotations for me that it does for you."

"Maybe not. I would think someone who's never had a real family would need one even more. But I guess I'm wrong."

"The timing is bad," Morgan said. "I'm dying. There's really no point in us...starting anything now."

"Now is the only time we may have."

Closing her eyes, Morgan lowered her head.

"Maybe…I have some things I need to work through. And I need to work through them alone."

"Well, you better work fast, Morgan, because if you think I'm going to stay away, you're wrong. I'll leave. For now. But I'm not going far, and I *will* be back. And I'll keep coming back, no matter how many times you try to throw me out. Understand?"

Morgan's head came up slowly, a frown between her brows. "No."

"No? You've never had anyone stick by you like that before, have you?"

"Only David. And he only did because he felt sorry for me. I didn't have anyone else."

"Maybe he stuck by you because he honestly gives a damn," Max said. "Kinda like me." She looked at her sister for a long moment; then, with a sigh, she turned and left the room.

Lydia watched her two companions drive away. The troubled Morgan was still sitting in her bedroom window, staring pensively out at the sea. David Sumner emerged from the house onto the patio in back, took a seat on a lawn chair and lit up a cigarette.

Squaring her shoulders, Lydia turned from her vantage point near the shore and began the long walk across the rear lawn toward where Sumner was sitting.

He looked up, spotted her coming, gave a welcoming wave as he got to his feet.

"You must be Lydia," he called.

She nodded, kept walking.

"I'm David."

"I know."

"Maxine and Lou have gone to a hotel in town,"

he said, a little less loudly now, as she drew closer. "I promised I would bring you along if you returned."

She nodded, kept walking.

"They thought you had gone into the village. I think they were hoping to run into you and..."

He let his voice trail off as she got still closer, until finally she stopped, a couple of feet between them. His eyes narrowed, brows drawing together.

"Hello, David. It's been a long time."

"My God. Oh my God."

20

Morgan lay on the table in a paper gown, with goose bumps rising on her arms and legs. Why the hell did doctors' offices have to be so cold? A tube ran into her arm from an IV bag on a pole. Clear fluid filled the bag. The doc had injected some kind of supercharged vitamin shot into the tube, as well. Not that any of that would help. She knew what she needed, and it was not in that IV.

Dr. Hilman came back inside, looking serious. David was sitting in a chair nearby. He'd stepped out during the exam but returned immediately after, and Morgan didn't have the heart to toss him out. She loved David, and she knew he loved her. She had a niggling feeling he was up to something though. She knew she shouldn't. She had never had any reason to mistrust David. He was the only person in her life she *did* trust, in fact. Besides Dante. Yet she had seen David today, alone with the blond woman. Lydia, that was her name. They'd been alone together, talking, and the atmosphere between them, around them, had seemed charged with some sort of intense energy. Morgan didn't know why. She had heard the car leave after Maxine's emotional goodbye. She'd expected to come down and find David alone.

Instead she'd found him deep in conversation with

Lydia, and they had both gone silent when they had seen her.

It still bothered Morgan. What could he have been talking about with the stranger?

David got to his feet at the doctor's reappearance. "Well?"

Dr. Hilman was over fifty but looked thirty-nine. Nice hair of nondescript brown, with a few gray strands but no sign of balding. He was in excellent shape. Must make most of his patients feel decidedly unworthy.

He drew a breath, sighed, smiled with his nice even teeth. "Frankly, Morgan, I'd like to get you admitted."

It took a second for her brain to translate. Then she blinked. "To the hospital?"

"Just so we can keep an eye on you. Your blood count is low, you're anemic, and you just don't look good."

"Can't you give me a blood transfusion and send me home?"

He exchanged glances with David. "If we could find a donor. You know you have a rare blood type."

"Yeah. I know." She lifted her head. "I have a sister, you know. A twin. But she doesn't have the Belladonna Antigen. How is that possible?"

He frowned at her. "Identical or fraternal?"

"I don't know. We look alike."

"Lots of fraternal twins look alike. You're sure she doesn't have the antigen?"

"She's healthy. Robust even."

He lowered his head, shook it slowly. "We don't understand Belladonna, Morgan. It doesn't behave the way other antigens do."

She nodded, having figured as much. "Look, Doctor, you're not going to be able to do anything for me in a hospital bed except make me sicker than I already am. I want to go home. I want to be in my house. I *need* to be there."

Narrowing his eyes, he leaned over her, removed the IV tube from her arm and applied a bandage as he asked, "Why?"

"I love it there. If I'm going to die, that's where I want to be, and if I'm not, then I want to spend the time I have left there."

"Really, Morgan," David said. "If it's only one night—"

"It's my life. I want to go home." She got to her feet. "You can't force me to stay in a hospital. I'm an adult. I'm going." Reaching for the counter where her clothes were folded, she took them. "You two can get out of here or watch me get dressed."

"All right, all right." The doctor turned for the door even as Morgan was pulling on her jeans. He stepped out, David close behind him.

She managed to wait until the door fell closed before she gripped the counter and held on. Dizziness, weakness. Damn, she'd gotten up too fast.

It passed slowly, fading until she could focus on the dull thrum of male voices outside the door. Buttoning her jeans, she leaned closer to listen.

"…something to help her sleep?" David was asking.

"I'll give you something to take home."

"I'll give it to her before bed."

The hell he would. She couldn't sleep. Not at night. Night was what she had been waiting and waiting for. She had to see Dante. She had to. She had to show him, to prove to him, that none of this was her, that she hadn't betrayed him. She edged closer to the door, leaned against it to listen.

"Tell me the truth, Doctor. How much time do you think she has?"

"You know I can't be sure of something like that."

"But you have an idea. I can see in your eyes that you have some idea. So what is it, Doctor? Come on. Months?" There was a pause. *"Weeks?"*

Still the doctor said nothing.

"My God, days?" David asked softly.

"Maybe. I'm sorry, David. I know how much you love her."

"There has to be something we can do."

"We could find a suitable blood donor," the doctor said. "That would give her a little more time."

"Then that's what we have to do."

"You realize...we'd only be buying time. In the end..."

"I realize it. I just don't accept it. I can't."

The pain in David's voice stabbed at Morgan's heart.

The doctor sighed. "I'll do everything I can to extend the time she has, David. I promise you."

Max tried to speak in the voice she always used as she continued narrating her most recent adventures into the telephone handset. "It was the damnedest thing, Stormy. Like she wanted me there, but at the same time, she couldn't wait to get rid of me. I'll tell you right now, hon, you're much more sisterlike than she is." She paused. "Anyway, Lou and I went to the hotel that Sumner recommended. Turns out he had called ahead. Guess he has clout, too, because you oughtta see this freaking place. We have a suite with two bedrooms, a sitting room and a little kitchenette. And the view—man, you've never seen a view like this, Storm. Great big windows looking out over the ocean. Waves and foam and rocky shore. Boats and gulls. Wait, you can hear them.'' She cranked open the window of the suite and held the phone out toward the screeching seagulls. Sea air rushed in, that fresh saltwater and fish tang, and an autumn nip.

"Did you hear them?" she asked, knowing there would be no answer. "You and I have to come back here when you're better. Stay in the same spot, you know? Of course, it's nothing in comparison to that house of my sister's, but it's nice. Hey, and when we come back, you can meet Morgan. You won't believe how much she looks like me. Only thinner and way prettier. Richer, too, but lonely. She's not happy. I don't know if she ever has been.''

And she was sick, Max added silently. Sick, maybe dying. Just like Stormy. For a moment she felt a weight settle onto her shoulders, a crushing, heavy, pressing weight. It made it hard to breathe.

"Anyway," she said, her voice thicker now, speaking, an effort, "Lydia finally showed up here an hour after we did. Guess she went out walking and lost track of the time. She said David Sumner gave her a ride. He was going out anyway, taking Morgan to, uh, some sort of appointment.''

She was being very careful not to say anything negative, anything frightening. Not only for Stormy's sake, but because she knew Storm's mom was probably hearing a lot of the conversation as she held the phone near her daughter's ear. She didn't want to upset the woman. And she certainly couldn't mention any part of the real reason why she was here in Maine.

"I love you, Storm. I want you to wake up. You know? So you can talk back, give me advice, tease me about Lou. It isn't fair, me doing all the talking. You'd damn well better wake up by the time I get home. Okay? Just wake up. Wake up, Stormy...."

She had to stop there. The tears were spilling over, and her throat contracted too tightly. She tried to get hold of herself, gulped in a couple of breaths.

"Easy, Maxie. Easy." Big, callused hands on her shoulders, heavy but gentle.

She glanced behind her at Lou; she hadn't even heard him come in. So much for the damn screeching gulls. He gave her a little boxer's massage. He did that a lot. It was the most physical contact she ever managed to get out of him, and she took advantage of it, because it helped. She leaned back a little, his chest behind her, solid, warm. She could almost feel herself drawing a little of his solidness and warmth into her body to battle the weakness and the chill. How could she bear to lose her sister and her best friend all at once?

"Maxine?"

She started, surprised to hear a voice on the line. For just an instant she thought—but no, it was Stormy's mother. "Hi, Jane. How is she? Is there any change?"

There was a long pause. Then, "She's no worse."

But no better, Max inferred. "Do you think she's hearing me?"

"I know she is, Maxine."

"Really? Was there any sign while I was talking to her?"

"I don't need any signs. I'm her mother. I know. You mean the world to her, and I know she's hearing everything you say."

Max nodded, sniffed, rubbed her cheek with the back of one hand. "I won't be here much longer. A day or two at the most."

"You do what you need to. I...I heard what you told Tempest—about finding your sister. That's the hand of God, young lady, that led you up there. Don't you doubt it. And don't take it for granted."

"I'm not."

Jane sighed. "We play the tapes you made for her, your voice reading to her. And the music you sent over, we play that, too."

"It's Tuesday, you know," Max said. "Her favorite show's on tonight."

"I know. There's a TV in the room. I won't forget. Goodbye, dear. Call again when you can."

"I will." Max lowered the phone slowly to the cradle, missed it somehow. Lou took it from her and put it in place.

"How's she doing?" he asked.

"No change." She turned slowly, slid her arms around his waist, let her head rest on his chest. He hugged her, rocked her back and forth a little.

"It's only been a day."

"Every day it's less likely she'll ever come out of it." She spoke against the fabric of his shirt but trusted that he heard and understood. "I'm losing two sisters at once, Lou. I'm not sure I can take this."

"You're tough, Max. Toughest kid I know. And I'm here for you, you know that, right?"

She nodded.

"Lydia's got a nice hot bath all run for you, and a

cup of that herbal tea she picked up when she was out exploring today. I want you to go soak and drink that tea, and then I want you to take a nap.''

She lifted her head, felt her eyes burning and wondered just how hellish she looked right now. ''When it gets dark—''

''We're going back to Morgan's place to stake it out,'' he said. ''Even though she and David both told us not to.''

Max nodded. ''You think you know me pretty well, don't you?''

''Am I right?''

''Yeah.''

''So that's why you need to rest a while now. You're all in.'' He ran a palm from the top of her head down over her hair, until it cupped her cheek. ''I don't like seeing you like this, Maxie. I don't like it at all.''

She smiled tiredly. ''That's 'cause you're nuts about me, just too dense to know it.'' She leaned up and kissed him on the mouth, softly, briefly. Then she turned away and headed into the bathroom.

Lou sighed as he walked back into the sitting area of the suite and sank into a plush chair. Lydia was sipping tea, tapping one foot, nervous.

''She needs you, you know,'' he said.

Lydia shot him a worried look. ''I'm right here.''

''She's hurting bad. She doesn't deserve that. She's a good girl.''

''I know she is.''

He stared hard into her eyes. ''You've got to tell her.''

"And what good do you suppose it would do her to learn that her mother was a whore? Hmm?"

"Come on, Lydia, that's not even close to what you are."

"It's what I was."

"You were a kid. Alone and clueless. Now you're a freaking hero."

She rolled her eyes.

"You think you're not? You got out of the slime alive. Barely. So what do you do? Get as far from it as you can, the way most people would? No. No, you lie on the goddamn ground and reach back down into the thick of it to pull kids out. One after the other, you haul their asses out of the muck, hose 'em off, tuck 'em away someplace safe. A place you *made* safe for them. Then you turn around and go back for more. You get dirty, you get splashed with that shit all the time. Doesn't bother you. You keep on going."

She faced him, and he saw that her eyes were damp. "That's the way Kimbra used to talk about our work. Like it was something noble. Some kind of divine calling."

"It is."

She lowered her eyes.

"You do all that for those kids. Those kids you don't know. Now you have a chance to do something for your own. Your own kids, Lydia."

"They're hardly kids, Lou." She set her teacup down on the coffee table.

He shrugged. "They need their mother. Max feels like she's losing everyone she cares about. And Morgan—God, that girl has no one, other than Sumner. You don't connect with her now, you may never get the chance."

She averted her eyes, maybe to hide a rush of wetness, he thought. "She wouldn't even embrace her twin sister. What makes you think she'd give a damn about *me?*"

"You won't know unless you try, Lyd."

"They've managed without me this long...."

"And they're both falling apart."

She bit her lip. He felt sorry for pushing her so hard and decided to back off. "At least I've maybe given you something to think about."

"You have."

"Okay. We'll drop it. You better get some rest. Maxie's gonna want to sit up all night watching her sister's place, and I know damn well you won't stay behind."

"No more than you would," she said.

"Of course not." He got to his feet and headed for the coffeepot in the tiny alcove at the far end of the room.

"She loves you, you know."

Lydia's words stopped him in his tracks. He thought maybe his heart might have ground to a halt, too, but no, that was wrong. It was pounding hard enough to pump hot blood into his face. He said, "She thinks she does. But that'll only last until some young buck her own age comes along and sweeps her off her feet. Till then, I pretend not to see it."

"For her own good?"

"And mine."

"Because you'll both get hurt in the end?" she asked.

He didn't answer, but he did find it in him to get moving toward the coffeepot again. Found a cup, filled it.

"You know, sometimes I think that if only I could have seen into the future, if only I could have known that loving Kimbra would lead me to this horrible, gut-wrenching grief of losing her, maybe I would have turned away from her the day we met. Maybe I wouldn't have taken that risk."

He nodded slowly, as if fully understanding.

"And then I realize," she went on, "that that would have been the biggest mistake of my life. God, when I think of the joy I would have missed. The days we had...the nights." She sniffed. "No. I'd suffer anything in exchange for the love we shared. Anything. I'd never trade it in. Not even if it meant my pain would vanish without a trace."

Lou sipped his coffee and pretended with everything in him that her pointed message was sailing right over his head. It wasn't, of course. But he could pretend.

21

"But it's not even dark outside yet."

"I know," David said softly. "But, Morgan, you're exhausted." His tone, his eyes, everything, so concerned. Full of love and worry. And yet he was keeping something from her. She knew he was. And it was more than just the fact that he was trying to drug her so she would sleep the night through.

She would be damned before she would let him.

"Come on, sweetie. Drink the tea and then go on up to bed. You need your rest."

She eyed the teacup. Laced, no doubt, with the tranquilizers Dr. Hilman had given him today. God, if he only knew that her life depended on seeing Dante again, on convincing him to do whatever it took to make her immortal....

She lifted the tea to her lips, pretending to sip. Lowered the cup again and then took the napkin from the coffee table and dabbed the poisoned moisture from her lips. "I'll do as you say, David, if you'll tell me what it was you and that blond woman were discussing when I walked in on you this morning."

He glanced at her sharply. "I already told you. I was just telling her where to find her friends. Offering to drive her into town to join them."

"It looked like a bit more than that."

He shrugged carelessly, but didn't hold her probing

eyes. "It wasn't easy trying to explain why you would throw your own sister out of your home, Morgan. If it seemed intense, it was because I was struggling to find a way to justify your behavior."

It was intended as a barb, and it hit home. It stung a little to have the one person who had never hurt her suddenly jabbing her that way.

He reached over, took her hand and held it gently. "I don't mean to hurt you, love. It's just so unlike you to be this unfriendly."

"It's unlike you to turn against me," she whispered.

"Oh, Morgan, no. Not against you. Never, ever against you."

"Then what were you and that woman conspiring about? You went dead silent when I walked in. You were discussing something you didn't want me to hear."

He ran his hand through her hair. "Only because I don't want anything upsetting you, as sick as you are right now. I didn't want her demanding explanations of you, and I didn't want you trying to offer them. That's all."

Tears were brimming in her eyes, and she blinked them away, telling herself that it didn't matter that her most beloved, most trusted friend was lying to her. She didn't need him. She only needed Dante.

"Drink your tea, darling. Come on."

He lifted the cup, held it out to her.

Taking the delicate china cup from his large hand, she nodded slowly. "I think I'll take your advice and go up to my room. I'll take it with me, sip it in bed."

"That's a good idea."

He helped her to her feet, and she carried the cup

with her to the stairs, started up them. "I seem to have become an awfully light sleeper," she said as he walked beside her, one hand cradling her elbow. "Must be all this time living alone. I've become used to silence, I guess."

"I'll be quiet as a mouse, love. You need your rest." He stopped, opened her bedroom door for her. She offered him a meek and obedient smile, kissed him on the cheek and went inside.

"Good night, Morgan," David said, and he pulled the bedroom door closed.

She walked across the bedroom to the French doors, opened them up and stepped outside. Then she tipped the little teacup upside down, pouring its contents toward the ground below. The stiff sea wind scattered the tea into a thousand droplets before it ever hit the earth.

Sighing, Morgan walked back inside, glanced at the neatly made bed, at her white satin robe hanging from the bedpost and the empty teacup in her hand. She would have to make it convincing. David wasn't a fool.

She set the teacup on the bedside stand. Then she tugged the covers back, rumpled them up a little. When she rearranged them, she put pillows underneath, working them around, plumping and flattening, over and over, before tucking the covers around them. Then she stepped back toward the bedroom door to look from the same point of view David would have when he checked on her, as she knew he would.

Good. It looked good. Just as if she were lying in the bed, burrowed beneath the covers with her back to the door.

She stripped off her jeans, her sweater, dropping

them on the floor in plain sight. Even her tennis shoes and white ankle socks. She pulled on the robe. Then, finally, as a last touch, she closed the French doors again and lowered the shades beneath the sheer curtains. She closed all her other bedroom shades, as well, blanketing the room in shadows. Now it would be even more difficult for anyone to tell she wasn't really in the bed, at least without turning on the lights, and she didn't think David would risk waking her to do that.

Finally she tiptoed to the closet, pulled a warm blanket-like shawl of soft black felt from its hanger and draped it over her shoulders. She slid her feet into a pair of tiny slippers, like ballet shoes, only velvet. Then she walked quietly to the bedroom door.

She had to pause there, because her breathing was out of control. Too fast and too loud to go unnoticed. Just the simple acts of the past five minutes and she was out of breath. It was getting worse. By the hour, it was getting worse.

She waited for her breathing to calm, her pulse to slow. Then, finally, she opened the bedroom door, just a crack, and peered out into the hall. It was empty. Silently, she crept out, closing the door slowly behind her. Then, step by carefully placed step, she moved toward the stairs. The living room loomed below her, empty. She started down the stairs, one hand gripping the railing in case she stumbled. So many stairs. God. Where the hell was he? Where was David?

She listened but didn't hear him. Looked but didn't see him.

Finally she reached the bottom, and that was when she heard footsteps above her. Snapping her head up, she saw David coming along the hall toward the top of the stairs, and she quickly got off them, ducked around them at the bottom and ran silently from the living room to the study.

Quickly she took her key from the pocket of her robe and let herself in, closing the doors behind her. Then she paused, leaning back against the doors to catch her breath.

It took time for her heartbeat to slow. Time for her breathing to become closer to normal again. When it did, she opened the safe and removed three of Dante's journals and the CD that contained the only copy of the new screenplay. The one she had been working on for months.

She closed her eyes, drew a steadying breath. She was doing the right thing. She had read the tale, in Dante's own words, of how a woman's love and betrayal had nearly cost him his life and that of his dear friend. She had to prove to him that she wasn't going to do the same thing. This gesture…this would show him.

She sealed the safe closed again, then listened at the doors and, hearing nothing, slipped out, relocking them quickly and moving into the dining room, into the kitchen. At the back door, the alarm panel stood at the ready, its red light blinking. David had armed the damned thing!

Breathlessly, she tried to remember the code, but her mind was whirling with other things. David was coming through the house now. Coming this way! Dammit, when had she told him the alarm codes? Hell, how hard was it for him to guess, even if she hadn't told him? Her birthday.

Right. Her birthday.

She quickly punched in the numbers. The green

light flashed on. David was coming through the dining room now, toward the kitchen. His steps got nearer and nearer. She yanked open the kitchen door and darted through it, hugging the books to her chest with one arm. Then she pulled the door closed quickly, but as quietly as possible. She raced toward the large willow tree, mentally counting as she ran. The alarm would reactivate itself in thirty seconds. Morgan hoped to God David wouldn't notice the green light before it turned red again. Reaching the tree, she ducked behind it and kept counting. When she reached thirty, she waited, staring back at the door, expecting it to burst open and David to come outside to see what was going on. But he didn't.

He hadn't even seen her.

Sighing her relief, she turned away from the house and walked down toward the shore and the spot where she had last seen Dante. Then she sat there, shivering and pulling her shawl more closely around her. Waiting. Waiting for him to come. What if he didn't?

The scene from the night before kept replaying in her mind. The way he'd jerked in pain, the blood oozing from around the bolt in his arm, and then him falling. Just plummeting.

How could he have survived?

But he wasn't human. He wasn't alive, really. Biting her lip, she looked down over the side. And there she saw what she hadn't seen before, in the darkness. A ledge. He must have landed on the ledge.

Frowning, she looked around, chose a spot and clambered over the side, lowering herself onto the wide stone ledge, like a natural balcony overlooking the sea. It wasn't easy to cling to the journals, the CD tucked into the pages of the top one, while making her way down. Thank goodness she hadn't tried to bring more of them.

She landed on the ledge. Here, she thought. He must have landed here. She ran her palms along the stone, as if she could still feel him. But she couldn't. Were the tiny stains she saw his blood? They could just as easily be droplets of salt water or rain or dew.

"Where did you go, Dante?" She looked to the left and right but saw nothing. Below, only sea and rock. He couldn't have gone into the sea, could he?

Sighing, wondering if she could manage to climb back up, she stopped and stared into the tangle of vines and the opening beyond them. "A cave," she whispered.

Parting the vines with one arm, she crept inside, into pitch, utter darkness and the constant chill of the deep earth. She drew her shawl closer, straining her eyes to see ahead of her. Stretching out her free arm, she moved it back and forth in front of her as she walked forward in slow, abbreviated steps. She expected cobwebs. There were none. Just smooth, cold stone beneath her slippered feet. She kept expecting to reach an ending of some kind. A drop-off, perhaps, and her feet slid cautiously. But the floor didn't fall away.

Her mind kept telling her to turn back. But everything else, her instinct, her heart and this mindless yearning for Dante, made turning back impossible. She was compelled to move forward. There was nothing to be afraid of, she told herself over and over as the darkness swallowed her. What was the worst that could happen? She could die? She was dying anyway.

She stopped swinging her hand and instead dragged it along the wall, until the wall curved away from her, and she stopped, startled. Okay, okay. She took her time, trying to get oriented, feeling her way. The walls hadn't vanished, just widened. She was in a larger area now. She patted the wall following it around until her hand felt a spot that was different. Steel rather than stone. Her fingers scrambled outward to its edges, and she realized she had found a door. She located the handle, an iron ring, and tugged, then pushed and tugged and pushed again until the thing moved, just a little. God, this wasn't going to be easy. Especially given how weak she felt today. Still, she set her precious books aside, summoned what little strength she could find and continued working at the heavy door until finally she managed to drag it open just enough.

Then she paused and leaned back against a bumpy stone wall, panting, breathless. And slowly, as she tried to will her heartbeat to slow, she felt something. Some...awareness. Some sense beyond the normal five—not a smell, not a sound—told her that she was close to him. Dante. He was here, somewhere. She wanted to sniff, but not that exactly. She lifted her head, searching with her mind, scanning the air for that sense of him, finding it, stronger now, thrumming in the very center of her forehead.

"Dante..." she whispered, her heart catching in her chest. That hollow yearning clawed at her belly. She pushed off the wall, bent to feel around until she found her books and hugged them to her, then squeezed herself into the space made by the slightly opened door and through it. "Dante, are you here?"

No reply. Pitch darkness, and yet her voice didn't echo as it should. She moved around, again, using her hand to gauge the shape and size of the room. Flat walls, not curved. And it smelled different. Her thigh bumped something that rocked, and her hand shot to it to steady it.

A small table.

And the item on it...a lantern. Then there should be...

Yes, she patted the table and found the matches. She must be in the room beneath the study, she thought, her heart tripping into a gallop all over again. Was this where he had come?

She set her books on the table, then fumbled in the darkness, lit a match and put its flame to the lantern's wick. When the light shone from the globe, she lifted the lamp and turned.

The coffin was there. Closed. Empty?

Swallowing hard, she looked down, and then she went still. Something dark red had been poured out on the floor. A lot of it, a puddle of it near the door, and then a ribbon that unwound, and another puddle beside the coffin. Oh, God, he had lost so much blood!

Carrying her lamp in a trembling hand, she moved closer, stepping around the drying pools, and for an instant she managed to tear her gaze away from the dull, dusty box and the life blood on the floor, to look around for a hook or... There was an ancient nail sticking out of one of the beams above her head. It was cocked up at an angle, as if it had been put there for this very purpose. She slid the lantern's wire handle over the nail and let it hang there. Then, nervously, licking her lips, she turned back to the coffin.

Was it dark outside yet? It hadn't been when she had found this place. But it had been a while now. Maybe an hour as she had slowly traversed the cave.

Only the length of her back lawn, but that was seventy yards, at least, every step of which had very likely been painted in Dante's blood. In complete darkness Morgan had inched the length of it. And then there was the time she had spent wrestling with the door. Which should have been locked. If Dante had been all right, he would have locked the damned door.

Her hands curled over the wood of the coffin's lid. She closed her eyes slowly, drew a breath for courage, prayed she wouldn't find a lifeless shell inside, and then she lifted the lid upward.

Its hinges, rusted with age and disuse, creaked and groaned.

Dante lay inside, perfectly still, utterly white. His face, so lifeless and yet so real. Pale. "Dante…" She touched his face, then drew her fingertips away quickly at the cool chill of his flesh. Was he dead? Had he bled to death from that hunter's arrow in his arm?

Tears blurring her vision, she tore her gaze from his precious face and looked at the rest of his body. He wore the black silk he seemed to prefer in shirts, and she saw that the left sleeve was torn away, his left arm bare except for the band of black silk that was knotted around it high on his bicep, almost to the shoulder.

Had he stopped the bleeding with his makeshift bandage? Would the faded lining of the casket reveal bloodstains if she inspected it?

Her eyes slid to his face again. "Oh, Dante, please be all right. You have to be all right. I need you." She whispered the words as she cupped his face in her hands and pressed her mouth to his cold, still lips.

Her own tears flavored the kiss. And he did not respond at all.

The words she had read in one of his journals and used in her first film came flooding back to her mind now. There were only a few ways a vampire could die, but bleeding to death was one of them. His wound—that would have healed by now, with the day sleep. Unless he had died before it had the chance.

She moved to his arm, tugging at the knotted silk until she got it loose, and then she unwrapped it from around his arm. There was no wound. Dried blood, yes, but no gaping hole in his flesh. It had healed. The books had told the truth about that.

Then they must also be correct about the fact that the blood he had lost could be replaced only one way. He had to take it from someone else.

"From me," she whispered. "Yes. From me." Leaning close to his face again, she stroked his hair. "I know you won't let me die, Dante. I know you'll do the right thing—and make me what you are—before you'll let me fade and die. I know you will. I trust you." Bending, she kissed his forehead. Then she straightened again and ran her hands over his jeans, checking the pockets, knowing he carried some sort of blade. She had seen him use it.

She found it, slid her hand into his front pocket to retrieve it, and as her hand slid intimately close to him, she realized that he was erect. It surprised her. And she knew instinctively that it wasn't the normal sleeping state for vampires. No. It was her. She was near, touching him, kissing him, and somehow, even in this state of near dormancy, he sensed it. And he wanted her.

Morgan dragged her hand over the front of his

jeans, caressing the hardness there as she brought the blade toward her. Opening her palm, she saw what looked like a small onyx-handled jackknife. But the blade she unfolded wasn't a knife blade. It was long and slender and looked like a Phillips head screwdriver, except that the X-shapes that crossed at its pointed tip were razor sharp.

She stared down at the device, and a little shiver went through her. If she jabbed herself in the wrong place and he didn't revive as she hoped he would, she might risk bleeding to death herself, she thought. She needed to be careful. Not the wrist. Not the throat.

Drawing a breath, she closed her eyes and tightened her fist around the odd little blade. Then, with one swift movement, she drove it into the palm of her other hand. Pain stabbed through her, and she cried out. The device clattered to the floor as Morgan gritted her teeth, opened her eyes and slowly opened her hand. Blood pooled into her palm. She looked past it at Dante. His nostrils quivered, and his hands were beginning to move sporadically.

"It's all right, my love. It's all right now." Fisting her hand to keep the blood from spilling, she moved it to his mouth. A droplet, then two, escaped her fist and touched his lips.

His tongue darted out to catch them. And then his hands sprang up like a trap, one closing on her forearm, the other pushing her palm to his open, questing mouth. Before she knew what was happening, he was fastened to her there, sucking at the tiny hole she had made, swallowing her.

The sensations coursed through her as they had before. Every part of her came alive, and some new kind of lust burned in her veins. She felt his teeth, his tongue swirling over her palm, lapping up every drop.

And then suddenly his eyes were open. Wide open, but unseeing. They glowed with a feral hunger, that predatory gleam she had seen before, as he took her hand from his mouth, held it away from him. He sat up suddenly, sprang from the casket, landing on his feet, still holding her hand at the wrist. His breath came fast, and each time he exhaled, there was a growl from deep within him. He jerked her body against his and ground his hips into her, his mouth trailing over her neck, sucking the skin between his teeth, nipping, drawing blood and moving on. The pain was sweet torture, and she arched against him. With one hand she managed to tug loose the sash of her white satin robe, and he pushed it off her shoulders as he nibbled a path over them.

"Take what you need from me, Dante."

One more low, deep growl, and then he pushed her with his body until she hit the concrete wall. He gripped her thighs in his hands, lifted them around his waist, and he drove into her. He was as cold, and hard as the stone at her back, and he filled her, rammed deeper and sank his teeth into her again and again. The bolts of pleasure and pain rocking through her mingled until she couldn't tell one from the other, and she screamed as she climaxed, her entire body shuddering with the unbearable force of her release, and still he kept pumping into her and sucking the life from her veins.

She clung to him, and she whispered that she loved him, that she would die for him, then feared that perhaps she was about to prove it.

* * *

Lou and Maxine sat in the car, a few yards down the road from Morgan's mansion. It was a good spot. They had a clear view of the back lawn all the way to the cliffs, and the front and one side of the house, as well. Max didn't think anyone would be coming or going without her and Lou seeing them. She had a Diet Dr. Pepper, and he had a mug of coffee. The sky was purple out over the water, darkening up higher, the water mirroring its progression.

"What time is it?" she asked.

"Quarter past dusk."

"Very funny." She looked toward the front door of the house, saw it open and that Sumner fellow fill the doorway. He spoke to Lydia for a second, then stepped aside and let her pass. "She's in."

"You thought she'd have a problem?"

Max shrugged. "Sumner said for us to stay away and give Morgan some space. I didn't expect him to welcome Lydia with open arms."

Lou shrugged. "She's a beautiful woman."

"Yeah, but she's not into men."

"More's the pity," Lou muttered.

Max punched him, maybe a little harder than if she'd just been playing.

"I meant for Sumner's sake, Max. Sheesh." He rubbed his shoulder. She had no doubt it really hurt.

"Ten to one she'll be back out here in five minutes," she said, smoothly changing the subject.

"I'll take that bet."

She scowled at him. "So what is it with you two, anyway?"

"Who? Lydia and me?"

She nodded. "Did you and she ever...?"

"She's not into men."

"Was once," Max said.

"How do you know that?"

"She told me she had a kid with some guy." Lou looked surprised as hell. "What, you didn't know?"

"Sure I knew. I just didn't realize she'd told you." She shrugged.

"What else did she tell you?"

"Nothing." She looked at him, and it was pretty damn clear in his eyes that there was something else. "Jesus, Lou, tell me it wasn't you."

"What?" He blinked twice, then gave his head a broad shake. "No. I didn't have anything to do with those babies."

Max tipped her head sideways. "Babies? There were more than one?"

He licked his lips. "This isn't our business, Max. You wanna know about Lydia's past, you ask Lydia."

"Fine. Don't get so damned defensive, will you? I just wanted to know if you'd boinked her or not."

He sent her a look of barely restrained impatience. "Not."

"Not that it's any of my business."

"You got that right."

"It's not like *we're* boinking on a steady basis."

"Or at all."

"Well, the night's young, Lou. Don't rule anything out."

Lou tipped his head back, thumped it against the headrest repeatedly and stared at the ceiling of the car. Max averted her face a little so he wouldn't see her grin. God, she loved teasing the man. She knew he reacted to it with a stirring of arousal. It wouldn't bother him so much if he didn't.

And she was going to tease the hell out of him

tonight. This was too good an opportunity to pass up. Stuck on a stakeout with him like this. Alone, all night, in the car. Just the two of them. What would he do, she wondered, if she were to reach over there and lay her hand on his lap? Probably leap out of the car and run for the hills. She looked down at her hand where it rested on the seat in between them. Neat, short, unpainted nails. She wished for a moment that they were long and sharp and painted like her sister's. Men liked that, didn't they? She inched her hand a little closer to his leg.

"Who the hell is that?" Lou asked, his head coming level, eyes sharp.

She resisted swearing out loud and followed his gaze. Then a tingling alarm raced up her spine as she saw the dark figure moving toward the house. He passed by the lamp post on the walkway, and it illuminated his face for a moment.

"It's Scarface!" Max said, squinting, staring harder.

"Is he the same man you saw the night of the fire?"

"I don't know. It was five years ago, remember?" she snapped. "He's ringing the bell. Come on, we'd better move."

She yanked open her door and got out. Lou got out on his side and hurried around the car to meet her in front of it. "Stay behind me, Max."

She didn't argue, but she would be damned before she would use him as a human shield. They reached the walkway just about the time the door opened.

Sumner said, "Who the hell are you?"

"The man who was attacking Morgan the night we arrived," Max called.

Both men swung their gazes around to face her and Lou. Lou had his gun in his hand. He didn't point it, just made sure they saw it. "I think it's time we had a talk, Mister...Stiles, isn't it?"

The scar-faced man nodded, his hands hovering about waist high, palms out. "Frank Stiles," he said. "And that's why I'm here. I want to talk." He looked at Sumner. "To all of you. I don't think you know what you're dealing with."

Sumner glanced at Lou. "What do you think?"

Lou walked up to the man. "Put your hands up, pal." The man raised his hands a little higher, and Lou handed his gun to Max, quickly patted Stiles down, then took the gun back again. "Sumner, you wanna hear what this guy has to say?"

"I think we probably should, don't you?"

Lou nodded reluctantly. "You try anything, I won't hesitate. You understand."

"I'm not here to hurt anyone," Stiles said softly. "I just want to help."

Sumner stepped aside. Stiles walked in, with Lou and Max right behind him. "Help?" Max asked. "Is that what you were doing to my sister when we arrived the other night? Helping her?"

"I was checking her to see if she'd been bitten."

Max lowered her gaze as they all trooped through the house into the small sitting room off the main living area. She imagined that was so Morgan wouldn't hear or see them if she happened to come down the stairs. "Where's Lydia?" Max asked as they all sat down.

"Upstairs, checking on Morgan." Sumner turned to Stiles. "If you have some explanation for attacking that girl, sir, I would suggest you give it now."

"I need to start at the beginning. If you'll just give me five minutes, I can make you understand—"

"Yeah?" Max asked. "You gonna make me understand why you put a bullet in my best friend's forehead, too, while you're at it?"

Stiles looked her dead in the eye. "I was there. It's true. I was at that apartment. But I did not hurt your friend. He did."

"He, who?"

"Dante. The killer I'm trying to track down."

"Vampires don't shoot people, Stiles."

"They do if they're trying to set someone up. Like me."

"So Dante framed you? Funny, the cops all seemed to think Lou did it. He was the one who ended up framed."

"Lou is a cop. They knew he hadn't done it almost immediately. I was the next obvious choice." Max rolled her eyes, but Stiles went on. "Listen to me. Please."

Throwing her hands in the air, Max sighed and paced away. "Fine. Fine, you have the floor." She sank into a chair. Sumner and Lou were already sitting, but Stiles remained standing.

"For twenty years I was an agent with the CIA's ultra-secret Division of Paranormal Investigations. Our headquarters was in White Plains. Our charge was the research and elimination of vampires."

Max nodded. She had already known all of this. Sumner seemed stunned as he glanced at Lou, then back at Stiles. "My God, you mean it's all true?"

"What I'm telling you is true. The vampires revolted, attacked the headquarters, burned it to the ground and killed most of the operatives. That was five years ago. It was a disaster. Our funding was pulled, the division completely shut down. Any surviving agents scattered, going undercover, as I did.''

''Why?'' Max asked.

''To avoid debriefing. We know a lot of things the government would rather not risk being made public.'' He eyed Max. ''That's why I threatened you that night. I couldn't afford for anyone to know I was alive.''

''And when I told someone, even though it was five years later, you knew somehow.''

He nodded. ''I still have a few connections in the Agency. One of them told me about Officer Malone's phone call.''

''So you went to Lou's place, lured my best friend there and shot her to teach me a lesson?''

''No! I went to his place to try to find out what he knew. That vampire was there, waiting in ambush. The girl was already unconscious. Before I could do anything, he shot her. Then he just gave me this evil smile and took off.'' He shook his head slowly and went on. ''I knew he'd come after Morgan next, that's why I drove all night to get to her. To warn her.''

''And why did Dante do all this?'' she asked.

''He knows what I've been doing,'' Stiles said. ''Searching for the surviving members of the DPI, putting them back together, re-forming our group as an independent entity. An elite unit of expert vampire hunters.'' He sighed, lowering his head. ''Dante wants to put me away. He figured if he made it look like I killed your friend, you and Lou would find a way to put me behind bars.''

Max leaned back in her chair, trying to digest all

he had said. "That doesn't explain what Dante was doing in Lou's apartment in the first place."

Shaking his head, he said, "Don't you get it? You and Lou were trying to find out who had killed that woman—Lydia Jordan's friend. It must have been Dante. He must have been afraid you were getting close and gone there to see what you had on him."

"It's a little farfetched," Max said, sighing, turning it over in her mind.

Lou said, "What I don't get is, why do you want to kill all the vampires?" Everyone looked a little surprised, but he shrugged and went on. "Hey, if they're anything like the way Morgan depicts them in the films, they aren't so bad."

"Morgan is under the control of a powerful vampire, Officer Malone," Stiles said. "Trust me, I know what they're capable of. He's got her completely mesmerized. She'll do anything he says, even turn against the people who love her in order to protect him."

"I don't understand that," Max said. "How is that possible?"

"Your sister has a certain blood antigen. It's called Belladonna," Stiles said. "And it's slowly killing her."

"How do you know about that?" Sumner demanded, getting to his feet.

"Whenever the antigen was identified in a mortal's blood, that information was forwarded to the DPI's files. There aren't many who have it. But those who do, attract vampires like honey attracts bees. They feed on them, suck the life out of them. That's why they all die young. It's not the antigen. It's the vampire it attracts. And unless we kill this one, he'll keep coming back, keep on feeding on your precious Morgan until she dies. But if we stop him, she'll live.''

Sumner averted his eyes, but Max saw the tears. "The doctor says it's the blood condition that's killing her.''

"But he doesn't know how or why. Everyone with the blood type dies young. I'm telling you what the doctors don't know, Sumner. It's because they become victims. Belladonna blood is the vampire's favorite kind.''

Max stared at him. "Are you telling me that she can get better? She can live?''

He nodded. "She can live. But we have to protect her from the vampire.''

Blinking, Max looked at Lou, silently asking him to tell her that he believed this man. God, she wanted it to be true.

But Lou shook his head almost imperceptibly. Before he could speak, though, Lydia came charging into the room, breathless, wide-eyed. "She's gone!'' she shouted. "Morgan is gone!''

22

Dante's body surged with pleasure but not vigor. It was an odd sensation. He was sated, yet still groggy, weak. Maybe he had only dreamed the pleasures of release, of possession....

He lifted his head, blinked his vision clear. And frowned, more disoriented than before. He was on the floor, his back braced against the cool stone wall. And the lantern was burning. He didn't remember lighting it. He didn't remember waking.

He wasn't wearing his shirt. His jeans were undone and halfway down his hips. He tasted blood on his lips.

And then he saw her, lying naked in a puddle of white satin.

"Morgan!" Dante surged to his feet, only to sink to his knees again at the wave of dizziness that drowned him. One hand pressed to his forehead, he forced himself upright and walked on his knees to her. She lay on her side, curled into a fetal position, hair covering her face. "Jesus, Morgan..." He caught her shoulders, rolled her onto her back. Her hair fell away from her face, and he stared down in horror at her white skin, her closed eyes, her parted, pale lips. He had to force himself to look at her throat, at her body. And when he did, tears welled in his eyes. *Tears*. He didn't remember the last time he had cried for anyone, much less a mortal. Her throat bore the marks of his invasion. And there were more. Tiny pairs of pinpricks on her breasts and shoulders. Her belly and thighs. It hadn't been a dream. He had ravaged her. Taken her in every way. Her body. Her blood.

"God, Morgan, what the hell have I done?" He returned his gaze to her face, cradling her upper body in his arms, bending over her. "Please wake up. Please, Morgan, live. I can't have done this. Not to you." He listened for her breath. He felt for her heartbeat. He scanned for her life force…and sensed it, still there. Weak, but there.

Her eyes opened to the merest slits, and her lips curled somehow into a shadow of a smile. "Oh, my love…"

"Hush. Don't try to speak. God, Morgan, I'm sorry. I'm…"

"I…brought something for you."

He shook his head, not understanding what she meant, but she shifted her eyes and his gaze followed; he saw the books on the wobbly table.

"Your journals."

"My journals…" He searched his memory. "I left instructions with an attorney. They were to be shipped to a storage unit for safe—oh, hell what does it matter now?"

"It matters," she whispered. Her jaw clenched; she swallowed, began again. "The script, too. On a disk, there with the books. The one I've been writing. Destroy it, Dante."

He stared at her, shaking his head.

"You have to know you can trust me. I brought them all to you—to prove myself."

"You're worried about whether *I* trust *you?* My God, Morgan, look what I've done to you."

"You did what I asked you to do," she whispered. Weakly, she lifted a hand, touched his face. "Tears? Why are you crying?"

His hands trembled in her hair as he bowed over her, holding her head to his belly, shuddering with barely contained anguish. "How can you ask that? God, Morgan, I'm so sorry." His voice broke, and he shuddered with emotion as he held her.

"Fix it," she breathed. And she spoke now as if each word was an effort. "Feed me. Make me immortal, like you are."

Tipping his head back, Dante closed his eyes, clenched his jaw.

"Dante...please. You won't let me die. I know you won't."

A hot tear rolled off his cheek and fell onto her face as he lowered his head to look at her. "I can't transform you, Morgan. Not now. I'm too weak. You wouldn't survive the ordeal, and if by some miracle you did, you'd be little more than a mindless zombie."

She expelled a long, wavering breath. "I don't understand...I thought—"

"Sharing the gift takes a vampire at his strongest. And even then it drains him, weakens him. Last night I nearly bled to death before the day sleep healed my wound."

"But you drank from me."

He lowered his head.

"It's because I'm so ill, isn't it? My blood has barely any life left in it. That's it, isn't it?"

He nodded without looking her in the eye. "I've

seen the effects of the gift gone bad before, Morgan. A vampire brought into this life with weak blood, or too little blood. Mindless shells with no reason, no thought, no personality, who exist only to feed. Monsters, truly monsters. I can't curse you to that kind of existence. I won't.'' Finally he met her eyes again. ''I'm sorry, sweet Morgan. I'm so sorry.''

''Well, you've done it again, haven't you, love?''

The voice was Sarafina's, and it came from near the entrance to his lair. Dante looked up at her. She wore red, full sweeping skirts of it, with a sheer black overskirt and enough jewelry to please a queen. '''Fina. Thank God.''

''Don't thank God for me, Dante. He has nothing to do with my existence.'' She narrowed her eyes on his face. ''Are those *tears* I see? My God, look at you. Reduced to weeping over a mortal.'' When she tossed her head, her earrings jangled.

''You have to help her,'' Dante said. He saw Sarafina's anger, felt it like a red hot cloud around her, but he had to try. ''She'll die unless you bring her over.''

She released a burst of air, waved a dismissive, ring-bedecked hand, and her bracelets rang. ''You want her so badly, bring her over yourself.''

''I can't. I'm too weak.''

''Oh, come now, Dante, you'd love her as an imbecile. She would obey your every whim. Be your slave forever, even better than a mortal one. They're so fragile, you know. She could hunt for you, serve you. Wouldn't you like that?''

He lifted his head. ''You're the one with the penchant for mindless drones, not me.''

''No, but you *do* seem to be the one more apt to

fuck a mortal to death. This makes what, now? Two?''

"She's not dead."

"Give her an hour."

"Why won't you help me?"

Sarafina lifted her brows. "Because you've turned your back on me, Dante. You've decided, quite obviously, that I am no longer enough of a companion for you. That you need to bring in someone new. To replace me."

"That's not how it is."

"No? It's how I see it. I'll tell you what, Dante. If you really want my help, let me finish the little bitch off for you. I would so enjoy devouring whatever small amount of blood you left in that pale, weak little body."

Anger heated his blood, and Dante gently lowered Morgan's head and rose to his feet. Standing straight, he faced Sarafina. "I'll kill you first."

She flinched. He saw it, a short flash in her eyes. A tightening of her lips. "And that proves what I've said, doesn't it? You'd kill me, your life mate, for her?"

"You are not my *mate*. Or my wife or my partner or even my lover, 'fina."

"I *made* you," she whispered.

"And therefore you own me?"

She stood so tense and so rigid that her entire body trembled. And then she said, "Damn you to hell for betraying me, Dante! Damn you with the rest of my kin. I need none of you!" Then she whirled in a swirl of skirts and a clatter of jewels, and fled through the door, a blur of speed and motion.

Morgan's soft but desperate sigh drew his attention

from Sarafina's pain—which he felt keenly. Logical or not, Sarafina was hurting. Now, though, he had no care for his dark mother's pain. Only for Morgan's.

"This is...all my fault," she whispered.

"Why did you do this, Morgan? Why?"

She shook her head. "You were so weak. I thought you might die."

"And it didn't even occur to you that you could die far more easily than I?" He knelt beside her, gathering her up into his arms, lifting her as he stood again. Then he shook his head. "No. No, you trusted that I wouldn't let that happen, didn't you?"

"This is my doing, not yours," she told him, leaning her head against his chest.

"I'm not going to let you die, Morgan."

She closed her eyes, but he saw her tears anyway, dampening and darkening her lashes from within. He carried her into the passage and along it, leaving the light far behind.

"The journals," she said suddenly. "You must bring them, Dante. And go to the house for the others."

"We can do that together, when you're well."

"They're in the safe, in the study. The year I found you—that's the combination. Nineteen ninety-seven."

"I'm not going to let you die, Morgan." He was weak, growing weaker by the second. But dammit, he could save her, save them both. He *would*.

"It's not your fault, Dante," she whispered.

He emerged from the cave and managed to hold her while climbing up the side of the cliff. Ordinarily he would have simply pushed off with his feet and jumped the distance. A small leap for one as powerful as he. But not tonight. Tonight he barely managed to clamber up the steep, stony path without dropping her, and when he reached the level ground, he was breathless, his muscles trembling with strain.

He started toward the house.

"Dante?" she whispered. "No! Don't take me back to them—I want to stay with you."

"You'll die without help, Morgan."

"Then I'll die in your arms. I'll breathe my last against your lips. Dante, don't make me go...."

He stopped walking and stared down at the woman who had risked her own life to preserve his. Who had trusted him completely and given selflessly. He had never believed anyone could love him the way this wraith-like creature must. His own family had turned against him. He'd lived his life trusting in no one. But he trusted her. And he realized, too late, damn him, that he'd known he could trust her before she had surrendered the journals or her work. Before she'd bled herself to the brink trying to save his worthless life. He loved her.

Leaning closer, cradling her head in his palm and lifting her face to his, he kissed her. Slowly, tenderly, he kissed her.

"Stay alive for me, Morgan. One night, so I can feed and grow strong again. One day, so the sleep can regenerate my power. Then I'll come for you. I swear I will. No army of mortals will keep me from you again."

He kissed her again, but this time her lips went slack against his, and when he lifted his head, hers hung limply and her eyes had fallen closed. He heard voices, saw her family and friends walking around the back lawn with flashlights, calling Morgan's name.

Lifting his chin, he called out to them. "Here. She is here."

"There he is!" someone shouted. "He's got Morgan!"

The gang of mortals came running toward him. Gently he laid Morgan down in the cool grass, bent to kiss her forehead and then, straightening, turned to flee. He had to live, to get strong again, so he could save her.

In three strides, the bolt penetrated his thigh. Pain beyond endurance shrieked through him as he tried to keep going. Weight on the leg intensified it even more, and he felt the blood pumping out of him. Three more steps. He went down hard, then tried to crawl, and finally, on his belly, he dragged himself toward the cliffs. Toward the edge. If he could pull himself over, maybe there was still a chance....

"Finally. You son of a bitch, I've finally got you." A hand clasped his shoulder and rolled him harshly onto his back.

The scarred man stared down at Dante. And then he smiled.

"Oh God, oh God, oh God..." Max knelt beside her sister. Morgan lay still on the ground, a white silk robe around her body, fresh puncture marks in her neck. No question now. "You see them, don't you? You see them, too, this time, don't you?"

Beside her, one arm around her shoulders, Lydia nodded. "I s-see them. I don't believe it, but I—I see them."

David said nothing; he was speechless, frightened to death.

Lou had his fingers on Morgan's wrist. He looked up, nodded once. "She's alive."

Max bent almost double, face contorting, sobs choking her, relief too powerful to contain. "Let's get her to the house."

Lou looked further along the lawn and frowned, getting to his feet. "Take her, David. I'll just be a sec."

Max followed his gaze to where Frank Stiles was leaning over the fallen form of the dark man who had done this to Morgan. Lou was striding over there, and Max got up, too. "Stay with her," she told Lydia, even as David gathered Morgan into his arms and started for the house. Then she ran to catch up to Lou.

Stiles said, "I've got you at last. You're not going to get away from me this time."

As Max looked beyond Stiles' vicious scowl to the man who lay on the ground, she caught her breath. He was exactly like the images Morgan had drawn— the ones that lined the walls of her study. "Dante, I take it?"

He nodded, but it was obvious he was in considerable pain. She looked him over, saw the blood gushing from around the metal bolt that pierced his thigh, and acted instinctively, dropping to her knees, tearing the denim fabric. "It must have hit an artery or something. My God, the bleeding…"

"His kind always bleed like that," Stiles spat. "Let him bleed out. He'll be dead in a few minutes."

"If I am," the fallen, dark man muttered through clenched teeth, "Morgan will be, as well."

"Don't you dare threaten my sister," Max whispered.

"I don't think it was a threat, Maxie," Lou said.

He dropped to one knee, clasped the bolt, glanced at Dante. Dante nodded once, and Lou pulled the arrow-like rod out in one smooth motion. As he did, Dante tipped his head back and howled in pain. Then Lou yanked his belt free of its loops, wrapped it around the thigh, above the wound, pulled it tight and watched as the bleeding slowed. He searched his pockets and emerged with a jackknife, then poked a hole in the leather so he could fasten the belt in place. He fastened the belt so tightly that Dante's thigh looked practically like an hourglass.

"I don't understand why you're helping him," Max finally said. "Why are we helping him, after what he did to Morgan?"

"No, no, Lou is right," Stiles said softly. "He's of far more use to my people alive."

Dante's gaze snapped to Lou's. And it surprised the hell out of Max to see what looked like the barest hint of fear in the vampire's eyes.

Lou drew her attention away from that, though, with his next words. "He brought Morgan to us. He called out to get our attention and got himself shot with that freaking crossbow of yours for his trouble. Where the hell did you have that thing, anyway, Stiles? I searched you before I let you in the house."

"It was in my car. I grabbed it the moment we realized Morgan was missing."

"He brought her back," Lou said. "He didn't have to do that. If he was trying to kill her, why would he have bothered?"

Stiles swore emphatically and rolled his eyes. "Doesn't matter. He's my prisoner as of right now. Get him out to my car and I'll take it from there. You people won't be bothered by him again."

Lou lifted his brows. "You're not taking anyone anywhere, Stiles. Get your ass to the house with the others or get the hell out of here."

"This is my project, Malone. I'm a fucking Federal agent."

"You're a *former* Federal agent, pal. My badge, on the other hand, is current, and unless you want to end up being *my* prisoner, I suggest you let me handle this."

Max saw Lou glance at her, his eyes searching. She looked at the creature on the ground, then at Lou again. Then she shook her head in disgust. She got up, gripped Stiles by the arm and tugged him along beside her back toward the house. He didn't fight her much. That worried her.

"You give that animal half a chance, he'll finish your sister off. Just like he did to your friend."

"Why don't you just leave and let us deal with this?"

"Oh, no. I'm not going anywhere."

"If you're staying, you're playing this our way. Otherwise Lou won't have to arrest you, because I'll do worse. You understand?"

Sneering at her in contempt, he nodded.

"Thank you," the vampire said.

"Don't thank me. I can't let you just walk away from this, you know."

"You have to let me go."

Lou shook his head. "What did you mean by what you said before? If you die, she'll die, too."

The vampire looked at him, searched his face. "I'm supposed to think you'll believe me if I explain it?"

"I don't believe any of this. But I do want to hear it."

Dante paused for a long moment, as if thinking. "I can save her. I'm the only one who can."

"How?" Lou asked.

Dante studied him, sighed. "I can't tell you that. Only that I need to heal, to get my strength back, before I can do a thing to help Morgan."

"Uh-huh," Lou said. "And how do you do that?"

The vampire looked away. "I have to feed."

"So you want me to let you loose so you can go bite some innocent and leave them as bad off as Morgan, or maybe worse?"

He helped the suspect up, drew one of the man's arms around his shoulders and started walking him toward the house. The guy was in some pretty intense pain, Lou knew that much. "I can't do that."

"I don't kill."

"And if you did, you'd admit it to me?"

Dante winced every time he put weight on his leg. "No. I suppose not."

"It's my responsibility to keep you in custody," Lou said, reasoning it all out in his mind as he went along. "That's the best I can do, just treat this like any other case. You're my chief suspect. From all appearances, you attacked Morgan. I can't book you and bring you up for a bail hearing—but I can keep you where you can't do any more harm until I figure all this out."

Dante sighed, and Lou wasn't sure if it was in compliance or despair. "Just keep her alive," he said.

"You know how sick she is, don't you? Even if she survives whatever the hell happened tonight, she's not gonna last much longer."

The vampire closed his eyes. "You just keep her alive. Promise me...."

Lou nodded. "I'll do my damnedest."

The vampire nodded. Then he said, "You seem like a decent man, for a mortal. Which makes me even more sorry..."

Lou frowned. "Sorry for wha—" He didn't get to finish. Something—a fist, he thought, though it felt more like a cannon ball—smashed into his head, and he went down in a heap.

Morgan's head turned back and forth as her body trembled. She was so weak, so incredibly weak. Max sat by her side on the sofa, doing her best to keep her sister still, as Lydia paced. David Sumner sat in a small chair in the corner, tears welling in his eyes.

Morgan whimpered and muttered. Every few unintelligible sounds she made were punctuated by one intelligible word. Dante. It was breaking Max's heart. She licked her lips, glanced up at the doorway when Lou came in. He was alone.

"Lou?"

"Sorry," he said, rubbing one side of his head. "He got away from me."

A string of curses polluted the room, and Max glared at Frank Stiles, who had been sitting in the shadows, observing everything. He snatched up his crossbow from the floor beside him and surged toward the door.

Lou stepped into his path. "It's not your place," he said.

"He'll kill again if you let him go. He has to, or he'll die himself. You saw how weak he was."

"I don't think he's gonna kill anyone," Lou said.

He looked past Stiles at Max and went on. "He could've killed Morgan. Hell, he could've killed me just now, if that was what he wanted."

"Lou, what if you're wrong?" Max whispered.

"What if I'm not?" Lou asked. "Max, he says he can save her. What if he's the one telling the truth here?"

"Oh for the love of—you honestly believe that? The word of an animal, for Christ's sake? Over me, one of your own kind?"

"Mr. Stiles, I don't think anyone in this room is one of your kind," Lydia muttered.

David Sumner looked at her, then back at Stiles. "Lydia, you can't be on the vampire's side in this. My God, look at Morgan."

"I am looking at her, David. And I'm listening to her, too. Are you? She loves him. She's dying, and all she can think of is him. Doesn't that say something to you?"

"It says she's in some kind of trance, just like Stiles told us."

"Or Stiles is lying and Morgan knows the truth," Lydia countered.

David jumped to his feet. "He put holes in your daughter's fucking throat, Lydia!"

She snapped her head up, eyes wide. Max thought her own heart stopped beating as she stared from David Sumner to Lydia and back again. "*Wha-what* did you just say?" Then, to Lou, "What did he just say?"

David dropped his face into his hands. "I'm sorry. It just—I'm sorry." His voice was muffled.

Max walked slowly to where Lydia stood. She stared at her for a long moment, searching her face, studying her features. Plumper than her own, more careworn. But suddenly there were similarities.

"You…you're…our *mother?*"

"I didn't ever want you to know," Lydia said, and it seemed as if she had to force the words through a space far too small.

"Why?" Max asked.

Lydia closed her eyes, shook her head quickly. "Oh, come on. Is this your fantasy, Maxine? That your birth mother was a teenage runaway who sold her body on the streets to get by?"

Max's eyes filled with tears. "This is too much all at once. I can't deal with this right now." She blinked rapidly, brushed her eyes with the back of one hand. "Jesus, where the hell is that ambulance?" She paced away, looked out the window, then dropped the curtain and turned again. "Did you know this all along? Is that why you had Lou introduce us?"

Lou spoke before Lydia could answer. "She didn't know, Max. I…I had a suspicion. I knew your birthday was the same day Lydia always lights a candle and spends the day weeping for the babies she gave up. And that was why I put the two of you together. So you could figure it out for yourselves."

Max stared at him, her face wet now. "You should have told me. How could you not tell me?"

"How could I tell you when I wasn't even sure myself?"

"Well, this is all very touching," Stiles said at last, stepping closer to the door. "But the longer I stand around listening to this soap opera, the farther that animal is getting from me." He started for the door.

Again Lou stepped into his path.

"Get out of my way, Malone."

"Give me the crossbow, Stiles."

Stiles smiled darkly, shook his head side to side. "Take it, if you think you can."

"That implies that you *don't* think I can."

The man's smile widened, twisting his scarred face into a warped semblance of a sneer. "You're saggy, baggy, out of shape and tired."

"Well, yeah...." Lou shrugged, pulled his revolver, and pushed the barrel into Stiles's belly, all in one smooth motion. "But I have this."

Stiles shot his hands up over his head. Lou reached up and took the crossbow from one of them. "Now, go sit down."

Stiles glared at him, but he went back to his corner and sat. A second later a siren screamed outside, growing louder until finally its strobes of red and white light were chasing each other through the room from beyond the windows.

Lou put his gun away and turned to open the door as paramedics came inside carrying red boxes of equipment. Max stood, watching everything happen and seeing none of it. She was disoriented, confused and angry as hell.

And then Lou was there, pulling her close to him. "You look shocky."

"You should've told me, Lou."

"You had so much else to deal with."

"No shit." Mentally, she went over the shocks of the past few days. She'd found out that she had a twin sister, met that sister and learned she was dying. She had seen her best friend lying in a coma from which she might never recover. She had discovered that the ex-hooker with the heart of gold she had been jealous of was her mother. And tonight she had met her first vampire. Face-to-face. Jesus.

"Go to the hospital with your sister. Watch over her. Keep him away from her."

"Dante or Stiles?"

"Both. You shouldn't have to worry about Stiles, though. I'm gonna keep him with me."

"And where are you gonna be?"

"I have to go after Dante."

The paramedics were muttering over Morgan and strapping her onto a stretcher now. Max watched them for a moment. Then, "Lou, you just stopped Stiles from going after Dante—a move I could kick you for. Now you're going after him yourself and taking Stiles with you?"

"I stopped Stiles from hunting him down like an animal. Killing him—or worse. That's not what I intend to do."

"No, you're gonna hunt him down like a human being, aren't you? Read him his rights when you catch him, that sort of thing?"

Lou lowered his head. "Something like that."

"He tried to kill my sister. He's not a human being."

"I know that."

"Know this, too." She took the crossbow from his hands as they wheeled her sister out the door. "You can protect him all you want. But if he tries to get near Morgan again, I'll kill him myself. And I won't let anyone stop me. Not even you."

Then she turned away, only to bump into Stiles. He nodded as if in approval and tucked a business card into her hand. "My cell phone number. You're the only one seeing things clearly here. You might need me.''

She shoved him aside and headed out the door after the paramedics, yanking a jacket off a hook on the way and draping it over her arm to conceal the weapon. She crammed Stiles' card into her jeans pocket. At the last moment she turned, glanced at Lydia. ''You and David can follow in the car, all right? I want to stay with her, in the ambulance.''

Lydia looked stunned, then relieved, as she smiled wetly and nodded. ''We'll be right behind you.''

Max faced forward again, started to leave. Halfway to the ambulance, she stopped. ''Lou?''

He was there, only a few paces behind her. She'd felt him following. ''Be careful, okay? Don't turn your back on that snake Stiles for a second. Or on Dante, either.''

''Didn't plan to.''

She turned her head, looked him in the eyes. She hated him for letting that animal go. No, she didn't. Not really.

''Ma'am?''

Max pulled her eyes away, turned toward the paramedic who'd called her. He stood holding the ambulance doors open.

''We have to go, ma'am.''

Nodding, she hurried to the vehicle and climbed inside.

Lou watched her go, feeling like pond slime. He had let her down. That was betrayal he had seen in her eyes. She had expected him to take her side, avenge her sister. Hell, part of him had wanted to, but you didn't spend twenty years as a cop and not assimilate the training. It was who he was, a part of him. Something about Stiles wasn't right. Something about Dante didn't fit the profile Stiles had laid out. Something was off, he felt it right to his toes, and goddammit, his gut was telling him the monster was the good guy in all this.

It made no sense, but there it was.

As the ambulance drove out of sight, David and Lydia following close behind it in Sumner's Mercedes, Lou turned to go back inside.

But naturally, when he got there, Stiles was long gone.

23

Under normal circumstances Dante would have been able to travel far faster on foot. But tonight he needed a car. So rather than struggling into some secluded place to rest, he limped weakly into the town and along the sidewalks, scanning the parked vehicles for dangling sets of keys. The other man's belt was still tied tight around his thigh, but every step he took caused blood to ooze from the wound. His jeans were soaked in it, and he was leaving an obvious trail, a crimson strand. The pain was blinding.

And fate seemed to be conspiring against him, because every car in the area was locked. Not a key in sight. In all his years he'd never mastered the art of car theft, and he regretted it now. If he survived this, it was a skill he would strive to learn.

Headlights shone in his eyes, and Dante instinctively backed into the shadowy recesses of a doorway. The car, a white Ford Mustang, pulled into an empty parking space, its radio blasting. Then it went silent and the lights died.

Closing his eyes, Dante focused his mind, casting a wide net and searching, sifting a thousand mental voices for those near him, then those nearer, and nearer still, quickly homing in on the driver. The young man was happily drunk and humming to himself, thinking about the girl in the passenger seat and

how willing she was. Thinking about how many times
he could do her before the booze he'd imbibed put
him to sleep and reminding himself not to drink any
more tonight so he could make the most of her.

Dante crept into his mind as silently as a burglar,
and every time his thoughts strayed toward the keys
in the ignition, Dante distracted him by gently nudging his mind back to thoughts of booze and sex and
the woman in his car beside him. It wasn't difficult
at all when they were drunk.

Within moments the young man was out of the car,
laughing as he came around it, slung an arm around
the girl and walked unevenly into one of the buildings
that lined the street. Dante sensed them going up the
stairs to the apartment above a shop. He let them get
inside before he withdrew from the young man's
mind. By then he was breathless, such a simple use
of energy damn near draining him.

Pushing himself upright, he walked, dragging his
wounded leg now. He made his way to the car and
saw with relief that the keys were in the ignition.
Yanking the door open, he got in, started the engine
and drove away.

He needed blood, and he needed stitching, to keep
himself from bleeding out before the day sleep could
heal him. 'Fina had abandoned him. Though the way
she saw it, he had no doubt abandoned her first. He
had to get to Belinda, the woman he kept in Bangor.

It took an hour to get to her place. Her apartment.
He had a keycard that let him in, and he made his
way to the elevators, all without being seen by anyone. The place was dark and nearly silent this time
of the night. Finally he reached her floor. Thank God.
He wasn't going to last much longer.

He fell against her door, thumping weakly with a fist. When she didn't answer, he opened it and stumbled inside.

Belinda lay across the sofa. She wore red and welcomed him with sightless eyes. No. She wasn't wearing anything at all. Her wrists were laid open. Blood had spattered over the walls, hit the ceiling in places, and soaked into the carpet and the sofa. Her body was covered in it. And it was old blood. Dead blood. Wasted.

"Did you think I didn't know about her, Dante?"

Dante spun, nearly falling over at the sudden movement.

Stiles stood there, grinning at him with that twisted mockery of a smile. "I couldn't leave your little human blood bank alive. You needed her too much. I knew you'd come here tonight."

"She was an innocent. God, you heartless bastard." Dante tried to lunge forward but slumped instead, catching himself on a table then standing there, bowed, weakening.

"The end justifies the means, though. What you don't know is that I've reorganized some of the men who used to work for the DPI. Oh, there aren't many of us. Only a handful. Survivors of that famous vampire uprising in White Plains."

Dante shook his head. "The government—"

"Has nothing to do with us. We're privately funded. Your kind should be careful who they feed on, Dante. Rich men like vengeance, and they can afford to buy it."

Panting, Dante managed to keep his head up, though it wanted to fall. "Glorified hit men," he muttered.

"Vampire hunters. When we aren't being paid, we do it...just for fun." Stiles stepped inside, and three other men came in behind him, carrying weapons. One had a gun, one a crossbow, one a stake. Dante closed his eyes at the cliché of the third weapon, shook his head. "I see you have a rookie."

Stiles laughed. It was a low, honestly amused sound, yet dangerous at the same time. "It's good that you can joke at a time like this," he said at length. "No, Dante, that's no rookie. The stake has been treated with a new chemical we think will do your kind in. But, of course, we won't know until we test it." Coming closer, he lifted Dante's chin. "Guess who gets to be our guinea pig?"

Dante put all the power he still had into the fist he drove into Stiles' belly. Stiles doubled over, staggering backward, and the other three rushed forward.

"Hold it right there."

Lou Malone, the mortal cop, stood in the doorway with his handgun drawn, and the men in the room went still.

"Drop 'em!" Lou shouted.

Weapons clattered to the floor.

"Up against the far wall. Come on, move it. Face in. That's it," he said as he herded them. "Hands behind your heads. Feet apart, forehead to the wall. That's better."

He jerked his head at Dante. Nodding, Dante made his way toward the door, but on the way he paused, dropping to one knee to pick up the wooden stake. As soon as he closed his hand around the wood, his skin began to burn, and he dropped it fast, clutching his wrist and staring in shock at the smoke curling from his seared palm. Struggling to his feet, he staggered into the hallway.

"I've got a car outside," Lou said. "Wait in it, and keep it running. I'll be out in a sec." Lou grabbed a telephone, dialed 9-1-1.

Dante went to wait in the car.

Lou clocked the men on the head with the butt of his revolver. Then he ran the chain of his handcuffs under an old iron radiator and put the cuffs on two of them. He locked the door and left them there, figuring that ought to hold them until the local cops arrived. They would be detained for at least a little while. Long enough for him to get his preternatural prisoner tucked away safe and sound.

He figured he would have another leg of *that* chase on his hands, but at least now he wouldn't have Stiles mucking up the works. So he was surprised to get back to his car to find Dante slumped inside. He couldn't believe the vampire hadn't run again.

He got in, drove the car back to the hotel in Easton, and used the rear entrance to get the vampire in and up to the suite. Dante came around slightly as Lou hauled him bodily into the hotel, straight to the elevator and up to their floor. Inside, he took the groggy vampire straight to the bathroom and set him on the floor with his back against the wall.

Dante was still. Shit. Maybe he was already dead. Lou was damned if he knew how to tell. Did you check for a pulse? Did a vampire even *have* a pulse?

He found some scissors, a needle and some thread in Lydia's makeup bag. Okay. So he could at least stitch the guy up. The damn blood was still leaking out of him, making a puddle on the bathroom floor.

Using the scissors, Lou sliced away the jeans from just below the makeshift tourniquet. He peeled the blood-soaked denim away, tossing it into the tub. Then he glanced from the slick red length of Dante's leg to the needle and thread sitting on the counter. "Shit."

He got up and went into the living room part of the suite, opened the little mini-bar and took out two bottles. Whiskey and vodka. Twisting the cap off the whiskey, he tipped it to his own lips and drank it down.

Releasing a breath, he twisted the cap off the vodka, carried it back into the bathroom, and poured some of it over the wound in the front of the vampire's thigh. It rinsed the blood away, and Dante groaned in pain. When Lou looked at him, his eyes were open.

"I was beginning to think you were dead."

"What the hell are you *doing* to me?"

"Correct me if I'm wrong, but I'm thinking this thing's gonna bleed to the last drop. I assume that's bad, even for a vampire."

Closing his eyes, Dante nodded. "Especially for a vampire."

"Thought so." Lou took the needle. It had a strand of black thread in it, and he poured a little vodka over it.

"That's not necessary," Dante said. "I'm not going to get an infection."

"You don't say." Shrugging, Lou leaned over the wound. "Brace yourself." He poked the needle through, surprised as hell by the howl of pain. "Hell, even I wouldn't yell like that. I thought you were tough."

Through clenched teeth, Dante said, "Sensations…are…magnified in my kind."

"Oh. I didn't know." Lou looked at him; his face was a twisted grimace of pain. "Should I stop?"

"No."

This time, when he pushed the needle into the man's flesh, Lou winced himself. Four stitches, nice and tight. That was all it took to completely close the wound. He nodded, satisfied with himself.

"There's another…just like it," Dante said. "On the other side."

"Christ." Lou reached for the vodka, drank what remained of it, and helped Dante to roll over.

It was agonizing to inflict this kind of pain on someone, vampire or otherwise. Lou was damn near to losing his lunch by the time he finished, and his patient was little more than a quivering lump. Still, the stitches held. Dante wasn't bleeding anymore. Not even when Lou hauled his ass off the floor, braced him over the edge of the tub and hosed the blood off him as best he could. Then he toweled the vampire off and helped him to the nearest bed.

He figured if Dante lasted the night, he would be all right. Lou had picked up enough from their earlier conversation to have figured out that vampires healed by day, while they slept. He cleaned up the mess in the bathroom, and then he made himself comfortable in a chair near the bed, planning to sit vigil over the guy until sunrise.

It was going to be a long night. Sighing, he picked up the phone, called the hospital, asked to be patched through to Max.

Her voice, when she came on the line, was strained, tired. Old. Way too old to be coming from a girl like her. He wanted to say something that would make it better. Comfort her. Something. But damned if he knew what.

"How's Morgan doing?" Stupid question. How the hell did he *think* she was doing?

"They're giving her fluids. No blood. No donors. She needs it or she'll die." Her voice broke though she struggled not to reveal that she was crying.

"I'm sorry, Max."

"Did you find him?"

"Dante? Yeah. He's not in very good shape, either. I did what I could. He's resting now."

"And Stiles?"

"He and some of his friends are visiting with the local cops tonight, if all went the way I hope it did. I don't expect they'll be bothering us at least until tomorrow morning. Maybe longer."

"So my sister's safe for tonight."

"As far as we know, yeah."

There was silence on the line.

"Max...I'm sorry I let you down."

She didn't answer. He lowered his head, trying to think of a way to break the silence. Finally he said, "I'm at the suite. You have the number, right?"

"Yeah."

"I'm gonna keep an eye on him until daylight. He can't be any problem in daylight if I'm understanding this right."

"From what I read in those files, that's right."

"I'll just stash him somewhere dark toward morning, and then we'll figure out what to do next. Okay?"

"Okay."

"You call if you need me."

"I've got it covered."

That hurt. It felt as if she was saying she didn't need him. Wouldn't need him. No longer trusted him to be the man she could depend on. He had let her down. Fallen off his goddamned pedestal.

"Okay, then." He drew a breath, sighed.

"Good night, Lou," she said, and she hung up.

The silence of the broken connection seemed smothering. Sighing, he put the phone back in its cradle. He made one more round of the suite, making sure the doors were locked tight, dead bolts turned. As an afterthought, he retrieved the two tiny booze bottles from the wastebasket and stood them in front of the door. If it opened, they would tip over, clattering against each other, waking him if he had happened to doze off.

Finally he went back to the bedroom, sat down in the chair beside the bed where the wounded vampire slept and let himself have permission to just rest his eyes.

"You're being awfully hard on him, you know."

Maxine turned from the telephone at the nurse's desk to see Lydia staring at her. "Is this motherly advice or just an opinion?"

Lydia flinched. But then she seemed to steel herself. "I suppose I deserved that. In your eyes, at least."

Max sighed, feeling a twinge of guilt and ignoring it. "How is Morgan?"

"The same. They've got her wired for sound in there, though. IV lines, monitors, the works." She lowered her eyes, but not before Max saw them welling. They were red, in fact, as if she'd been shedding tears all night. "God, I hope I get the chance to...to tell her."

"That you're her mother?" Max asked. "You already had the chance, Lydia. But you didn't say a word. Not to Morgan, and not to me."

The older woman looked up slowly, met Max's eyes. "I hope I get the chance to tell her I love her. That's all. I never intended to tell her—or either of you—the rest."

Max swallowed the knot of guilt that rose in her throat. "Why?"

"I thought I explained that to you. Just how do you feel about knowing your mother was a whore?"

Max flinched this time. It was as if the woman had slapped her with her words. "You're ashamed of what you were."

"No. No, I'm not ashamed. But I knew you would be, and so would your sister in there, if she knew the truth."

"Know us that well, do you? After all of...what? A few days?"

A nurse came to the desk, and they both fell silent as she shuffled papers, gathered charts. Max turned to her. "Can you have them turn on the phone in my sister's room, in case I need it again?"

"I'm sorry, no phones in ICU. But there's a convenience phone in the Intensive Care waiting area. TV, too. It's just across the hall from your sister's room."

She nodded. "If I get another call, could you put it through to there?"

"Sure."

Max glanced at Lydia, inclined her head and started down the hall to the waiting area. As they passed the

Intensive Care unit, she could see into Morgan's room through the large safety-glass window. David was in there with her, holding her hand, speaking to her. "Same scene, different hospital," Max muttered.

"Here it is."

Max looked toward Lydia, who was holding open a door on the other side of the hall. She went inside, looked around. There were three vending machines—snacks, soda and coffee. A television, a radio, a phone—not a pay phone either, but a real phone. Several chairs and a couple of futons completed the room. Max propped the door open, then took a seat that gave her a clear view of her sister across the hall.

Lydia dropped coins into the coffee machine and waited for her cup to fill.

"You said you're not ashamed of what you did for a living all those years ago," Max said slowly. "I'm curious about that."

Taking the cup of creamed coffee from the dispenser, Lydia sipped and grimaced. "Because I had no choice."

Max waited, but Lydia didn't seem inclined to continue. "Come on, Lydia. Don't you think I have a right to know the whole story?"

Walking to a chair, Lydia sat down slowly, took another sip of coffee and then set the cup on a small table beside her chair. "I suppose. It's not pretty."

"The truth rarely is."

Nodding, Lydia seemed to gather herself. "When I was ten years old, my father died. When I was eleven, my mother remarried. My stepfather was abusive."

How cool and clinical she sounded, Max thought. "He beat you?"

"Beat me. Raped me. He hurt me in just about every way he could think of. My mother, too. She didn't have it in her to leave, but I did."

"So you ran away from home? When? How old were you?"

"Fourteen. That's how long it took me to realize that my mother wasn't going to protect me. She couldn't even protect herself. And it was getting worse. I figured if I didn't get out soon, he would end up killing me."

"Where did you go?" Max studied her. Lydia's eyes were stark. Empty.

"Nowhere. There was no place I could go. I lost myself in the city, lived on the streets, made friends there. The drugs helped ease the pain. The people helped me learn how to survive. It seemed horrible at first, the idea of selling my body for money. But when you get hungry enough, it stops seeming so bad. Hell, it was far better than what was happening to me at home. I was in control. I got to say when and how and who—or at least that's what I told myself—and I got paid for it." She shrugged. "I got by for a while—until I got pregnant."

Max's stomach was tied in knots. "You didn't…make them use protection?"

"I didn't *make* them do much of anything, Max. It's dangerous out there. You piss off the wrong john, you end up bearing scars, or worse."

"You're lucky all you got was pregnant."

"You're right."

"So then what happened?"

Lydia lowered her head. "There was this old woman. Mary Agnes Brightman, but everyone just called her Nanna. She had a big house in White

Plains. Word was she took in pregnant teens. So I paid her a visit.''

"And she took you in?"

"Yeah. She wasn't incorporated, didn't have a license. Just a big house and a big heart. There were six of us staying there full-time while I was there, and countless others in and out. Nanna fed us, clothed us, talked to us like we were intelligent human beings, you know?" She sighed. "Some decided on abortion, and when they did, she paid for it, took them to a good doctor, got it done right, made them go to counseling before and after. Some decided to keep their babies, try to raise them. She helped them find housing, jobs, day care, file for public assistance until they could get on their feet. Some decided to have the babies and give them up for adoption. Nanna had a son who was a lawyer, and he helped them arrange that, no charge.''

Nodding slowly, Max said, "That was the choice you made."

Lydia lifted her head. "Nanna and her son, Brian, took me once to see the couple who wanted to adopt my baby. Oh, I didn't get to meet them. Didn't know their names, nothing like that. But I watched them. They were shopping. They'd moved up to the top of Brian's waiting list, so they knew that they'd be likely to get a baby within a year. They were shopping for furniture. Cribs, walkers. And I watched them. She got misty every time she held up some tiny outfit or teddy bear. Got actual tears in her eyes. He would say something funny, joking about baby names or something until she smiled again. They looked…so good. You know? Nice. Normal. And that woman, God, she wanted you so much." Lydia drew a wavering breath.

"That night Brian showed me some photos of their house, though he couldn't tell me where it was I had no idea it was so close—right in White Plains."

She lifted her eyes to Max's. "I knew you'd be happy there."

Max felt a little misty herself. "But they didn't want us both?"

"They didn't have the chance to make that decision. When we learned I was having twins, Brian let me assume both of you were going to that same home. But that wasn't the case. He placed your sister with a different family."

"Why?"

Lydia's voice had turned coarse now. "Oh, he thought he was doing a good thing. Helping out a dear friend on the West Coast who desperately wanted a child. I don't think he meant to harm anyone. But he did. I never knew the truth until after Nanna died some ten years later. She had found out, somehow, and was furious with her son over it. She left me her house, with the explanation that I had been wronged when she had only wanted to help me, and that she owed me reparation."

"And you kept her work going," Max filled in.

"I had been going back there often, helping out with the new girls in between my other jobs. Legitimate jobs. One of Nanna's conditions of helping girls like me was that we promised not to go back to the life. I was one of the few who kept that promise. Kimbra was another. I first met her at Nanna's house." She shrugged. "So when Nanna died and left the place to me, I knew almost as much about running it as she did. Turned out Kimbra had a great head for business. She helped us incorporate as a non-profit organization. Haven House.''

Max drew a breath and looked Lydia in the eye. ''And you thought Morgan and I would be ashamed of this story?''

Lydia looked away. ''Just the beginning.''

''Just nothing.'' Licking her lips, Max impulsively gripped Lydia's hand. ''You were right about that couple. I had that idyllic childhood you wanted me to have. And if that lawyer hadn't taken her elsewhere, Morgan would have, too. My adoptive parents were wonderful, Lydia. I never suffered the lack of anything. Most of all love.''

Lydia closed her eyes. ''God, you don't how much hearing that means to me. Letting you go…it was so hard.''

''I can imagine. But I think you did the right thing. And I'm grateful.''

''The right thing…for you, maybe. But Morgan…''

''Don't give up on Morgan just yet. She comes from good stock.''

They both turned to look across the hall, through the glass to where Morgan lay. Lydia nodded. ''I, um, I'm going to go sit with her for a while.''

''David looks like he could use a break.''

Lydia got to her feet. Max did, too, and then hesitantly, awkwardly, she gave Lydia a brief hug. Lydia squeezed her hard, then let her go.

''I think I'll call Lou back.''

''Good idea,'' Lydia said. She gave an encouraging nod and left the room.

Lou fell asleep in his chair, his head hanging to one side, ear pressed to his own shoulder. Something woke him. Two somethings. One was the sudden shrill ring of a phone. The other came first, though. It was Dante's voice. And it was coming from close to him. *Very* close to him. Like in his face.

Dante said, "I'm very sorry about this, Malone. But I have no choice."

Then the phone rang, and Lou's eyes popped open. Dante was leaning over him, and Lou flung his arms up to push the vampire off, but the chair went over backward and Dante came with it to the floor. He sank his teeth into Lou's throat as Lou fought to pry him off.

Lou swung out an arm, knocking the stand over. The phone fell to the floor. Vaguely, he could hear a tinny voice repeating his name.

"Jesus!" Lou gritted his teeth against the sensation of being drained. "I saved your fucking life!" He intended to shout it, but it came out weaker than that. "I helped you!"

His heart pounded harder than he thought was healthy, and he kept struggling to push the creature off, but his efforts were useless.

Finally Dante lifted his head and let Lou's fall backward to the floor. "You're still helping me," the vampire said, and he looked...different. Stronger. His eyes glowed, and his skin seemed to plump with life.

Yeah, Lou thought. *My* life.

Dante wiped his mouth with the back of his hand, then he scooped Lou up off the floor and dropped him on the bed. Turning, he picked the phone up from the floor, set its base on the stand and brought the receiver to his ear. "Your boyfriend needs you, Maxine. He's waiting for you at the hotel. You'd better hurry. I didn't drain him dry, but I was damned thirsty.''

He hung up the phone.

Lou moaned, reaching for it, knowing full well what the vampire was doing. Trying to lure Max away from her sister so he could get to her himself. Dammit.

Dante looked down at him in the bed. ''I really am sorry. There was no other way.''

Lou tried to sit up as Dante turned and left the room, but he only managed to raise his upper body a couple of inches before falling backward again, into darkness.

24

"**W**ait!"

The phone went dead, and for an instant, Max felt panic creeping up her spine and wrapping its cold claw around her brain. But only for an instant. She shook it away, stiffened her spine, depressed the telephone's cutoff, and then dialed star-six-nine.

The mechanical voice recited the digits of the last number to call the line she was on. It was the number of the hotel. The vampire hadn't been lying about that.

Then maybe he'd been telling the truth about Lou, as well.

She slammed the phone down, ran to the door. She had to get to him, help him.

Then she stopped still as she stood facing her sister's room, seeing her lying there in the bed, helpless. Why had Dante told her what he had? Out of the kindness of his heart? No. He wanted her to leave her sister unguarded.

Dammit! How was she supposed to choose between her sister's life and Lou's?

It occurred to her then that she didn't really need to choose.

She went back into the waiting room, picked up the telephone, dialed 9-1-1, then told the dispatcher where Lou was and that he was near death from blood loss.

Then she dug in her jeans' pocket for that other number. The one that sleaze-bag Stiles had given her. As she dialed, she hoped that whatever Lou had done to the bastard to keep him tied up with the local police all night had failed.

It was very dark, like standing outdoors on a still night, in a thick fog. Mists swirled, and Morgan floated, without the will or the strength to move. The girl with the spiky blond hair floated out of the mists, looked at Morgan and said, "Hey. I know you."

Morgan shook her head slowly. "No."

"Yes. You're her. I heard Maxie talking about you."

Her head lifting slowly, Morgan asked, "You know Max?"

"You're the long-lost sister, right?" The blonde smiled. But then her smile slowly died. "Max keeps telling me to come back. And I want to go back. I just can't find the way."

Morgan sighed, every part of her too tired even to nod her head. "I know the way," she said. Her words were slow, expressed more as a sigh than a sentence, and that only with effort. "But I don't have the strength."

Tilting her head to one side, the blonde said, "Gee, do you suppose we could help each other? I mean, work together?"

"I don't think it works that way. I'm supposed to die. I've always known it."

"I don't think so. I mean, have you seen how fast some of them come through this place?"

God, her head was heavy. So tired. "I haven't seen anyone."

"What do you mean? Of course you have. Look! There goes one now!"

Morgan saw only a streak of light flash across the deep blue backdrop of the swirling silvery mists. "I thought those were shooting stars."

"Uh-uh. I've been watching them. I think they're just like us. Only they know where they're going. And we're kind of…stuck. Because we don't. That must mean something. Right?"

Morgan shrugged, too tired to care.

"Look, I'll help you. I'm strong, I'm just lost. I'll help you, and you tell me the way. All right?"

"I…can't."

"Sure you can."

The blonde bent down and clasped Morgan's hand. Energy melted into her, a pool of life. The girl tugged gently, and Morgan rose to her feet as if weightless.

"Now," she said. "Which way?"

Morgan surfaced slowly, unsure what was going on, knowing only that she ached for Dante. God, where was he? Why hadn't he come for her?

She couldn't raise her head to look around the hospital room, and her hearing was distant, as if all sound was muffled. She saw through cloudy vision as Maxine, her sister, spoke to Lydia and David.

"They'll be bringing Lou into the ER any minute. Please, go down there and wait for him. And if…if it's really bad…come back for me. Otherwise, though…"

"We understand," David said, his eyes solemn. "Be careful, Max."

Max nodded, and Morgan wondered what was going on. What had happened to Lou Malone? And why did David feel the need to warn Max?

He must be afraid Dante would come for her. Oh, God, Morgan thought desperately, please let him come for me!

After David and Lydia left the room, Maxine opened the closet door, stepped inside it and closed it again.

What in the world…?

Morgan waited silently, her heart hammering. The lights were all turned out. The glow of the various monitors surrounding her bed painted the skin of her hands with a faint green tint. It seemed to Morgan that she could hear every tick of the clock as she waited, waited, wondering what her sister was up to.

The window slid open. A soft breeze moved the curtains. They danced like ghosts; then a dark form climbed through. Morgan's heart leapt in her chest as Dante landed on the floor easily. He looked at her, met her eyes, and everything in her seemed to sing. She wanted to speak, to cry, to leap up and run into his arms, but she couldn't move, couldn't speak. A tear welled in her eye, rolled onto her cheek. Dante saw it, and it seemed to Morgan that love shone in his eyes as he hurried to her bedside without even looking around first. His long, slender hand stroked Morgan's hair away from her face. And Morgan saw the glimmer of a tear on his cheek, shining in that greenish glow.

"I'm here," he whispered. "It's all right now, my love. I'm here."

He bent to press his lips to hers, and she tasted his

kiss only briefly. The door burst open suddenly, and Dante jerked his head away.

Frank Stiles, the scarred man, burst in from the hall, as three other men—his cohorts it seemed—appeared as well, two from the adjoining bathroom, another from behind the bed curtain. Weapons were drawn, aimed at Dante, and Maxine stepped out of the closet. "Back away from her, Dante," she ordered.

Morgan's heartbeat raced. She tried to form words, lifted a hand in weak protest, but she was ignored.

"You don't know what you're doing," Dante said softly, staring at Morgan, his eyes gleaming with emotion. "Please, she's going to die, Maxine. Your sister is going to die unless you let me help her."

"I'm sorry. I don't believe a word you say, Dante. Not after what you did to Lou."

Lou? Morgan wondered. What had Dante done to Lou?

Stay calm, my love. Malone is fine, I promise you. Dante's thoughts rang in her mind, soothing. *Stay alive. I'll come back for you, I swear it.*

He started to turn for the window.

Stiles fired a weapon, and Morgan caught her breath. It wasn't an explosion but a small pop, as his gun shot a dart into Dante's shoulder. Whatever it was, it worked instantly. Dante buckled, dropped to his knees. One of the other men yelled, "It works!"

Dante looked up at Maxine with pained eyes. "For the love of God, don't let this happen."

Max moved closer to him. "You blew your shot at getting any sympathy from me when you attacked Lou Malone. He was the only one who wanted to give you the benefit of the doubt, you know. The only one who wanted to help you. And you turned on him.''

''You don't realize what you've done.'' He turned his gaze from hers to Morgan's, his eyes filled not with sorrow, but with promise. He would come back, he would find a way. He swore it to her without speaking a word.

''Get back, Ms. Stuart. We'll take it from here,'' Stiles said. He nodded to one of his men, who opened a pack and took out a rope with several pulleys and latches attached. He tied off one end and dropped the other out the window.

Maxine backed off.

''You're just fortunate we weren't detained by the police after all,'' Stiles went on. ''Luckily your boyfriend the cop only had one pair of handcuffs on him. He had to leave one of my men free, who managed to free us before the police showed up.''

One of the men bent over Dante, who was completely unconscious now. As Morgan watched in horror, unable to do a thing to help besides move one finger over and over on the call button at her pillow, the man snapped a belt around Dante, then flung him easily over his shoulder. ''Ready, sir.''

A nurse stepped into the room from the hallway, went still, eyes wide, and said, ''Just what the hell is going on in here?''

''We're Ms. De Silva's private security team, ma'am. This man broke in here. We're taking him right back out again.'' Stiles wiggled his gun like a finger, and the nurse's face drained of color as she looked at his scarred face. ''Now you just stay quiet until we're gone, hmm?''

The nurse backed into the hall, turned and ran,

shouting for security. The big guy who had Dante over his shoulder sat on the windowsill with his back to the open window, the rope in his gloved hands. He put his feet to the windowsill, pushed off, then rappelled down the side of the building with Dante anchored over his shoulder. The others clambered out just as quickly, bagging their weapons and taking them. They were gone in seconds, as if they had never been there. Almost.

Maxine went to the window, removed the rope and dropped it after them. Then she closed the window and returned to her chair, sinking down tiredly.

Two hospital security men dressed like cops, came crashing through the door, looking ready for all-out war. Maxine looked up at them as if vaguely irritated. "What is this?"

"We were told there were armed men in this room, ma'am." The leader jerked his head, and the other man went through the room, the closet, the adjoining bathroom, checking everywhere and finding nothing and no one. He even looked out the window, but Stiles and his cronies were too fast to be spotted so easily. And well hidden in their black clothes, on a night as dark as this one.

"Armed men?" Max asked. She faked an incredulous laugh. "I suggest you have whoever told you that fairy tale tested for drugs," she said. "There's been no one here for hours."

Frowning, the men muttered among themselves and finally left her alone, but Morgan noticed one of them remained in the hall outside the door, just to keep an eye on things.

Maxine sighed, and she closed her hand around Morgan's, glancing down at Morgan's face and finally realizing that Morgan's eyes were open and staring straight into hers.

Morgan strained to force words, and even then, only the barest whisper emerged. "You get him back," she rasped. "Or I'll die hating you for this, Max. I swear I will."

Dante's captors sat around a table, smoking, talking in low tones. Dante had been rendered temporarily unconscious by the drug, whatever the hell it had been, but already its effects were wearing off. He was still weak. Far from fighting strength, but at least he was awake. Able to listen, smell, try to discern his surroundings. He was on a table, he thought. Flat and hard. His arms and legs were restrained. He smelled only tobacco smoke and the moldy, musty smell of age and disuse. He opened his eyes a mere slit and saw bare lathe and crumbling plaster, spiderwebs and broken boards. Shattered windows with razor shards of glass still in them. An abandoned house?

"The drug works. You did it, Frank. You reproduced the old Rogers formula perfectly!"

"Yeah, and just in time, too. Man, he went down fast," another man said.

Stiles spoke next. His voice was beginning to become familiar to Dante. Familiar...and hated. "It works, but we have no idea how well, or for how long. I only had partial notes on the process. The rest were destroyed in the fire."

"Well, he's out," said one of the others. "That says all I need to know."

"Then you're a fool."

The men went quiet for a moment. Then, "What

are we going to do with him, boss? You said we weren't ready to keep prisoners yet.''

"We aren't. The cells in our new headquarters aren't even finished. And even when they are, capturing them will never be our goal. I want you to remember that, men. That's where we differ from the old DPI. Our mission is to eliminate them. Wipe them out. The entire race. However, keeping a few for experimentation will help hone our weapons for maximum effectiveness.''

Dante suppressed a shudder. This man was singlehandedly re-establishing the DPI—and making it more bloodthirsty than ever.

"This one, though, we kill. But we can at least keep him alive long enough to see how the tranquilizer works. He might as well serve our purposes before we slice him open and watch him bleed out.''

Gently, Dante gave an experimental tug on the restraints. They felt solid, and he sensed he wasn't yet strong enough to break them. And then he wondered why he even bothered to try. If he couldn't save Morgan, what was the point? God, why had he waited so long to acknowledge the bond between them? She hadn't. She had known it for what it was from the very start. She was his. Meant to be with him. It had taken him centuries to find her. And now she was being taken from him. And there wasn't a damn thing he could do about it.

"Go see if he's still out," Stiles ordered.

Footsteps came closer. Dante relaxed his features, lay perfectly still, limp.

"Still out," the man called.

"Make sure," Stiles said.

The man was quiet for a moment. Dante heard him

puffing on his cigarette. Then the puffing stopped, and Dante felt heat near his neck. It got hotter, and then the tip of the cigarette pressed to his skin. He clenched his jaw to keep from crying out as the skin seared. Pain screamed through him. He did not react. He couldn't, or they would kill him. And dammit, then it really would be over. But as long as he drew a breath and she still lived, there was a chance. Slight, but real. Very real. He had to survive, escape and get to Morgan.

The hot brand moved away, but its burn remained, sizzling skin cells. Dante smelled his own burned flesh.

"I'm sure," the man said. "He's really out."

Morgan lay very still in the bed, watching, too weak to do more. Even speaking exhausted her. She wasn't going to live much longer; she knew that with a dire certainty. And she didn't care. Dante. He was all she cared about. God, if she couldn't be with him, then death was a far more desirable prospect than that of life without him. But she could not bear the thought of him in the hands of those evil men. She couldn't bear it.

Tears slid down her face in utter silence as she lay there, unable to howl her anguish. Her longing for him was so deep and so sharp that it cut into her very soul. And the pain was unbearable. She barely heard her so-called sister as the girl sat beside her, telling her all the reasons why she'd had to betray the man Morgan loved. He'd shot her best friend, she said. He had attacked Lou. He was a killer. They were words. Far less convincing, less moving, to her than the words of a madman on the pages of a diary.

The door opened. Morgan watched with dying eyes as Lou Malone walked in, a bandage on his neck. He looked fine. Healthy. Pink.

"Lou!" Max jumped from her chair and flung herself into his arms. "Oh, God, are you all right? I can't believe he did that to you—and after you tried to help him! I can't believe…" She let the words trail off. "Where are David and Lydia?" she asked.

"I sent them back to the house to get some rest." Lou wasn't looking at her though. He was looking at Morgan. She held his eyes and prayed he could see the plea in hers. She parted her lips, tried to speak. "Dante" was the whisper that emerged.

"I thought he would have been here by now," Lou said. He clasped Max's shoulders, put her away from him, searched her face. "Have you seen him?"

"Seen who? Dante?"

Lou nodded. "I assumed he was coming for Morgan." He closed his eyes. "I was so afraid you would get in his way. He's damn dangerous when it comes to her. I don't think there's anything he wouldn't do—"

Max lowered her head. "He came," she admitted. "I knew he would. I had Stiles and his men here waiting."

Lou blinked. His gaze shot to Morgan's, to her cheeks, where hot tears rolled in slow motion, then back to Max again. "Did they kill him?"

"They shot him with some sort of dart. I don't think it killed him, but I don't know for sure. Then they took him out of here."

"Where?"

"How would I know? Jesus, Lou, don't look so concerned about the guy. He tried to kill you."

"No," Lou said sharply. "He didn't."

"What do you mean, he didn't? He...he *bit* you. Drained your blood."

"And told you where to find me. They gave me two pints. Two pints, Max. The doc in the E.R. said I'd have been fine even if they hadn't brought me in. Tired, dizzy, weak for a couple of days, but fine."

"He attacked you." Max lowered her eyes. "And he shot Stormy."

"He made sure I would be found. He made sure not to take enough to do me any harm. And let me tell you, I think he could have used a lot more, as weak as he was."

Shaking her head as she kept her eyes cast down, Max said, "He came here. He came after my sister."

"Even though he must have known there was a chance he would be ambushed. He knows you're not stupid, Max. Sure, he thought he might lure you away, but it was a slim chance. And he came anyway. Risked whatever hell he's in right now to get to her."

"To kill her," Max snapped.

"Or maybe to save her."

"No. You're wrong. You have to be wrong."

Morgan's heartbeat sped up, and her breath was coming faster. God, they were so close. So close to understanding. They had to save Dante. Please, God, let them save him from those men.

There was a tap on the door. A nurse poked her head inside. "Ms. Stuart? You had a message at the desk from, uh, Lydia. She said someone had been trying to reach you on your cell phone with no luck and finally left a message with her at the house. You're to call this number." She handed Max a slip of paper.

"I turned the cell phone off. There was a sign."

The nurse nodded. "They can mess with certain equipment in hospitals. But, um, between you and me you can use it in here if you want. Just stand near the window."

"Thank you." Max opened up the folded slip of paper, reading the number on it as the nurse walked out of the room. Her head came up slowly, eyes meeting Lou's. "It's the hospital in White Plains." Her eyes fell closed. "Oh, God, it must be Stormy. She must be gone, Lou. Oh, God, she's gone."

Lou wrapped Max up in his arms. Part of Morgan felt that her sister deserved to lose someone she loved, after what she had done to Dante. But most of her wept to see her sister in pain.

"You'd better call," Lou said. "Her mother will want to talk to you."

Nodding, Max straightened away from him and started fishing in her purse. Lou snatched a couple of tissues from a box on the bedside stand and caught her chin in his hand to hold her face still while he dabbed her tears away.

Sniffing, Max poked numbers into her cell phone, held it to her ear and waited. And then she said, "Hello? Mrs. Jones, it's Maxine."

There was a pause. Then she cupped the mouthpiece, spoke to Lou. "She can't bring herself to tell me. She's putting someone else on." And then suddenly her eyes shot wider, her hand moved, and she spoke into the mouthpiece again. "Oh my God. *OhmyGod,* Stormy? Is that you?"

Her face crumpled, and her voice became a series of laughs punctuated by sobs, with a few words in between as she spoke to the friend she had thought was dead. When she finally got herself under control, she said, "I want you to know that we got the man who did this to you. He's not going to hurt anyone else, not ever." Slight pause. "Yes, yes, we're sure." Then her eyes shot to Lou's. "Just to be safe, though, can you describe him?" And then, very slowly, the color left Maxine's face. Her jaw went lax, and she turned slowly to Morgan. "Oh my God. No. No, Stormy, everything is fine. Listen, you just rest, get strong again. I have to go, but I'll speak to you soon, okay?"

Finally she hit the kill button. "The man who was waiting in your apartment that night to shoot Stormy had a horribly scarred face."

"Stiles," Lou growled. "And if he lied about that, I'm betting he lied about everything else, as well."

Max turned to Morgan, her eyes wide, wet. "Oh, God, what have I done? Morgan, I'm sorry. I'm so, so sorry."

Morgan held her eyes, begging her. "Please..." she managed.

"I know. I know." Max turned to Lou. "We have to rescue Dante."

"No shit. But how the hell are we going to find him? Stiles could have taken him anywhere."

For the second time that night Morgan's window slid slowly open. Again a form climbed inside. But this time it wasn't Dante. It was the woman Morgan recognized as Sarafina. She was stunning, with masses of jet hair and ebony eyes, lips of blood red, and skin as pale as snow. She stared at them, her gaze potent enough to send chills up Morgan's spine. She wore red velvet, and she said, "I may have a suggestion."

"Who the hell are you?" Max asked, stepping between Morgan's bed and the woman standing near the window.

"Brave, for a mortal. My name is Sarafina. I am Dante's sister. And his aunt, and his mother."

"You're a vampire," Max said, and it sounded like an accusation.

"Your powers of observation are astounding," the woman said, sarcasm dripping from every word. "Yes. I am a vampire. Not the tooth fairy, not the sandman, a vampire. And you will either help me get Dante back or pay for his life with your own. Are we clear on that?"

Max stood her ground. "How do I know I can trust you?"

Her brows rose. "Well, the fact that I'm going to offer myself as bait for the vampire hunter ought to be sufficient for that, don't you think?"

Max and Lou stared at her, stunned.

"Come now, it's the only way. Dante's not sending signals strong enough for me to pick up mentally. I can't find him on my own. But I know he's alive. I can feel it."

"Alive," Morgan whispered, fresh tears welling in her eyes.

"Yes. Which is more than I can say for you, mortal."

Morgan smiled at her, weakly, unsteadily. She didn't care that she was hovering on the brink of death. She didn't care—so long as Dante would be all right.

"Come, we've little time. You," Sarafina said to Max. "Contact the scarred man, tell him you have another vampire. That I've been injured, can barely function, and that you've bound me and will hold me for him. Tell him to meet you at the house, near the cliffs, if he wants me. Then gather up your sister and bring her along as quickly as you can.''

She turned then to Lou. ''While she does all that...'' She held out her arms, wrists pressed together. ''Bind me and take me to the cliffs to await the vampire hunter.''

''Lou, I don't think you should go with her. Not alone.''

''Afraid I'll kill him, are you?'' Sarafina asked. She rolled her eyes. ''Mortals. Fine, if you want me weak enough that I pose no threat, we can arrange that, too.'' She drew a dagger from her pocket. ''Just see to it I don't faint and bleed out entirely.'' Lifting her arm, she brought the blade to her wrist.

Lou caught her hand, stopped her from slicing herself. ''No.'' He looked at Max. ''We have to trust her, Max. We need her at full strength or we risk losing the fight. Stiles has at least three other men working with him, and maybe more, all of them armed.''

''Not to mention trained,'' Max said. Then she paused, turning to Sarafina. ''Can you help my sister? Dante says he can save her. Does that mean you can, too?''

The woman looked at Morgan, licked her lips. ''Frankly, I fear she may be too far gone to survive the transformation at all at this point. Add to that the fact that if I were to try, it would leave me too weak to fight for several hours, and by then, Dante might well be dead.'' She looked away.

''But there's a chance.''

''There's a chance. But I won't do it.''

"And you expect me to trust you?" Max asked.

Lou clasped her arm. "Be reasonable, Maxie. If she tries and it fails, we lose them both. If she tries and it works, we save Morgan and lose Dante. Do you think that's what Morgan wants?"

Morgan tried to say no, but it emerged as a groan instead.

"Her way, we have a shot at saving them both."

Closing her eyes, lowering her head, Max finally nodded. Then she gripped Lou's arms. "Be careful, dammit."

"I will."

Max turned to Sarafina. "I don't give a damn what you are. If you hurt him, I'll find you and I'll kill you."

The woman looked surprised, and perhaps a little amused. "I do believe you'd try." Then she turned to Lou. "Come," she said. She flung him over her shoulder as if he were a rag doll, turned and leapt out the window.

Max cried out and lunged to the window, hands braced on the sill, looking down. Then she sighed in relief.

"Call," Morgan whispered. "Call."

"Yeah. I'm on it." Max took out her cell phone again.

25

"Stiles. Thank God you're still there. Listen, I don't know what the hell to do. We've...we've got another one."

"What?"

"Another one. Of *them*." Max swallowed hard, her eyes locked with her sister's ever-weakening gaze as she spoke on the phone. "I think *he* sent her. She tried for Morgan. Lou was here, they struggled, and she wound up going out the window. He didn't mean to push her, it just happened. She damn near took Lou with her."

"She was injured?"

"Yeah. Pretty badly, by the looks of it. I don't know, she was unconscious. We tied her up, but I'm not sure how long we can hold her. If she comes around..."

"Where is she now?"

"Lou took her to the house. He figured he couldn't very well hold her here, where someone might see. He's going to lock her up there or something. Told me to tell you he'd wait for you by the cliffs."

"I'll be there in twenty minutes." Stiles rang off.

Nodding her head slowly, Max pocketed the phone and sat down beside her sister, stroking her hair. Morgan's eyes were mere slits. "Just a little longer, babe. Hang on, okay?"

A nod so slight her head barely moved. Then the door opened, and Dr. Hilman walked in. "Maxine, you wanted to see me?"

"Yes," she said. She got to her feet to face him, lifted her chin and squared her shoulders. "I want to take Morgan home."

"Impossible." He said it quickly, without even thinking about it first.

"Let's just drop the bull from the beginning. We both know it's *possible*. Maybe not advisable, but possible."

Shaking his head slowly, the doctor said, "She may not survive the trip, Maxine."

"C'mon, Doc. Do you even expect her to survive the *night?*"

Licking his lips, he lowered his head. "Frankly...no."

"Then what's the difference? She wants to die at home. In her own bed, in the house she loves. There's nothing you can do for her here except maybe prolong her life a few extra hours. But you *can* do something for her. You can grant her last wish. I'll take full responsibility."

He lowered his head, pressing his lips together.

"If you say no, I'll take her anyway," Max added.

With a sigh, the doctor moved past her, bent close to Morgan, touched her face. "Is this what you want, Morgan? You want to go home, even though you might last a little bit longer here?"

She managed to nod, even pulled her lips into a ghost of a smile.

The doctor straightened, inhaling deeply. "All right. I'll get the paperwork."

"Time is a factor here."

"I'll be quick."

He was—amazingly so. Ten minutes later Max was signing beside the X and wheeling her blanket-wrapped sister out to the waiting taxi. A short while later they were pulling into the driveway, and Morgan sighed her relief audibly at the sight of the old house again. God, it really did mean the world to her.

Max studied Morgan's face for a long moment. She didn't look the way she had looked only days earlier. Her face was sunken, deep purple wells had appeared beneath her eyes, and her cheeks were concave. Her lips were pinched and chapped. She looked like an old woman.

Max paid the driver, got out of the cab, went around it to open her sister's door and hugged her gently. David came out of the house, and when Max moved aside, he scooped Morgan up and carried her easily into the house, up the stairs, and, moments later, was tucking her into her bed. Max stopped off in the study to take one of the smaller charcoal drawings of Dante from the wall. She carried it upstairs with her. When she got to the bedroom, she placed it in her sister's hands and saw just a hint of the former light flash in the dying woman's eyes.

"Hold on, Morgan. If you feel yourself slipping, look at Dante's face and know he's coming for you. I'm going to bring him to you myself. I promise."

A slight nod. A breath of relief. A single whispered word. "Hurry."

Max glanced at Lydia, at David. "Stay with her."

"You know we will. Be careful, Max," Lydia said, and gave her a quick hug.

Max hugged her back and whispered in her ear, "Tell her. It might be your last chance."

* * *

Sarafina lay on her side on the cool, damp ground above the cliffs. Her hands were cuffed behind her back, her ankles bound together with duct tape. She lay still, motionless, eyes closed, hair in disarray. She'd rubbed clumps of soil over her dress and her arms, smudged a bit on her face, hoping to look more convincing in the darkness.

Lou banked a hint of admiration for the woman. Brave. Then again, she had reason to be. She was stronger than ten ordinary men. Still, this was a risk. She must care a great deal about Dante.

"So I'm still not clear on your relationship with Dante," Lou said softly. He stood beside her prone form on the cliffs, watching the night, listening for Stiles to arrive. "You said you were his mother, sister and aunt. Just how the hell does *that* work?"

She opened her eyes, looking up at him without moving her head. "Sister, because all vampires are siblings. We come from a common source, we share the same blood. The same antigen that makes us unique. Mother, because I am the one who changed him from dying mortal man to powerful immortal creature. I birthed him into this life."

Lou nodded slow. "And aunt?"

"The usual way. Great-great-aunt if you want to get technical. I was his great-grandmother's sister."

He nodded again. "So you changed him be-cause—"

"Hush! They're coming." She closed her eyes again. "He'll know the cuffs alone won't hold me, mortal. He'll try to drug me, as he did Dante. We can't let him."

Lou strained his eyes and ears but didn't see or

hear a thing. Then again, her senses were supposedly working at some elevated level. Just how elevated, he could only guess. He didn't question their accuracy. Hell, after that jump from the third-story hospital window, he figured there wasn't much she couldn't do.

Eventually the sounds of footfalls in the grass reached his substandard ears, and he focused in that direction. Stiles's shape emerged from the darkness. He was wary, looking closely, moving slowly. He approached the fallen Sarafina the way Lou figured he would approach a sleeping tiger.

"She's unconscious," Lou reassured him. "She was hurt pretty badly in the fall."

"That's what the redhead told me on the phone," Stiles said. He drew a syringe from his pocket, held it upright and checked its contents, then took another halting step forward. And another. He started to reach for her, then drew back.

"Oh, for Pete's sake, will you do it already?" Lou asked.

Stiles finally moved closer, dropped down on one knee, brought the syringe toward Sarafina's arm. She flung her head up suddenly, slamming Stiles in the chest, knocking him off her and the syringe to the ground. Lou threw himself at her, and they struggled for a moment as Lou picked up the syringe and quickly squeezed its contents onto the ground, hiding his actions from the other man.

"There, goddammit," Lou growled.

Sarafina went limp, let her head fall to the ground, closed her eyes. Lou got up, disentangling his limbs from hers, brushing himself off. He handed Stiles the empty syringe. Stiles eyed it, then him. "Thanks," he said.

"Bitch tried to kill me," Lou said. "That's twice in one night. You were right about them, Stiles."

Stiles nodded. "She won't try again." He dropped the syringe to the ground, bent and scooped Sarafina up into his arms. "Remember," Stiles said as he turned to trudge back toward the house. "You tell no one. This is over. You and everyone else involved just need to forget all about it. Understood?"

"I won't forget," Lou said. "But I will keep it to myself." He forced a smile. "Hell, who'd believe me, anyway?"

"Exactly."

Lou walked with Stiles around the house to where the man's car waited. He winced when the bastard tossed the woman into the trunk. She landed hard, and then he slammed it closed. Stiles said, "You won't be seeing me again."

"No offense, Stiles, but I sure hope you're right." Lou waved him off as Stiles got behind the wheel and drove away.

As soon as the taillights vanished around a curve in the road, Max pulled up in Lou's car, flung open the passenger door, and Lou jumped in.

"It's been so long," Lydia said, pacing the bedroom an hour later. "Why haven't they come back by now? God, it will be dawn soon."

David put a hand on her shoulder. "Try to have faith, Lyd. It's going to be okay. It has to be."

She smiled at him in a way that told Morgan there was something between them. Something they'd kept from her.

"Max was right," David said softly. "You should tell her."

Lydia held his eyes for a long moment before turning to Morgan. Sniffling, she came to sit on the edge of the bed, clasped Morgan's hand. Lydia's felt strong and warm around it. Looking Morgan in the eyes, she said, "Morgan, I am the woman who gave birth to you and Max. I'm…I'm your mother."

"Mother…." Morgan whispered the word. She wasn't entirely shocked by the news. She'd wondered why Lydia seemed so connected to Max, why she seemed to care so much about her, when they'd only just met. She'd caught the woman crying over her in the hospital, and, knowing she was adopted, it hadn't been such a wide leap.

"I gave you both up for adoption because I thought you would be better off. I wanted you to have a good life. But I was told you were both going to the same family. It was a decade before I knew you'd been separated."

Sighing, Morgan nodded with her eyes. She was too weak to move her head. Then she slid her gaze to David. "Father?" she asked, despite the effort it cost.

"No," David said. "Though we thought for a time I might have been." He came closer, too, sat down on the bed. "I was one of Lydia's…clients. Young, wealthy. I always liked her. When she told me she was pregnant, I agreed to be tested. And when I learned you weren't my children I…I walked away. It was a mistake, Morgan. It haunted me. I looked Lydia up again a year later, and she told me you'd been adopted, though she didn't know the details, except that you were happy. So I hired an investigator to find you. Maxine was fine, in a loving, healthy family. But you…" He shook his head. "I didn't like the people who'd adopted you. And I didn't know how the hell to undo what had already been done. So I moved to the West Coast, and became your adoptive father's best friend. It was the only way I could stay close to you, watch over you. And I was compelled to do that. I didn't contact Lydia again to tell her, because—well, because I knew it would kill her if she realized she'd handed you over to people like that.''

He leaned down to kiss her cheek. "I'm sorry, honey. I'm sorry I never told you the truth.''

She closed her eyes. "Love you.''

When he sat up, he had tears in his eyes.

Morgan wanted to tell them both that it was okay. That she didn't hold anything against either of them. But she couldn't. This damned weakness was robbing her of the ability to do much of anything. She was existing from one breath to the next, more uncertain with each one she drew whether she would have the strength to draw another. But she tried to tell them with her eyes. And that was the best she could do.

"What's taking them so long?'' David asked.

Max stopped the car when she saw that Stiles had slowed down. She'd been driving without headlights, in pitch darkness, guided only by the distant red glow of his taillights. It was risky at best. Stupid at worst, but it was for her sister. She couldn't believe how badly she had managed to screw up. She had to make it right.

She put the car in reverse, saw no traffic behind her and backed up with nothing more than her own reverse lights to guide her. When she was out of sight of Stiles' car, she put the headlights on and found a place off the roadside to park. Then she shut the car off and turned to Lou. "This is it."

"Not for you, it's not. You take the car and go. Get some backup out here. I don't care what you have to say, just get some cops to head this way. I'm going in alone."

"The hell you are." She whipped out her cell phone, dialed 9-1-1. Then she frowned at the thing when nothing happened. "Dammit, we're out of range."

"Like I said, you go for help."

"Even if I did and help came running, they wouldn't get here in time. We have to do this now, Lou. You and me. With maybe a little help from the Mostly-Dead-Duo in there, if we're lucky and they're in a good mood." She left the keys in the ignition, got out of the car, not even waiting for Lou to reply, and started trudging forward.

He caught up to her in short order. "You could get hurt, Max. I couldn't live with that."

"My sister's dying, Lou. I caused it. I have to do this. If I don't, and she doesn't make it, how the hell do you think *I'm* gonna live with myself?"

He swallowed hard, staring at her in the darkness. "Dammit, you're so fucking stubborn."

"Yeah, and you love it."

"Here." He slapped a gun into her hands. Small. His handgun.

"What about you?"

He lifted his opposite arm, and she saw for the first time the dark outline of the shotgun he carried. "I figured it was time to break out the big guns."

"Good thinking."

They strode side by side along the road until they

could make out the shape of Stiles car in the overgrown driveway of a falling-down house. It looked abandoned. But there was light coming from inside.

"Do you think Sarafina is still in the trunk?" Max whispered.

"He'd be an idiot to leave her there."

They moved in closer to the house, leaving the car for now. If Sarafina were in the trunk, she could probably get out, Max thought, and there was no sense wasting time or tipping off the enemy by rattling around trying to open a locked trunk. She assumed Lou agreed when he passed by the car without stopping.

They were approaching the rotten-looking front steps when Max felt a gun barrel in her spine. "Move and she dies," a man said.

She jerked her gaze sideways and saw Lou looking at her, a horrified expression on his face. "Okay, okay, easy," he said. "We're friends."

"Drop the shotgun."

Lou bent at the knees, laying the gun on the ground, and straightening again.

"You, too, hon," the man said.

"I don't have a gun to drop," she said. "You wanna loan me yours?"

"Fine, I'll get it myself," the man said, and he started patting her down, apparently certain she carried her gun taped to her crotch, judging by the amount of time he spent groping the area. He finally located the gun Lou had given her, took it and then nudged her forward. "Get inside. Both of you."

Lou and Max walked forward into the dilapidated house. Its door hung crookedly from one hinge. Max blinked in the white light of a gas lantern as she was prodded into a room where Stiles and two other men sat at a table.

"Well, what have we here?" Stiles asked, rising.

Through a doorway to the left, Max could see Dante strapped to a table and Sarafina strapped to another. She pretended not to notice them. "Impressive," she said, addressing Stiles instead. "So this is the new DPI headquarters? Talk about high tech."

"This is a temporary holding area," Stiles said. "So, do you want to die now, or would you prefer to tell me what the hell you're doing here first?"

Lou interrupted her before she could zing Stiles with a sarcastic reply. "I followed you."

"I knew it."

"Hey, if you knew it, why did you leave?"

"What are you talking about?"

Lou licked his lips. "After you left, I picked up that syringe and saw that there was still some of that drug left in it. I was worried she might not be out after all and jumped in the car to come and warn you."

Stiles lifted his brows, nodding as Lou spun his lies. He whistled long and low when Lou had finished. "And here I thought this was all a setup so you could get Dante out of here. So tell me, Lou, where did you leave your car? I didn't hear it pull into the driveway."

"Ran out of gas," Lou said. "Just a little ways back."

"Right." Stiles looked at the man behind Max. "Take them out back and shoot them."

Max shot her eyes to Lou. He stared back at her, and she saw that he was afraid—for her, not himself. Then the other man grabbed him and shoved him out of the house. She was being shoved right along behind him. They marched the two of them around to the back of the house, shoving her forward until she and Lou stood side by side, their backs to the men.

"Get on your knees."

"I'll die standing, thanks," Max said.

"Have it your way." The gun barrel moved from the small of her back to the base of her skull.

Lou moved suddenly, ducked low, and jammed the man behind him with an elbow. Then he turned and threw himself at the one with the gun to Max's head. The gun went off, deafening her, but she didn't feel pain, and reasoned that the shot had missed. She found herself on the ground, probably the shock of that gunshot next to her ear, but she got up as she saw one of the goons scrambling for his dropped gun. She went for it, too. He got it first and leveled it on her. Lou was grappling with the other man, both of them rolling around in the weeds.

Max held up a hand instinctively, and the gun, aimed right at her chest, went off. As it did, a dark form lunged between her and the shooter, like a black streak. Another shot, from behind her. Lou had won the fight for the other gun and shot her would-be assailant in the chest. The man went down in a heap. Behind Lou, his partner lay bleeding and unconscious.

She heard a car, tires squealing. Stiles and the one remaining thug getting away, no doubt. But she was too horrified to go after them. Dante, her sister's only hope, the man who had just taken a bullet for her, lay on the ground, bleeding, gasping, clutching his chest.

"Oh, God," she whispered.

"Just...stanch it." He ground out the words

through clenched teeth. "Just get it stopped before I lose too much."

Nodding, she tore a strip from her blouse, balled it up, pressed it to the wound. Held it there.

Dante caught his breath. "Now...get me to Morgan."

"Lou, get the car," she said.

Lou ran into the darkness to comply. Sarafina came out of the house, looking at Max, at Dante in her arms. The handcuffs were still on her wrists, dangling like bracelets, their chain snapped in two.

"If you try to transform her tonight, it won't take," Sarafina said coldly.

"You don't know that."

"She's too far gone. And now you're wounded. Not at full power."

"I'll make it work."

"It could kill you."

"Then I'll die."

Sarafina lowered her head, closed her eyes. The car came screeching back. Sarafina went around the house to meet it, and Max wondered why. When she returned, Lou was at her side, and she held the roll of duct tape he'd used to bind her ankles. She tossed it to Max.

"Cram more padding into the wound. All you can fit. Then wrap him tight in this tape, all the way round his chest. Tight as you can make it."

Max didn't question her. She nodded her compliance, tore more fabric from her blouse and did exactly as Sarafina had instructed her.

When he was bound up tight, Sarafina said, "Now step away."

Max eased Dante's head to the ground, and Sarafina knelt beside him. "You have made your choice, Dante. Between me and this mortal woman you crave. You've chosen her."

"Why must I choose at all?"

"Will you come with me now? Leave her behind?"

He grimaced in pain. "I can't do that."

"Then you've chosen her." She brought her arm to her lips, bit a gash in her wrist, and pressed it to his mouth. Dante clutched her hand and drank as Sarafina went on. "This is the last time I will ever help you, Dante. You'll never have the chance to betray me again."

She jerked her wrist away, grabbed a strip of cloth Max had left on the ground and twisted it around the wound, using her teeth and one hand to knot it tight.

"I haven't betrayed you. Sarafina, wait...."

Without another word or a backward glance, she walked away, into the night, skirts dancing in the wind, bracelets and bangles jingling like bells. Dante closed his eyes. Aching, Max thought.

"Come on, Lou. Let's get him into the car. We have to get him back to Morgan."

Lou glanced at the sky as they hoisted Dante between them. "It'll be dawn soon."

"She won't last another day. It has to be now. If we're not already too late." She searched Dante's face. "Was she telling the truth about that? That it might not even work."

"If she's too near death, if I'm too weak..." Dante sighed and shook off their supporting arms, walking the rest of the way to the car unsteadily, but under his own power. He got into the back seat. Lou and

Max got in the front. "It'll work," Dante said as Lou started the car, backed out the driveway. "It has to."

Lou put the car in drive, and stomped the accelerator to the floor.

26

Dante got out of the car, faced the house. The deepest sense of dread he had ever known swelled in his chest, overwhelming even the pain of the bullet hole. He could feel her inside. Her essence was weak, tenuous, and fading more with every breath.

His own body swayed with weakness, reminding him yet again just how closely they were linked to one another. Max grabbed his upper arm, steadied him. "Are you all right?"

"It's her. God, she's so weak."

"I know. Come on."

He let her lead him, and he noticed that Lou stayed below as they started up the stairs. He couldn't stop thinking that if Morgan died, it would be his fault. He should have listened to her from the start. He should have changed her right away, when she was strong. Now, even if he managed to save her, she would never know the preternatural strength she would have had if he had acted sooner.

He hated his selfishness. His fear. Yes, he'd been afraid of her. Afraid of the power she had over him. She could hurt him, destroy him. She would—if she died.

They reached the upper floor, and Max walked him along the hallway to the bedroom door. She tapped once, then opened it.

Lydia and David were beside the bed, but Dante's gaze barely swept over them on the way to Morgan. Oh, God, Morgan. He closed his eyes, lowering his head. She looked like a ghost already.

Max went to Lydia, to David. Spoke to them softly. Dante watched them as they each bent to kiss Morgan's forehead, then walked past him on their way out of the room.

Then Max leaned over her. "I've brought him, just as I promised I would."

Dante steeled himself, schooled his face into an expression of calm, and finally moved into Morgan's range of vision. When she saw him, her weak smile of welcome tore at his heart.

Then she shifted her gaze to her sister again. "Thank you."

Max nodded. "I won't see you again, will I?"

Morgan didn't answer, and Max leaned down to hug her gently. Then she straightened and backed away. "Be happy."

Dante glanced at the window. It was nearly dawn. He knew they would both be weak after the transformation, if it even worked. They would be vulnerable. He couldn't do it here. He needed her in a haven, safe from the sun. Gently, he bent over her, sliding his arms beneath her and lifting her from the bed. She was light as a dried stalk as she gazed up into his eyes. God, how he loved her.

He looked once more at Max. "Thank you for helping us."

"I only wish it hadn't taken me so long to figure out who the real monsters were."

Turning, Dante carried Morgan to the balcony, her white nightgown trailing down his side. He braced

himself and leapt over the rail. The landing was jar-
ring. It rattled his teeth, but he managed to remain
upright. Then he carried her away from the house,
toward the cliffs. He could feel Max's eyes on them
as he walked into the night. He could feel her tears,
as well.

He took Morgan into the hidden place beneath the
house. As far as he was aware, she had never told
anyone, not even her sister, about this place. It should
be safe. He wouldn't put her in the coffin, not now.
Not considering how near death she was, how frightened she must be. Instead, he tore the lining, and satin
pad from it, and made them a cozy nest on the floor.
Then he reclined there, his back against the wall, with
her resting across his body. He bent to press his lips
to hers.

She kissed him back. He felt it, sensed her re-
sponses, even though, physically, she could barely
move. He touched her chin. "You'll be with me now.
Always with me, Morgan. I'll never doubt you
again."

"Yes," she whispered.

Lifting her chin, he pressed his face to her throat,
bit down and pierced her jugular. Inside him, fires
licked to life. Her pulse, fluttering against his tongue,
the warm flow of her blood, the arousal he felt waking
in her body, even in its weakened state, combined to
create an answering need in him. And the hunger
raged, as the hunger always raged in his kind.

He mustn't take too much, he reminded himself.
Only a little. He felt her slipping away and drank
deeply, until he pushed her into the shadowy realm
between life and death. Her heart stuttered, skipped.
He lifted his head away and stared down at her half-

lidded eyes. A breath escaped her. A rattling, broken breath.

Quickly he tore the flesh of his wrist, and when the deep red blood welled, he pressed it to her lips. The touch of that fluid sparked her. She swallowed, and as her mouth filled, swallowed again. And then she began to suck, to draw the liquid from him. She needed a lot, and he knew what she felt. Not only because he had felt it himself, but because he felt every sensation that went through her. They were one while she fed at his wrist. Everything she experienced registered in his brain. Everything from how deeply she loved him to how badly she wanted him.

He weakened, and she sucked harder. Dizziness came, and still she drank. His head fell sideways, and his vision grew dark around the edges. He tugged his wrist slightly, but she held on and kept drinking.

Finally he gave a firm yank. He bound the wrist in a strip of fabric.

She fell backward, her back arching over his arm, her eyes falling closed.

Dante gathered her upper body, cradled her in his arms. "Please, don't die. Not now. God, let this work. Let it be enough. Let it work!"

Her lips moved, just slightly, right against his ear. Her breath, a whisper, weak but insistent. "Make love…to me…one…last…time."

He closed his eyes in misery. "It can't be the last time, my love. It can't." Pulling her over him, he dragged the white gown up her body, bunching the fabric around her waist. She was naked underneath. Her body lay against his chest now, her legs parted around his hips, linked behind him. He reached down to free himself from his jeans and immediately pressed himself into her. She was wet and yearning, ready for him. The blood lust did that. Even in this state, her hunger was for his body as much as for his blood, and it always would be. He clasped her hips, pushed himself deep inside her. She would have moved if she could have. He knew she couldn't, so he did it for her. Gently, slowly, as tenderly as he knew how. He kissed her and held her and moved very gently inside her. He had never made love this way—not in either of his lifetimes.

They were still locked together when the sun rose. And as she sank into slumber, he couldn't tell if she were dead…or undead.

And then he slept.

Epilogue

A month later

Dressed to the nines, Maxine sat and admired the way Lou looked in a tux. She was clutching his hand in one of hers and Lydia's in the other. Lydia, too, was glamorous tonight. Sequins, daring neckline, gorgeous cascading blond ringlets. She'd been drawing hungry looks all evening, from both men and women. Everything was beautiful, and yet bittersweet.

"This is incredible," Stormy said, leaning over Lou to grin at Max. "I can't believe you managed to get an extra ticket for me."

"For Best Original Screenplay, the nominees are..." the stunning female presenter on the stage said.

Stormy sat back in her seat as all of them focused on the stage. Max was practically holding her breath. David sat on the other side of Lydia, and from the look on his face, he was as nervous as she was when the starlet on the stage said, "And the award goes to...." and tore open the envelope.

Looking up, blinking back emotion, the actress said, "Morgan De Silva for *Twilight Hunger.*"

The audience roared with applause. The emotional favorite had won. People rose to their feet, the five of them included. They hugged. Max and Lydia both cried liberally, and David made his way into the aisle and onto the stage as a voice announced, "Accepting the award on behalf of the late Morgan De Silva, David Sumner, her producer, director and dear friend."

He took the podium, nodding sadly as he shook the pretty presenter's hand, accepted her kiss on the cheek. He took the golden statue in his hands, fighting tears and waiting for the applause to die down. The big screen behind him was suddenly filled with a larger than life photo of Morgan, before the illness had ravaged her.

"God, she was so beautiful," Max heard someone say. "So young."

Slowly the crowd retook their seats and the applause died down.

David spoke. "Thank you. Morgan would have been so thrilled and so honored by this. I only wish she could be up on this stage tonight, accepting it herself. This film—not just this one, but all three of her films—meant the world to her. And through them, I like to think her spirit lives on. Thank you. Thank you so much."

Applause thundered again as a pair of models led him off the stage.

Lou walked Max to the cemetary in the wee hours of the morning. Once there, though, he stood back. Gave her some space.

Standing alone, holding the golden statuette in both hands, Max stared at the beautiful rose granite headstone that had Morgan's name engraved on its face, along with her date of birth and date of death.

Sniffling, Max held the trophy out toward the headstone.

"You did it, my beautiful sister. You won."

Morgan stepped out from behind the headstone. She couldn't wipe the smile from her face as she took the statue and hugged it to her chest. "I did, didn't I? Oh, God, this is incredible! I won! I won!" She spun in a circle, tipped her head back and laughed, loving the rich, clear, powerful tones of her own voice, ringing in the night.

Dante came out of the shadows, as well, and stopped her spinning by catching her in his arms. Strong arms that she relished feeling around her. "Let's not forget whose story it actually was."

"Oh, please," she said, smiling up at him. "It was lifeless until I turned it into a script."

"Your script was lifeless until you fed it my story," he teased.

"Fine. We'll share the trophy, then."

Dante kissed her, and her laughter died away. "As we share everything," he whispered, and his deep voice so close to her ear sent delicious shivers up her spine.

Max cleared her throat exaggeratedly, and Dante finally released her. "You get to see her a lot more often than I do," Max said, opening her arms. "Do you mind?"

Dante waved his arm in surrender. Grinning, Morgan hugged Max hard. Her sister. Her very own *sister*. Morgan could barely believe how much she had come to love Max in two months' time. But it seemed, once survival had stopped being foremost in her mind, she had time to think about what it really meant to have Maxine in her life.

"You look wonderful," Max told her, holding her at arm's length as her green eyes danced over Morgan's face. "Healthy. Vibrant. Okay, a little pale, but I guess that goes with the territory."

"I *am* wonderful, you know," Morgan told her. "Better than I ever was, Max. Stronger. More powerful. I feel more alive than—than when I actually was. All thanks to you."

Max lowered her head. "I nearly got you killed," she whispered.

"No, love. You saved me. You showed up when I needed you most. You stayed, even though I tried to chase you away. You kept me alive, and you rescued my love and brought him to me." Still, Max's eyes were downcast. Morgan caught her chin, lifting it, holding her gaze. "Darling, if you hadn't come, Stiles would have done us both in. Even though it took you a bit to see the truth, it was your presence that made the difference. I'm convinced of that."

Max sniffed and hugged her again. "I'm just sorry it was so close. I should have listened to you from the beginning."

"That was a mistake I made as well, Maxine," Dante said, speaking softly. "In fact, I think Malone was the only one who was clear on things from the start."

"Clear my ass," Lou said, finally coming to join them. "I thought I'd lost it."

"Thank goodness you hadn't." Reaching out, Dante shook his hand.

Morgan took Max by the hand and led her away, leaving the two men at the graveside to chat. "We need to talk," she said.

"All right."

The two sisters walked together amid the stones of the rural cemetery, along its winding paths, among headstones that cast eerie shadows on the lush grass, fresh flowers and dead ones. Leafless trees swayed in the brisk night wind. The scent of flowers on a fresh grave, and the approach of winter, flavored the air.

"I wanted to talk to you about the house," Morgan said. "You've barely used it at all since I...well, since my funeral." A little chill of cool air whispered over her nape, and she shivered. "God, it feels funny saying that."

"It's your house, Morgan. You still need a place to live. I don't want to take it from you. I mean, the will was just a formality. It's only mine on paper."

"No, I meant it. I want it to be yours," Morgan said. "Besides, I can't occupy it openly and not risk discovery. I want you to have the place. Use it. Run your business out of it, if you want. It would be best for both of us."

"For both of us, huh?" Max asked. She paused near a bench that had been placed alongside the path for visitors and, turning, sat down. Morgan sat beside her. "Just how does it benefit you and Dante? Having relatives around all the time can't be a passionate young couple's dream come true. You guys are as giddy as newlyweds."

"You don't know the half of it," Morgan said, averting her face. "He's incredible," she whispered. "I never thought I could be this...complete. For so long I had no one. Other than David. Now, suddenly, I have you, and I have this man who...he would die for me. He loves me that much. I still can't quite get over it."

"All the more reason to let you have your privacy,'' Max said. ''My moving in wouldn't have one positive benefit for you two.''

Morgan blinked against the moisture that came to her eyes and the catch that entered her breathing whenever she pondered Dante's love. ''Yes, it would,'' she told her sister. ''If you were there, I would have cover.''

''Cover?''

Nodding, Morgan paced in front of the bench where Max sat. ''As it is, I have to be so incredibly careful not to be seen. If you were here and someone saw me, they would just assume it was you. I could go out in public again, once in a while. Go to a movie, or go shopping.'' She stopped pacing, crouched down in front of Max and clasped her hands. ''On top of that, if the place is occupied by my surviving family, strangers won't come snooping around.''

''People have been snooping?'' Max asked, looking concerned.

Morgan nodded. ''Yes, every now and then. Curious fans, local kids. Hey, I'm famous. I won an award, you know.''

Max smiled. ''Yeah, I heard that somewhere.''

''So?''

Max thought about it for a long moment. ''It really would make a great place for the business. But, um, well, Stormy is my partner. She would have to come, too.''

Morgan nodded slowly. She had only observed the blonde from a distance, but there was something oddly familiar about her. ''Does she know about me?''

''I haven't told her,'' Max said. ''But I think she suspects. And I do trust her. You know, she's convinced that she met you while she was in the coma. She goes on and on about how you led her back to the land of the living again. There's no telling her it was just a dream. So she feels she owes you. You can trust her not to betray your secret.''

Morgan smiled just slightly as the memory that had been eluding her finally clicked into place. She *had* met her sister's best friend before—in a dream, when she was hovering between life and death in that hospital. Or…maybe it hadn't been a dream at all.

''And of course there's Lou. I have to consider him,'' Max went on.

''Do you think he'll agree to move up here? To work with you?''

Max shrugged. ''I think I've got my work cut out for me to convince him to give it a try. But he was talking about a little cabin on the beach, and a fishing boat. He retires from the force soon, you know.''

''Then what's stopping you, Max? Come on. Do it.'' She clasped her sister's hand. ''I miss you. If you were here, we could have more time to make up for all the years we missed.''

Max licked her lips. ''If you're sure you want us here.''

''You're my sister,'' Morgan said, smiling now, knowing Max would agree. ''You know I want you here.''

Finally Max nodded. ''Okay. I'm here then. The Supernatural Investigations Service shall be based in Easton, Maine.''

''SIS,'' Morgan said, with a slight nod. ''I like it.''

''I kind of thought you would.''

Arm in arm, they rose from the bench and walked back to join the men at the grave. Morgan curled herself into Dante's arms, and he held her gently, lovingly. "It'll be dawn soon, love," he told her.

"I know." She smiled at her sister and the man who stood at Max's side, looking uncomfortable. "I'll see you soon?"

"Very soon," Max promised.

Morgan and Dante turned, moving into the shadows.

"You know, she's happier now than she has been her whole life," Max said, watching them walk out of sight. "She's so lucky."

"How's that?" Lou asked. He started toward the car, and Max fell into step beside him.

She shrugged. "Isn't it obvious? They're soulmates. Madly, wildly, eternally in love. I can't imagine how gratifying it would be to have a man love me the way Dante loves Morgan. It's pretty special, what they have together."

"I guess you're right," Lou said, sliding a casual arm around Max as they walked along the path toward the parking area. "Some folks go through their whole lives without finding that kind of thing."

"Yeah. And some have it right under their noses and refuse to see it."

"You think?" he asked, glancing down at her.

Max rolled her eyes, shook her head. "Yeah," she said. "I think."

Lou shrugged and kept on walking.

From the darkest shadows, Sarafina watched Dante talking and laughing with the mortals, finally leaving them with his lover held tightly in his arms.

"I'll love you forever," he whispered to Morgan. "I think, in some way, I already have."

"We were meant for each other, Dante. You know that now, don't you?"

"I've always known it on some level. The first time you said it, I got a chill." Gently, he kissed her. "I'm sorry it took me so long."

She smiled and kissed him back. "Just don't let it happen again." Then she danced away from him, her eyes sparkling with life and love. "Race you back to the house!" And, whirling, she laughed and ran off, nearly as rapidly as Sarafina herself could have moved.

Dante raced after her, never looking back.

So this was what he wanted. He had a new family now. He had turned his back on her. Dante—the last remaining link to her own family, her heritage, her blood.

Damn him.

He had betrayed her. Just as surely as every other member of her family had betrayed her.

It didn't matter, she thought, as she walked into the open and sat on the ground in a pool of spilled moonlight. She was a vampiress. She did not need a family. She didn't need anyone at all. And she never would.

No. Not ever again.

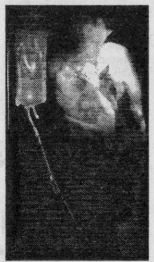

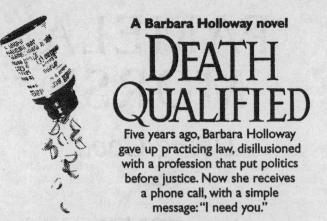

PAMELA MORSI

Doing Good

One more chance...please!

Jane Lofton is so busy rescheduling her next liposuction, shopping for clothes she doesn't need and bragging about her latest real estate sale that she hasn't noticed the callus forming around her heart. Her husband is cheating on her, and she talks to her daughter through a therapist. No, life is *not* perfect.

Very suddenly, Jane's problems become incidental when she is involved in a traffic accident. She barely escapes a tragic end, but not before making a solemn promise to "do good" for the rest of her life.

So how come "doing good" is so complicated?

Available the first week of March 2002, wherever paperbacks are sold!